WENDALL'S LULLABY

Kip Koelsch

This novel is a work of fiction. Names, characters, businesses, places, events and incidents are either the products of the author's imagination or used in a fictitious manner. Any resemblance to actual persons, living or dead, or actual events is purely coincidental.

ISBN: 9781522021100
Imprint: Independently published

For my parents, Art and Marilyn—for always encouraging me to follow my dreams.
For my wife, Jules, for loving and believing in me.

WENDALL'S LULLABY

Kip Koelsch

Day One

Wednesday, February 19, 2008

Chapter 1

107 Miles off the Coast of Galveston, Texas

Baseer wiped the tears from his eyes. Peering through the dim, red light he craned his neck to glimpse the two sleeping men, sharing less space than the inside of a small car. The moment--and the irony-- nearly overwhelmed him. He wondered how he had managed to keep his secret as the three of them reached this extreme level of intimacy. Over the past 13 months, during their training and deployment, they had shared their personal traumas—the loss of their families, the destruction of their villages—and their hopes for vengeance and salvation through their service to Allah. He shared their grievous losses, but not their passion for revenge, not their passion for salvation through violence.

It had been his dream to open a medical clinic in his village, but, while studying medicine at the University of Florida, one of his brothers had been seduced into making a coordinated suicide attack on the NATO outpost just over the hill from their home. His subsequent, and premature, home-coming was not what he had planned—no greetings from his proud parents, no mullah with blessings at the opening of his new clinic—just the sadness and anger of the mass funerals that so often accompany the cold retaliation of a drone attack. He could still feel the firm hand upon his left shoulder, as he sat head-in-hands on his suitcase amid the rocky rubble of his home. Looking up into those brown eyes, he knew it was time for the killing to stop.

Yet, here he was. Shaking his head at the irony, he reexamined a small notepad—his time-distance calculations—and eased the sub to a depth of just five meters. Satisfied with his location and positioning, Baseer flipped the cover from the detonator switch and firmly pressed the black button.

Senate Committee on Commerce, Science and Transportation Washington, D.C.

"Dr. Clarke, I'm sorry we didn't quite finish with your testimony last night. Thank you for coming back first thing this morning to answer one final question." Almost everyone in the room knew that the senator had purposely put off his last real question for Dr. Clarke—wanting the anticipated answer to resonate through the final day of testimony and the day's news cycle. But now, Senator Hulme paused for a different reason--Rear Admiral Lawrence Collins—the current Undersecretary of Commerce for Oceans and Atmosphere and administrator of the National Oceanic and Atmospheric Administration—had just hustled out of the hearing room.

"Dr. Clarke, for the benefit of those new to the hearings and for the record, would you please restate your name, title, and the agency for which you work?"

Dr. Clarke nodded. "Dr. Angela Tatum Clarke, National Director of Marine Mammal Health and Stranding, National Marine

Fisheries Service, National Oceanic and Atmc
Administration."

Third Floor Hallway, Senate Office Building
Washington, D.C.

Tucked into an alcove within view of the committee room doors, Admiral Collins stared at the "highest priority" message on his Blackberry: "CONCH detection success. Threat neutralized."

The first phase of the system had been online for only two months, so Collins was anxious for details. He entered a secure number and, after the connection was apparent, whispered, "Location? Vessel? Survivors?"

He stared without focus at the nearby wall, waiting for the reply, already planning the political maneuvering necessary for the funding and deployment of the system's final phase.

The practiced monotone on the other end of the line was succinct in its reply. "Detection success 107 miles southeast of Galveston. Refineries probable target. Mini-sub. Initial report— detonation was premature and prior to on-water intercept. Investigation in progress."

Senate Committee on Commerce, Science and Transportation
Washington, D.C.

Dr. Clarke had finished her formalities and the senator looked to the committee room door—nothing.

Shaking his head, he poured a glass of water and took a small drink. As one of his fellow senators cleared his throat, the door opened and in came the admiral — grinning and strutting with more than his usual SEAL swagger. Senator Hulme nodded in his direction and turned to Dr. Clarke.

"Now, Dr. Clarke, these mass die-offs, what do you call them?"

"Unusual Mortality Events, Senator. UME's."

"Unusual Mortality Events, yes, thank you." Looking down his nose at a list of mass whale and dolphin beachings from the last 10 years, the senator nodded at the clarification, "And, in your expert opinion, there hasn't been any definitive link, any peer-reviewed scientific evidence..." There was silence as he inhaled — shoulders rising — and exhaled--shoulders dropping--using his hulking frame and powerful voice to orchestrate a little extra drama before continuing, "...and no known human cause for these Unusual Mortality Events?"

"That would be correct, Senator."

Senator Hulme leaned slightly forward in his chair--looking left and right at the rest of the committee. Sensing they were all in agreement, he said, "No further questions, Dr. Clarke. Thank you. You are dismissed."

Tucking a long, frazzled strand of blonde hair behind her left ear, Dr. Angela Clarke gathered her papers into a manila folder, slid it into her black briefcase and headed for the door. Her three days of meticulous, rational and emotionless testimony were over. Her boss,

National Marine Fisheries Service (NMFS) Director Jake Hamilton, side-stepped across the back row and followed her out through the dark double doors.

"Well done, Angela. Well done."

Jake maneuvered his still nimble — though slightly heavier — body of a former Coast Guard Academy lineman, around a small school group and a wooden bench. He planted himself in front of Angela. Frowning, she resisted the urge to take a step back from her boss. She was not normally uncomfortable with how close — almost belly-to-belly--the director can get when he talks one-on-one.

"I'm sorry the senator dragged you in for one more question. I'm sorry you had to be the one he used to punctuate his agenda."

Angela looked down at her skirt and heels and then back to the director. "All dressed up and no place to go." Snickering and shaking her head, she continued, "Sometimes science is facts--data. You know I love data. But, sometimes it's theory. Even I recognize that sometimes we need theories..." The director raised his large, black hand and stopped her mid-sentence.

"They're politicians. They have enough trouble with facts."

"You're a politician — a damn good politician."

Director Hamilton grinned and nodded while glaring into her unblinking brown eyes. The look was broken by a buzz from Angela's briefcase — her cell phone. Looking at the screen, her eyes narrowed and she shook her head.

Jake was just about to step around her and head back to the committee room when Angela grabbed his shoulder and stepped back, "Hang on. This might be something you want to hear…"

She opened the phone, "Hello, Angela Clarke."

"Angela? Angela, it's Kurt—Kurt Braun."

"Yes, Kurt. I recognize your number and your voice." Kurt usually emailed any stranding-related information. It had been at least four years since he had actually called her—even his congratulations on her promotion to National Director of Marine Mammal Health and Stranding were emailed.

"Uh…Angela? The hearings…" Kurt was caught off guard. "I thought maybe I'd…I figured it would go to…I'd get voicemail…hoped I'd get voicemail. Are you done with the hearings already?"

"Already? After *three days* I'm finally done."

Director Hamilton was getting anxious to return to the committee room—Angela held up the wait-a-minute finger.

"You didn't call me about the hearings, did you? I really don't have time to get into it with you right now."

Kurt interrupted, "It's not all about you…or us…or what was *us*. I expected that kind of treatment from you, Ang…but…but, no…no, that's not what I'm calling about." He paused. During day two of the hearings, Angela had spent three hours debunking and discrediting Kurt Braun and the very public and extraordinary conclusions he had reached linking several Texas stranding events with human causes—particularly waste water discharge from local oil refineries. "No, I'm not calling about *that*. Seriously, there's been a mass stranding of bottlenose dolphins…um…*Tursiops truncatus*," Kurt made sure to correct himself and use the scientific name of the species with Angela, "…at least 150 over a mile of beach."

Impatient, Jake started walking towards the committee room — Angela stepped in his path, stomped one foot and narrowed her eyes. She mouthed, "Wait!"

With the 300-pound director again standing belly-to-belly with her, Angela continued the call. "Why didn't you call me sooner? You should have called me sooner!" Stranding occurrences of that size were rare and would typically stretch out over days, weeks or even months, and Angela immediately assumed that Kurt had been negligent in contacting her. He was eerily silent and Angela thought that was a guilty confirmation. She prodded, "*Tursiops*? *That* many? How many days or weeks ago did it start? I don't understand why you didn't call me when it started?"

"If it had been weeks or months or days. I would have called you already. You would have seen it on the news." He paused. "A jogger made the initial call *this morning--today* — 6:30am. East Beach. You know how popular that beach is for runners and walkers. Someone would have seen them if they were coming up for the last couple of days. So, it must've happened overnight. I was off the island last night and I'm…I'm fifteen minutes out."

"Shit! Today? You're kidding, right? Overnight? Any alive? How can you *know* it's that many? Who is on site?" She knew a one-day stranding of this magnitude was unprecedented in the United

States--that it was of bottlenose dolphins was even more surprising. She knew that bottlenose dolphins typically travel in small social groups—the largest being mother-calf-female associations rarely larger than 15 animals. The males typically travel in pairs or alone—forming slightly larger groups only for cooperative hunting or mating. A group *this* size was more than unusual. Dr. Clarke pulled a legal pad from her briefcase and Jake watched her start to put pen to paper as Kurt responded.

"Who's on site? They're my most dedicated First Responders--mom and her son. Rehabbed Wally and got hooked. Very passionate, but very reliable. By the book. Not the typical dolphin huggers you love to hate. They counted with…"

"Shit! You're breaking up! Call me back when you get an accurate count and an initial on-site assessment!" He was gone and she closed the phone.

Jake shook his head, "You said *shit* outside a Congressional committee room. No, you yelled *shit* outside a Congressional committee room--*twice. This* can't be good."

Angela looked up and down the wood-paneled hallway—noting that the profanities didn't seem to draw any extra attention. "*Not good* would be an understatement. If what he is telling me about this stranding is true—the numbers, the timeframe—well…" Angela was a little flustered—she showed him the number—150—that she had written and circled on her notepad, "…it's beyond *not good*. It's a catastrophe—a UME in the making."

After gently dropping his large hand on Angela's shoulder, Director Hamilton whispered, "Then *you* need to make sure it is handled properly." She nodded. Jake broke his serious, momentary stare into her eyes and turned — walking down the hallway and back through the committee room doors.

Beacon Island Beach, Plettenberg Bay, South Africa

David made a smooth landing on the beach, tucked his surf ski under his beefy, tanned arm and, with a face-filling grin, shook his wet, shoulder-length hair like a model. Lifting his chin in Robin's direction, he yelled, "That was sick, brah!"

Robin had landed first — but, not so smoothly. He sat on the sand next to his 20-foot ocean racing kayak, scratching at the red blotches on his hairless, chiseled calves and shaking his head. "Aw, right — sick for you, maybe." While glaring at his training partner, he stood and shouldered his boat for the walk back to the car. "I don't know how you avoided those damn bluebottles when you fell in three more times."

"I got back on my boat faster — too fast for the jellyfish. Besides, be happy--you got the best rides." David looked back at the huge waves cresting and crashing off the beach. "Your last ride linked some sick waves — you shredded it for at least 300 meters!"

"Yeah, till I whacked my bloody rudder while landing in a heap on the sand. Great day. Just unlock the car." Robin slid his surf ski onto the roof rack next to David's and headed toward the back of the car. Ducking his head into the car, David started fishing through their tie-down gear.

"Robin, your mobile is bleeping."

"Bleeping mobile! Where are the straps? Let's get these things tied down."

David tossed him two straps, "Here you…"

"Ach!" Robin had been staring at the damage to his kayak-- the straps hit him in the back and fell to the ground. *"Domkop!"* Looking over his shoulder at David, he narrowed his eyes. "Rudder shaft ripped right through the hull. I don't have the time to fix…" Robin frantically scratched at his legs and bent to pick up the straps. "Fucking jellyfish bites are itching like crazy."

"Your mobile is *ringing* now!" David walked to the back of the car and slapped the phone into Robin's water-shriveled hand.

"Hello…Vee…Howzit? What?" He threw the straps at David and stalked away from the car. "Finish tying this down for me."

"Trusting a *domkop* like *me* to tie down your ski?" David shot him a puzzled look, but Robin was already out of earshot and kept walking.

A perennial contender in the South African Surf Ski Series, Robin Nicely was serious about racing the long, narrow, sit-on-top kayaks that had evolved from the wider and more stable craft used by Australian and South African lifeguards. Typically, he was on the water six days a week, in the gym strength training for two days a week, and, when his other commitments didn't get in the way, running or cycling a few times as well. The unexpected phone call from Vee was just one of those other commitments.

Ten minutes later, Robin was back. David had tied down the boats and settled into his beach chair and a discreetly held Carling Black Label — watching the last flickers of the sunset battling with the black.

Robin grabbed the can of beer and swallowed what was left. "Get up! Bloody dolphins beaching on Bazarutu." He crushed the can and threw it at David.

"Mozambique? Can't their people handle...?"

"I don't even know if I can handle it." In addition to being a competitive long-distance ocean paddler, *Dr.* Robin Nicely was a world-renowned marine mammologist, the assistant director of Plettenberg Bay's Dolphin Study Centre and founder of the Pan-African Marine Mammal Stranding Network — the organization responsible for investigating the beachings of whales and dolphins for most of the continent.

David folded his chair and tossed it in the back seat. "How many, brah?"

Shivering in his wet rash guard, Robin peeled off the skin-tight top — revealing a faded tattoo of a dolphin leaping over a kayak on the right side of his upper back. After pulling on a pilly, gray fleece, he looked at David and kicked a clump of sand. "Fuck!" Robin closed his eyes and ran his fingers through the salt and pepper crew cut stubble on his head. "Vee says at least 300."

Chapter 2

East Beach, Galveston, Texas

Kurt had never seen a single stranding this large — even over several months. He stood at the edge of the massive dirt parking lot and looked from side to side. Bottlenose dolphins were strewn a half a mile up the beach in both directions — some with tails still moving, struggling to breathe, but obviously alive. More than half were clearly dead. Volunteers were keeping all the dolphins moist and covered, spreading sunscreen on the live ones and keeping gawkers back from the animals. People were everywhere, but there was little chaos other than a few gawkers shooting video and taking pictures. Just to the right, on the beach, stood Shari Casseine, gesturing and pointing in front of a group of seven people.

The group went trotting off to the right and Shari walked over to where her son Bryan was managing the blowhole of one of the dolphins — he was making sure the water used to keep its skin moist didn't get sucked into its lungs. It was Bryan that first saw Kurt — it was hard to miss his lanky, six-foot four frame wrapped in a red Texas Marine Mammal Stranding Network (TEXMAM) windbreaker and topped with a Cousteau-like, red wool cap. The boy tapped his mom to turn around.

Kurt waved her to him. Shari lumbered across the soft sand and met him at the parking lot.

"Wow." He stared right into her bloodshot eyes.

"I know it's awful." Shari paused to catch her breath. "I never thought I'd see something like this--so many."

"The 'wow' was for you." He reached out and steadied her hands. "On the phone earlier...I'm sorry I doubted you...your estimates. You've organized an amazing operation. Well done."

She smiled, holding back tears that wouldn't have come anyway. "Good training."

He let go of her hands and turned to the beach. "So, what do we know?"

"Well, Bryan's initial count *was* a little inaccurate—a little low."

"Low? When I called NMFS I low-balled it even more. I said 150. Most people see something of this scale, are overwhelmed and overestimate." He looked northeast up the beach toward the jetty. "How low?"

"I assigned four volunteers to count--two starting from each end. I also assigned two pairs to walk further along the beach to look for more strandings."

"How many?"

"207 on the beach. We think a few may have been pushed off before we got into action, but we haven't seen any come in since we've been here. I told the volunteers to let me know if they had any new additions."

"I need to get an initial assessment to NMFS ASAP. Have you noticed anything with the animals? Lesions? Rashes? Phlegm? Blood? External parasites? There has to be something."

Shari just turned and looked up the beach. "Kurt, what are we going to do? We can't take all these animals to Caldwell. We can't save them."

He knew she was right. The Caldwell Aquarium's three hospital tanks could hold maybe six animals—only three if they wanted to keep individuals isolated in their own pools. There was no comfortably accepted protocol for a stranding of this size. But, he knew there *was* a protocol.

"They've closed the beach—police are at all the beach access points keeping the public at bay as best they can. The stranding phone tree has been activated—a statewide call for volunteers." Looking up the beach he could see a few other people sporting the red TEXMAM windbreakers. "I see some of our volunteer leaders have already arrived. Dr. Menke and his vet techs from the aquarium are on their way."

"Good. That's good." She looked down at her sand-caked shoes. "But, what can they do?"

"You're right. We can't rescue all of the live ones. I hate to do this—I hate to make this choice--but *I* need to choose a dozen that I think might survive. We'll have Dr. Menke's team reevaluate them and choose six to transport."

Bryan had taken a break from his animal, sidled up to Shari and heard the last bit of conversation. The short, slight boy poked his mop-topped head out from behind his mother and asked, "The...the rest? What happens to the...what happens to the rest of the live ones?" He stayed slightly behind his mother-- still a little intimidated by his respect for Kurt.

"Bryan, for an event this large we need information first and foremost. Everything from length and girth to blood samples to teeth."

He stepped out from behind his mother, "And then what?"

"We may try to push the few survivors out." Kurt hesitated.

Bryan persisted, "And then what?"

Kurt looked over the water into the hazy, grey brightness. "I guess we send as many dead animals as we can to the aquarium or the NMFS lab to necropsy and to refrigerated storage. We necropsy the rest on the beach."

Bryan was silent. He scrunched up his face, turned and ran back to his dolphin. Shari sighed and started leading Kurt up the beach.

"It's okay. He needs to hear stuff like that. Reality. He needs to always remember how to face and deal with it."

A firm believer in the power of positive reinforcement, Kurt stopped walking to emphasize his point. "You're doing better than that with him, Shari. After what he went through with his dad...well...you are doing an outstanding job." Kurt looked from side to side up the beach. "...you are doing an outstanding job."

Shaking her head, she laughed, "You should have seen me when I first got here. It was like I had the DTs again." Shari turned and pointed to the neighbor's car she had borrowed with her still shaking hand. "Sitting there rocking and sobbing."

"But, you got it together."

"*Bryan* got me together."

"And, you organized quite a crew."

She smiled again. "Good training — very good training."

"Yes, well..." Uncomfortable with the compliment, Kurt changed the subject. "When the rest of the stranding volunteers get here we'll need to assign them duties and..." Kurt's phone rang. He looked. "Dr. Clarke at NMFS. I need to take this." He flipped the phone open while still talking to Shari, "If I'm still on the phone when the rest of the team starts to arrive, brief them — get them started."

He turned away, "Hi, Angela..."

Chapter 3

Dolphin Towne, Tortola, British Virgin Islands

"Whoa!" Jasmine immediately reached and turned off the outside shower, shaking her head. It was a frantic bring-me-back-to-the-present, not a sexy, slow-motion look-at-my-great-hair-shake.

"Sorry, I…" Adam—who had touched her lightly, tentatively on the shoulder--recoiled, stumbling in his flip-flops on an uneven tile. "Shit!" He regained control of his long, thin legs and stood a few feet away.

Jasmine Summers was the young founder and spiritual guide of Dolphin Towne—an experimental experience in human-dolphin interactions. Looking at Adam, Jasmine held up her hand--her face serene. "Adam. Adam." Taking a deep breath and a step into his space, she continued in an almost too-quiet-to-be-heard voice, "No, I'm sorry. Unexpected. I was caught in some sort of negative energy whirlpool. Bee was odd. All of the unconscious light emptied from the lagoon, from Bee, from me. Dark. Confining. Cold. I had to pull out…break the connection. I had another 35 minutes in the water—but I couldn't stay. I couldn't stay in the dark water with Bee."

Handing her a towel, Adam turned his back and took a big step away—continually shifting his weight from foot to foot. After three years he was still intimidated by her comfortable nakedness and voluptuous beauty. More in control at a distance where he couldn't feel the warmth of her breath on his face, he got to the reason he came to find her in the first place. "I wanted to remind you to complete your encounter log before you get too distracted back at Eli House—especially now. The Encounter software is updated and working again across all platforms. Vid-Mind Sync is even updated, running and linked--so, the Theta Wave Meditation Meld should run even smoother." To Adam, her silence just reinforced his perceived disinterest on her part—disinterest in the advanced client services his technological prowess produced and disinterest in him. He glanced back at her--Jasmine was just wrapping the towel and tucking it between her tan and lightly freckled breasts. He quickly, guiltily looked at his watch, "I should have the other enhancements and updates completed before the weekend retreat."

"Are you with Bee today?" Jasmine couldn't let go of the unpleasant experience she had just had with her favorite resident dolphin—for her, that five-year bond with Bee was intimate.

It was October of 2003 and Road Town had suffered a near miss from Hurricane Bee--*near* enough that most of the coastal resorts were shut down for major repairs, but *miss* enough that there was only one human death on the island.

While her 50-foot sailboat *My Calypso* was secured at a local marina, Jasmine weathered the storm in a tastefully decorated bungalow on Cappoons Bay. She woke up well after the storm had passed—courtesy of multiple glasses of a special punch at the Bomba Shack's pre-hurricane blow-out. Back on *My Calypso*, with a big mug of freshly brewed Ethiopian coffee in hand, she rang Dolphin Cay — the next stop on her most recent "cruise of self-discovery."

One of the few major hurricane casualties had been the waterfront Tortola Inn and its swim-with-the-dolphins program — Dolphin Cay. The tanks and lagoons were intact and the dolphins, safe, but the supporting infrastructure was devastated — no electricity, no pumps, no filters. When Jasmine heard the news — no dolphin programs for the foreseeable future — she was devastated. But, instead of just moving on — drifting with the tide or blowing with the wind with no particular plan — Jasmine had an idea that lit her up inside and kept her from sailing.

Despite the hurricane damage and typical "island time" delays, Jasmine was able to call in immediate help from the US — industrial pumps, filters and generators arriving within 24 hours. The Road Town locals were astonished at the efficiency of what looked like a typical lazy-ass, drifting, dreadlocked American hippie. Jasmine had always embraced the passion and free spirit that was such an obvious part of her life — now, she embraced the trust fund and powerful connections that she had worked so hard to hide.

Even with Jasmine's airlift and donation of materials, the real estate group that owned the Tortola Inn and Dolphin Cay couldn't afford to keep the dolphins on-site *and* rebuild the resort. Cash was short and they had already started to put out feelers to aquariums and other "swim-with" programs — "dolphins for sale." After walking along the twisted deck of the damaged dolphin lagoon, dangling her feet in the water and feeling the energy move through her toes, up her legs and into her heart, Jasmine offered them another option.

Within four days of the hurricane, Jasmine had bought an old "resort" at the foot of Windy Hill on Ballast Bay. She had temporary tanks flown in, moved her pumps and filters from Dolphin Cay and made an offer. Encouraged by BVI tourism officials who wanted to see the Tortola Inn rebuilt *and* keep the dolphins on the island—as well as an above-market cash offer--the owners accepted.

Eight days after the hurricane, another bottlenose dolphin-- "Bee"--arrived. Bee had beached at Little Lambert Bay near an artists' enclave. The residents had heard about Jasmine's place and loaded Bee into a truck for the bouncy trip to what the locals were already calling "Dolphin Town".

At a loss for what to do—Bee was not eating and was unable to keep herself upright in the water—Jasmine flew in the world's leading marine mammal veterinarian, Dr. Aldo Menke, and his team from the Caldwell Aquarium at Texas A&M, to help nurse Bee back to health and to train her and her new staff to care for the rest of the dolphins.

Jasmine and Bee--it wasn't the first time Jasmine had held a dolphin in the water. It wasn't the first time that she had looked one in the eye or traced the outline of its smile with her finger tip. But, it was the first time an encounter affected her the way she always imagined—personally communicating at a higher, spiritual level-- and in a way she didn't—filling her with an overwhelming urge to finally stop wandering the world and put down roots.

While standing in the above-ground pool that was one of her makeshift tanks-- supporting Bee during her rehabilitation--Jasmine designed a uniquely interactive dolphin-human community in her mind. Outside the tank, she consulted with environmental architects from the Solar Living Institute, Dr. Menke and his team and then broke ground for an off-the-grid, high-tech, high-concept meeting place for dolphins and humans. By June of the next year, Dolphin Towne (she added the stylish "e" to the locals' name) was opened and Jasmine was confident in her decision to set down roots on Tortola.

Adam sailed into Ballast Bay seven months later and stayed after he cleaned a nasty virus from Dolphin Towne's nascent computer network, helped with Sammy's initial rehabilitation and made a memorable full-moon trip to the Bomba Shack with Jasmine.

Now, Adam stood inches away from a towel-wrapped Jasmine—the dreadlocks were long gone and her long, red hair framed a lightly freckled face that was, to Adam, angelic. Lost in thought, Jasmine's ever-so-slightly irritated voice snapped him back to the present, "Adam! Are you with Bee today?"

"No--Sammy. I want to check on his bad eye as well as get my daily swim fix. I figure we both get something out of it that way. Good karma, right?"

Jasmine turned toward the path to the women's locker room. "Sammy. He's pleased to have you spend so much time with him. Some guests…they shy away from his mutilations. They don't realize the beauty he holds on the inside."

Stopping, spinning, she stalked back into Adam's face. "Is anyone with Bee before the new pod of guests arrives Saturday morning?" Jasmine often referred to groups of guests with the term used to describe groups of whales and dolphins.

"She's scheduled for an Off-Cycle." An *Off-Cycle* was a time of minimal human contact—usually at least 24 hours long. It was something Jasmine instituted to allow the dolphins to "regenerate" from the emotional intensity of human contact. For Adam, it was a time to observe the dolphins' more natural behaviors. After looking at the schedule on his Blackberry, Adam concluded, "Her next swim is Tommy's weekly Theta Wave Meditation Meld--8pm Friday."

Chapter 4

Capital Beltway, Maryland

"207? You're not pumping up the numbers are you? I want this done correctly—accurately." Angela paused as she tried to manage the phone and pay attention to road signs obscured by whirling snow flurries. "And, *Tursiops*? Are you sure?"

"Yes, 207. And, yes, *Tursiops*--I *have* seen a few bottlenose dolphins in my time. Count is holding steady. No new strandings since the First Responders arrived."

"Unbelievable—in a single day."

"Yes, in a single day." Kurt took an audible breath and continued, "It's awful." Angela could hear another sigh. "We're starting to lose more of them."

"I figured. Your plan?" Angela knew that a stranding of that size was, for most people, for most stranding networks, an unmanageable event—something beyond the scope of rescue and barely within the scope of disciplined data collection. She hoped that at least some of the comprehensive procedures she had implemented during her tenure at TEXMAM were still in place under Kurt's leadership.

"We have room for six at the aquarium. We're pre-selecting 12 candidates and Dr. Menke's live animal team will select the six for transport. They're already on the way here."

"Good. The rest?"

Kurt sighed. "You know."

Of course she knew. Angela was the co-chair of the working group that developed the current National Contingency Plan for Response to a Mass Marine Mammal Stranding (CPRMMMS). And, according to CPRMMMS, data collection was the number one priority.

Kurt knew his answer wouldn't stick--she wanted to know that he worked out the details. He knew he was being tested. He knew his time would be better spent getting started. But, he indulged her and sighed. "We'll split our people into three groups—live animal management and data collection, carcass transport for necropsy at the aquarium, and on-the-scene necropsies. Of course, data collection will be our priority."

"Okay. You have enough trained people?"

"The live animal folks will collect the standard data. When we are finished with those we'll let the volunteers do what they always want to do—shove them back out to sea."

She was impatient now. "Okaaaay…but do you have enough people?"

"I have eight locals qualified to do the live animal sampling. Plenty of bodies to move the carcasses onto the trucks. I put out a statewide call…" He hesitated.

Angela filled the pause. "And the necropsies?"

"The usual suspects will be with Doc and the rescued animals at the aquarium. Same folks—Sarah, Eric, Frits...anyway...So, the vet students from College Station that we've been training—that Doc's been training to assist with necropsies--are three hours out."

"What's the temperature there?"

"What? Cold. Low 40's. Overcast—barely any sun poking through. Pretty dreary--appropriate. It's February."

"Okay...keep dousing the animals with water. Dead, alive—doesn't matter. Let Doc take his six. Don't move any of the other animals—dead or alive. Clear? I need to see this...I need this done right."

"You're not in your office anymore are you?" He could tell that, in her mind, Angela was already on-site managing the stranding—revising his plan.

"Almost to Andrews." She paused—trying to focus on the entrance gate signs at the Air Force base. "The UME Working Group has been notified. I'll be landing in Galveston in less than three hours." She tried to create a dramatic pause, but she didn't get to continue.

"You're taking over. You don't trust me to handle this and you're taking it over. Shit..." She couldn't see it, but he was alternating nodding and shaking his head from side to side. "Going over me..."

"We both know the rarity and severity of..." Angela paused, not wanting to further stir up old emotions. "You aren't a scientist. Director Hamilton has ordered me to take charge. He wants the science done right. He wants me to coordinate it. An event of this magnitude...with the hearings and all..."

"Ah, the hearings. Let's not get into a discussion about the hearings." *Bitch.* Kurt kept the bitterness to himself and continued,

"Yeah, the wonders of the internet." The MARMAM list serve was *the* way people with scientific interests in whales and dolphins kept in touch—details of Angela's hostile treatment of Kurt's stranding theories during the hearings were almost immediately posted online. Kurt knew everything she had said about him. "C'mon! What's *your* plan? We're wasting time."

"Okay—here's something *you* can get started on. Start moving as many as you can to cold storage. The NMFS lab adjacent to the A&M campus has more refrigerated storage space....more room for necropsies of this scale." Angela had given in just a little— nixing her previous idea of leaving them all on the beach until she arrived. "I'll set things up—let you know what building and such. For now, make sure you do a detailed site map. Tag, label, photograph and measure all the carcasses before they're moved. Keep perfect records."

"I know your proto..." Her pause hadn't been for him to talk, but for her to think.

Angela cut him off and went on, "Wait for me for to start the necropsies. The director says specifically that I'm to supervise that."

"Andrews, huh? NOAA jet?" He knew she had that kind of clout now.

"Yes."

"Fly fast. I'll have a sheriff's deputy meet you at the airport. We'll be here waiting for you." He knew she'd like the opportunity to make a dramatic entrance.

"Thanks."

"You're in charge, *Dr.* Clarke."

Satisfied, Angela smiled and continued, "Of course, I'll want to see the site first. In the meantime have the vet students ..." But, Kurt had already hung up.

Third Floor Hallway, Senate Office Building
Washington, D.C.

"Thank you for the notification, director." Upon his return to the hearing room, Director Hamilton had sent a short text message to his boss, Admiral Collins. Now, following the adjournment, they stood in a small alcove.

The admiral spoke first. "What is the current situation?"

Director Hamilton peered into the hallway. "Dr. Clarke is on her way to Andrews, admiral--sir. She should be on site within three hours. She has already contacted the site coordinator and assumed command of the operation. But, sir, why..." Director Hamilton stopped as Admiral Collins began shaking his head. It had been two months since the admiral requested immediate notification of *any* marine mammal incidents in five specific coastal regions of the US. The admiral had given no reasons for his special interest and, in this face-to-face discussion of just such an incident, Jake had hoped to get some answers.

"Jake." The admiral stopped shaking his head and smiled. "I have a special interest in marine mammals — particularly dolphins and whales. Have since my time in Nam. Not for any sentimental reasons, but...well, as you know, the damn critters have been both an integral part of our national security plan and a hindrance to that same plan. I'm not sure if this incident will fall into either category, but I do know it is significant enough for us to watch very closely. Understood?"

Director Hamilton nodded and the admiral continued, "Good. Dr. Clarke is a great asset…I'm glad she is on her way…make sure she understands…make sure that if anything unusual develops, if…"

"Sir?" Director Hamilton was unsure of exactly what the admiral was looking for, but he had the utmost confidence in Angela. "Dr. Clarke will make sure that the site is managed properly--that the science is done correctly…"

The admiral interrupted. "The science is important. But, keeping anything unusual between Dr. Clarke, you and myself…well, that may be more important."

"Dr. Clarke is all about protocols and procedures, sir. She'll understand that nothing—no information, and certainly no speculation, is to be communicated to the outside…"

"To anyone outside the three of us."

"And, Kurt Braun, sir?"

"Inconvenient. At least her current boyfriend may be useful."

"Sir?" Director Hamilton was unaware that the admiral was so well versed in Dr. Clarke's personal life.

The admiral smiled at the innuendo that went with the director's tone, but continued his own line of thinking. "I'll check into a clearance for Dr. Nicely. As for Braun…Dr. Clarke hit him hard the last three days. Can't imagine any warm-fuzzies remain."

"No, sir." Director Hamilton knew that relationship was long done. "I'll make sure she only passes along what he needs to know as the operational head of TEXMAM."

Nodding, the admiral shifted subjects. "Do you think she'll be able to find anything?"

Jake Hamilton smiled. "She is thorough, admiral — very thorough."

"I just hope *we* were thorough."

"Sir?"

The admiral was distracted by a buzz from his briefcase. He looked at the phone and then at Director Hamilton. "I'll expect an update later today."

The meaning from the admiral was clear — *we're done here* — and Jake walked away. Still in the alcove, Admiral Collins looked again at his latest text message and the accompanying photos:

> *Arrived at stranding site. Confirmed: just over 200 casualties.*

East Beach, Galveston, Texas

Message sent, Dr. Menke closed his eyes. He replayed the day six years ago that Admiral Collins had arrived, unannounced, at his office in Galveston. Only for *this* man would Menke have cleared his full schedule of appointments and listened to a research proposal well beyond his current field of expertise.

Following his pre-med BS from UCLA, Aldo Menke enlisted in the army, trained as a medic and in 1970 was sent to Vietnam. He rationalized the decision with an eye on the practical experience and the hope that the army would eventually put him through medical school — but, he really was sincerely convinced that fighting communism in Southeast Asia was worth the sacrifice of a delayed and profitable medical career.

In Vietnam he was attached to the 9th Infantry Division, 34th Artillery. His unit was based on the *USS Freehold* — a huge tank landing ship anchored 40 miles up the Mekong River. The *Freehold* had been converted to house troops and act as a floating base for coordinated movements of the 9th Infantry and the Brown Water Navy. The forward part of the ship housed 175 soldiers, while the rear quarter of the ship was the headquarters for the Navy's river patrols in the sector and home to a platoon from SEAL Team 2. Two large barges were tied along the port side — one for storage, the other for recreation. The starboard side sported a wide fuel barge and a floating wooden dock. Tied to the stern were two SEAL team riverine attack boats and a sunken net enclosure with a small floating dock.

Vietnam was not only the first testing ground for the Navy's elite SEAL teams, but for the Navy's experiments in using trained dolphins for war. SEAL Team 2's "D-Platoon", from the Little Creek Amphibious Base in Virginia, had spent two months at the Navy's top secret marine mammal training facility in San Diego prior to being deployed. The unit developed the skills and relationships with the dolphins that would allow them to work as an integrated team. That team was deployed and based on the *Freehold* following an attack on a similar floating base on the My Tho River in 1968. There, the *USS Westchester County* had been destroyed by mines attached to the hull by Viet Cong frogmen. Three of the five dolphins based on the *Freehold* swam regular patrols around the base — trained to locate, identify, and if necessary attack, enemy swimmers. The other two dolphins were used further upriver — helping the SEAL fast attack team locate mines and underwater obstructions as they neutralized Viet Cong outposts, intercepted enemy supply boats and prepared the interior for regular troop movements.

One afternoon, while Menke was on the recreation barge smoking and writing a letter to his mother in Fresno, there was an explosion in the water about 60 yards off the bow. The men from D-Platoon were in their boats and then in the river almost before the last drops of water hit the surface. One boat returned to the stern with two dead Viet Cong. The other swung around to the big floating dock calling for a medic. Menke rushed up the ladder, across the deck, and down the starboard side ladder to the dock. Stopping short, he saw four SEALs laying one of the dolphins on the dock. Running over, medical bag on his shoulder, he called for more help. The deep laceration, consistent with a shrapnel entry was obvious, but Menke did a quick full-body evaluation. The SEALs did the best they could to hold the powerful dolphin still and keep it moist. Menke started to probe the bloody laceration. The dolphin arched and nearly threw all of them overboard. Menke reacted, poking the dolphin with a sedative before the SEALs could stop him. The arching stopped immediately — breathing stopped at few seconds later.

With the help of smelling pungent smelling salts, Menke woke up about ten minutes later in a familiar place — the *Freehold's* sick bay. Apparently, a SEAL named Collins knocked him out with a hard shot to the right side of his head. Apparently, dolphins couldn't be sedated—they need to be conscious to breathe.

The concussion kept Menke in the sick bay overnight. He awoke the next morning to the smell of fried eggs and bacon. Sitting next to his bed was the SEAL with the powerful and stealthy left hook—Master Chief Lawrence Collins. After the assault, Collins had been chewed a new asshole by the 9th's Colonel Stampel. He was made to understand that no charges would be filed if Collins took the time to apologize profusely to what all aboard considered their best medic.

Collins took the deal a step further—putting it on himself to educate Lieutenant Menke about *Tursiops truncatus*. He wanted this medic prepared to deal properly with any future casualties amongst his bottlenose teammates.

Following his return to the US in 1971, Menke opted to stay in the Army, but instead of requesting the opportunity to attend medical school, he decided to attend veterinary school at the University of California--Davis. His Navy friend Collins worked a deal to have him assigned as an intern/assistant to the Army veterinarians who supervised the care of the dolphins, belugas, and sea lions in the Navy's Marine Mammal Program (NMMP). Collins also made sure that Menke had the transportation to make the long trip at least once a week. Upon graduation, he joined the NMMP vet team full-time. Within five years, *he* was the head veterinarian. Over the course of more than 20 years, he managed captive breeding programs, assisted with, and lead, a variety of research projects, got to know several hundred dolphins and sea lions, met a number of SEALs and managed the transition to exclusive, marine mammal specific special operations teams (MSOTs).

Collins had recognized something special in Menke then, and had come to his office in Galveston in need of those talents and attitudes.

"*Invitation* or *order*?" He remembered asking the admiral for clarification.

"A call to duty," was the admiral's answer.

Menke could still see the unblinking blue eyes and feel the punctuated drop of the admiral's right hand on his left shoulder.

"Doc!"

"Shit!" Dr. Menke's eyes popped open, looked at the hand now on his left shoulder and followed the arm out the box truck window. "Kurt."

"Need a little more coffee?"

"Just thinking through a few things. It's all a little overwhelming."

Doc stepped out of the truck and extended, then pulled back his slimy, rubber-gloved hand.

"You've already made your initial exams?"

Dr. Menke and the live animal team from the Caldwell Aquarium arrived before Kurt had finished with Angela's call and had set to work evaluating select animals for transport. Walking around to the rear of the truck, they could see Doc's team loading a third live dolphin.

Kurt scribbled at his clipboard and then stared blankly toward the water. Doc took a clipboard from one of his students and flipped through the data sheets. "We're almost ready to roll this bunch — TT18, TT43, and TT192."

With no response, Doc continued, "We're almost ready to roll the first truck. We should be able to turn it around for the other three animals in less than an hour."

Um…that's great — great work. Which dolphins are loaded?"

Doc repeated the shorthand designations that indicated the species — *Tursiops truncates* — and an identifying number.

This time, Kurt made a note on his clipboard. A news helicopter buzzing over the water and circling the beach caught his eye, but he quickly returned his attention to the clipboard — flipping repeatedly through a series of checklists.

Dr. Menke could see Kurt's distraction. "Angela's coming isn't she?"

"You heard?" Kurt hadn't told anyone yet. It was next on his list of things to do.

"I figured. This is her type of show — lots of moving pieces to manage. She was made for this." Doc knew them both from their early years working together at the stranding network. "Besides, she's the only one I ever saw who could get you this flustered." Only partially joking, Doc quipped, "And, this organized."

Kurt turned and started toward the beach—Doc followed. "You're right—she's on her way." He stopped after a few feet and turned back towards the box truck. "I'm assuming you'll stay at Caldwell?"

"I'll be sending Randy and the same crew back. Fresh bodies are meeting us at the tanks." Dr. Menke brushed off some sand and a few strands of sea grass and led Kurt to the back of the truck. "See you at Caldwell when things calm down."

Doc climbed in and Kurt helped close and latch the rear door. Three dolphins were away.

"Kurt!" Shari had come up from the beach. "I spread the rental trucks out in the parking area—less distance to carry. That should help get the necropsies going at the aquarium."

He turned her toward the beach with a touch of her shoulder and started walking. "Smart." Struggling for the right way to say it, "But…we're in a holding pattern right now. We can't start the necropsies until…"

"What?" They were at the soft sand again. Shari pointed. "Look at this! We need to know what caused this. We need to get the animals sampled…" Kurt put a quieting finger to his lips and his other hand on her shoulder.

"I know. But, the protocol. It…"

She pulled back and leaned against the creaky wooden railing. "We're following the protocol aren't we? We need…" He sighed and she stopped mid-sentence.

"The protocol allows the NMFS Director of Marine Mammal Health and Stranding to appoint an On-Site Coordinator for any UME. In this case, the director is appointing herself."

"Well...well." Agitated, Shari struggled with the idea that Kurt was being replaced. "You're doing a fantastic job. Your volunteers are doing a fantastic job. She can't run things from Washington!" Her tone was haughty and the affront she perceived was personal.

Kurt put on his best face, "She--Dr. Angela Clarke — she's not in Washington. She's amazing with large, complicated situations like this. She'll be here in a few hours to oversee the necropsies and manage the stranding." Touching her shoulder, he tried to find some reassurance to share. "It's okay. It's a good thing." Pointing towards Bryan — wash from the surf lapping at the boy's legs--still managing the blowhole of the same dolphin, Kurt found a true smile. "He's doing a great job." He gave her a bear hug and released. "You go right. I'll go left. We can still start transporting the carcasses. Let's update the troops."

Out on the beach, Shari turned right. Two years ago she wouldn't have talked to any of these people. Two years ago they wouldn't have listened. Two years ago she was alone and in rehab.

Her husband, Eddie Casseine had been an alcoholic — but, he was far from a violent drunk. Shari thought he actually got kind of cute — sappy and quiet. When he got quiet, she used to tell Bryan, "Daddy's thinking. Let him be." They still did family things — he'd take them to the Galveston Seawall. It was his favorite place. It was the family's favorite place. He'd throw a baseball around with Bryan, barbeque some hotdogs on their little hibachi and, before they headed home, Eddie would always take a few minutes to sit on the wall by himself — quiet.

Shari paused and looked over her shoulder — Kurt was well up the beach. Her head turned to the limp dolphin carcass lying on the beach — it's lifeless tail moving only with the subtle pulse of the surf. It was just over three years ago — Wednesday, December 1st — when Eddie didn't come home from the Office Depot where he worked in the stock room. The following day, an elderly couple out walking their dogs spotted Eddie's misshapen body wedged against a rock groin near Stewart Beach. Her mind blended the two images — Eddie's body and the dolphin carcass. She closed her eyes and started to rock.

"Shari!"

Startled by the shout from a volunteer, she opened her eyes and took a slow, deep breath.

"Shari, what…are you okay?"

Taking another deep breath and nodding, Shari said, "Eric. Okay. I guess the early morning is finally catching up with me."

The volunteer smiled and Shari took a firm step into his space, "We need to do a full work-up on all the animals — dead or alive. I want you to handle the master site map — make sure all the animals — even the ones Dr. Menke just transported--are properly labeled so that we can cross-reference the individual records when the time comes. We need that done ASAP—before we can start moving the carcasses. Got it?"

"Yes, ma'am!" He looked down the beach at the other volunteers.

"I'll brief the others on the individual data we need."

Nodding to herself, Shari marched down the beach. She really didn't remember much immediately after Eddie's death. When the police found his Astros jacket and two bottles of Jack Daniels on the seawall--she wondered why he went there, instead of home to her and Bryan, to celebrate his promotion. Her own low-level alcoholism blossomed and an attempt to pick Bryan up from school while intoxicated resulted in an ugly encounter with the school's police officer, a court-ordered and supervised stay at the Salvation Army's Adult Rehabilitation Center and the state taking custody of her son.

Shari approached the last group of volunteers and paused—again closing her eyes. Her involvement in TEXMAM—her choice for fulfilling her court-ordered community service hours—and Kurt's patient leadership had been hailed by her Salvation Army case worker as an integral part of her recovery. But, standing on the beach, with that blended image of dolphin and husband again in her mind, she knew it meant so much more.

Chapter 5

Bazaruto Island, Mozambique

"Ay, Robin! Over here!" Vee wiggled a flashlight to get the scientist's attention in the subdued light.

Dr. Robin Nicely and his South African stranding response crew had touched down, in a small jet on loan from one of DSC's major donors, at the Bazaruto Lodge's airstrip less than six hours after the call. The urgency was a testament to his dedication and to the Centre's endowment.

"Howzit?!" Vee extended his hand, but Robin slapped it aside and grabbed him in a hug.

"Honestly, I'm still itchy from those fuckin' blue bottles yesterday. Antihistamines, my ass."

"When are you going to stop swimming with the jellyfish? I thought the idea was to stay in the kayak." Vee grinned as he grabbed Robin's carry-on, "You'll end up on the beach like a dolphin someday."

"Surf ski. It's a surf ski." Robin glanced at the bag. "Careful, my laptop and sat phone are in there.

"Let's get your gear in the *chapa* — the truck--and get out to the lighthouse."

"Vee." Robin steadied his hand on the tall, young man's shoulder and nodded at the modified pick-up truck, "let's see them."

While Dr. Robin Nicely's early fame as a scientist was in the study of the social structure and behavior of bottlenose and long-beaked common dolphin communities, he was currently best known as the hands-on director of the fledgling Pan-African Marine Mammal Stranding Network.

The idea for the network was hatched while Robin was still at the University of Cape Town and the university hosted the International Marine Mammal Conference. During several after-hours socials with US colleagues, the free-flowing pitchers of Windhoek turned the conversation to the recent stranding — over the course of four weeks--of 400 bottlenose dolphins near Zanzibar and the data that was lost because of the lack of trained personnel and modern lab and communication equipment. Most of the scientists simply bitched and moaned over their beer. But, Dr. Angela Clarke confronted Robin and his South African colleagues — she said it was *their* responsibility to respond. *They* were the only ones on the continent with the resources. It was the honest power of her directness that managed to cut through his beer buzz and plant the idea in his mind.

Six months later, when he left his post at the University of Cape Town and joined DSC, he had the freedom and funds to move on the idea. After six years of development, the network of stranding teams currently stretched from Angola to Egypt. Robin's collection of scientists, students, expatriates and locals now had the basic equipment and scientifically accepted protocols to respond, collect data and communicate it to the rest of the marine mammal community.

Vitor Mabila — *Vee* to his friends--had been one of those first eager students — eager enough to eventually graduate from the biology program at Eduardo Mondlane University in Mapoto, Mozambique's capital. Now, a graduate assistant in the pathology of marine mammals at the University of Cape Town, Vee had been in Bazaruto starting field work for his thesis on the relationship of *morbillivirus* and pneumonia in bottlenose dolphins. Because of his long association with Robin and the network, the local stranding team from the resort passed the on-site leadership to Vee.

From the passenger's seat Vee turned his head while pointing at a small trail of tiki torches leading up from the base of the dunes, "Ay, we'll park there and walk over to the beach. You won't believe it."

Robin put on his headlamp and grabbed a small backpack while the crew loaded the fat-tire beach wagons with gear. He and Vee slogged up the steep dunes towards the beach. Cresting the dunes he stopped and dropped to his knees. More tiki torches lit the beach — piles of dolphins filling the islands of flickering light.

"The photos you emailed, they... I really...." The words stopped. *Fuck* — it was all that came to his mind. There was little movement on the beach and only a few labored, wheezing blows amongst the piles of dolphins. The local stranding team was working with those few live animals and struggling to keep the already dead fresh in the 80 degree heat.

Robin shook his head. "Fuck. No rescuing here."

"That's a given in Mozambique." Twenty-plus years out of its civil war, Mozambique was finally restoring its people and infrastructure, even attracting tourists from Europe and the United States, but there still weren't the facilities to rehabilitate dolphins. Robin made a mental note about future Centre allocations, turned and plunge-stepped back to the crew struggling to push the first wagon up the torch-lit dunes. Vee went back to help the second.

Robin yelled back down the dunes, "Vee! Can you get us more local help? We need help to keep them from rotting too fast and to move them quickly. We need to necropsy as many as we can. We need tents, better lights and tables…"

Vee was composed. He looked at his watch, smiled and hustled back up the dune so he wouldn't have to yell, "Fishing boat is coming from Inhassoro…filled with ice…still about three hours out." After catching his breath, he continued, "The resort will supply us with food and drink. Dr. Lindelo is already in flight with six students from Mondlane, two generators, lights, old military tents, lanterns, and whatever lab supplies he could spare. He'll be here within the hour."

Dolphin Towne, Tortola, BVI

The Eli House — named for the famous dolphin communication researcher, isolation tank inventor and beyond-the-fringe thinker Dr. Livingston Eli — was an ecologically friendly, Key West style lodge overlooking Ballast Bay. Jasmine and Adam sat on the wide back deck enjoying the salty sea breeze and an organic lunch.

Jasmine set down her fork and looked at Adam, "I know it's not typical. I hate to intrude. But, on Friday, can we watch Tommy's swim with Bee? In the Window Room, of course."

"We really have a lot to get together for the weekend retreat." He took another bite of romaine and chewed. "I know *I* need to finish my software updates and get the incoming pods' profiles and logins up on the network. Retest the suction cup transponders, service the filters. They'll be arriving at 8am on Saturday." He gulped green tea with fresh mint.

Jasmine was focused. "I'm afraid that Bee is going to take him to the same place. I know she'll have been through the cleansing of an Off-Cycle, but I'm still being drawn into the darkness at odd times. It's very cold. Bee is there, but her luminescence is not — her warmth is not. Darkness. Cold. At odd times." Jasmine shivered.

After more than three years, Adam was mostly over the New Age spring that flowed from Jasmine's mouth, mind, and heart. He still enjoyed the time he spent swimming with the dolphins, but felt none of Jasmine's, or the other clients', profound spiritual connections. His experiences were increasingly scientific.

Part of him stuck around slimly hoping for a repeat of that seemingly long-past full moon night on the beach at Cappoons Bay. It was a life moment for Adam — the thin, awkward, brainy boy who had been advanced several grade levels and had never felt socially at ease among his older classmates. Jasmine had grabbed his hands and dragged him into the bay — collapsing haphazardly, but together into the surf. The rich red hair that typically fell all the way down her back was now soaking wet, and wrapped around his back. The breasts that were always just out of reach were now pressed warmly against his chest. Adam knew the moment was fueled somewhat by the Bomba Shack's special full-moon "tea", but couldn't help hoping that there was magic beyond the mushrooms.

When he woke up the next morning he was lying alone on a rickety lounge chair that the night's vigorous gyrations had collapsed onto the sand. Jasmine was just coming in from a swim. Before he could get past her raw naked beauty, before he could get a word out, she shouted, "We need to get back to Dolphin Towne--three new pod members coming in tonight."

They never spoke about that night and from that morning on, to Adam's disappointment, Jasmine seemed to treat him more and more like a brother. But, on other levels the arrangement suited him. He lived for free at Dolphin Towne — trading his time and expertise for a fully furnished apartment in the Eli House, organic meals made to order, and a loose purse that allowed him to purchase and experiment with the latest software and electronics. It was the stress-free antithesis of his MIT research disaster.

Content, Adam was almost always agreeable. Putting down his fork, he looked across the table, "I'm good with that. We can watch Tommy and Bee on Friday. But, let's get to work on that retreat stuff. I want to get as much done now as we can."

"Thank you." Jasmine reached across the table and held one of his hands in the two of hers. She closed her eyes. "Blissful. You work on your computers; I'll take care of the rest."

Chapter 6

NOAA GS-3, somewhere between Andrews AFB and Galveston

M-A-R-C-O-8-9. Dr. Angela Clarke typed in her password and logged onto her laptop--reviewing the protocols her working group had developed for sampling stranded marine mammals. It was one of her first accomplishments as the new National Director of Marine Mammal Health and Stranding. She was proud of it--but even after three years of tweaking the minutiae, she never considered it quite "finished." Still, Director Hamilton had signed off on the procedures, so she was confident in the process. He wasn't the type of man who signed off on anything questionable — his stated formula for a steady rise to the top of the government marine science hierarchy. It was an approach Angela admired and mimicked.

Unfortunately, she didn't feel comfortable that it was the approach that Kurt would take in Galveston. Kurt was the head of TEXMAM — the Texas Marine Mammal Stranding Network — and generally respected in the marine mammal community for the basic work of dealing with beached whales and dolphins. But, he was not a scientist — and, because of his wild theories about the causes of those strandings, most scientists still considered him a bit of a flake. She knew him better than that — his creativity, his passion, his power and his agenda. She knew like no one else.

Or, do I? Angela wondered if he was finally sleeping with someone new--sharing his life with someone new. The thought interrupted her fifth read-through of the protocols.

Despite no hard, unbiased evidence, and even though strandings were recorded as early as the second century by the Greek poet Oppian, Angela knew Kurt was still convinced that cetacean *mass* strandings were a human-related phenomenon—specifically that human impacts on the marine environment were at the root of the problem. He was convinced in a passionate way that she knew biased his stranding work—that she knew was not good science.

At the recent hearings when his stranding data was admitted, she had to deconstruct and debunk *his* credibility, *his* methodologies, *his* results and *his* conclusions. She could do nothing else. Ignoring Kurt's hyperbolic conclusions would have hurt the status of the Marine Mammal Protection Act and future funding for all stranding networks and research. Angela knew it would hurt Kurt. It *had* hurt Kurt.

She knew that was nothing new for Kurt. Shifting in her seat, Angela's stare moved out the window. He was used to her hurting him.

Angela first saw Kurt while she was a PhD student at Texas A&M. He was speaking as part of a public lecture series offered by the university. Granted, "The Mythology of Marine Mammals" wasn't at the top of her list of ways to spend her time at College Station. Her trips to the University's main campus were usually short and business-like—with a direct drive back to the coast and the marine mammal facilities at Galveston. But, Dr. Blaire, her advisor, said Kurt Braun was reputed to be quite a speaker—worth the extra time. Angela wasn't disappointed.

Though the topic proved more interesting than she imagined, it was Kurt that held her attention — as well as the audience's. It was the way he spoke about the temple of Delphi and Apollo's transformation into a dolphin — a confident, powerful passion born of thorough knowledge and understanding. From that night on, she just called it *the voice*.

Angela wondered if she had heard *the voice* when she talked to him earlier on the phone. It was something that was hard to sense over a bad cell phone connection. Angela flipped her notebook open again to start her sixth time through the protocols. Flipping it shut again, she closed her eyes and her thoughts drifted back to that night.

Shuffling out of the mythology lecture with the rest of the crowd, Angela found herself in a mild panic. She *had* to have more — but, was hardly dressed to fit in with the invitation-only, jacket and tie set at the post-lecture reception. Never one to be deterred by decorum, and harnessing some serious motivation, Angela confidently approached the entrance to talk her way in. Maybe it was the confidence with which she approached, or her relentless argument, or maybe it was the effect of her low-hip jeans on the man at the door. Whichever, she didn't care — she was in.

Once inside, Angela spotted Kurt alone, sitting off to the side — a plate of food in balanced on his lap. Making a quick pass of the buffet table — she was still on a graduate student's budget after all — she took her piled plate and sat next to Kurt. Looking at him, she knitted her brow.

He recognized the look--and the question that most often followed—and answered, "I'm good with large crowds...at a distance," he had said. "Or, small groups of intimate friends."

Angela remembered smiling and not hesitating to say, "A small group of *my* intimate friends is going camping down at Galveston Island State Park this weekend. Join us?"

More "formal" introductions followed, as did the exchange of cell phone numbers and email addresses. Later that evening, after the long, sleepy drive back to Galveston, Angela emailed the details of the weekend camping plans. She followed that, mid-morning, the next day, with a 47-minute phone call.

Kurt brought Angela's intimate camping group up to eight people. It was a mix of marine mammal and fisheries graduate students—males and females. The seven friends were already out on the beach, some lounging, some surf fishing, when Angela got a call from Kurt. He was at the campsite, alone. She walked back, helped him settle into one of the three tents and then led him to the beach to make the introductions. While Angela had noticed at the lecture that Kurt was "cute", it wasn't until she saw him in his board shorts and tank top that she could tell he did something to keep himself in top shape. *Bonus*, she thought.

While it was clear to Angela that Kurt's near silence signaled more than a little discomfort around new people, she did her best to pull him aside at regular intervals to give him tidbits of insight on the rest of her friends—Christy and Thad were engaged, Thomas was gay, Delia was a vegetarian--actively trying to accelerate his acculturation. At about five o'clock Kurt headed back to the campsite—told Angela that he would get the grill started for the fish that Thad and Thomas had caught. But, she could sense that he was a little overwhelmed and just needed time alone. As much as she wanted to, Angela didn't follow.

When the rest got back to the campsite, Kurt had hot coals in the grill and a roaring fire in the pit. He was sitting in his rusty old-style lounge chair with a carefully concealed beer on the ground and a dog-eared copy of Homer's *Odyssey* in his hand. Angela looked at the book, then at the beer on the ground, then at the book, then right into Kurt's eyes. "Some things I just won't give up on." She remembered him saying that—in *the voice*—and his penetrating, grey-blue eyes.

Just before Kurt had headed back to the campsite, the conversation had turned to his job, career, and life plans. Angela could see that the questioning made him uncomfortable—he went from sitting crosslegged on his beach towel to lying back, blank-staring into the blue sky. She was about to attempt a save and ask him in some flirtatious way to go for a walk on the beach, when *the voice* kicked in. Kurt explained that had he met any of his former high school classmates at this point in time, the ones who had gone through years of honors classes with him, they would have expected him to be nearly transformed into the second coming of Jacques Cousteau—exploring the undersea world in his own version of *Calypso*. But, he wasn't. Instead, about halfway through his freshmen year of college he had a confrontation with the second coming of calculus. His first confrontation had been in crusty, funny old Abe Finegold's honors calculus class his senior year in high school. It did not go well. Kurt's second battle with derivatives, inverse functions and implicit differentiation went worse—halfway through the semester he withdrew from the class and all his work suffered from the depression of his retreat. Angela remembered him sitting up on his towel, looking directly at her and saying, "I quit. On calculus and on the marine biology I knew I couldn't get through without the math. I quit." It was still hard for her to forget *the voice* and the images associated with it--even from so long ago.

So, Kurt explained, because his ineptitude in math wouldn't let him *do* the science, he decided to study how *others* did science. His eventual PhD in the history of science focused on the study of marine mammals from Ancient Greece to present. At the time of the camping trip, Kurt was a financially struggling adjunct at A&M—spending his off time looking for a full-time teaching gig and running just to stay in shape.

Angela's memory went back to the campfire and the *Odyssey*. "Some things I just won't give up on." That's what he had said. Kurt told her that he had only read the *Cliffs Notes* in high school, but that while surveying Greek texts for his thesis that he picked up the full text and a real appreciation for the work. A true romantic, he loved the epic quality of the poem and Odysseus' persistent drive to get home. Kurt carried it and re-read it to remind himself never to quit again.

The rest of that evening on the beach was more of a giddy blur to Angela — the dwindling fire, the inevitable lull in the conversation, her grabbing Kurt's hand and nuzzling him towards the beach. Smiling, she could feel the warmth of the sun and the smell of the salt water bringing back the image of waking up on the sand next to Kurt. When her eyes moved back to her computer screen, Angela frowned — her distant, happy memory replaced by the emailed images of dolphin carcasses strewn near that idyllic beach.

Chapter 7

Dolphin Towne, Tortola, BVI

Adam could lose himself in his computers the way Jasmine could lose herself in a discourse centered on the healing properties of swimming with dolphins or the dolphin link to the universal consciousness. He was in that kind of flow focus now — sitting in his network control room tweaking software and creating user profiles for the 15 guests coming for the weekend's retreat.

The network control room was in the Education Center and contained servers, a small high performance computing cluster, 13 small high definition video monitors, Adam's main computer station, and the fiber optic links to two satellite dishes and landlines within the property. This was both his playroom and his workroom. Even in the peaceful, lush campus of Dolphin Towne, it was where he felt most at home.

Upon finishing, he closed his eyes and rotated in his chair towards the bank of monitors — first checking out Sammy. Sammy had been mutilated by a fisherman and left for dead — found on a beach along East End Harbour on Jost Van Dyke. The obvious rope scars on his body pointed to some type of net entanglement — the loss of the top of his dorsal fin, his entire right pectoral fin, and a gouge near his right eye pointed to how the fisherman had articulated his rage with a large, serrated knife. Over the phone, Dr. Menke had recommended euthanasia — Jasmine convinced Adam to help her treat and keep Sammy. Now, as Adam watched on the monitors,

Sammy swam with no apparent handicap. Smiling, he turned his head for a quick look at the new image on his computer. "Nice!" He had to shout, the new subcutaneous transponder that he had implanted during his earlier "swim" with Sammy was working perfectly—brainwaves, heart rate, body temperature. Setting his software to "continuous record", he turned to Bee's video monitor.

As Jasmine's soul-mate, Bee inhabited the largest of the seven natural-looking lagoons on the Dolphin Towne property. It was one of two that actually abutted Ballast Bay—separated by an expensive walkway-topped, perforated Plexiglas wall that allowed the free flow of water and smaller fish.

What? Adam couldn't tell whether he yelled in his head or out loud, but he repeated it out loud, "What? What was that, Bee?"

He thought it was an anomaly—that it wouldn't happen again. But, Bee chased, caught and ate another small fish.

Bee had been in captivity almost since the beginning of Dolphin Towne. Her stranding was blamed on the hurricane and she bore the storm's name. Exhausted, emaciated and dehydrated, she had only a minor respiratory infection when Dr. Menke did his initial examination. Tube feeding began immediately—fluids with glucose, electrolytes and antibiotics. As she improved, her tube-fed diet changed to fish shakes. Eventually, Bee was trained to eat whole dead fish. By that time she had gained weight and was, in Dr. Menke's evaluation, a clear candidate for release. But, Bee failed the next step. She failed it again and again over the next month. She failed it for weeks after Dr. Menke packed up his team and headed back to Texas.

Bee simply would not eat live, free-swimming fish—the last, and most important, prerequisite for release. And, as far as Adam knew, nobody had given her that opportunity again.

"Shit!" After the third catch, Adam rolled his chair over to the main video control console and hit "record". The scientist in him kicked in—he had to find out what had changed.

Chapter 8

East Beach, Galveston, Texas

Angela arrived with the deputy sheriff and a two motorcycle escort. She had called Kurt upon landing and he was in the parking lot to meet her.

Her fit legs were the first thing he saw — she was still wearing the just-above-the-knee skirt from the hearings that morning.

Kurt approached her with arms wide, "Angela."

Cell phone plastered to the side of her head, she held him at a distance with the wait-a-minute finger and continued walking towards the beach. Kurt followed her and waited.

"Thanks. I'll swing by the tanks once I get the necropsies started — 60 to 90 minutes or so." She hung up just as the entire beach came into clear view — and stopped. It was like someone took a roller of black paint to the earlier, happier images of her and Kurt lying out the beach under the starlight.

"Kurt." She finally turned to him. He grabbed her in one of his famous bear hugs — thinking that even Angela the scientist cum bureaucrat was a little emotionally overcome by the sight. But, what had already been a half-assed return hug on Angela's part suddenly went limp. Kurt just sighed.

Angela pulled away, running toward the beach as she yelled back, "Damn it! There are people out there without masks!"

He caught her and stopped her at the bottom.

Angela glared at Kurt. "And gloves! Some don't have gloves. You know the protocols!"

"Of course I know *your* protocols. But, we've had different crews of volunteers working with them in shifts for hours — we just didn't have enough gloves or masks when we started. But, the master site map is complete. The on-site data collection is complete. We've started moving carcasses. We need to get the necropsies started and the few remaining live animals off the beach." Hearing all the shouting, Shari walked up from where she was compiling the data collection sheets and stood shoulder to shoulder with Kurt.

Angela's shoulders tensed. Her face tightened. She forced her breaths. In. Out. In. Out. She glared at Shari. "The masks and gloves should have been handed out from the start. That is the first step-- first step. Protect the volunteers — protect the data."

Shari reluctantly stepped in, "We didn't have enough and once we started tending to the live ones and collecting the data we just didn't think of it." She pointed to the supply van in the parking lot, "We can make sure that..."

"Too late! The data are screwed already." Angela glared again, and then closed her eyes to focus while turning to Kurt. Taking a deep breath, she opened her eyes and looked directly in his eyes. "Yes, still get the masks and gloves to everyone. I'm heading over to brief the vet students and supervise the necropsies." She looked down the beach at the volunteers working to load carcasses into the box trucks. "Keep them coming. I got us room in the NMFS labs at Fort Crown to set up the necropsy stations. Building G — it backs right up to the Caldwell rehab area. I'll have a student outside directing your drivers there instead of to the fridge."

It was Kurt's turn to close his eyes—knowing she had already improved the situation. She really was *that* good. Kurt shouted at her as she ran toward her car, "And me?"

Sand on the parking lot ground into the pavement as she stopped and turned. She paused and pursed her lips in thought, then spoke, "Half-hourly data collection on the live ones. Keep the carcasses moist. Don't screw it..." Her phone rang and she put up her finger while she answered. "Excellent--thank you so much for your help. Please contact Kurt Braun when your people arrive."

A self-satisfied smile on her face, Angela turned back to Kurt and shouted, "The Red Cross is sending volunteers with tents, generators, lighting and weather gear. I'm still working on the food and hot drinks." She looked down at her phone again—it was a different, specific ring. "Keep things going." She turned away and covered the mouth piece. "I'll call you once I get the necropsies started."

"Thanks!" Kurt shouted, but she was already out of sight.

Wide-eyed, Shari looked at Kurt. "Wow. You have a serious history with that woman, don't you?"

Kurt looked through her and nodded.

Chapter 9

NMFS Laboratory, Galveston, Texas

"Dr. Clarke?" Director Hamilton's assistant had her on hold for the entire 10-minute ride from the beach to the aquarium.

"Yes, Milly."

"Here's Director Hamilton." Milly patched her through.

"Jake." Even through the phone he could hear her voice was solemn.

"Not getting all squishy over a few carcasses are you?" With no answer on the other end, he tried being a little more upbeat — adding a little sing-song to his voice. "How goes it, Dr. Clarke? Got everything running smoothly now?"

Nothing. He wasn't used to Angela getting emotional or using silence to dramatize anything.

"Angela?"

"It's…" After another short pause, she continued, "It's more than a few carcasses *and* it's more than one location. I just got the call- -there's been another *Tursiops* mass stranding."

"Crap." It slipped out, subdued, but not unheard. "Where? Texas?"

Angela continued her short walk from the aquarium parking lot to the old buildings of the Galveston National Marine Fisheries Service laboratory. "It's in your neck of the woods-- Virginia Beach." She looked at the notes she jotted while on route. "A…um…Little Island Park. Surfers saw them beach. Crazy surfers were out in that winter storm you've got brewing!"

"How many?"

"It looks like another live stranding." Angela had just walked into the small classroom on the ground floor of building G— oblivious to the thirty veterinary students milling about, talking. "Their guess was *hundreds*." The classroom went quiet and she finally noticed all the students.

Stepping back into the hallway and closing the door, Angela continued, "I've already been on the phone with Ed Bordon. His stranding team from the Virginia Aquarium is loading their truck now—ready to roll in 30 minutes."

Jake sighed, his mind going back to the day's earlier conversation with Admiral Collins. "No."

He couldn't see taking steps in Virginia Beach without consulting his boss. He also couldn't see sending volunteers out with a winter storm warning in effect. With that, Hamilton knew he had the perfect excuse--unarguable. "Call them off *now*. Tell them to go home—stay home. It's not just an average winter storm. With the weather coming in, with the winter storm warning--we just can't risk human life out there…"

"Really?" Angela paused, calmed herself and got professional. "Director Hamilton. You know we need that data. I could fly in tomorrow morning…we could use staff and…"

Jake cut her off. While they were talking, he had pulled up a map of eastern Virginia, noticed all the military bases, and formulated a better plan. "You sit tight—nobody will be flying in anywhere near Virginia Beach tomorrow. Cancel the volunteers--

now. The wind is already up to gale force and they are calling for two to three feet of snow--possible freezing rain behind it. The travel advisory is telling people to get to their final destination in the next two hours or stay put. It's just not safe. We can't have you flying and we *cannot* put volunteers at risk for this."

He knew Angela couldn't argue with that, but he also knew she'd want some type of response. So with another look at a map of the area, he took a creative whack at a response plan. "Admiral Collins might be able provide some help — provide a team that can handle this weather. The area is littered with naval bases. He still has strong connections at Little Creek and the other naval facilities in the area. Maybe can see if there are a few un-deployed SEALs there — those men can take the cold weather and keep the public away…keep the public safe." Little Creek Naval Amphibious Base is the Navy's east coast training center for amphibious combat operations — part of a number of important naval installations in the area and home to several SEAL teams.

With no immediate response, Director Hamilton continued, "Bob knows the protocols…"

"Squires?" Angela was livid. The Director of the Office of Protected Resources, Dr. Robert Squires, was her immediate superior. "He is a great administrator, he might even know the protocols, but he's never been on a stranding. He's not been in the field in years…"

"Stop!" The director's voice boomed. "I'll brief Bob. My priority is getting him to the site — getting someone with authority from NMFS to the site--but I'll brief him. I know the protocols *and* I have been on more than one stranding. Remember, I watched you coordinate that two month-long manatee event in Fort Myers four years ago." Angela's seamless management of that red tide related stranding — from the initial assessment and rescues to the meticulous necropsies and tissue sampling--convinced Director Hamilton that she was what Admiral Collins had been looking for in a new national stranding director. With the admiral's enthusiastic blessing, she was given the job.

His voice booming through the phone, Jake continued, "Under the circumstances, this is the best, the safest, thing we might be able to do."

"I wish I were there. Dr. Menke, Kurt, they really would have done just fine." She looked through the small pane of glass into the classroom — the vet students were talking loud enough to be heard in the hallway. "I've got to brief my necropsy teams. Let me know how you make out with the admiral. Have Bob give me a call after he gets on site."

Director Hamilton wanted to reassure his protégé. "You're going to make sure they all do better than *just fine* in Texas. It's what you do best. It's what I hired you for. Here, well, we'll be lucky if the dolphins even stay on the beach in these conditions--it's getting *that* bad."

"You're right. I can't be everywhere at once. I can have a greater impact here. Make sure Bob checks in with me ASAP. I want that stranding managed as correctly as possible." Angela hung up and opened the classroom door.

Chapter 10

Office of Admiral Collins, NOAA
Silver Spring, Maryland

"Thanks for holding, Jake." Admiral Collins had set down his personal cell phone and was once again speaking to the director of the National Marine Fisheries Service on his office phone. "Lieutenant Commander Medlin will be the officer in charge and your on-site contact."

"That's good news, admiral. I'm glad Little Creek can spare a few men. I wanted to delay Dr. Clarke from acting — with our earlier conversation in mind…plus--the weather--I didn't think it was fit for volunteers. I noticed all the bases in the area and remembered the SEALs you work with at Little Creek and…well…I tried to think fast, sir…anyway…" Director Hamilton's thoughts wandered and then he continued, "For site coordinator, I was sending Bob Squires, Angela's direct supervisor, Director of the Office of…"

Admiral Collins interrupted with a relieved sigh. "Squires sounds like the right man for the…situation." The admiral pulled out his personal phone--sending Squires' contact information and personnel file to his contact at Little Creek while he continued. "Lt. Commander Medlin will set up a rendezvous point with Squires. They'll take him to the site in a vehicle suited for the conditions."

"Impressive." Jake knew that the admiral still had tremendous pull, and interest, in the Navy. "Are these SEAL units that have trained at NMMP in San Diego?"

"No. Not SEALs. No."

Director Hamilton understood the admiral's tone — though much of the Navy's work with marine mammals had been public knowledge for over 10 years, the existence of the Marine Mammal Specific Special Operations Teams (MSOTs) — special forces teams qualified to work with dolphins and sea lions and trained at the closely guarded Navy Marine Mammal Program facility in California — was classified. Jake moved on, "Yes, sir--got it."

Collins drummed his fingers on the edge of his desk. "Thanks for calling me before allowing Dr. Clarke to act in Virginia Beach — well done. *This* is a situation I definitely want handled with the special sensitivity of a national security event. Information is to be shared only via my approval and only then on a need-to-know basis."

Jake knew this wasn't a time for questions. A graduate of the US Coast Guard Academy and a veteran of six years on active duty, he knew when to follow orders. Besides, in the past the admiral had generously upgraded his clearance--to assess the environmental impacts of certain defense projects that required at least a cursory review by NMFS. Jake respected that special trust in his expertise and the man who extended it.

"Understood, admiral."

"Again--I will expect you to be in *frequent* contact." Admiral Collins hung up, pulled another cell phone out of his desk drawer and texted:

BLADE

Unanticipated consequences? Galveston, Virginia Beach — plans in action. New York, San Diego, Tampa?

On his laptop, there glowed a special map of the United States. Labeled "CONCH," the screen displayed five coastal areas highlighted in green — other areas of the US coast were red. He finished texting:

Anticipate needed actions now. Assets must be located or inserted and on ready alert. Advise.
ACRET

Day Two

Thursday, February 20, 2008

Chapter 11

Bazaruto Island, Mozambique

"Vee!" Robin called him on the two-way. "How's the loading going?"

Vee looked into the ice, and now, carcass-filled hold of the fishing boat. "We've managed to get 63 into the hold. That's the most we can get in and keep covered with enough ice."

"Sweet. Come over to the tent."

Six active necropsy tables were under each of the faded, green military tents. Robin supervised one tent, Dr. Lindelo managed the other.

"Vee." Robin was shaking.

"You need some food." Vee motioned to a cooler in the corner of the tent. "Come over here."

"I don't have time…" At six-foot two inches and 185 pounds, Vee was no longer the skinny school boy Robin had met six years ago. Robin was two inches shorter, but the intensity of his surf ski training earned him the lean, hard body—and sometimes the hard mind--of an elite athlete. However, Vee recognized the signs of bonking—a serious and potentially debilitating drop in blood sugar. He knew that even the super-fit Robin was human. Grabbing his mentor by the shoulders, Vee persuaded him to move towards the cooler. "I'm sorry, sir. We need you to stay strong."

With a reluctant mouth full of banana Robin mumbled, "What are you scheming?"

"I'm going to take the boat back to Inhassoro and make sure they get stored properly in the ice house. I'll recruit some local help to move them."

"Yes. Hang on." Robin stood up and helped one of the volunteers bag a sample from a liver biopsy, then came back to Vee and the cooler. "Take some of the unused equipment with you and start setting up. We'll be done here late tonight. Any carcasses we don't get to will be too rotten by then. I'll have the locals burn the rest." He looked out at the beach and then sat back down. "The plane should be able to have us there sometime around 10."

Robin paused and stared--the banana peel sat in his lap. Vee prodded, "Keep eating."

"Yes--off with you then." He grabbed a granola bar and held it up for Vee to see. "I've got to make a call to the states. Someone there needs to know about this."

Vee shot him a sly look and then headed back up the beach.

Building G, NMFS Laboratory, Galveston

"Bob! How's it going there? I can barely hear you!" Angela shifted herself upright and the blanket slid off her and the cot she had been napping on when she got the call.

"It's the wind — gusts up to 50 mph! You wouldn't believe it. I barely made it here — if the Navy team hadn't met me…the roads, well…there's two feet of snow on the ground already and they're calling for a lot more! It's a crazy, swirling whiteout!"

Angela ran her fingers through her tangled bed-head hair-do. "The dolphins—how many? What's the status? I don't really want a weather report." She knew she sounded a little grumpy—irritable in fact—but didn't care. Angela had settled down for her first nap since leaving Maryland just 40 minutes before the phone rang. She was tired and didn't care if she was demanding.

"Okay." Bob paused, absorbing the directness he knew well from working with Angela at headquarters the last three years. He tried to make his answers just as direct. "247. *Tursiops truncatus*. Well-beached, but the tide is out at the moment. Dying fast...from exposure I would assume."

"Don't assume!" Angela started to make her way back to the impromptu necropsy labs in the depths of Building G. She spotted a vending machine and managed to make it eat her crumpled single and spit out a Diet Coke. She took a couple of gulps. "What's your plan?"

"These Navy guys have got this area closed like it's Fort Knox, so no public getting in our way. I have four corpsman that Director Hamilton and I briefed..."

"Jake? Jake is there?"

"No, no. Satellite uplink on their all-weather, portable workstation. Nifty piece of hardware-sent video and photos too. We could..." He found himself drifting off point and self-corrected before she caught it, "We're just about to start data collection—blood, etc.--on the live ones. We figure the dead will be well-preserved. But, we are expecting the worst of the storm later and a *big* high tide at

11:30 this morning. Like I said before, it's already deteriorating…worse than expected."

While staring at five vet students working at the closest table, Angela tried to put herself on that snowy beach in Virginia. "If you can, detail some of those Navy boys to move as many carcasses as you can up the beach—above the high tide line. The cold will preserve them enough for sampling after the worst passes."

"I'll call you early afternoon with an update." Bob sighed directly into the mouthpiece—knowing he wasn't in a situation of his own making or in his field of expertise. "We'll do the best we can." He hung up.

Angela closed her eyes and tightened her jaw, wondering why people always had to qualify that statement. She wondered why they couldn't just do the job. For some reason, Kurt's favorite Yoda quote popped into her head, "Try not. Do or do not. There is no try."

She opened her eyes. The vet students were a godsend. Dr. Menke was right—they were anxious to impress and excited to work on something more exotic than cows and chickens. It showed in the quality of their efforts. Angela was happy with how the necropsies and the tissue sampling was proceeding, so she gave everyone the thumbs up as she walked by on her way out to the med tanks.

East Beach, Galveston, Texas

The beach looked like a small, ramshackle army encampment. The Red Cross had not only brought the weather gear, tents and lights Angela had requested, but heaters and cots for volunteers working through the night. Carcasses still lined the beach — transport had slowed as the necropsies started and the refrigerators at Caldwell and the NMFS labs neared capacity.

Kurt surveyed the morning scene from the top of the beach patrol building. He hadn't slept. Most of the volunteers had only catnapped in the Red Cross tents. He was happy that the local Starbucks had started bringing fresh coffee and muffins — happier that they'd be back every two hours with more. Standing there with a *grande* cup in his hand he waved to get Shari's attention — she was organizing another small group of volunteers.

Remembering when he first saw her — shuffling to the back of the TEXMAM classroom with Bryan — an empty row of metal folding chairs separating the two of them from the 15 other people in the room that first Saturday morning — Kurt whispered to himself, "You've come a long way baby."

That back row was no place to hide. After Kurt's general "hello," he proceeded to greet each student personally — starting with the back row, starting with Shari and Bryan. After reaching the front row, Kurt then asked each student to tell the group why they were there. This time, he started from the front row — allowing Shari plenty of time to spin a tale other than her truth. After the others had gone, he smiled and nodded at Shari. He knew she was there doing community service and he wanted her to feel safe enough to tell these people the truth — she could immediately see *that* in his eyes.

Like the others, she and Bryan stood up—her left hand on his right shoulder. Shari looked down at Bryan looking up at her. She looked at Kurt. He smiled and nodded again.

"I'm Shari Casseine, and this is my son Bryan. I'm an alcoholic and seven months ago I was arrested for a DUI. After six months in rehab, I'm here to start my community service hours and spend time with my son." There was so much more to it than that, but Kurt smiled at the big step Shari had taken and nodded again. Shari and Bryan sat down. Bryan reached over and hugged his mom tight.

When Shari finished with her small group of volunteers on the beach, she acknowledged Kurt's wave and came up the steps—stopping one short of the top.

"I was just thinking of your first day at TEXMAM—how brave you were that day. You told the truth. I was thinking about all the office work you've done for me—not missing a Monday afternoon for two years. And then…and then there was the help with Wally's rehab—that was above and…" She put up her hand and he stopped.

She looked at her sandy shoes in silence.

"Day two." Kurt looked down, smiled and chuckled. "Did you or Bryan get any sleep?"

"I slept between three and four." Shari looked back toward the water, where Bryan was still on blow-hole duty. "Bryan doesn't want to leave Pirate."

"*Pirate*?" It was posed as a question, but Kurt knew that someone had gone and named the dolphin. He also knew the emotional attachment that came with a name.

"He said one of the campers here first thing this morning named it Pirate. Bryan just closed one eye, scowled and said *arrrrrrrrgh* when I asked him more about it."

Kurt tensed his face and bit his lip. "I don't even know what Ang...what Dr. Clarke is going to want us to do with the few live ones left."

"Four." Shari shifted from the top step to the flat top of the boardwalk and leaned against the railing. "There's only four live ones. Can't the aquarium..." She stopped when she saw Kurt shaking his head "no".

"The protocol." Kurt looked out towards Bryan. "Dr. Clarke's protocol in an event this large, if we can't get them to a facility..." It was difficult when he knew that even the best volunteers got attached to the live animals. "...is to euthanize them on the beach."

"*You* can't do that. Not you."

Kurt looked down at his feet—sand filled the dry-rot cracks in his old duck boots. He looked back up at Shari. "Dr. Clarke will make that call."

Shari noticed the coffee in his hand and the Starbucks van over his shoulder. "I'll let the volunteers know about the fresh coffee and..." She could see they had food there, but wasn't quite sure what.

Kurt saw the question in her eyes and finished her sentence, "…muffins." He nodded thanks for the not-so-subtle change of subject. "They'll appreciate that."

Chapter 12

Roland Summers Marine Mammal Rehabilitation Facility
Galveston, Texas

"Angela! Over here!" Dr. Menke spotted her just coming through the gate separating the NMFS buildings from the aquarium. Angela joined him on the wide wooden deck that ringed Med Tank C.

"Status, Doc?" The lift from the Diet Coke had come and gone.

"Well, good morning to you too." He smiled — knowing Angela too well to take offense to her directness and to miss an opportunity to tease. "Long time no see…"

"Sorry, I…"

Dr. Menke cut her off with a wave of the hand. "No need for sorry."

He smiled again and touched her on the shoulder to direct her over to a small table on the platform. There hung six clipboards — the status sheets from each of the dolphins. One clipboard was hung backwards. "We're down to five Angela. The sixth wouldn't take any fluids. At about four this morning, he started arching and gasping."

Bottlenose dolphins had been kept in captivity in the US since the 1930s. More was known about *Tursiops truncatus* than any other dolphin species. But, even with that knowledge base and the relative success of rehabilitating stranded bottlenose dolphins over the last 20 years, Angela had seen that behavior — arching--plenty of times. The dolphin's whole body abruptly arches into a "C" shape and holds that position for tens of seconds. Then, it releases--relaxes. Then, it repeats. Sometimes it's violent and volunteers need to leave the tank. Sometimes the animal is so weak there is no risk.

Angela nodded at Dr. Menke.

He continued, "We euthanized her by lethal injection at 4:30am. Time of death 4:33am."

Angela peered down at the two dolphins in Med Tank C. Volunteers were supporting both animals, managing their blowholes and sponging water over their skin, and said, "We'll need a small euthanizing team on the beach shortly." One of the volunteers in the tank turned his head quickly in her direction — sound carries amazingly well down and into a round tank. Angela noticed his wide eyes and turned away from the water. "Kurt tells me there are four still alive at the state park."

"I have a new shift of vet students in at nine…three that have worked with me before. All professionals. All experienced with this sort of thing."

"When they arrive we can brief them. I'll go too — someone will need to explain to the volunteers. I don't want Kurt absorbing their frustration — he has to work with those people in the future."

Dr. Menke smiled.

"What?" Angela blushed.

"Sweet of you to play the bad guy."

Her face went white. Turning and waving her hand at the clipboards, she moved on, "Tell me what else you've got now."

"Well now, princess," Dr. Menke knew just how much he could joke with her--and, just how much she needed to be joked with at times like these. "With such a large group you would expect some commonalities to show up." He frowned, "But, from these six...now, five...we're not seeing any beyond the emaciation and dehydration..." Looking at Angela he continued, "...which I would think is less pronounced than in the carcasses you've been looking at?"

Angela looked back into the tank. "Not by much...but, yes, I'd say so. Still, it looks like none of them have eaten in..."

"Months." Dr. Menke caught her quizzical look that he recognized as "Don't exaggerate, Doc." He got a little more precise. "Four to six weeks--easy." Angela got a little more impatient.

"What else?"

Menke shot her a look that only someone she really respected could dish out. She gave him a closed eye apology — mouthing, "I'm sorry." Doc was one of the few people Angela respected enough to extend the liberty of her preciously small supply of patience.

"We've learned more about *Tursiops* in the last 30 years than in the previous 2000. In the last five years we've learned more than at any time in the last 30." He paused, picked up the first clipboard and flipped a couple of pages back. "Still, in some cases I can't tell whether the presenting conditions came before or after the feeding stopped. Was it the cause or the effect?"

"And I thought you were the Dr. House of marine mammals...the Sherlock Holmes of pathology..." Angela chuckled and let that hang in the air while she looked over the clipboards. Dr. Aldo Menke was unarguably the world's leading marine mammal veterinarian. When Dr. Menke retired from the Army and the Navy Marine Mammal Program, he moved to teaching at Texas A&M veterinary school—mainly because of their involvement in the stranding network and their plans for the as-of-yet un-built and unnamed Caldwell Aquarium. Now, Dr. Aldo Menke stood on the deck of the country's leading marine mammal rescue and rehabilitation facility. His extensive experience with marine mammals—particularly bottlenose dolphins—commanded the respect of anyone in the marine mammal community.

Still, Angela harrumphed and said, "We'll have blood work when?"

"The basics shortly. More by four. Cultures, well, that takes more time." Seeing that Angela was impressed, he smiled, winked and shared his secret. "The kiddies do good work fast when a senior faculty member asks."

Angela nodded, "I've been very pleased with their work." She smiled and headed for the steps. "I'll check back in later. Thank you."

Chapter 13

Director's Office, NMFS, Silver Spring, Maryland

"Director Hamilton's office, this is Milly, how may I help you?"

"Hello, Dr. Robin Nicely here. Dolphin Studies Centre in South Africa. Is the director in?"

Milly wrote the name on a piece of scrap paper next to the phone. "He's on another line Dr. Nicely, can I connect you to his voicemail?"

"Aw, no. I left a message on Dr. Clarke's already. If I don't hear back I'll try again. Cheers…uh…thank you."

"You're welcome, Dr. Nicely. Bye-bye."

Milly took the scrap paper with the name and slid it onto the director's desk. She pointed at it several times — like she was typing the same letter over and over with her index finger.

Jake Hamilton covered the phone with one hand and shoed her out with the other and a quiet "Thank you."

"Sorry, senator." Without even glancing at the note, "My assistant couldn't wait to pass me a message." He could sense Senator Hulme getting typically impatient. So, while the senator was sighing, Director Hamilton looked at the name, whispering, "Nicely, Nicely." He wondered why Dr. Nicely would be calling *him*.

"Director Hamilton?" The senator took back control of the conversation. "Are things under control in Virginia Beach?"

With the winter storm filling most of the local news time from South Carolina to Maine, there had been no coverage of the stranding at Little Island Park. And, with the Navy team now on site there would be no coverage, period — as the admiral wished.

Ever the cautious political bureaucrat, Director Hamilton chose his words carefully — he didn't know how the powerful, four-term senator had found out about the stranding and he wasn't about to give too much away. "Well, a team from Little Creek has the area sealed off — they'll be sure to keep the curious or heroic public safely away from the animals and out of the dangerous weather."

"Seems our *retired* admiral still has many connections..." Senator Hulme let the sentence hang in silence.

Hamilton didn't bite, "Bob, um, Director Squires from Protected Resources is managing the site and working with the Navy medics to collect whatever data they can in those horrendous conditions. We just couldn't risk exposing volunteers to that weather, senator. It seemed like our best option."

After a brief silence, Hulme continued, "Nice use of the available resources, especially given the weather. Um...how goes things in Galveston?"

"Dr. Clarke's cautious with any details, senator." Director Hamilton was thankful for slight change in topic. "She's pleased with how the necropsies are going — her data collection is clean, by the book. She's stating only the obvious commonalities — the species and the emaciation of the dead. No detailed blood work until later today. Carcasses still on the beach are relatively fresh. A team should be on their way to euthanize the four still alive on the beach. Five of the six at the aquarium are still swimming…" A heavy sigh from the senator stopped Jake mid-sentence.

"Please keep me in the loop, director, you know my interests."

Jake ticked them off in his head, *Oil production and refining, space and defense industries, commercial shrimping and fishing.* Jake tried to put the pieces together, but couldn't afford a prolonged, thoughtful pause. "Of course, senator."

Chapter 14

East Beach, Galveston, Texas

"I think you should talk to him." Kurt had intercepted Angela and the vet team that was going to euthanize the remaining four live dolphins.

"You know the kid, Kurt. I'm sure he respects you." Angela was backpedaling on the main reason she had accompanied the team—to talk to the volunteers and absorb their ire--to protect Kurt. Or, was she just back to challenging him to do things outside his comfort zone?

The vet team stood off to the side, gear bags in hand and just within earshot—waiting.

"This kid and his mom, they've been through a lot. They were the first TEXMAMers on site yesterday. Can't we just save Pirate?"

Angela shook her head and thought, *Pirate? Why do they always name them?* But before speaking, her line of thought was interrupted.

One of the vet students stepped closer and said tentatively, "Dr. Clarke?" Angela looked over to the approaching young woman--astonished at the interruption. The young woman continued, "Sorry to be eavesdropping, but when they euthanized TT 18 this morning that opened up a space in the med tanks. We could transport Pirate and…"

Up went the hand. Angela nodded at the student and turned to Kurt. "We're all stretched thin. You know the human and financial resources that live animal care uses. Is it worth it to save one more animal? Is this kid really that special?"

Angela had seen that look before. It was the look—confident and unyielding--that went with *the voice*—though this time, the look itself was sufficient. Angela whipped out her phone and dialed. "Doc. I'd like to bring in one more live one." She listened and stared off towards the boardwalk. Kurt could tell she was really only humoring Doc by listening to his arguments against transport—he knew that if her mind was already made up, she would get her way. She always got her way. Doc finished on his end and Angela let the silence linger for a few powerful seconds. "If we have space for one more, I want to use it." Smiling she turned to Kurt and then to the student. "Randy and the live transport truck will be here within 30 minutes. Keep tending to...to Pirate."

Kurt knew Angela was smiling only because of her power to persuade Dr. Menke, but he thanked her anyway. "Well done. We'll have one much happier 12-year old."

"It was the right thing to do. We had the space. We may learn something from *Pirate*." She motioned to the students. "Now, let's get on with it."

Chapter 15

Little Island Park, Virginia Beach, Virginia

"Dr. Squires!" Lt. Commander Medlin patted the director on the shoulder. Bob Squires turned around. The wind made anything less than a shout at close range inaudible. "We could use some help with that one!" Medlin pointed to an exceptionally large dolphin that appeared to be dead.

Squires trotted over with the Navy crew and took up station — as directed--on the dolphin's tail. An office person at NMFS for the last 10 years, Squires didn't have much recent hands on experience. He would have been happy to have been in the field if it weren't for the weather and for having to take orders from golden child, Dr. Clarke. Well, *Director Hamilton took care of that*, he thought. *He put me in charge here.*

Focused and somewhat blinded by his snow-caked glasses, Squires waited for the sailors to coordinate the move. He couldn't see the rest of the dolphin--obscured by the hulking men in their weather gear. He couldn't see the corpsman stick the not-quite-dead dolphin with 100 milliliters of adrenaline. Arching violently, the dolphin flipped its fluke--sending Squires spiraling backwards into the icy surf.

Office of Admiral Collins, NOAA
Silver Spring, Maryland

"Thanks for holding, commander," Undersecretary and NOAA Administrator Rear Admiral Lawrence Collins rotated his chair to look out his floor to ceiling window — it vibrated in the wind and the view was nothing but white. "I wanted to pass that status report to Director Hamilton at NMFS ASAP and let him know that you would be his on-site contact until the weather breaks."

"Yes...*sir*." The slight hesitation in Lt. Commander Medlin's voice was covered by his respect and loyalty to the admiral — by his emphasis on the word "sir." Rear Admiral Lawrence Collins was the first SEAL to reach flag rank, the first to command a fleet and a stateside base — the first appointed to a civilian position at the Undersecretary level. He was also the man who championed the creation of the Marine Mammal Specific Special Operations Teams (MSOTs).

For the elite men of the MSOTs, men like Medlin, Admiral Collins' record and reputation were legendary. His first action was in Vietnam, clearing underwater obstructions and mines, and Viet Cong guerilla camps to allow Brown Water Navy patrols to control the Mekong Delta. He was famously awarded the Silver Star and the Purple Heart while working with a platoon of the 9th Infantry to re-secure a top secret forward operations base on the Cambodian border. His combat experience, work with the first active dolphin team and subsequent creation of MSOTs made him a legend in the special ops community and a mentor to "dolphin men" like Medlin.

Exploiting that status, Collins requested and was granted participation in the continuing education of all of the nation's SEALs and MSOTs. At least one weekend a month, he traveled to teach. Sometimes he was in the classroom—lecturing on everything from jungle combat strategies and urban assault tactics to current trends in world politics and the basics of dolphin training. Often, he was with the teams in the field—observing and critiquing their training exercises. This availability helped secure a very real and intimate bond with the men.

Because he was currently based at NOAA in Maryland, and because he was the former base commander, Admiral Collins most frequently visited the teams based at Little Creek. On more than one occasion he had lectured or observed Lt. Commander Medlin— enough that he thought he had the measure of the man.

"Continue as directed, Lt. Commander." The admiral again scrolled through Medlin's service record on his laptop and, again, noticed that his father was a career Marine--killed in the Beirut Barracks Bombing in 1983. Typically, an event like that created just the type of man he needed. "You're doing a fine job. Your father would have been damn proud, son."

"Yes, sir. Thank you, sir."

Admiral Collins glanced at the clock on his computer, "As per Commander Kirk's orders, you will continue to report directly to me for this mission. I'll expect your next report at 1300. Understood?"

"1300. Yes, sir."

Chapter 16

Roland Summers Marine Mammal Rehabilitation Facility Galveston, Texas

"Hey, Randy!" Angela had just returned from East Beach — supervising the euthanasia of the three dolphins after the recovery team had toted TT 7, Pirate, back to Caldwell.

Dr. Menke's protégé turned and shushed her. He walked over to the edge of the tank's deck and squatted down. "Doc's in the tank with Pirate."

Angela just smiled and gave Randy a thumbs up--she already moved on to her next thought and had her phone to her ear.

"Thank you for calling Dr. Robert Squires, Director of Protected Resources…"

She redialed. "Thank you for calling Dr. Robert Squires…"

"Voicemail." Angela grumbled and started walking towards Building G to get an update on the necropsies and to start the process of shipping out tissue and blood samples. She stopped and dialed again. "Thank you for calling Dr. Robert Squires, Director…" This time, she let the greeting play through and left a message, "Bob. Angela here. Call me with an update ASAP. I need to know what is going on there. ASAP, Bob."

Angela couldn't deal with not knowing what was going on in Virginia — she dialed Director Hamilton's cell phone.

"Angela, how are things in…"

She cut him off. "I can't get a hold of Squires."

She noticed one of the vet students, a necropsy team leader, trotting up to her. Angela looked him in the eye and gave him the hand, then the wait-a-minute finger. He walked closer and she noticed a Ziploc bag in his hand. "I called three times and finally left…" Angela paused, finally getting a glimpse of what was in the vet students bag. He held it up for her to see.

A little flustered, she stammered on the phone, "I'll have to…have Squires…" Angela took the baggie and held it up to her eye. What she saw focused her for the moment. She looked at the phone — Jake had already hung up--and looked again at the little metallic cylinder. Then, she looked questioningly at the student. "From one of ours?"

"We saw a very slight lump under a small scar, we thought it might be some kind of cyst, so we incised it and this popped out."

Building G, NMFS Laboratory, Galveston, Texas

Angela had to see for herself. Drew, a third-year vet student, led her through the old building's narrow hallways to the dolphin in question.

She looked at the incision four centimeters anterior and to the right of the blowhole—it was obvious to her that the small, cylindrical metal object had come from that location.

She turned to Drew, "Did you photograph or video the procedure?"

Drew handed her the digital camera and helped her scroll through. "Here's the scar before our incision." He scrolled again.

"Video of the procedure. I knew it was metallic — bone, cysts, they don't feel like that."

"I'm going to take this camera and download it to my laptop." Angela looked at the bag again. "Where's the chain of custody sheet?" All samples that moved from hand to hand or where shipped anywhere were tracked on a physical chain of custody sheet and an Excel spreadsheet. Every time the spreadsheet was updated the new file was emailed to Angela and Kurt. Drew handed Angela the sheet for samples from TT 27. She looked down the list for the metallic object and printed, signed and dated the line to the right. Handing it back to Drew she said, "Well done."

He didn't turn away — just stood there, waiting.

"Drew?"

"I worked in a Humane Society clinic last summer." He looked at the jar in her hands. "I spent a good bit of time getting practice doing minor surgeries — chipping cats and dogs."

Angela motioned for him to follow her and then stopped in a small alcove away from the rest of the team. Quietly she said, "I don't want any wild conspiracy theories leaking out."

"We all know the public information protocol, Dr. Clarke. No one would jeopardize their standing working with marine mammals."

Angela knew that marine mammal work was coveted by more marine biology students than there were positions available. "Okay. I hope so." She looked at the bagged sample again. She looked at Drew.

Drew again answered the implied question, "Understood."

Angela walked down the hall into the lab that had become her makeshift office/bedroom. She set her laptop on the old yellow wood desk and powered it up. "Idiot!" Her mind moved back to Virginia Beach. She hadn't heard back from Squires; she had hung up on Director Hamilton—all for what was probably just some strange piece of marine trash.

There was nothing on her cell phone voicemail, but there were two messages on her office phone. "Robin?" Her smile was weak. They'd talked for two and a half hours two weeks ago—then, nothing. She knew that sometimes he liked his space—so she didn't initiate contact—but, two weeks without even an email was unusual and infuriating.

Her thoughts stopped as she tapped in her voicemail code and focused on his message. "...Bazaruto, Mozambique. It's a small archipelago midway up the Mozambique coast. *Tursiops*, 306 carcasses. Bloody, stinking mess in the heat, but thanks to you we'll get quality data from most of them. Nothing conclusive at the moment. All are very emaciated. We're moving what carcasses we can to an ice house—the heat is taking its toll. Call me on this sat phone number when you get a chance. I'll email photos sometime Friday. Cheers, love."

Pulling out the old metal desk chair, Angela flopped down—slouching low, legs spread wide and shaking her head. Too agitated and fidgety to sit, she stood and paced—stopping to close her eyes. "Damn it," she whispered—angry at herself for being angry with him. He'd obviously been working in Mozambique for a while—300 carcasses don't just wash up overnight. Chuckling and shaking her head at the absurdity of that thought, Angela still wondered why it took him so long to call or why she hadn't heard about or seen any online posts about a stranding of that magnitude.

Walking to the desk, she grabbed her phone and dialed Director Hamilton.

"Angela." Jake Hamilton's voice was firm enough to not allow her a reply. "Squires is in the hospital."

"What!? Why didn't you..."

He cut her off sharply. "*You* hung up on *me*. Now, *you* listen." Jake wasn't in any mood for the control-the-conversation games Angela usually played. "He was helping the team move a carcass, or what they thought was a carcass." He paused, but Angela respected his silence. "It wasn't dead. It spooked and sent them all flying. Bob went into the water. In the commotion it took them a few minutes to get him out. Luckily it was the Navy men and not some volunteer team."

She couldn't hold her tongue any longer, "And he's..."

"Let me finish!" It was one of the few times Angela had felt the director get agitated with her. "The cold water...his diaphragm must have went into spasms and caused him to inhale the slushy seawater. He almost froze his lungs. Right now...well...he is stable, sedated and on a respirator—breathing some warm, moist O-2. The docs at Virginia Beach General say the corpsman's training—and, their tracked vehicle's ability to move him quickly in the snow--saved his life."

Angela let the pause hang long enough to know it was okay for her to talk. "I guess we are lucky that we didn't have our regular volunteers there. Good call on your part. Who did you send over to coordinate?"

Director Hamilton knew this would be the hard sell — but, he was now under orders from Admiral Collins. "No one. The weather won't allow anyone but the Navy team and their tracked vehicles to move. We're lucky they got Bob out and to the hospital. We can't risk another civilian injury in this weather. So, the commander — Lt. Commander Medlin--is my — *our*--on-site coordinator until the weather changes." He anticipated her next outburst, "No *buts*. That's an *order*."

She was stymied, but had to say something. "Okay, but now you're starting to command like the admiral."

Director Hamilton was deft enough to deflect the intended sarcasm with a chuckle and move on. "Your Dr. Nicely is trying desperately to get in touch with you. He even left a message for me with Milly. Didn't you give him your cell phone number? The admiral has approved information sharing with him. Thought his expertise might be helpful. I'd like you to return his call ASAP."

Chapter 17

Inhassoro, Mozambique

"Vee!" Dr. Robin Nicely strolled into the huge ice house—the blast of cold air was a welcome relief from the heat and humidity.

"Robin!" Vee spread his arms wide and turned his head back and forth--prompting Robin to check out the interior of the ice house. "Welcome."

It was quite a sight 63 carcasses neatly stacked to one side. A huge glass window separated the ice house floor from a large office that Vee had obviously converted into a necropsy room. Robin and his crew from Bazaruto moved in that direction. "Well done. I'm afraid that someday someone is going to pull you away from the science you love and turn you into an administrator!"

"Dr. Nicely!" One of the locals who had been outside unloading the truck ran into the ice house. "The mobile in the truck--it's ringing." Robin turned and marched back to the truck.

The satellite phone wouldn't work inside the ice house, so Robin had left it behind—sitting on the truck's dashboard. He reached through the open window and managed to get it before his voicemail kicked in—but before he could look at the display and see who might be calling.

"Hello. Nicely here."

"Robin! Angela."

"About bloody time, girl. Where have you been?" He really wanted to know, but he also *knew* the question was sure to provoke her. Robin was the only one who seemed to rattle and unsettle Angela — the only one who could disrupt her composure or get her to respond in a way that was anything but all business. Robin loved to have that power and, to use it.

"For the last two weeks I've been sitting by the phone waiting for you to call. Checking my email. Looking for smoke signals…" Angela knew the sarcasm was mildly playful, but she missed him enough to allow a little of the hurt and anger she felt sneak through.

"Obviously, you've been sitting by the wrong phone." Robin opened the truck door and climbed in — getting comfortable. "At work I left two voicemail messages. I even called Director Hamilton's office."

Angela's seriousness returned. "Um…cell phone? Mobile? Anyway…Yes, that's why I'm really calling. Jake…um…Director Hamilton wanted me to call about the stranding." She had to say something, *had* to say something else. Her voice got weak, "It's been two weeks. I was worried that…but, with 300 animals in Mozambique I figure you've been pretty busy. Is that where've you been all this time? Why didn't you try my mobile? Why didn't you call me sooner?"

There was serious silence on the other end. Robin had to say something, "I just arrived yesterday, love. The animals started hitting the beach in small groups four days ago. Apparently, the biggest lot — over 100--was on the last day."

Angela repeated her last question, "Why didn't you call me sooner?"

"There's not time to go into that now." Robin closed his eyes hard, "Just know that you've been on my mind every day." He opened the door again to turn on the light and fished a thermos of coffee from the mess on the floor. "Now, want to hear the latest?"

Angela, in one of her most practiced moves, pushed her feelings aside. "I've got two strandings myself."

"Two?" Barely managing a laugh through his tired, sunburned face, Robin countered, "We had 306 on the beach and..."

"207 in Texas. At least...who knows...250 in Virginia Beach. Two *mass* strandings idiot!" Angela's voice was more than a little pissy.

Robin swung his legs out of the truck and stood. Some serious expletives were on the tip of his tongue, but his thoughts quickly turned inward. "In three places? Over 700 total." His voice became anxious, "What species?"

"*Tursiops*. Both locations." Knowing Robin's temper, Angela waited.

"Fuck!" He hurled the now empty thermos into the darkness. The old-fashioned glass liner shattered. "Shit! Here as well." Robin's tone bordered on anger. While pacing and pawing at the dusty ground around the truck, he shouted into the phone, "What the fuck is up with that?"

Realizing that was all he had to say at the moment and that he was seething on the other end of the line, Angela had to continue, "Now, ask me over how many days."

There was silence.

She tried again, "Ask me."

Robin stopped pacing and leaned against the external spare tire. He pursed his lips, wondering why she was so insistent. "Over how many days?"

"Single day events. One day."

Covering the mouthpiece he cursed again, "Fuck!" He knew she didn't like how much he used that word, so he kept that one to himself. "That's insane — in one day? That's just not right. Mine came up like "normal" at least — over four days according to the people at the resort."

"*Tursiops*?" Angela waited nearly ten seconds for Robin's reply.

"Yes, and I know what you're thinking. I'm thinking it too." Lost in the situation, Robin was sitting in the dirt next to the truck. "They are *never* in groups this large. Never." He stretched out on his back to look up at the stars, his fatigue catching up with and sidetracking his train of thought. "Remember that June night on the beach in Zakynthos just lying there looking at the constellations…trying to imagine how the old time Greeks turned that seemingly random assortment of lights into a dolphin?" Robin rolled over and stood up. "Well, let's not fabricate connections that don't exist…mine was over several days and yours was…shit…all at once? Does yours look like *morbillivirus* too?"

Angela's sigh was audible — even across 9000 miles. "No." She hesitated. "I mean…we'll have some data from Galveston in a couple of hours…Virginia…who knows. Big winter storm there."

"Okay?" Robin knew she was struggling to share. He prodded a little more, "C'mon--even for me? I know you don't have all the data, but what do *you* think?

"Entirely off the record?"

"Hang on," Robin waved away Vee—who had come out to see what was taking him so long. It was really a sarcastic gesture— lost on everyone but himself. "All clear now. Off the record. Hush-hush. Yes."

"I've seen about 50 of the carcasses up close. Maybe two or three with the obvious lesions and...."

Robin started walking back towards the ice house. Angela continued, "Not enough to steer the others to their doom...at least based on the stranding behavior we've seen in the past. What about yours?"

"An epidemic. When we get all the labs back, when I get to look at the photos of those we didn't get to necropsy...I'll bet we'll see it in 98%. Still, Vee thinks there is something unique about how this particular strain manifests itself."

"Looks like we both have our own mystery to solve."

"Right. Vee will make short work of the pathology. He's gotten *that* good." Angela had met Vee enough times over the course of the last seven years to be intimately familiar with Robin's pride in his protégé's continued accomplishment. "Now, we just need to get that eminent dolphin social biologist, Dr. Nicely, to figure out how the hell—or, why the hell—so many banded together and hit the same beach." Back at the door to the ice house, Robin paused. "I need to get back to the necropsies — they'll think I'm out here taking a little kip."

"I'm sure they know how much you love your naps." She paused, startled when her minded wandered to something she hadn't asked. "Wait!"

"C'mon, Ang…need to go."

She got to the point. "Is *anyone* using a subcutaneous chip for tag and recapture? *Anyone?*" Angela described the metallic cylinder and its location in TT 27.

"You almost forgot to tell me about *that*?" Sarcastically, he ventured to tease, "I love you too." Robin closed the ice house door — still standing outside in the night heat. "Seriously, love…no — no one using anything like that — still using photo ID for most studies. Chip-tagging like dogs and cats? Too cumbersome and resource-intensive. You know that. You sure that's what it is? Could just be marine rubbish — part of a buoy clip or something? I can't imagine it's relevant. Are you sure that's what it is?"

Without hesitation Angela said, "No, but one of the vet students thought that's what it might be. He worked in a vet clinic and…I haven't asked…I guess I need to…"

"Smash it open! Let me know what you find. Gotta go, love. Work to do." He opened the ice house door and could feel the air chilling his sweat soaked shirt.

"Love you!" Angela shouted quickly into the phone — hoping Robin hadn't just hung up.

He hadn't. This time, Robin replied sincerely, "Yes, love you too."

Chapter 18

Dolphin Towne, Tortola, BVI

While Adam had finished his preparations on Wednesday for the weekend retreat, he told Jasmine he still needed more time — completing software updates, system defrags, virus scans, and profile creations. Every time she asked, he rattled off a list of technical jargon that he knew she really didn't understand. In reality, he spent most of the day in his network control room — conducting the research he began once he knew he had gained Jasmine's trust. He couldn't get over his ideal situation — a severe contrast to his brief graduate school run at MIT.

Adam Reich had been a prodigy — his math and science skills put him out of high school at 16. A voracious appetite for learning had him a double major in biology and physics by 19. His aptitude for tinkering with computers — software and hardware — and other electronic devices complemented his intellect.

Courted by world renowned humpback whale and bottlenose dolphin researcher Dr. Harvey Lykes, Adam entered a highly-competitive, cooperative PhD program at the Massachusetts Institute of Technology. The cooperative work was done through Woods Hole Oceanographic Institute, where Dr. Lykes was hoping that Adam's interest in bioacoustics and a more directed approach to his hands-on electronics work would enhance the groundbreaking work his team was already doing on dolphin communication. After a month-long sailing vacation that took him and his father from their vacation home on Anna Maria Island along Florida's west coast to the Keys and Bahamas and back, Adam packed his car and made the drive from their home in New Jersey to Boston.

While most new students in the MIT-WHOI program spend their first two years mired in classes with only the summers for serious research, Adam worked with some brilliant graduate students, post-doc researchers and professors from the beginning. His reputation earned him that special treatment and a special burden. Lykes was currently trying to isolate which portion of the dolphin brain triggered specific dolphin sounds, but was having a hard time synchronizing the data from his recording hardware. In his first month, Adam redesigned and rebuilt the two needed transponders and wrote an algorithm that had solved the problem.

Adam struggled for the first time in his academic life — trying to balance his required full course load with his expected contribution to Dr. Lykes' project. He still managed "A's" in his class work, but they were marginal — his professors constantly questioning the lack of creativity and enthusiasm in his approach. It seemed Adam was reserving all of his originality and passion for the dolphins. Endless cans of Red Bull, frequent trips to Starbucks by a sympathetic roommate, and two to three hours of sleep seemed to be all he needed. But, at the end of his first full year, Adam was frazzled. He was looking forward to joining the Lykes team heading to the Bahamas for two months of field research — collecting acoustic and behavioral data on wild bottlenose dolphins, participating in his first tagging captures, spending everyday out on the water with his fellow students. The hope was that the trip would be relaxed and regenerative—like his family's vacations in Florida.

But, the trip never happened. Adam was not invited to join the Bahamas team and instead received a summer teaching assignment on top of his duties to continue Dr. Lykes' captive dolphin communication research program. Two weeks into the summer session, Adam was again reworking the electronic transponders and rewriting software. After 65 hours of tinkering, two trips from Boston to WHOI and back, and a few too many Red Bull-Mountain Dew cocktails, Adam's roommate found him on the floor despondent and shaking—notes for his 8am lecture strewn around the room. The MIT health center pumped him with IV fluids and a mild sedative. Adam woke up 18 hours later—he had missed his class. Ashamed and unable to handle the pressure, he didn't even return to face his roommate.

Credit card in hand, Adam was on the next flight to Sarasota, FL. After reaching the family vacation home on Anna Maria Island, he stocked their sailboat and headed south.

At Dolphin Towne, Adam was able to indulge and expand his intellect and creativity in Jasmine's low to no-stress environment. In his short time at MIT, he had developed an interest in dolphin brain waves—something that his time working on Dr. Lykes' communication projects didn't afford him the liberty to thoroughly explore. Jasmine's money allowed him to do that—and, to create an electroencephalogram transponder that was smaller than anyone had ever used.

The subcutaneous transponder was the next step in his research—allowing him to monitor a dolphin's brainwaves without any obvious external devices and with a lower likelihood of accidental detachments. Now, he could collect data 24/7 without Jasmine knowing. Sammy was the ideal first subject—his excessive scaring allowed Adam to practice the hypodermic insertion technique without worrying that a botched job would attract attention. It was Sammy's transponder signals that he was monitoring at the moment—ensuring proper synchronization with a video journal of the dolphin's activities. With the old external transponder, Adam had collected over two years of data—brainwaves matched to Sammy swimming, eating, interacting with clients, sleeping, echolocating, and socializing with the other dolphins. It was enough for Adam to write his first scientific paper—now in the hands of the editors and peer review panel of *Marine Mammal Science*.

With his synchronization program running smoothly, Adam turned to Bee. He had been recording her activities since her successful hunting the day before and decided to review the last 24 hours at 10 times normal speed. Since the lagoons were usually unlit at night, Adam had a double camera system in each that included a standard high resolution video camera and an infrared system. It was the infrared video that he was deep into now.

Adam noticed two shapes swimming along the clear bayside wall of Bee's lagoon. He slowed the recording. "Two dolphins! Shit!" Adam watched as Bee swam alongside the wild dolphins—albeit on her side of the wall. Back and forth, back and forth—47 minutes of real time. He didn't observe any hunting behaviors in the 47 minutes of the encounter—but they had to be teaching her to eat free-swimming fish.

Adam verified that he was still recording video of Bee's activities. Then, he flicked on the hydrophones in Bee's lagoon and hit "record"—curious as to what was being said between Bee and her two wild friends.

Chapter 19

Little Creek Amphibious Base, Virginia Beach, Virginia

Lt. Commander Medlin stood at attention while on the phone. "Admiral Collins, sir. Everything is proceeding as you ordered, sir."

"I don't need to remind you of the sensitivity of this mission, do I commander?"

Medlin did not hesitate, "Sir, no, sir!"

"Be sure that…"

The admiral was cut off by a beeping in Medlin's ear. "Pardon, sir, call waiting. It's Dr. Clarke on the other line, sir."

"Very good. Give Dr. Clarke your report—as we discussed."

Medlin switched lines. "Dr. Clarke?"

"Lt. Commander Medlin?"

"Yes, ma'am." Medlin relaxed and sat on the desk in the small, heated guard house. "First, I have some bad news to report Dr. Clarke. My father always taught me to give the bad news first."

"Squires?"

"No ma'am. Dr. Squires is stable and improving the last I heard from the hospital. He was injured under my watch, so I requested periodic updates. My men did all they could to…"

"I'm sure they did, commander."

Looking through the frosted window and across the snow-lashed field, Medlin could see his men carrying out *his* orders—the subtle glow of the base incinerator lighting up the swirling snowflakes. "Ma'am, the worst of the storm hit yesterday at approximately 1000 hours. We abandoned our efforts and returned to our vehicles to secure the perimeter. The east winds at 50 mph drove in an exceptionally high tide at 1130. When the storm and the tide receded the carcasses we had left on the beach were gone."

"Gone?"

"Gone. Apparently the outgoing tide..."

"How many? How many did you lose?"

"Ma'am." Medlin wasn't used to this kind of impassioned questioning. He paced small circles in the cramped office. "All but nine."

Angela held her anger in check. "Please explain, commander...please explain how more animals were not moved above the high tide or into trucks or..." She stopped and sighed.

Medlin clicked into damage control mode, "I understand your frustration, Dr. Clarke. We had loaded nine animals before Dr. Squires asked us to start concentrating on moving the animals higher up the beach. His hope was that their position would be safe and that the cold would preserve them for sampling when the storm passed." Medlin opened and closed the Velcro closure on his side arm. He did it again—and a third time. "We work in these types of environments—beaches and estuaries that is—all the time. The consensus of our team was that the movement was sufficient for the conditions."

"But you were wrong." Angela quipped.

"Yes ma'am. We were wrong." Securely closing the Velcro on his sidearm, Medlin stopped his pacing and leaned on a desk. "Prior to the change in plans we did manage to safely store nine animals in one of our vehicles. We tended to Dr. Squires…we did manage to collect your basic data set on 74 animals. My team of corpsman collected blood and teeth from 33 animals before we took refuge in our vehicles. Honestly…" Still leaning on the desk, he started playing with the Velcro on his sidearm again. "Honestly…my team did an exemplary job under the circumstances. I'm certain a civilian team would not have been able to do a similar job."

"I'm sorry if I came off a little…well… unforgiving. I've been dealing with another mass stranding in Texas and…"

Medlin cut her off. "No need to apologize, Dr. Clarke. We, of all people, recognize the stresses of managing complex events like these. Director Hamilton informed us of your situation in Texas during our initial briefing with Dr. Squires." Four more tracked Navy trucks backed up to the incinerator. Medlin stood and just stared out the window.

"Commander?" Angela wondered about his silence.

"Sorry, ma'am. I'll email you the data we collected when we leave the site. We'll stay until morning to see if any of the carcasses reemerge. When the weather clears enough to put a chopper in the air, we'll scour the coast. If we can get you more…"

"Understood, commander. Now, the nine carcasses you *did* preserve?"

"We'll transport them to the stranding team at the Virginia Aquarium tomorrow morning." Medlin slipped his heavy cold weather gear back on and handled the door knob.

"Excellent. I'll let Ed Bordon know you are coming, do you need…"

"Director Hamilton forwarded me his contact information. I'll call him with enough time for them to be ready. Anything else, ma'am?"

"That will be all, commander. Thank you."

"If we…" Medlin stopped when he heard the dial tone. Sighing, he whispered, "okay" to himself. He pulled up his hood, pulled down his goggles, and headed across the field.

Chapter 20

Roland Summers Marine Mammal Rehabilitation Facility
Galveston, Texas

"C'mon, Bryan!" Shari yelled into the men's locker room. Determined to get Bryan to school one more day this week, she put her foot down—no more overnight shifts. He had just finished back-to-back four-hour shifts with Pirate. She had spent the second shift entering data from the beach and emailing her preliminary spreadsheets to Angela and Kurt. "Bryan! You have homework, boy!"

Bryan emerged—gym bag over his right shoulder and dripping wetsuit in the crook of his left arm. "Okay, mom. Okay." He was just *a little* whiney. Shari was *a lot* tired.

"Let's go. We've got to catch the 8:27 bus and get you ready for school tomorrow." Shari walked behind pushing him forward— out through the security gate and down the road towards the bus stop.

Bryan stopped a block from the bus stop. "When are they going to let you get your license back?"

The headlights of the bus were just coming into view. "Move it, young man." They both shuffle-ran towards the stop.

Once settled on the bus, Shari responded. "Sorry. You know if we missed this bus we would've been here another half an hour..."

"...and we could've gone back to watch Pirate. He's doing so much better. He's finally opened his one bad eye and I just want to spend every minute..."

"Honey." Shari put her hand on his shoulder and looked down at him. "I know he means a lot to you. I know you are learning a lot of good things." Moving her hand to his she continued, "But, there are other things you need to learn too. You need to be in school. You need to do your homework. If we want your custody to be permanent...if we want me to get my license back..." Shari looked out at the cars at the stoplight. "Well, we need to do the right things — that means going to school as well as helping Pirate."

"I understand."

Shari bent over and picked his wetsuit off the floor. "We can do double shifts with Pirate on the weekends. One shift during the week." She looked hard at his sad face and stayed tough. "We can check his status on the aquarium website — they have a webcam on the tanks and one of the vet students is helping Dr. Menke with updates. And, we still need to be helping Kurt on Mondays — by then, he'll have a mountain of paperwork to get through. That's it."

Bryan just stood and hugged Shari hard — his big smile perched on her shoulder.

Day Three

Friday, February 21, 2008

Chapter 21

Office of the Director of National Intelligence
Washington, D.C.

"Sir?" The Director of National Intelligence's administrative assistant poked her head through his partially opened office door. Director Stanley Shaw looked up from his computer screen and nodded. His assistant walked in, set down a large, fresh mug of coffee and continued, "Sir, it's Jenna Damne from the UEAR team at the Operations Center. Line two."

UEAR, the Underwater Early Acquisition and Response team, was responsible for monitoring the nation's sophisticated electronic coastal defense systems. Shaw took a sip of his first coffee of the day, then waved and nodded at his assistant. She got the message — scurrying out and closing the door behind. He picked up the phone.

"Ms. Damne. I'm assuming that you have an update."

"Sir, *that* would be correct."

Since mid-November, the UEAR team — based at the Operations Center of the National Counterterrorism Center — had been on high alert. Though CONCH was currently online in only five of its 12 planned locations, rotating teams of five were responsible for round-the-clock supervision of the sophisticated technological monitoring network protecting the nation's coasts. High alert status came as a result of the threat level for the nation's ports being elevated to red — severe.

Director Shaw flipped to a clean page on the legal pad to the left of his computer—ready to write. "Continue."

"Sir, it seems that our elevation to Threat Level Red on November 17 was prudent. As you know, CONCH detected an unidentified submarine vessel off the coast of Texas at 0138 hours yesterday. Bearing indicated destination Galveston. Detected speed would have put them within reach of multiple commercial strategic targets within four hours. Two ships were in the area—the cutter *Perception* and the frigate *Holmes*. *Perception* was closest, though *Holmes* was more mission capable—both moved to intercept. Perception detected and visually verified the detonation from a distance of 5.7 kilometers."

"Nice summary of what we knew yesterday," Shaw sighed. "Now, what new information do we have?"

"Sorry, sir. *Holmes* took up station and the investigative team began immediate operations—MSOT dolphins investigated the debris column—mainly for survivors--while a Robotic Assessment Sub scoured the sea floor for debris. There was one large piece on the bottom—consistent with a submarine of the size determined by CONCH. Apparently the weapon was designed to direct the blast upward."

Putting down his pen, Shaw interrupted, "Sounds like they were carrying one hell of a payload."

"Yes, sir. It would appear that it was a large conventional payload. Based on the sonic signature recorded by Perception and Holmes and the size of the remaining hull—we'd estimate the blast at approximately 0.25 kilotons. Recovery operations are on-going. We are doing everything we can to determine the nature/origin of the explosives, the vessel, the crew — anything that might lead to a source."

"Well done. Please extend my congratulations to your team for their diligence and thoroughness." Refreshing his dormant computer screen, Shaw typed and sent a short encrypted email:

ACRET
Confirmed CONCH success. But, detonation was self-inflicted. Device conventional. Vessel debris recovery in process. Investigation continuing.
BLADE

"I'll be sure to do that, sir. But, it's my understanding that the intelligence estimate that necessitated our move to Threat Level-Red was based on the movement of multiple vessels with possible multiple targets. I'm assuming we are to maintain our diligence until those vessels are accounted for, sir."

"You are correct — we had credible, corroborated evidence that attacks with potentially grave consequences were planned for multiple targets. Unfortunately, the time frame — the imminence — of those attacks was not verifiable. Apparently the time frame is upon us and we simply cannot assume that all of them will detonate prior to reaching their intended targets..." Shaw's voice trailed off into a slight pause, and then he continued, "Ms. Damne, make sure I get the names of all members of your team — I want to make sure they are properly recognized for their efforts to protect our homeland."

"Yes, sir. I think that will go a long way to helping maintain their morale and attentiveness."

"Exactly." He scanned her file to reaffirm the team leader's first name, "Keep up the great work."

After hanging up, Shaw stood and paced around the room — stopping at his book shelf. Amidst the books was the framed fragment of a burned and shredded American flag — the flag that had been flying at the US Marine Corps barracks in Beirut the day that it was bombed on October 23, 1983. One finger touched the glass and traced the outline of the fragment. Four words throbbed through his head--*credible, corroborated, imminent, catastrophic* — the accepted criteria for evaluating security threats. A former marine intelligence officer, Shaw had been a young CIA analyst attached to the US Embassy in Damascus. In September of 1983, his Syrian contacts provided detailed information about an imminent attack on the multinational forces in Beirut. His superiors, convinced that such an attack was not possible, had not passed the intelligence along to the US commander in Lebanon.

Shaw walked back and sat at his desk, happy that times had changed and that he had been an integral part of that change.

Senator Hulme's Office, Washington, D.C.

"Admiral? I didn't expect to be hearing from you only one day after the hearings. And, while I do sincerely appreciate the call — the personal touch — your Director Hamilton has already updated me on the UMEs currently in progress."

The true tone of confidence in the admiral's voice ignored the senator's arrogance. "We confirmed a detonation 20 miles southeast of Galveston yesterday. One of the projects you fought so hard to fund…"

Senator Hulme slid to the edge of his seat as he looked at the phone to make sure they were on the correct secure line, then excitedly asked, "Which one?"

While Senator Billy Hulme chaired the committee that exercised a tremendous amount of power over the admiral's current position at NOAA--the Committee on Commerce, Science and Transportation—he was also a powerful member of the Defense Appropriations Subcommittee. He was particularly proud of this 2005 appointment, which made him privy to many of the nation's top secret military and security projects. Reveling at being *in the know*, Hulme enjoyed playing both cards with the admiral.

After a moment, the admiral answered, "CONCH."

"Neutralized?"

"Yes and No." Collins paused—wondering how such a man-child could wield so much political power. "The cutter *Perception* received an alert at about 22:30 last night and moved to intercept. They reported being about six kilometers from the target when it detonated. Hell of an explosion they said."

Collins continued, "When the National Counterterrorism Center's Operations Center received the initial Verification of Credible Threat from CONCH…we…um…" The admiral still had a hard time remembering he was *technically* retired, "the Navy moved certain assets into each area. Our Navy intercept and investigation team was only 20 minutes behind the cutter. They are leading the current investigation."

The senator was smiling--*worth the risk*—funding CONCH had been a protracted battle in committee. CONCH was one of the few "unacknowledged" Special Access Programs—those not published in the federal budget and whose funds are hidden in another budget entry—to pass through *both* of the senator's committees. This lack of detailed disclosure made his wholehearted support of the program even harder for his more pennywise colleagues to handle.

But, with the continuing instability of the civil wars in Iraq and Syria, a resurgent Taliban controlling nearly two thirds of Afghanistan and almost nightly reports on new extremist groups with increasingly more sophisticated weaponry and tactics popping up in the desolate reaches of the world, "homeland security" was an argument that few could resist. It was an issue that the senator had driven home to his Alabama constituents and his defense industry backers during his 2004 re-election campaign and one he would not renege on because of a lack of detail.

His resolve to be a leader in homeland security policy—and to push funding for CONCH and similar programs--was further strengthened after a conversation he had with Admiral Collins at a White House reception. Hulme had never met Admiral Collins before, but was immediately taken in by his charisma—by the gravity of his presence. Collins pulled the senator aside and spent nearly 20 minutes extolling the virtues of projects he—as a now *retired* Navy officer—should have known nothing about. Regardless, something told Billy Hulme that Collins was still a very serious player—so he listened intently. The substance—what little there was--of the admiral's spiel was that many of the projects—especially CONCH-- would protect the homeland while allowing the continued liberal deployment of the majority of the military—ground troops, special forces, planes, and ships—where needed for overseas counterinsurgency and counterterrorism operations.

Trusting the admiral, as well as his own national security team, Billy Hulme pulled the lever and took a gamble--seizing on and politicizing the repeated attacks in Paris and London, the downing of a Russian airliner and the bombing of the US Embassy in Ottawa. His spin through the network morning shows and his colleagues' offices, and his dramatic and energizing presence in committee, sealed the deal for any homeland security-oriented defense appropriations. Both committees unanimously supported all of the Department of Defense's "unacknowledged" programs—including Admiral Collins' precious CONCH.

Vindication--he reveled in the success. The funding he worked so hard to secure—political favors he had freely granted-- had not gone to waste. Senator Hulme practically jumped through the phone to probe for more. "So...the craft that exploded? The weapon? CONCH did *what...exactly...*to ensure their destruction?"

"I am sorry, senator." And, Collins loved pulling this on that arrogant ass of a useful politician, Billy Hulme. "That information is beyond your clearance at this time. I just wanted to pass along a little good news concerning a project you were instrumental in funding."

"And, how, Rear Admiral Collins, US Navy *retired,* are *you* privy to that information?"

"I'm afraid that is also beyond your clearance, senator."

Senator Hulme sat fuming at the admiral. He did not like to be on the outside of anything. But, he was also anxious to know if there was any way to cash in some immediate political capital from the victory. "And how and when will my constituents — my country- -thank me for my less than public successes?"

"Senator, let's just say that the American people will start thanking you in Iowa and New Hampshire in a few years."

The dial tone signaled the admiral's abrupt departure — but the senator didn't really care. He rocked back into his big leather chair and kicked his feet up onto the desk with a thump and thought, *President Billy Hulme. No, President William Howard Hulme.* He smiled, not really caring that he still had no idea what he had fought so hard to fund.

Chapter 23

Building G, NMFS Laboratory, Galveston, Texas

To say that the vet student and TEXMAM volunteer necropsy teams were efficient would be an understatement — Angela continued to be impressed with how professionally they handled the assembly-line process she had put in place. Since starting mid-day on Wednesday, the teams had completed 84 necropsies. With the remaining carcasses finally off the beach and into cold storage, Angela was ready to give the teams a more substantial break — allowing two teams to cycle out every four hours. She knew she could give them more of a break once the next wave of students arrived that evening.

With the new schedule communicated to the necropsy teams, Angela turned her attention to the "chip". Since speaking to Robin on Thursday, she had found a hammer in the lab's maintenance closet, but hadn't succumbed to the barbarity of his suggestion. Now, Angela sat at the desk in her makeshift office, holding the Ziploc bag with the cylindrical metallic object. She knew it couldn't be anything. Still, she was curious — it looked just a little too refined to be marine debris. "Smash it open!" he had said — but, she knew that wasn't typical Robin. While he looked like a gladiator, he paddled — he made love to her — like a poet. Smiling and staring at, but not seeing the chip, Angela realized she had wandered way off task. She really didn't know how she got from debating what to do with the chip to the last time her and Robin were together at the sea cave on Middle

Caicos. *Back to the chip, Angela.* First, she thought it. Then, shaking her head once, she said it, "Back to the chip!"

"Back to what chip?" Kurt appeared in the half-open doorway. He looked at Angela's flush face and then to the bag in her shaky hands.

Angela closed her hand around the bag. "What are you…?"

"8:30 conference call, remember? You, me, Menke, your boss. I figured I'd come by a little early and check out the necropsies." He lifted his chin, motioning at her closed hand, "What gives?"

Angela waved him in and motioned for Kurt to close the door. She looked at him hard. "No jumping to conclusions." She held out the baggie. Kurt held it up to the light.

"Don't get on me for assuming, but I assume this came from one of our dolphins." He looked at her for approval.

Angela nodded. "Yes, TT 27."

Looking at it closely, Kurt tried to stay analytical, "It's too symmetrical to *not* be manmade. Too symmetrical to be…what? Looks like one of those chips they found in Scully's neck on the *X-Files*…a little larger, but very similar. Somebody tracking our wild dolphins?"

Angela shook her head and snatched the bag, laid it on the desk and picked up the hammer, "Do you think I should…"

Kurt shook his head, intercepted the hammer and completed the question, "…look at it under a binocular microscope?" He handed her back the hammer and then answered the question himself. "Sure, let's have a look."

"8:10. We have a few minutes." Angela picked up the bag and brushed past Kurt to the door. "Follow me."

Spinning, Kurt followed her out into the hall. "Have you found more?"

"Just this one...the only one...so, it's probably nothing..." Angela hesitated, "I probably shouldn't even waste my time — our time — with it. Still..." She continued down the hall, and then stopped--looking at the sign on one of the lab doors. "Here." She knew she'd find the type of microscope they were looking for in the plankton lab she had passed in her travels through Building G. They walked in and spotted what they needed.

"What's going on in Virginia Beach?" Kurt pulled the vinyl cover off the microscope and toggled on the light.

She was startled--no one had put out an official release on that stranding. Angela wasn't used to being caught off guard — twice. "How'd you...?"

"I did a quick check of MARMAM first thing this morning to see what people were saying about our stranding." Kurt got caught in the stream of that tangential thought, "...amazed at the size. Shock at the single day nature of the event. Lots of crazy speculation — even from the hard science types. Praise for what they've heard about the management. I ran out of time to really..."

"And Virginia?" Angela had forgotten about the chip for the moment. "Who posted something about Virginia?"

"Ed Bordon—Virginia Aquarium. He..." Kurt hesitated. Looking down at the chip in its Ziploc bag and then back to Angela, "Ed said they were called off by you and Director Hamilton."

Angela nodded, *yes*. "The storm and..." Never one to pass the buck unless it was sincere, "it was Director Hamilton's order. The weather was..."

This time, Kurt got to give *her* the hand, "I know—even during an event like this I try not to live in a box like you...I need to know what else is going on in the marine mammal community...in the rest of the world. I've seen the weather reports online. I think it was a good call to protect the stranding volunteers. Weather like that...mix it with frigid water and 500-plus pound wild animals— very risky. Even keeping it quiet could be rationalized for public safety—the curious, the voyeurs come out in any weather." He looked again at the small, metallic cylinder, sat down in the swivel chair in front of the microscope and spun to face her again. "I know having the Navy team there was a very convenient, even smart option...but it still...to me, anyway...feels a little...um...weird?"

"Kurt!" Angela knew the theory was next. "Convenient and smart. Safe." She was firm. "They really were the best qualified for those conditions. They have tracked vehicles, proper clothing and winter training. They really did a great job." She paused, wondering whether she was trying to convince Kurt or herself. "Admiral Collins, the NOAA Administrator, is the former base commander there—he pulled some strings at the director's request. Jake made the call to try and get the people best suited for those weather conditions in there to save the data. They performed heroically." Angela looked at her watch, "Please...please put any connections, conspiracies or conclusions out of your head for now. I know the kind of speculation that can run rampant on the discussion groups and I know how your tangents can..."

Kurt didn't allow her to continue. He hadn't touched her hand in a long time, but he reached out, and she didn't pull away. "They're saying nothing but good things on the message boards at the moment. They're hoping that the Navy managed to save something to analyze — anything. They know the volunteers would have been out of their league in that kind of storm." Angela started to look uncomfortable, so Kurt let go — turning back to the chip and the microscope. He picked up a set of forceps and opened the baggie. "I just get a little uncomfortable when I start seeing chip implants, the military acting on American soil, and over 200 dolphins stranding in three locations. I really start to hear the old *X-Files* theme in my head."

Angela's head and eyes moved from the microscope to Kurt. Kurt knew the look said, "What?"

"Yes. I've also heard about the stranding in Mozambique." He focused for a second and using the forceps lifted the chip and placed it on the microscope's stage. "But, I'm sure that is *someone else's* worry."

Angela ignored his snide tone, "Yes...yes it is. But, they beached over three or four days and they have a pretty good handle on the cause…" She pulled a chair next to Kurt. "…an epidemic of some new strain of *morbillivirus*."

"Hmmph!" It was unusual for his commentary to be so brief, but Kurt was now focused on the cylinder. Using the forceps, Kurt rotated the chip as he looked through the eye pieces. "It definitely looks man-made. Very regular, symmetrical. No numbers, letters — no markings…look at this!" He pulled away from the eyepieces and she leaned into the space between Kurt and the microscope.

"It looks like a faint seam near one end." Angela groped at the microscope looking for the magnification control.

"Yes! Yes! That's what I thought." Kurt was excited and wanted to look again, but Angela was still fumbling for the magnification.

"That's better…oh!" She was excited, "Definitely a seam, but not one that looks like it was made to be opened."

Angela sat up and Kurt jumped back to the eyepieces. "At least not opened by anyone other than the maker…or user." Sitting up, Kurt put the chip back in the labeled baggie. "Do you know of anyone using anything like this for tagging?"

"No, and I called Robin…" Angela sighed and turned away from the microscope and Kurt--not knowing how he would react to hearing Robin's name. "I called Dr. Nicely and he didn't know of anyone either. For field research he really didn't see the point. The tagging operation, logistics and range would be too…" Angela could see that Kurt's mind had drifted a little. "Kurt!" Turning back to face him, she continued, "Robin said the range of a package that small would be too short for field research — that the risks to the animals during capture would be too great. He said to whack it open with a hammer."

"A hammer? Neanderthal." Kurt zipped the bag closed and took a deep breath. "No hammer."

Angela grabbed the bag, stuffed it in her pocket and headed for the door. "Time to go — conference call. Doc will be there waiting."

Putting his arm across the doorway, Kurt blocked her path. "We need to get that thing open. No one is using that technology that we know of…then, who? Then, why? And, of course, did it contribute to the stranding?" His eyes went into a blank stare as he continued to block the door. "Have you told Doc about the chip?"

"It's nothing — let's go."

He persisted, "Have you told Doc about the chip?"

Angela struggled with an answer while standing in a very uncomfortable space. "No." She slapped his arm from the doorway. "But I will tell him about the *object* during the call." Striding off down the hall, Angela hollered, "Let's go!"

Kurt stood in the doorway for a moment, thinking, *A well-healed scar would blend with a bottlenose's typical rake marks and scratches — natural camouflage. But, why hide a tag? Maybe it's not hidden. External tags often come off — these would be permanent--as long as the power lasted. How do you power something that small for that long? How do you power it for the needed transmitting range? But Angela would know. The great Dr. Robin Nicely would surely know. They're in the know.* He could see Angela stick her head back around the corner she had just turned.

"Kurt!" Angela waved at him. "Doc is here. 8:28. Let's go!"

He took a couple of steps and paused when Angela again disappeared around the corner — "Doc." Kurt mumbled as he worked through his thoughts--*Army Veterinarian. Navy Marine Mammal Program. Doc.* Picking up his pace, Kurt hollered, "Ang!"

Chapter 24

Inhassoro, Mozambique

"Right! Thanks mate." Robin turned back toward the icehouse after sending his first truckload of samples on its long journey back to Dolphin Study Centre in South Africa. While Vee was doing a great job running tests of blood and tissues with the network's portable lab, there were some things that needed to be done using the more advanced equipment available at DSC.

Back in the icehouse, Robin's chest heaved as he sighed — half happy to be back in the cool and half sad at the loss of carcasses caused by the summer heat. Inside Vee's makeshift lab, Robin moved to his laptop — linked to the outside world via satellite phone and an antenna finally rigged to the roof of the building. Robin booted up his laptop and Vee looked across the room — noticing his mentor's wallpaper.

"Dr. Nicely," Vee's tone was immediately, humorously, sarcastic — the result of knowing Robin too well and not wanting to miss a chance at teasing what most people considered a very manly man. "Very romantic sunset photo of you and Dr. Clarke." Vee paused for effect as Robin swiveled around in his chair. "Those are some beautiful roses she's holding. Can you remind me...which *conference* is that from?"

The volunteers and assistants in the lab laughed hard — even the locals recognized the irony of the hard-bodied, beer drinking and often foul-mouthed doctor in such a phoofy setting. Robin crossed his arms, forced a smile, and shook his head. "Fuck you. Fuck you all." Everyone laughed harder. Robin forced a grin, shook his head some more, swung back around and hunched over his laptop.

It was difficult to keep his language formal, but he took some solace in knowing he'd follow with something more personal later.

Dr. Angela Clarke
Director of Marine Mammal Health and Stranding
National Marine Fisheries Service, NOAA

Dr. Clarke,

I wanted to take this opportunity to pass along our preliminary findings RE the 17 February, 2008, mass, single-day stranding of Tursiops truncatus on the northeast beaches of Bazaruto Island, Mozambique.

There were no live animals rescued. Of the 306 animals on the beach, 42 were necropsied on site, 63 in process at our makeshift facility (commercial icehouse) in Inhassoro. Due to the intense summer heat, the remaining carcasses quickly deteriorated beyond acceptable necropsy standards. Basic data (length, girths, teeth, photos, etc.) were collected for all. What carcasses could not be necropsied on site or removed to the icehouse were burned on the beach.

The vast majority of animals necropsied to date show some or many signs consistent with cetacean Morbillivirus — emaciation and overall poor body condition, ulcerative stomatitis, white blood cell and protein rich plasma in the alveoli (consistent with interstitial pneumonia), and lymphoid depletion. Tissue and blood samples are on route to the Dolphin Study Centre in Plettenberg Bay, SA, for further analysis.

I have attached photos of the stranding site and a sampling of photos from individual carcasses.

I have also attached an Excel spreadsheet with basic data from all 306 animals. As we complete more of our analysis, I will update you at convenient intervals.

I also look forward to continued updates (as time allows) RE your strandings in Texas and Virginia. I vaguely remember seeing something about a chip similar to that metal object found by your team. When I finish in Mozambique and return to DSC, I'll see if I can recall the reference.

Finally, at this time I wanted to take the opportunity to officially thank you (again) for providing the inspiration for us to establish the Pan African Stranding Network. Without your encouragement, we would not have had the resources in place to collect the data necessary to better understand these unfortunate events.

Kind regards,
Dr. Robin Nicely
Dolphin Study Centre

Robin hit send and rocked back slightly in his chair. As he looked from face to face in the lab, everyone still managed to smirk. Turning to Vee he blurted, while laughing a little himself, "Fuck you!" Robin put a serious look back on his face. Using his head, he motioned "follow me" to Vee.

Outside, they both sat on some packing crates haphazardly "stacked" under an awning. Robin stood up and paced a few steps away, turned, paced back, and turned again. "Vee." He turned around and looked right at his colleague — his young friend. Robin started again. "Vitorio…"

Vee laughed, "Must be serious if…" Seeing Robin's glare, he stopped.

Robin rolled his eyes and then brought them back to Vee. "I'm going to ask her to marry me."

Vee stood straight up. "What? When? Where?" Then, he shook his head, "After seven years? Finally manning up?"

Sitting back on the crates, Robin turned to his friend. "David...David's been building me...building us...well, I've been helping with the finishing...anyway, building a house on the water at Plettenberg. It will be done in a week. I've already moved in. I was hoping..." Robin drifted away. "I was hoping to fly her in at the beginning of March, to propose on the dock at the house...sunset. Now..."

"Now what? Seven years in the making and you're hesitating? Where are your balls, man?" Vee stood and took a couple of steps away from Robin.

He ignored the comment and continued, "You were so busy and so focused on your research. Then, we had this stranding and...you've done a first-rate job." Robin stood, and Vee took another step backwards. "I should have told you sooner—about everything." Waving his hand, Robin signaled Vee to sit back down. "There have been two mass strandings in the US—Texas and Virginia." Robin could see by Vee's look that he wanted details. For the moment, he stuck with the strandings. "Unlike our event, these *Tursiops* stranded in one day and likely in one group. Hundreds of animals--like ours. Only a few obvious Morbillivirus symptoms—*not* like ours."

Vee was stunned. "So, *your* lady is very busy." He winked, "She need any help from a tall, dark and handsome African pathologist?"

Steering around the comment, Robin answered, "She needs to put together a puzzle with no — at least not yet…," he paused. "…a puzzle with no common pieces. She needs help finding out who might be using a subcutaneous chip tag. *That* is what she needs help with."

"Too bad we are so busy. It would be nice to visit the states again." Vee scratched at the small tuft on his chin. "Chip tag? That technology exists? I mean…for more than first-world dogs and cats? I just can't imagine it being practical for wild populations. I've never heard…" He stopped at Robin's shaking head *no*.

"I keep thinking I have a vague memory of someone talking about the possibility of developing something like that, but…" Robin's tired eyes glazed over as he faded into his memories, but he still couldn't recall the reference.

"Well, can't get much more definitive than that. Still, small battery with lots of power to transmit…sounds like aliens to me." Vee laughed and then lost his smile, "Or, military." Slumping back on the crates, Vee kicked at the dirt. "Seriously, one chip in over 200 dolphins — over 400 if you count the other stranding. Sounds like a dead end waste of time. An anomaly. Not like your Angela to waste too much time or effort on something like…"

"Agreed. Hmmm. Kurt. I bet Kurt knows and already has a theory like yours…but, I can't imagine Kurt pushing her to waste time on something like that." Robin stood up and paced back and forth in front of Vee. "It's been too long for him to be able to..."

Vee just shook his head, "Angela's...um...ex? Kurt?"

Tight-faced, Robin answered, "It's been too long to call him that — but, yes, him."

Vee stood up and shook his head some more — then, walked over to Robin and put his hand firmly on his mentor's right shoulder. "It's been too long for you to worry about him, Robin. If she's wasting time on this chip thing, she's doing it for her own reasons — not for some long ago boyfriend."

Robin hugged Vee and stepped back. "Hey, I need to send her... Angela ...I need to send another quick email..."

"...then back to work." Vee finished the sentence and then grabbed his mentor in another hug. "What we were talking about before you brought up the chip...do it. Ask her." He broke the hug but stayed nose to nose with his mentor and whispered. "She's a good woman and a beautiful woman — a challenging woman. But, she makes you happy." They both walked toward the door. "Um...Robin? Do you think she has any idea?"

"Of course not..." He knew she didn't have a clue about the house...or his intentions. His parents knew. David knew. Half of Plettenberg Bay knew. Now, Vee knew.

"Robin." Vee's voice and another hand on Robin's shoulder was firm — breaking him out of his mind drift.

"Sorry Vee, I..." Robin leaned on the door. He closed his eyes.

Vee needed to reassure him, the way Robin had reassured him about leaving Mozambique to go to school in South Africa. "The last time I saw the two of you. May--last year...in Cape Town again. Remember?" Robin nodded and Vee continued. "We took the DSC van to drop everyone—Angela too—at the airport. We could all see what the two of you have. There was no way she wanted to fly back to the states. If you would have asked her, she would have got back in that van and went home with you then."

Robin opened his eyes, smiled and pushed open the icehouse door.

Chapter 25

Building G, NMFS Laboratory, Galveston, Texas

"Angela. Kurt." Dr. Menke looked at the clock on his open laptop—8:29—and while winking at both of them asked, "What have you two been up to? Not rekindling a long-dead romantic disaster I hope…"

"We were in…" Angela started, but Kurt dropped his manila folder and the papers spread all over the floor. Angela paused in the confusion and Kurt picked up the answer to Doc's question.

"Like you said, Doc—long dead. Angela was showing me her necropsy operation—quite a set-up. Your students are doing great work with the volunteers." Squatting in front of the desk, Angela tried to sneak in a questioning look while handing him the papers from the floor. Kurt stuffed the papers back in to his folder.

"Angela?" Dr. Menke set his cell phone on the desk. He knew Kurt was lying—he had just visited the necropsy area on his way to the meeting.

Angela stood, again glanced at Kurt, and walked around to her laptop on the other side of the desk. "I told you before how impressed I was. Drew…what's his last name?"

"Fiedler. Drew Fiedler."

"He gave us a nice summary of where they're at and…" Angela was interrupted as three cell phones rang in unison—albeit with distinctly different tunes.

"Menke."

"Dr. Clarke."

"Kurt here."

"Whoa! That's a little too overwhelming." Director Hamilton replied.

Angela suggested, "We're in the same room—that way we could…let's just use the speaker on my phone." Kurt and Menke nodded agreement and hung up.

Director Hamilton started again, "Good morning, all. How are things in Texas today?"

Flipping open her laptop and bringing it out of hibernation, Angela moved to her summary file quickly. "Well, of the 207 original animals…"

Jake cut her off. "Hang on Angela. First, I want to know how the three of you are doing—mentally, physically. You are running an important project and I want to make sure you all are up to speed." The director let that sink in for a moment. "Kurt? Haven't seen you in a while—how are you faring?"

Hunching towards the cell phone on the desk Kurt replied, "Thanks for asking—I'm fine. Once we had all the animals off the beach, I moved back to the office at A&M. I have a cot there. Last night I managed four hours sleep. Volunteers are bringing me good things to eat. My second cup of coffee is kicking now. No worries."

"Dr. Menke?"

"Doing well. Great team of volunteers, vet students and techs, so I've gotten about four hours of sleep each night. I'm a little shriveled from spending so much time in the three med tanks, but other than that, well." He sighed and then continued, "Really, we're all good but still have a lot to do." Doc looked at Angela, rolled his eyes and shook his head.

"Two sets of three hours last night." Angela nodded and jumped in without Director Hamilton's prompting. "Two Diet Cokes and some cereal this morning." Chuckling, she added, "My hair looks great."

"It always does." Director Hamilton chuckled himself, then continued, "Kurt, since your initial phase of the response is largely over, why don't you go first."

Angela shook her head, looked at Doc and mouthed, "What?"

Opening his folder, Kurt started, "Well...we received the initial call at 6:00am Central Time. Two of our First Responders were on the scene by 6:45am. They organized the people already on the..."

Angela and Dr. Menke tuned Kurt out while they tapped at their laptops.

Angela opened her email. There was something formal from Robin and she sighed. The note said that his stranding was definitely *Morbilli*—but a group that large was still atypical. He mentioned vaguely recalling seeing something about a tracking chip? She knew that with his mind for trivia, he'd eventually remember. Smiling at his nice comment about her help with starting the Pan-African network, she forwarded the email to Director Hamilton—always looking for points with her boss. Then, her thoughts drifted back to the chip.

Angela glanced up at Menke and Kurt—both engrossed—and wondered why Kurt was concerned about sharing information about the as-of-yet unidentified metallic cylinder. It was likely nothing and if it were a tracking chip of some kind it was still likely to be inconsequential. Sipping her third Diet Coke of the morning, she went back to her inbox—there was a too short, personal email from Robin. She smiled again, but hearing her name she turned to Kurt.

"...so because of the mask and glove situation, Angela, I'm sure, will call some of the data into question. After rectifying the situation, we also noted which animals were tended without proper protection..."

Mostly over that issue, Angela went back to her thoughts and her email reply. She missed Robin and wanted to put a buzz in his ear—it was time for another romantic rendezvous. She didn't want to seem overly anxious. Shaking her head she snickered a little to herself—how could she be overly anxious after seven years? She smiled and closed her eyes. With Doc's summary next, Angela typed—*Robin, see you as soon as this is over. I love you.*

Kurt rambled on. He had never lost his gift for lecturing--even nine years after his adjunct professorship was "de-funded". Not wanting to waste time listening, Dr. Menke composed:

ACRET
MK6Chip RECOVERED GALVESTON. NOT
IN SECURE HANDS. ADVISE.
FREEHOLD

Doc hit *Send-E—Send Encrypted*—and turned his thoughts back to Kurt and Angela. Drew had told him about the chip—but why didn't Angela relay the information herself? He was sure she had told Kurt. He stared at Kurt — shaking his head in disbelief — knowing that some connections, no matter how tenuous, just never break.

Doc had arrived at Texas A&M just as Angela was finishing her PhD. She was coordinating a project that combined her efforts with those of two vet students and six senior undergraduates — looking for biases and errors in the analysis and reporting of 10 years of stranding data for the entire Gulf coast from the Florida Keys to the Mexican border. The re-examination of hundreds of paper and computer files was complemented by a re-analysis of over a thousand banked tissue and blood samples. Doc, a new addition to her thesis committee, recognized her promise not only as a scientist, but as a scientific leader. Her keen orchestration of the research team and completion of that complex project lead to well-received articles in *Marine Mammal Science* and *Nature* and a consequent minor bout with celebrity within the intimate world of marine mammal research. Offered a prestigious post-doctoral fellowship at the Woods Hole Oceanographic Institute — an opportunity that would have allowed her to do similar research on North Atlantic strandings — Angela declined. She made the trip, did the interviews and went out on a pilot whale stranding at Cape Cod. She even looked, briefly, at apartments. But, when it came to signing the contract, when it came to leaving Kurt in Galveston, she hesitated — then, she declined.

Their relationship had progressed quickly after their first "date" at Galveston Island State Park — especially when funding cuts axed Kurt's position at College Station and gave him the "freedom" to move to Galveston. For a year, Kurt worked on a book based on his mythology lectures. For a year, he ran miles to stay in shape "and think." For a year, he lived in Angela's apartment and largely off her A&M post-doc fellowship stipend. For Angela, *the voice* was slowly getting softer--weaker.

But, if passion is a powerful camouflage for some, comfort and steadiness were camouflages for Angela—at least for a while. Angela declined the Woods Hole offer and, instead, cobbled together a plan that she hoped would re-vitalize her partner and seal their bond. TEXMAM was in need of an executive director, but Angela, in all her organizational glory, convinced the board that co-directors could better deal with the growing volunteer network and the increased frequency of strandings—she would handle the actual stranding logistics and any science while *Kurt* would manage the volunteers.

With stacks of research notes but only 47 written pages, Angela persuaded Kurt to abandon his book—*for now*—and join her at TEXMAM. *The voice* seemed to strengthen as they shared the day to day management of the network and the training of the volunteers. Kurt excelled with the volunteers—he was a powerful teacher and that came to the surface again. Over the first year, the quality of their non-work time improved as well, with Kurt and Angela often running together on the beach and along the sea wall.

The only mass stranding of 2001 changed all that. Eight spinner dolphins beached at South Padre Island. Angela's logistical plan would have impressed any military commander — but, in action it would have awed them. In contrast, Kurt's volunteer *plan* was great — but the *execution* was obviously lacking. Kurt was flustered — his phone and email lists were outdated and his mobilization of volunteers was haphazard and slow.

A few weeks before, Angela had noticed a few of Kurt's book research folders and a Greek-English dictionary carefully tucked under volunteer files on his desk at TEXMAM. Under the desk was the messenger bag he carried back and forth to work every day. Lying on top of the bag was his old copy of *The Odyssey* — the book hadn't even been on their nightstand in more than a year. Angela, wrote it off — he was doing a pretty good job.

The South Padre Island stranding changed everything. Kurt wavered, and Angela, without hesitation, said, "Lead, follow, or get out of the way, Kurt." From that point, Kurt waffled somewhere between "follow" and "get out of the way."

Angela soared — using her organizational skills as a baton and directing what the stranding community was soon praising as an "exemplary response". MARMAM was a-twitter with praise for her and Kurt — for TEXMAM. Angela was livid — knowing that *she* had been the one. *She* was the leader. It was a life moment — the beginning of the end of her and Kurt. Dr. Menke could see it then, and thinking about it now — stuffed close to the two of them in that small office in Building G--made him smile as he looked at Angela, then at Kurt. He knew she was done with him — long done with him.

After 10 minutes of "summary", Director Hamilton tried moving things along, "Thanks, Kurt. Very thorough. Seems like your volunteers did outstanding considering the nature of the event."

"They still are, sir—assisting with necropsies, the live animals..."

"Yes. Well done." The director obviously wanted to move on. "Doc. What have *you* got for us?"

Dr. Menke closed his email window to look at his summary. "Well, I'll try to be concise." Gesturing with his hand, Doc started, "Six live animals. We did lose one that we replaced later with another from the beach." Kurt was smiling, Angela was still looking at her computer. "All showed signs of a prolonged debilitation— emaciation, dermal sloughing, mouth ulcers. All but TT 18 immediately responded to fluids and are showing improvement. TT 43 was even doing short, independent bouts of swimming last night. Recovery is always a dicey thing, but I think..."

"The causes, Doc? The causes?" The Jake's patience had been used up on Kurt—the only one of the three he really didn't know closely enough to prod.

Angela looked up, surprised.

Director Hamilton continued, "Yes, it will be a great accomplishment if we can rehab and release, but—and I can't stress this enough—the priority is to find out what caused this disaster."

Dr. Menke was a little startled with the Director's abruptness, but continued a little more formally, "Okay. Two have *Morbillivirus*— their prognosis is not good. Three have pneumonia—but each is a different strain. The last has a bacterial infection that appears to have entered through a relatively old shark bite." Re-opening his email, Doc sent a blank message to the director. "I'm sending you an overall summary, a summary of the values for each animal, and my comments." He sighed audibly, but smiled to himself — knowing there was no need to embellish. "Honestly, director, from my analysis of these six animals…no real causal commonalities…I just can't imagine what would send 200 of them into the beach." Admiral Collins had been in touch with him — concerned about the locations of the two strandings — but, Menke now thought his old friend and mentor was overreacting. He decided to move the conversation forward. "Your turn, Angela?"

"Well," she was still scrolling through some of the spreadsheets Shari had emailed her the night before. "Nothing — there's nothing." Angela couldn't hold back her obvious surprise.

Doc got up and circled around to look at Angela's screen. "Jake? I'm skimming her spreadsheets now. She's right — there's nothing. Go figure."

"Nothing? That many carcasses and you have nothing?" Director Hamilton wanted better answers.

"Hang on." Doc reached over Angela's shoulder and moved through her spreadsheet — looking at rows and columns that were hidden. "Okay, interesting…"

"What, Doc?" The director grew impatient with the short silence.

Doc pointed to the rows and columns that recorded the sex and maturity of the dolphins. Angela nodded.

"Doc?" Director Hamilton queried again.

Angela answered, "Well, it appears that most of the animals are females — sexually mature females — only...one...two...three sexually mature males — and calves. The calves are a mix of males and females."

"That is even more catastrophic." Kurt interjected, "Huge mortality event and few females or calves to replenish the stock. The ecological impacts..."

"Yes, yes, understood, Kurt — devastating," Director Hamilton interrupted. "But, does this shed any light on the stranding itself."

Doc answered, "Honestly, I don't know. Angela?"

"Not my specialty — but, I can certainly inquire with..."

"Let's keep this among ourselves for now. Make the time to do a literature search, Angela." The director was back to controlling the conversation. "Now, let's move forward. External evaluations, blood work, necropsies are revealing what? Let's go, Angela."

"Okay. My external evaluations are similar to Doc's-- emaciation, dermal sloughing, mouth ulcers. Many..." She looked at her summary notes for the hard numbers. "141 had at least small patches of *Balanomorpha* — barnacles. A typical sign of prolonged swimming at slower than normal speeds — especially in *Tursiops*. Necropsies also revealed a variety of possibilities. Of the 84 completed to date, 11 showed typical internal signs of

Morbillivirus—lymphoid depletion, interstitial pneumonia. 28 had some other pneumonias. Obviously, we're having a number of cultures done from lung tissue. Same for the bacteria. Blood values, liver enzymes...consistent with the stated infections..."

"So, bottom line." Director Hamilton's voice wearily interrupted, "Nothing as definitive...as neat and clean as Dr. Nicely's 306 *Morbillivirus* carcasses."

Kurt's eyes opened wide as he turned to Angela and seriously, silently mouthed, "What? That many?" The Mozambique stranding was noted on MARMAM, but the post was sketchy—it contained no real details.

Angela ignored him. "It will be a few days before Robin has hard confirmation of *Morbilli*, but..."

"...but according to the email you forwarded from him the external examination and necropsy reports overwhelmingly point to it."

Kurt was still looking at Angela and shaking his head in disbelief. He closed his eyes—sad because she couldn't share everything with him any longer. Opening his eyes, he glared at her.

Ignoring Kurt's stare, Angela sighed, "Even with my well-known, and well-respected, propensity for protocol and biases, I would say that with that number of necropsies that..." She paused, knowing that she still struggled with being definitive. "...that at least the final cause of the Mozambique stranding...was *Morbillivirus*. Yes, I could state that with conviction."

"But for our situation," Doc chimed in, looking at Kurt and Angela in rotation, "For us, I don't see that kind of definitiveness." In agreement, Angela nodded. Kurt nodded.

"Kurt?" Obviously, the director couldn't hear their head movements. "Angela?"

She looked at Kurt and answered for him. "We agree with Doc."

"Fine." Jake wanted to move forward. "I'm assuming the samples are on their way to other labs for testing...and, to our national tissue bank for storage?"

Angela didn't know why, but she looked at Kurt. "The first batch is going out this morning—one set to the lab at College Station, the other to Patel Pathology Associates in Houston. Of course, a set is also going to the tissue bank."

"Angela?" Doc had a question. "Do we have enough to send a set to Colonel Rice at the Armed Forces Institute of Pathology?" Making sure not to look at Kurt, Menke continued, "With their nearly 25 years of handling our past samples their team might have a unique insight into the analysis. Because of the unique circumstances of this event, I think it is warranted." Prior to the 1992 creation of the National Marine Mammal Tissue Bank, samples were tested and archived at AFIP—that, and Doc had a special connection to the institute. AFIP oversaw the Army Veterinary Corps and the animal care team that worked with the Navy Marine Mammal Program. AFIP had also overseen research in which Doc and the admiral had a special interest and of which Director Hamilton had a special knowledge.

Though Kurt's stare—it was a look that said, *No conspiracies here, Angela?* —caught her eye, she answered Doc without hesitation. "I think that's a great idea. That's not a problem. The more eyes we have on this the better." Looking at Kurt, she shook off his questioning glare with a condescending grin and nod.

"Excellent work...everyone." The director's tone was sincere. "Angela? Theories?"

"Well," Dr. Menke had again been scrolling through Angela's summary tables over her shoulder. Ignoring the director's inquiry of Angela, he answered. "This is interesting. The emaciation, based on carcass weights, seems more advanced than would be typical at the observed stage of many of the pneumonias, *Morbillivirus*, etc." Looking at Angela for confirmation, and seeing it in her eyes, he continued, "To me that suggests that the decline of body condition, some fall-off in eating or nutrient absorption, pre-dated the onset of the infections."

"But nothing conclusive. Thank you." Director Hamilton interrupted–it seemed that was all he wanted to hear, "Obviously, much more to be done. Doc, Kurt...thank you for your dedication. Keep it up." The conversation was ending, "Angela—as always..." Jake let that hang for a second, and continued down another path instead, "Angela, can you call me back? 10 o'clock."

"Yeah, I can..."

"Talk to you then." Director Hamilton was gone.

Doc closed his laptop, grinned and shook his head at Angela—then, he left the room.

Kurt couldn't find anything to say—let alone find his voice. He just sat a few moments with his elbows on his knees and his head in his hands—frustrated that he hadn't had the balls to speak up about the connections he was mapping in his mind. Without looking at Angela, he bolted upright and headed toward the door, a cursory, "I'll be in my office", coming out as he passed into the hallway.

Chapter 26

Virginia Aquarium and Marine Science Center

Virginia Beach, Virginia

Lt. Commander Medlin's team was nothing if not efficient — at 0830 they met Curator of Marine Mammals, Dr. Ed Bordon and two volunteers at the aquarium's loading dock. Medlin and his detachment of six MSOTs made quick work of transferring the nine carcasses from their two trucks to gurneys and finally into the massive walk-in freezer. Also transferred were 33 sets of samples from the lost carcasses.

Medlin removed the NMFS chain of custody sheet from his folder, slid a signed duplicate into another green file folder and passed it to Bordon. "Dr. Bordon," Medlin wasted no time — talking while striding back towards the loading docks, "I will email the data sheets and photographs to you later this morning, sir."

The curator passed the folder to one of his volunteers and followed the now exiting MSOT leader. "Lt. Commander Medlin." Ed Bordon pulled up his hood--bundled against the weather in an alcove at the still mostly snow-covered loading dock. "Considering the weather, you and your men did an outstanding job. I can't imagine what it…" He shuffled to the edge while Medlin made his way down the icy stairs. "We couldn't have managed that kind of effort with our few volunteers. I'm amazed that you…"

"Dr. Bordon, sir." Medlin shouted in the still strong wind. "We appreciate your kudos, sir, but we need to be getting back to the base." Looking relieved and relaxed, the commander turned toward the tracked Navy truck.

Bordon shouted, "If you or your men ever want to bring their families...just call me. Admission is on the house."

Medlin turned around. He sighed. "Thank you, sir. I *will* let them know."

Office of Admiral Collins, NOAA
Silver Spring, Maryland

Rear Admiral Lawrence Collins stared at a photo on his desk—himself and Aldo Menke kneeling on the dock behind the *Freehold*, and CC. CC was holding his permanently smiling dolphin head out of the water. Only two weeks after that photo was taken, CC was killed by a mine explosion—clearing the way for a SEAL team landing and the destruction of a Viet Cong supply camp. CC was an unfortunate, but necessary sacrifice. A frame on the other side of the desk held a more somber photo—the smoking, post-attack, pre-collapse, World Trade Center towers. Tucked in the right hand corner of that frame was a frequently handled, wallet-sized photo of a young man in a jacket and tie. Shaking his head, he thought, *It's not really a different kind of war. It's still a war that requires sacrifices...not shopping.* His attention snapped back to email and he clicked open a new, encrypted message.

> *ACRET,*
> *Latest satellite update of MK6C dolphins--2 Feb--*
> *shows two chipped animals in Galveston area, three*

in Virginia Beach area. Suggest SEAL team scan Virginia Beach stranding. Recovery op for discovered Texas MK6Chip-- in process. Will advise 2000 hours.
THE FEW

"THE FEW"--it wasn't what most people would consider a typical email signature, but Collins wasn't a typical email recipient. Officially, he was Rear Admiral Lawrence Collins, US Navy (retired), Undersecretary of Commerce for Oceans and Atmosphere and administrator of the National Oceanic and Atmospheric Administration. It was a post that seemed a step down for a man decorated for valor in Viet Nam, Lebanon, Grenada, and operations never to be public — a man who, to most, seemed to thrive in actual combat operations. Yet, those who knew him intimately knew of the varied and balanced path he walked — mixing special operations combat with an ambitious climb through the naval administrative hierarchy. For a short time he directed the Navy Marine Mammal Program in San Diego, and then was commander of Naval Base Coronado in San Diego. Eventually he moved to Little Creek and a subsequent promotion to Rear Admiral and Commander, Navy Region Mid-Atlantic. He seemed a prime candidate for moving to the top spots in the Navy and Department of Defense. Instead, Collins retired, finished his PhD in public policy to complement his MA in Environmental Policy and his Naval Academy BS in physical oceanography.

After a year of relative obscurity — except to his professors and to the special operators he continued to work with at Little Creek and across the country—Collins was nominated for the rather obscure post of Undersecretary of Commerce for Oceans and Atmosphere. But, to Collins—to THE FEW—the appointment made perfect sense.

In the late 1990s, US Navy ships—partly in response to the development of quiet-running diesel-electric submarines that would allow an enemy stealthy access to coastal waters—began testing and training with new low frequency active sonar arrays in shallow water areas. Within a year of the new testing and training exercises, detailed necropsies showed that the new ship-board, active sonar array was responsible for the beaching and deaths of several beaked whales in the Atlantic and Pacific Oceans and the Caribbean. The carcasses from the Canary Islands were the most damning--revealing severe hemorrhaging in the brain. The outcry from environmentalists and animal rights groups was intense and the subsequent, lengthy lawsuit ended up in the US Supreme Court in 2004. While the court ruled in favor of the Navy, environmentalists rallied enough support for restrictive legislation to move through Congress and to be signed into law by the newly inaugurated, environmentally leaning President.

Funding for further sonar development, testing and exercises was to be tied to a strict, new set of environmental regulations. Warships using the sonar were now hamstrung—in the opinion of most in the Navy and the supporters of a strong national defense--by the new operational guidelines required during training and testing. Training with existing systems required the cooperation of marine wildlife monitors who had the power to halt the exercises if whales or dolphins were detected within the training zone. New sonar systems were to be rigorously tested for adverse impacts on a variety of marine wildlife—not just whales and dolphins. Research methodologies and results were to be reviewed and approved by the head of the National Marine Fisheries Service—a division of the National Oceanic and Atmospheric Administration.

Collins was "placed" in his position to make sure that the Navy's contribution to national security was never compromised in that way again. As administrator of NOAA, Admiral Collins was exactly where he wanted to be—in a position obscure enough to keep a relatively low profile, but still allow him access to the people and policies essential to forwarding an important part of his national security agenda.

The admiral's pro-active passion for a comprehensive national security agenda was deeply shared by a group known by its members simply as "THE FEW"—of which he was an original member. A name bestowed on the group by one of its five founders in half-sarcastic deference to the then newly approved Marine Corps marketing slogan (*The Few. The Proud. The Marines*), Collins preferred his own interpretation of the name—citing Winston Churchill's 1940 speech to the House of Commons during the early days of World War II: "Never in the field of human conflict was so much owed by so many to so *few*." In Collins' mind, it was always the few who protected the many—in this case, it was THE FEW's four other original members who had signed off on a group email.

The aim of his group was simple--ensuring the smooth approval, development and deployment of military projects they deemed necessary for national security. Originally, they wanted to ensure that the men on the ground had the latest and greatest equipment, training and intelligence in the world and to avoid embarrassing failures like the 1980 attempt to rescue the US hostages in Iran or the Beirut Barracks Bombing in 1983. But, the World Trade Center attacks of September 11, 2001, revealed the group's initial shortcomings and the short-sightedness of their approach. Motivated to new levels, they worked to better address the government's obvious intelligence errors and expand their vision to push projects designed to protect the homeland. Collins' placement had been carefully orchestrated and was a key part of that later aim.

While THE FEW still numbered less than 10 individuals, the current or former military men cultivated a network of interested parties at all levels of government and in the private sector. Many were given security clearances well beyond what would be considered typical for their position—some permanently, most on a project by project basis. The foot soldiers of the group were men like Lt. Commander Medlin—individuals with psychological screenings, work or military records that fit a specific patriotic—love of country, love of God, children of distinguished military parents, etc.—and psychological profile that the group deemed "useful." Information and enhanced security clearances were given to them only on a very limited, need-to-know basis.

Somewhere on General Booth Boulevard
Virginia Beach, Virginia

From the passenger seat of one of his team's tracked vehicles, Lt. Commander Medlin phoned in an update, "Admiral, sir. We just dropped the samples at the aquarium and…"

"Shit." Admiral Collins interrupted. "Sorry, Lt. Commander."

"Sir?" Medlin shifted, fidgeting in the passenger's seat. He looked out the ice crusted window—people were stirring and beginning to shovel or blow or play in the snow.

"You're efficiency got ahead of us, son."

"What's that, sir?"

"Medlin. I just received confirmation that at least three MK6Cs were deployed in the Virginia Beach area. It's my fault really. I should have covered that…ordering you to scan for those dolphins."

"Begging the admiral's pardon, sir." The confidence returned to Medlin's voice, "Once we had the beach secured…as a precaution, sir…I had my team scan for MK6Cs, sir. I deemed it prudent…"

"Medlin! There was a civilian on site. That technology is top secret. Please tell me that Dr. Squires did not compromise the security of that project."

Not sure how to proceed, Medlin stumbled a little, "Yes, sir…I mean, no, sir…What I mean to say, sir, is that Ensign Ramirez completed the scan from one of our vehicles, sir. Dr. Squires was neither in the vehicle nor in any way aware of the procedure, sir."

"You are sure, Lt. Commander?"

"Absolutely, sir!"

"And, your scan results, Medlin?"

Knowing the praise would eventually come from his superior, Medlin continued, "Negative, sir. Ramirez detected the presence of no MK6Cs, sir. I would have notified you if the scan had been positive, sir. Of course, we've never used the equipment in that kind of weather sir and…"

"Well done, Lt. Commander — well done. I'm happy to see an MSOTs commander with the courage to go beyond his orders when necessary — especially when the result is a win for us." Ever mindful of his role as a powerful mentor, the admiral continued, "Medlin, just be sure to always adequately weigh the costs to your men and to the country in every situation. Exceeding your orders is nothing to be done on a whim."

"Sir, yes, sir!"

"Again, well done. Now, please email your photos and files to myself, Director Hamilton and Dr. Clarke — then, destroy them." Medlin did not fill the admiral's pause. It was obvious Collins would continue. "You will also dispose of the carcass ashes and make sure they get buried at sea."

"Sir?"

"A helicopter crew will meet you at Little Creek at 0900 to assist. Captain Patrick will call you when he is 15 minutes out. Understood?"

"Sir?" Medlin lied to cover his overly questioning tone, "Sorry sir. We just went through base security and…sorry again, sir." Pausing to emphasize his understanding, then saluting with his voice, Medlin shouted, "Understood, admiral, sir!"

"That is all, Lt. Commander." Collins was firm.

"Yes, sir!" Medlin hoped his faked enthusiasm was not obvious to the admiral or his teammates. After hanging up, Medlin leaned his head against the icy window — tired — and closed his eyes in thought. "Need to know. That's what the admiral said on Wednesday." Medlin pictured all those dolphins and shook his head — at this point, he needed to know.

Chapter 27

Building G, NMFS Laboratory, Galveston, Texas

"Angela." Director Hamilton was happy that she was precise—1000 hours exactly. "I'm getting Doc on the line in a minute as well. I know Kurt did an outstanding job managing the volunteers and the site, but…"

Slouching in the old swivel office chair, Angela cut in, "Better than I would have imagined--really. I guess without me around he's had to step his game up a little… but…I understand your *but*—he can be…what I'm trying to say is…"

The director let her off the hook, "Well, the conclusions you dismembered in the Senate committee hearings—they…well…you did a masterful job debunking Kurt's unsupportable and somewhat outlandish stranding theories."

Angela closed her tired, burning eyes—knowing that she had to do that. There was no malice. Kurt's methodology was not sound. She knew there was no malice. The data did not support his conclusions. "There was no malice." Whispering it to herself, she wondered if it were true. "Of course, it's true." She was still mumble-whispering with the mouthpiece of her phone turned away, "Science is not malicious. I'm not malicious." Shifting her weight as she put her feet up on the cot that had become bed, dresser and file cabinet, she noticed a little jab in her right hip pocket.

Jake continued, "And, what is Kurt's theory on your…your so-called chip?"

Angela sat up and removed the labeled baggie from her pocket. "Metallic cylinder. We really don't know what it is yet. But, I was talking to myself, out loud, when Kurt came early for the call. We looked at it under a binocular microscope—there's a seam...at least it looks like a seam and...we really don't know..."

"Dr. Menke." The director cut her off as Doc clicked into the call. "Thank you for joining us. I was just asking Angela about the object your students found. Seems she and Kurt found a seam at one end."

Angela looked at the little cylinder in the bag—realizing that Drew had told Doc about the chip but that Doc had said nothing to her.

Doc filled the silence, "I spoke with Drew about it this morning—quite an outstanding student, Drew—I'm sure Dr. Clarke will also give him a glowing recommendation. He said the cylinder resembled the chips now used for identification in cats and dogs. I don't..." The sentence tailed off, but it was obvious that it was not to be completed.

Angela couldn't sit. She fidgeted—shifting from cheek to cheek and finally standing. Stuffing the baggie back into her pocket, putting her phone to her ear, she walked into the hall. "Jake, you asked about Kurt. He didn't have time to theorize. We had to get back for the conference call. But, he's always suspicious. He likes to make connections...it's how his mind works...like the Navy team at Virginia Beach and..."

"Navy at Virginia Beach?" Dr. Menke chimed in. "Admiral Collins help you with that?" Doc knew about the stranding and the MSOTs deployment, but feigned his surprise — and, certainly didn't offer up that the "Navy team" was one specially trained in symbiotic special operations with marine mammals.

"Of course." Angela answered. "And, Kurt saw and examined the cylinder. He heard about the Navy team on MARMAM…" Without letting either comment she continued, "…of course it's on MARMAM — everything gets mentioned on MARMAM." Walking towards the building's exit, Angela finished, "He makes connections — even if they are not there. It's how his brain handles information — complex webs of data that is all interconnected."

"The speculation will likely live and die quickly on MARMAM, Angela." Doc had a surety in his voice that he hoped would leave no doubt. "Nobody has the technology that would make *that* a practical tool for wild dolphin research. The same cat/dog technology would work in a captive setting, but why? Other identification…re-identification techniques — like photo ID--work so well. Regardless, even if it is more than just marine debris, it's one object in 200 plus animals — not relevant to the stranding."

"Doc, I totally agree. And, it certainly doesn't make sense for any captive monitoring telemetry." Angela was unusually non-confrontational. She opened the door and stood in the cool air. "But, I still think we need to determine what it is…it looked too…too refined to be trash…the seam…I just need the right tools…fine tools…I'd just feel better knowing." She headed for the main NMFS office on site. "Jake, I'm going to see if someone in the office can help me find some tools or a technician that can help." She hung up before getting approval—or denial—and wondered why she was still so interested.

Dr. Menke's Office, Caldwell Aquarium, Galveston, Texas

"Jake, you still there?" Doc sat at his desk, an interesting cylindrical schematic on his computer screen.

"Yeah. She sure is strong-willed—dashing…"

"Jake…" Menke hesitated—not knowing the level of the director's involvement or knowledge. He knew he had to be careful. While thinking, Doc clicked over to his email—then clicked "new message" and started typing. He wrote:

ACRET
MK6Chip POSSESSION CONFIRMED: DR.
CLARKE. ACTION REQUIRED – STAT.
HAMILTON CLEARANCE? STAT.
FREEHOLD

"Ha, you knew *that* when you hired her…promoted her…put *her* in charge of *this* stranding. I really don't think this *chip* is anything. Maybe it's a piece of something the dolphin rubbed against in the wild…fishing tackle, buoy clip maybe? I haven't seen it, but who knows?" Doc continued to obfuscate with his own list of theories for several minutes and then paused. "It's certainly not the cause of the stranding. I don't understand how someone as logical, as level-headed, as Angela could waste time pursuing this. But, I'm sure some technician at the NMFS lab here in Galveston has the tools."

Director Hamilton followed the logical line of thinking, "Right. I'll make sure she passes it off and doesn't waste her own valuable time on it. Thanks."

"Not a problem. Tomorrow's update at 8:30am again?" Doc was tapping at his keyboard again. The needed communication between Director Hamilton and Angela Clarke had been facilitated.

"0830. Yes." Jake hung up and Doc hit "Send-Encrypted".

ACRET
MK6Chip RECOVERY HOLD PENDING TRANSFER AND NEW LOCATION CONFIRMATION.
FREEHOLD

An almost instantaneous reply blinked into place:

FREEHOLD
Recovery operation in place — authorized for final recovery at NMFS location. 0=1230 HOURS pending location confirmation. Hamilton clearance: NEED TO KNOW only.
ACRET

Menke rocked back in his chair — still wondering why Angela would think the chip noteworthy. Was it something she saw? Was it something Kurt said? He clicked back to the detailed, cylindrical schematic on his laptop. He needed to give Director Hamilton a few minutes before calling Angela and finding out where in the NMFS lab she was taking the chip.

Chapter 28

Director's Office, TEXMAM, Galveston, Texas

Kurt threw his stranding file onto the desk — on top of his copy of the *Odyssey*. Flopping into his chair and leaning back, he closed his eyes. He knew what Angela had been thinking after the conference call and yelled, "Why do I care?" Slumping forward--elbows on knees--he buried his head in his hands. All he had really wanted was to love her — or, for her to love him.

He sat up and rolled the chair to his desk. Reaching under the thick file, he pulled out the tattered book. Flipping through the dog-eared pages he frantically searched for some highlighted passage, a note of his own in the margins, some Homeric insight to inform or inspire. His impatient rage was punctuated by the book hitting the wall. His regret was punctuated by the soft silence of loose, yellowed pages floating to the ground. Curling into a ball on his chair, Kurt sobbed.

Chapter 29

Building C, NMFS Laboratory, Galveston, Texas

"Dr. Clarke!" Sami Singh waved as Angela swung through the door. "This way Dr. Clarke." The entrance hall "T'd" 20 feet in and the young woman quickly disappeared around the left hand corner.

Angela took quick steps so as not to lose sight of the woman. "Wait!" Rounding the corner herself, Angela saw Sami standing outside an open door. "Ms. Singh?" The receptionist at the main NMFS office had quickly put her in touch with the lab's electronics technician.

"Sami Singh." The woman smiled and extended a hand, "You must be the infamous Dr. Clarke."

"Infamous?" Angela handed her the specimen bag with the chip. "Dr. Angela Clarke, yes." She followed Sami through the door, closing it behind her, and started down a flight of stairs — disregarding Director Hamilton's order to just pass off the chip to the tech. "Infamous. If that gets me what I need, I'll take it. I'm sure that all of what you've heard about me is true. Now, we're headed to..."

"My electronics workshop."

The basement hall was narrow and dim. Built in the 1890s as part of Fort Crocket, the walk through Building C revealed that structural maintenance had been low on this lab's list of budget priorities. Open drop ceiling panels revealed masses of wires dangling just above head height. The heat and humming from what Angela assumed was some kind of antiquated heating unit was just enough to be annoying. Angela paused and looked at the exposed wiring in an open breaker panel.

Sami noticed her worried look, "It's an on-going process — we were low on the list for repairs already — even lower after the last hurricane. The guys should be back from lunch shortly." She pointed at the tool belts, empty coffee cups and coils of new wire just down the hall. "Annoys me to no end. Power on. Power off. Power surge. It was supposed to be done eight months ago. The budget cuts..." Turning through another doorway, Sami paused and, with a little extra dramatic flourish, flipped a light switch and smiled, "At least they left the power *on* today."

The workshop was not what Angela expected — not a ramshackle pile of circuit boards, gutted televisions, piles of wire. It was an oasis amidst the chaos of the hallway — spotless, labeled bins and shelving, two new computer workstations, neatly stacked file folders on the desk — obviously the product of an organized mind. Looking at Sami, Angela nodded approval.

Sami grinned slyly as she sat on a stool in front of her work table. "You're infamous in your world, and I'm infamous in mine." Setting the chip bag on the table she rolled right and opened a black tool cabinet. "I've found that focused, strong-willed women get what they want. Most men would rather give in than deal with the inevitable confrontation. It seems to work--and my ass isn't even as nice as yours."

Angela's laughter was drowned out by the concussion of a large explosion elsewhere in the basement—"Shit! Sami?" That was all Angela could manage shouting before the pressure threw her hard into a storage locker. Sami was sent rolling backward on her stool — violently smashing into a desk and crumpling over. Smoke filled the room through the now unhinged door.

Dr. Menke's Office, Caldwell Aquarium, Galveston, Texas

Admiral Collins hissed through the phone, "Risky? You didn't think of that when you gave me the location of the lab? Of course it was risky! Calling *me* on an unsecure line about *this* is risky! Get off the phone now!"

"Larry...Angela..." But the line was dead. Angela's injuries were minor, but he still had trouble reconciling the risk of the operation and the risk to such an exceptional person. He should have known Director Hamilton's order for her to pass the chip to the tech and get back to the necropsies just wouldn't stick with Angela.

Menke, rocked back in his chair and rotated from side to side-- looking around the room. His eyes settled on the same photo that sat on Admiral Collins' desk — the two of them in Vietnam with CC. "Sacrifices," he sighed and whispered to himself, "The greater good. Is the MK6C program worth it?"

Doc's computer bleeped--*new mail.* He knew it was from the admiral and sat back up in his chair to read.

> FREEHOLD
> *Item recovered with your assistance. Expect personal contact. Injuries regrettable but unavoidable. You know the costs and the benefits. Do not question the benefits. The needs of the many*

outweigh the needs of the one. Proceed as planned.
Do not break protocol again.
ACRET

Menke understood. Rocking back in his chair and staring at an old, poster-sized black and white photo of CC's permanently smiling dolphin face on his wall, he forced his own smile and jealously thought, "If only mine were built-in like yours."

Director's Office, TEXMAM, Galveston, Texas

Kurt dialed the phone—and hung up. He dialed and hung up again. "I can't do it!" He dialed and hung up again. Under his breath he repeated, "I can't talk to him. I can't do it. I can't talk to him. I can't do it." Standing up, he paced between his desk and bookshelf--back and forth. Stopping at the book shelf on the fifth trip, he picked up a small smooth stone. The stone was from Galveston Beach State Park—collected during their last camping trip together. Kurt stood there rubbing the concave backside slowly. "I can't talk to *him*."

It was September of 2001 and their relationship had been deteriorating since the South Padre Island Stranding in June. Angela was bitter—criticizing Kurt behind his back *and* to his face. She criticized him on MARMAM and in her final stranding report to NMFS. She criticized him in front of their friends. She not only criticized his work at TEXMAM, but everything else he did—nothing he did was good enough for her. But, Kurt did nothing to rebuild the trust or respect that Angela once had. Openly back to writing his book, he simply let his TEXMAM duties slip even more.

The Labor Day Weekend camping trip had been planned for over a year--a reunion of the gang that they hung with during the last year of Angela's PhD. The first night, amongst old friends and memories, around the campsite's fire and with a few slushy margarita's, Angela seemed to warm to Kurt again. They laughed, snuggled close, and held hands. When the conversation lagged and their gazes transfixed on the pulsing red embers, Angela pulled on Kurt's hand and led him to the boardwalk, over the dunes and down to the deserted beach. They made love on the beach and, to Kurt, all seemed right in the world.

A collector of things to remember significant events, Kurt slid a smooth stone into the pocket of his jeans — he hoped it marked a fresh start. The rustling brought a smile to Angela's face and she rolled over and kissed him on the cheek before jumping up and scurrying for the campsite. Kurt relaxed on the beach and fell back to sleep.

When Angela returned to the campsite, the others were still conscious and sitting around the campfire. Thomas pulled her aside and confronted her with a stream of questions, "Ang? What are you doing? What are you doing to yourself? What are you doing to Kurt? That..." He gestured at the beach and squinted in the new morning light, "I know what you did, girl...that just wasn't fair — wasn't right, Ang. I *know* you don't have any intention to..."

Angela turned to Thomas, gave him the you-don't-want-to-go-there stare and walked to where Christy and Todd were starting to make French toast. Looking at them both shaking their heads, she passed them and continued walking towards the bathhouse. She knew Thomas was right—she wasn't moving forward with Kurt. Before the trip, she had seriously considered the power of *the voice*--the power of Kurt--that once moved her. She had tried to go back to that place—but, it was gone.

When Kurt returned to the campsite, Angela was cold and aloof—rebuffing any attempted affection, sitting as far from Kurt as she could, and ignoring anything he said. It was a complete disconnect. She moved out of their apartment two days later.

Overwhelmed by that deep, painful memory, Kurt tensed his entire body and squeezed the stone in his hand. He wanted to hurl it at his office wall—but restrained himself, internalizing his anger and shakily setting the stone on the corner of his desk. He muttered to himself again, "Fucking Nicely. I really don't want to talk to him...don't want to talk to him." Walking around the desk, Kurt squatted where he had thrown the *Odyssey* and haphazardly shoved the pages back into the mangled book.

The book had not been in that bad of shape since Cape Town--since the Marine Mammal Conference; since his embarrassment at finding out about Angela's Southeast Regional Stranding Director job from their colleagues around the table instead of from her; since Angela walked out of the bar that evening with Dr. Robin Nicely and then walked in with him, arm in arm, to the conference gala the next evening.

There was nothing in Kurt's mind as he slumped from his squatting position to lie against the wall. His eyes were wet and red and vacant. His head moved, almost imperceptibly, side to side. "No. No. No." Snot ran down his face and onto the book in his lap. He lay there for 10 minutes--20 minutes.

Crawling to his desk, Kurt opened the bottom drawer. On top of the fourth draft of his manuscript, he dropped the *Odyssey*. On top of the *Odyssey* he dropped the rock. He closed the drawer, pulled himself back into his chair and dialed.

Chapter 30

Dolphin Towne, Tortola, BVI

Tommy arrived on schedule—7pm--for his swim with Bee—a Theta Wave Meditation Meld. Adam snickered as he booted up the software, "Meditation Meld...silly people."

As a cover for the serious brain wave research Adam knew Jasmine would likely not approve, he created the Theta Wave Meditation Meld—a New Age technological ruse to please her most fanatical customers. Theta waves are alleged by some to be the ideal meditative state—opening the mind to an expanded consciousness. Swimming with dolphins has been anecdotally reported to induce that state in humans. Using Adam's Wave Meld software program, Dolphin Towne's powerful computers created wave images to show clients the parallel changes in their and the dolphin's brain waves during the swims. Eventually, they went into what Adam called a "synchronized Theta Wave State"—a shared meditation. The clients loved it—some staring for hours at the mesmerizing wave images while working on their encounter logs in the Education Center or back at their rooms. Jasmine loved it because it was a package that attracted passionate repeat clients with deep pockets—clients like Tommy.

Of course, only Adam knew the Meditation Meld was a complete fabrication—the software randomly individualized and matched patterns based on a standard model of Alpha, Beta, Delta, and Theta waves. That was what the clients saw. What Adam saw and had analyzed were the brain wave data his transponders were really collecting.

Upon his arrival, Tommy went through the typical pre-swim processing. Jasmine or Adam personally screened each guest prior to every visit. Questions were mostly medical — to protect the dolphins from any human transmitted illnesses. But, both Adam, and especially Jasmine, also tried to sense the guest's mental and emotional states. Adam did it mainly because it was what he knew most of the guests expected; Jasmine did it because she wanted to protect the dolphins from stresses that even their "souls of light" couldn't heal.

Most guests also went through the simple, required physical cleansing routine — a shower with mild organic soap followed with a serious rinsing with specially filtered water. The serious visitors took much more elaborate steps. Tommy was one from that more serious "pod."

Following his screening with Jasmine, Tommy went to the locker room, disrobed and headed to the dry sauna. He paused outside to select music (a low frequency Buddhist chant) and went inside to sweat. Tommy emerged 15 minutes later and completed the basic shower. Finally, he returned to the dry sauna to sweat for the final 15 minutes before his encounter.

Tommy had experiences with all nine animals at Dolphin Towne. And, at times he still swam with each. But, most visits he spent with Bee--with her, his encounters were "simply the most vivid." He'd write in his personal encounter log for two to three hours after each session, but those four words were the most he shared with Jasmine or Adam.

After the screening, most guests were isolated from human contact until the completion of their encounter logs following the swim. This was partly for modesty — the discerning guests preferred to swim in the nude—and partly to enhance the one-on-one mental/spiritual link with their chosen dolphin. Typically, their only connection to the outside was through a small transponder of Adam's design that each guest wore on their wrist and that could be activated in case of emergency. Jasmine despised the device for its intrusion into the experience, but Adam had finally convinced her that it was a small price to pay for the benefits of isolation and to minimize their legal liability. All of the active transponders were monitored by the network and tied to an alarm that would sound throughout the compound and on Adam's phone. Gradually, Jasmine warmed to the benefits of the transponder and the other electronic interfaces he made available.

While Tommy was cleansing, Adam brought Bee to the side of the lagoon and put three small suction cup transponders on her head. These were the latest, Jasmine-approved external versions — each about the size of a quarter. Each could transmit Bee's brainwaves, heart rate and temperature—but, they were still antique compared to what he had just tested with Sammy. Tommy had two similar transponders that a flexible strap allowed him to wear around his head. Twelve digital video cameras completed the Vid-Mind Sync that was part of the more expensive "packages"—including Tommy's Theta Wave Meditation Meld--at Dolphin Towne.

As soon as he finished with Bee, Adam joined Jasmine in the Window Room. She was standing, staring at the control console. Adam shoed her away and joked, "Did you bring the popcorn?"

Jasmine gently closed her eyes and whispered, "All this technology...disturbing, unnatural energy..." Taking a deep breath and opening her eyes, she continued, "Can we have it on all the screens?" Jasmine shuffled across the middle row of the stadium seating and sat.

Attached to the Education Center, the Window Room was used for viewing when dolphins were not encountering humans. The "windows" were metaphorical—13 high definition screens— including one that was 12 by 24 feet--brought the viewers intimately into the dolphins' natural lagoons without getting wet.

Adam fiddled with the video at the control station. "I'll have the 'tracker' image on the 12 by 24 and individual screens for each of the cameras."

"Nice images. You really are a wonder with these things." Excitedly, she moved to the edge of her seat, "Here he comes!" Tommy was sliding gently into the lagoon via the sandy sloped ramp.

Adam plopped down in the same row as Jasmine—with an empty seat between them--and rocked back slightly in his chair. "Sure wish I had that popcorn."

"Adam! This is seriou..." Jasmine was about to administer one of her very infrequent, and oh-so-calm as to be ineffective scoldings when a graceful grey shape flew across the screen. "There's Bee!"

Adam scoffed, "She's swimming normal--tail going up and down and all."

Tommy floated at the surface near the ramp while Bee made two accelerating ellipses through the lagoon.

"Adam!" Jasmine shivered, reached across the empty seat and grabbed his hand in a firm, non-romantic way. In 12 by 24 foot high def they both stared as Bee rammed Tommy hard — driving him back up the ramp and out of the water.

Jasmine screamed, "Darkness! Bee!" She pulled Adam out of his seat and towards the door. "Your cell phone! We need help now!"

Day Four

Saturday, February 22, 2008

Chapter 31

Plettenberg Bay Airport, South Africa

Upon landing, Robin's satellite phone immediately began to beep. It was the tone that signaled "new voicemail." He dialed and punched in the access code.

"Dr. Nicely, Kurt...Kurt Braun here..." Robin could hear the bit of a tremor in Kurt's voice. "Got your sat phone number from Angela's notes. Dr. Nicely...Robin. She's in the hospital. She's okay. She'll be out Saturday morning. She...she's okay—just overnight for observations. She'll be fine. There was an explosion at one of the labs—old wiring and old boilers or so the story goes. Electrician just coming back from lunch rescued her and the tech. Fire destroyed the basement workshops. She's okay. Has her cell phone at the hospital." There was a pause and a sigh from Kurt, "I'm sure she'd love to hear from you." Another pause and then, "Dr. Nicely, I don't think this was an accident. Angela and the tech, I'm sure they were looking at the chip. She told you about the chip? Of course she told you about the chip...you told her to smash it...anyway, maybe it's more important than we imagined...the chip...well...I'm certain the chip is missing." Robin could hear the end of time beep on the message. "Robin, call her."

Kurt Braun was the last person Robin would've expected to be leaving him a message—especially about Angela. They were not exactly friendly—what happened at the Cape Town Marine Mammal Conference made sure of that. Robin knew any feelings of guilt over winning were long past—after all, it was Kurt's fault and it had been seven years. Still, he couldn't help feeling something for the guy that lost Angela.

That second to last night of the 2001 Cape Town Marine Mammal Conference had many of the same American and South African scientists gathered around the same table in the same bar where Angela had directly confronted her South African hosts about their need to get off their asses and start a real African stranding network. Robin was there. Kurt was there.

The beer was flowing again and the conversation ebbed back to the establishment of an African stranding network. Everyone remembered Angela's challenge from the previous night and Rudi Ramirez from Miami half-sarcastically, half-jokingly, half-drunk said, "After you get settled in as Southeast Stranding Coordinator in January maybe you can send these boys a plan!" Kurt turned abruptly to Angela and mouthed, "What?" She grinned, nodded at him and continued the conversation, waving a mug in the air. "I'll send *all of you* a plan next year." They all raised a glass to drink. They cheered. Kurt kicked back from the table and hustled outside while shaking his head—his displeasure with Angela was obvious. She didn't notice. She didn't follow. An hour later, when Robin and Angela left together, Kurt was still lingering on a bench outside the bar. Angela didn't see him. Robin did, and quickly scooted her off in the direction of his flat before Kurt could react.

The full Kurt and Angela story didn't come until Robin invited Angela to Plettenberg the following August--to help him plan the stranding network. That's when he really fell for Angela, when she opened up about her past relationships and when he really understood what Kurt had lost.

"Dr. Nicely!" Kora, one of Robin's post-doc researchers— broke through his memories. She had made the short drive to pick up her boss, the gear, and the new batch of samples. Once everything was secure in the DSC van, Robin jumped in the passenger's seat and dialed the satellite phone.

John Sealy Hospital, Galveston, Texas

Angela cringed as she opened her eyes--the light magnified the throbbing in her head. Her cell phone was ringing and she wondered why she had chosen that hideous Caribbean ring tone. The number was odd, but even in her slight narcotic haze Angela quickly recognized the country code and answered.

"Robin, how did you..."

"Kurt. Kurt called me, love."

"I'm sure he didn't call you *love*. But, I'm happy he called you." Angela closed her eyes and smiled.

"You're smiling aren't you?"

"I love you, Robin." Angela sat up taller to try and relieve her pounding temples.

"Right—me too...um...I need to talk...but you're busy with...so, how are you doing? Physically, I mean."

"Wicked headache running down through my stiff neck...throbbing temples." Sighing, she noted his inability to say "I love you," then continued, "Light makes it worse. Very, very minor concussion. Minor lacerations. The tech, Sami...she...she broke her back."

"Fuck! Uh...sorry." He knew she hated how he used that word a little too much and quickly moved on. "What's going on? Kurt said something about your chip being gone and...well...what's up with the Navy responding to strandings now?"

"Chip? Navy? Did he tell you all of that?" Even with her head aching Angela swung her legs over the side of the bed and hobbled to the window—lightly stroking her finger across the glass.

"No. It was a voicemail and MARMAM. He must've called while I was on the plane..."

She interrupted, "You're in South Africa *now*?"

"Right. Vee's finishing things up on site. I wanted to supervise the start of the lab work at DSC...missed my paddling...flabby me needs a workout." Robin paused. "Like I said, Kurt left a long, but still sketchy voicemail--mostly about you. Mentioned the chip being lost in the fire and how it might be more important than you let on...I was on MARMAM while in the airport at Maputo—saw the bit about the Navy there and well, Vee said he thought the military might be able to..."

Angela interrupted, "The weather. The Navy team was there because of the winter storm. Kurt said that was on MARMAM too." A little dizzy, she went back to her bed and sat. "Don't you start weaving conspiracy theories—leave the paranoia to Kurt. Are you just joking with me? Although with that little cylinder now missing...missing or destroyed? Mmm...my head. Makes a difference, doesn't it? Damn piece of trash! It's really not relevant. It didn't put those dolphins on the beach. Still...Any luck with your chip reference? Ahhh...my head hurts."

"Right, joking love—plenty of folks have ground-truthed the weather. But, Kurt isn't the only one spreading theories on MarMam. I won't contribute to the speculation—here or online. Now...the chip...I can still look into that when I get back home...almost to Plettenberg...I'll crash at the hou...I'll have a few hours sleep and head to DSC."

Angela swung her legs back up and slumped back into her pillow pile. "I'll be out of here at 11am—if not sooner. Like 11am means anything to you—or me--right now." She closed her eyes and rolled slowly onto her right side—the slight narcotic haze was burning off and her mental clarity was returning. "I'll be in Texas another day and a half at least. They don't want me to fly until I have a follow-up MRI tomorrow. So...out of here late tomorrow at the earliest and we still have a butt-load of necropsies to wrap up. Then I'll go to headquarters via Virginia Beach Aquarium. This will make quite a report."

"Any connection with Virginia Beach? Any similarities?"

"We've got 33 samples and nine carcasses that survived the storm and the tides. I know—not many. But, the weather was storm-of-the-century bad. You heard that. Did you hear about Squires? Unfortunate...but he is recovering...anyway, the Navy commander said Dr. Squires suggested *Morbillivirus*...but Squires is no expert—

certainly no pathologist--just going by the photos in the stranding binder. The carcasses were hard-frozen and I just don't know — honestly--if we'll have enough evidence to be conclusive. The necropsies won't get started until tomorrow."

"Your rambling a bit, I..."

"Hang on." A beep in Angela's ear signaled another call. "Shit." The phone's display showed a number with area code 727. "Robin, I've got a call from St. Petersburg...from Florida...I need to..."

"Another stranding?"

"Don't wish that on me. Hey, I need to..."

"Go love...go!"

Robin was gone and Angela switched lines.

"Hello. Dr. Clarke here."

"Dr. Clarke...you don't know me, but my name is Ellie Prinz. I'm a biologist with FWC...that's the Florida..."

"...Fish and Wildlife Conservation Commission. I know." Sighing, Angela straitened herself up in bed. "Ms. Prinz, I was the NMFS Southeast Regional Stranding Director for two years and worked closely with my colleagues at the FWC." Angela closed her eyes and the throbbing in her head returned. "Now, what can I do for you?"

"Okaaaay." It was obvious—by the way she drew out the word--that Ellie was taken a little aback. "The local NMFS office told me to speak to you directly." A loud hum filled the pause.

"Ms. Prinz, please don't tell me that there's been another stranding. *Tursiops* and there are hundreds of them?"

"Uh...no. No stranding. I do manatee aerial surveys and...well..."

"Speak up," Angela shook her head from side to side — trying to shake out the fuzziness. "What is that droning noise?"

"The plane, Dr. Clarke. I'm in the air right now. They are massing."

Angela reached to the rolling tray table for her legal pad and pen. "Manatees are massing? It's February, it's pretty typical for manatees to...but you know that — that's why you're in the air, counting." Her mind moved right to the potential problems. "What's the water temperature? Are they not in a warm water refuge? Where are they massing? What's the water temperature, *Ms. Prinz*?"

"Ellie." The stress on the name stopped Angela's tirade of questions. "Call me Ellie. And, they're dolphins, Dr. Clarke — definitely dolphins. Schooling like fish just east of the south end of Egmont Key. It's at the mouth of Tampa Bay...but you probably are familiar with the area...anyway...maybe 200 animals. Just swimming in a big circle..."

"Yes, yes--I'm familiar with Egmont Key." The barrier island was once home to coastal batteries that protected Tampa Bay — now, there was a lighthouse, a small Coast Guard outpost and a pier for landing a tourist ferry. A state park and a wildlife refuge, Egmont Key was a protected area. East of the island were extensive, shallow water grass flats—a prime fishing area and a great place to seek shelter from the larger winter waves of the Gulf of Mexico.

"Really? Really that many? Shit! Some sort of pre-stranding behavior maybe? What the hell is going on here? Damn. Ellie…shit. Sorry. We're stretched really thin right now. I'm stretched…" Angela put her phone on "speaker" so that she could start scrolling through the contact files for the NMFS office in St. Petersburg.

"I figured. I read about the other strandings on MARMAM— saw the Texas one on TV-- and figured that our stranding people and the local NMFS office might handle it. But, my manager directed me to David Tilton at NMFS St. Pete and he directed me to you. I don't know how you can manage…"

Angela interrupted, but in a softer, reassuring tone, "We'll manage—I'll manage. I need an accurate count. I know you need to do your manatee survey, but at this point this has got to be a higher priority. I need GPS coordinates, photographs. I'll alert your superiors at FWC--inform them of your mission change. We'll need to mobilize additional staff—FWC and NMFS." Angela closed her eyes and the throbbing arched aggressively from her forehead to her temples.

"Dr. Clarke? I have the survey to…"

"You did the right thing reporting this. It is not only unusual, but also—if it is indeed *Tursiops*—unprecedented. You are the only asset on site right now. You can provide us with critical real time data. I don't know what we can do, but we need to be ready." In her head, Angela started running through the list of organizations with rescue teams in the area — FWC, Clearwater Marine Aquarium, Mote Marine Laboratory in Sarasota. "Ellie, I'm sure your manager will be fine with me re-tasking you for something of this magnitude. I'll make a call, but the need is immediate. You good with that?"

"Yes, ma'am. You're right. This is…"

"Okay." With Ellie convinced, Angela was back to business. "Call me back within the hour with a better count and coordinates…Do you have any way to email me photos from the air?" Angela was simultaneously outlining an action plan on her legal pad.

"Best I could do is with my cell phone. I don't have a good camera with…"

"That will do. Send them right to this number. Get me a good photo with that phone."

"I'll do my best."

"I expect you will do better than that. Now, just do it — get me the count within the hour — get me a photo. Thank you."

Chapter 32

Dolphin Towne, Tortola, BVI

"Adam!" Jasmine rarely raised her voice, but shouted to him across the Eli House's main dining room—he was having some multigrain pancakes and fresh fruit. As she sauntered across the room, Jasmine continued, "I just got off the phone with Tommy. Breathing's still a little raspy from the lung puncture, but he has been breathing on his own since midnight. Four broken ribs. He thinks he'll be out in two days." She sat at the table, picked up one of Adam's strawberries and took a small bite. "He already is asking when he can come back. I told him…"

Adam sat back in his chair—away from the table. "I've been filming Bee 24/7 since your unsettling incident with her on Wednesday. I wanted to see if she was doing anything…"

"And? And? What did you see?" Jasmine was curious, but agitated. "Invading her private time like that? I hope…I hope you saw something worth the intrusion! So, what did you see?"

Trying to calm her, Adam slid back up to the table to hold her hands. She quickly pulled them away and folded her arms across her chest.

"Two things. First, I saw her catch and eat live fish. Second…"

"A live fish?" Jasmine shifted to the edge of her chair. "A live fish?"

Adam took a deep breath — in through the nose, out through the mouth. "No. Not *a* live fish. Fish — plural. Fishes. I have video of her from the last three days eating multiple live fish."

Slumping back in her chair and pulling her knees up to her chest, Jasmine got quiet. Her contemplative look turned to sadness. "And, second?"

"Wild dolphins have been swimming along the lagoon's bayside wall. Bee's been swimming with them. The wall's permeable enough to allow fish through...and vocalizations. I've recorded vocalizations coming in and going out. She has some new friends."

Jasmine was still curled in her chair. She rocked ever so slightly, "She...she wants to leave me."

Adam didn't know where to go with his discussion — he didn't know what level of disclosure would expose his research. "Jasmine." Adam looked at her and then turned away — sliding his chair back and standing. He paced back and forth on his side of the table. "Last night I looked at Bee's heart rate, body temperature and brainwaves from her attack on Tommy and..."

Jasmine put up her hand and slid her legs back down to the floor. "What did Tommy do? How did he provoke her? What negative energy was she trying to drive from her space? My Bee could never do this."

"I looked at Tommy's data as well and..." And, this was true, "...his brainwave patterns were the same as those I've saved from previous encounters." Adam snickered and grinned, neither Tommy nor any of the other Theta Wave Meditation Meld clients ever saw the real brainwave data. "I only had that brief bit, but it was an identical match to his previous visits."

Curling back into her chair Jasmine started to cry, "Bee isn't bad. Bee isn't violent. Bee...Bee is love and light and..." She wiped her eyes on her sleeve and raised her voice, "Bee is good."

Adam sat back down and locked eyes with Jasmine. "Bee is a wild animal. Sure, she's been in captivity for...five years...she hasn't killed a fish in five years..." He reached out this time and she sat forward, letting him hold her hands. "Jasmine. There is love and light and good in her being wild."

Gripping his hands tightly, Jasmine closed her eyes. "Arrogant, human, selfish me. What do I do now? What do I...what do we do now?"

"Well, first we don't let any of our soon-to-be-arriving guests swim with her. We isolate her from the rest of the pod—human and dolphin. We rearrange the encounter schedule. We make it work."

Jasmine opened her eyes wide, "I'll call Dr. Menke. I'll fly him in for a consult...maybe it's a physical illness manifesting itself..." She looked at the clock on the dining room wall. "The group starts arriving at 9:30. I have some time. I'll call him." Rubbing her thumbs gently on his grasping hands, Jasmine smiled and Adam's hands relaxed. "Thank you. Thank you for enlightening me."

Keeping his eyes locked on hers, Adam slowly pulled his hands away, slid the chair back and stood. He smiled like he was the one who was filled with light. "I'll make sure we're ready for the guests."

Chapter 33

Director's Office, NMFS, Silver Spring, Maryland

"Angela?" The concern in Director Hamilton's voice was genuine. "Doc, Kurt, said you were…"

"I'm fine. The drugs are wearing off and my mind is coming back. Just a little headache and a few scratches."

He knew she wouldn't like the suggestion—he wasn't even sincere—but, Jake felt he had to make the offer. "I can put Kurt or Doc in charge and have…"

"Don't you dare. This is my show and I'm going to see it through. I'll be out of the hospital today and we'll have most of the necropsies wrapped up by the time I'm cleared to fly sometime tomorrow. This stranding is unprecedented and I don't want it screwed up by changing things now. I'm the best qualified and…"

"Relax. You need to relax. You are still in charge, Angela. Just remember who is letting you stay in charge." He shook his head and drummed his fingers on the desk. "And, why would you need to fly anywhere yet? Virginia Beach is being managed. Just get your rest."

There was a long pause. "I just got a call from St. Petersburg."

"Shit." Jake moved one hand to his mouse and woke up his hibernating computer. "Manatees? Pygmy sperm whale?"

"Sick, Jake—sick, wishful thinking. No--dolphins."

"What the hell is going on?" Director Hamilton reviewed his conversations with the admiral. Collins never elaborated on the potential national security implications, but Jake never dug deeper.

Now, the NMFS Director started to wonder about some of the connections TEXMAM's Kurt Braun had made about the Navy and the stranding—and the chip. While tapping a quick, but pressing, email message to Admiral Collins he continued with Angela. "Shit. Where? How many?"

"The information is still from a sketchy, first-hand account. They've not stranded yet...but, it appears that they're massing. Maybe 200 off Egmont Key—that's west of the Sunshine Skyway bridge. The mouth of Tampa Bay. Massing and swimming in a circle..."

"Who? Who reported...?"

"Biologist with the state—Fish and Wildlife—doing manatee aerial counts. This might be a chance to...

"I know, I know. It's an opportunity to learn something at the very least. At best..."

"Let's not hope now. Not after what we've seen already. Anyway, the girl called me from the plane. She's getting me GPS coordinates and an accurate count...hopefully a photo. I told her this took priority over her manatee survey. I don't really have any authority..."

"You exude authority, Angela. I'm sure *that* was enough."

"Right. I called her superiors. I must have been convincing-- they phoned her with their approval." She paused, and then continued, "It may be another 200 animals. They are swimming in a circle approximately a quarter mile in diameter."

Jake didn't know what to say when she paused again. He checked his computer for a reply from Collins — *nothing*. The admiral's order to keep him informed kept pounding through his skull.

Angela broke the silence and the director's train of thought, "This has got to be a precursor…damn…some kind of pre-stranding behavior…sorry. It's just…I didn't mean to jump to conclusions. But, the inshore massing is too unusual to discount. Unusual is an understatement. Inshore bottlenose dolphins…well…I don't know if they are…there just aren't *that* many locally…hmmm…anyway, I'll have the count, the coordinates and, hopefully an image…but…"

"But what?"

"But, I really think we need more monitoring…boats on the water…a plane in the air…I don't want to see another 200 animals die. And, if they are already on their way, I want to learn as much about this as we can. I've already made some contacts and have started to outline our rescue efforts…" She paused because she was feeling a bit overwhelmed — not realizing the dramatic effect. "We have to mobilize…"

"You're saying we need a major effort here. I get it." Jake swiveled in his chair and pulled up to his desk. He looked at his email — nothing. He checked his cell phone — nothing.

"Remember Norway a few years ago when they tried to free the two whales from the iced-in fjord?" She left no time for a response — everyone even remotely involved with marine mammals was familiar with the multi-million dollar effort and the media hoards that brought it to the world. "*That* kind of effort."

A double bleep moved Jake's eyes back to his email.

Director Hamilton,
We cannot miss this opportunity. Further instructions forthcoming. Stand by.
Admiral Collins.

"You listen to your doctors. Get better. I'll contact our St. Pete office as well, get the admiral's go ahead to use other NOAA staff in state if need be. I'll also contact Florida FWC about keeping their plane in the air. *You* stay put and get better. You are not to fly until the doctors clear you. Understood?"

"Yes. I'll email you the action plan I've already outlined and the contact information…I'll make sure it gets CC'd to the folks in St. Pete…but, I'll be out of here before noon if all is well…and, I'm sure it is. *I* want to be on site—in Tampa ASAP."

"If all is well with the doctors *tomorrow*, call me. I'll have one of the jets waiting for you in Galveston. Now, get well. Make sure things are staying on track there…and let me know what more you hear from St. Petersburg. I'll do likewise. But, I *do* want you coordinating that effort as well. It's too important to leave it to anyone else." Jake hung up and waited for the "further instructions" promised by Admiral Collins.

Chapter 34

Dr. Menke's Office, Caldwell Aquarium, Galveston, Texas

"Jasmine!" Doc put down the results of Pirate's latest blood work and, with the phone to his ear, turned to another photo on his desk. "Always a pleasure...I could use a little dose of your positive energy...how's it..."

"It's Bee. She's..." The tone didn't match the glowing smile of the photo or the energy of the moment it captured — Doc, Jasmine and Bee in the waist deep water of Bee's new "natural" lagoon. Jasmine had flown him in for the transfer — to monitor all the dolphins as they were moved from the temporary tanks to the seven natural lagoons that had been created on her property.

"She's not well, is she?"

"Changed, Doc. She's changed."

Dr. Menke got up from his desk and went over to the cabinet where he kept the files on all of the Dolphin Towne residents. Pulling two folders — one thin, one thick--from the drawer, he sat back down.

"Changed? Blood values? Eating habits? Behavior?"

"Yes. Um...well...eating and behavior. I've lost contact with her. She's...she's darker now...cold...not the light of Dolphin Towne."

Doc smiled and tried to cheer her, "You're the light of Dolphin Towne and..."

"She rammed a swimmer. Dark. Cold and black--very dark. He's...broken ribs...a lung puncture...he's going to be fine...already wants to schedule his next swim to mend things with Bee…not right when I swam with her Wednesday…I feel hollow, empty, washed out thinking about it…nauseous…she's eating fish…live fish and…"

"Live fish?" Doc closed the thick file he had started to flip through while Jasmine droned on. "Five years and now she's eating live fish? That is a change. You're sure? Live fish? You saw it?"

Jasmine's rambling continued over Doc's questions, "Adam. Adam's video…after my swim and the darkness…sorry, it's so hard…I get drawn into that frigid, lightless place…so empty…black…and, so draining for me."

Real or perceived, the connection Jasmine felt to Bee was powerful. Dr. Menke knew this and knew to respect her overwhelming sincerity. Gently, he asked, "Adam recorded Bee eating fish? That's it?"

"Yes." She appeared to compose herself. "Yes, Adam recorded her eating live fish. Several times. And…"

"That's fabulous! After all these years, Bee might be a real candidate for relea…" He stopped cold and moved fast to recover. "And, what?" He tried hard to lead her to finish the thought he had interrupted. "Eating live fish and what?"

Doc knew the silence was Jasmine digesting his slip. He waited. She sniffled.

"Adam also filmed her swimming with wild dolphins…that is, swimming along the bay wall with wild dolphins. Two…two wild dolphins. She wants to leave me. The darkness is her disconnecting-

-shutting me out. Shutting *me* out." Jasmine's voice was cracking. She sniffled again.

Knowing she was crying, Doc searched for the right thing to say. He remembered back to Bee's original rehab, wondering if he ever came up with the right words when he was almost certain the release might happen. No, he didn't recall coming up with the words, but he'd been through the routine eight times with other animals and volunteers at Caldwell. The volunteers get so attached. Still, they weren't five years attached — like Jasmine and Bee.

The right words didn't come, so Doc took another line. "Adam's a real asset. I'm glad you've given him a place. You…you know about his time at MIT and Woods Hole of course. Adam was quite the rising star of dolphin research — a prodigy. At least, he seems to fit his aptitude for high tech gadgetry in well with your goals for Dolphin Towne. We may yet see some great things from him." Doc paused and closed the file on Adam he had also retrieved from the cabinet. "Anyway, the video is a good clue…"

Jasmine's voice was serious, "A good clue to his other research motives." And then she lightened up, "But, that has never concerned me. Adam's love for the dolphins…his love for me…that is sincere."

Doc revived MS Outlook on his computer and started through his calendar. "I don't think this is medically urgent, but we should set a time for me to come down and re-evaluate. I need to be here at least another week because of the stranding and…"

"Stranding?" Jasmine's voice sank with her heart. "How many? When?"

"I think we can save the six we have at the aquarium now." Doc knew that wasn't enough for Jasmine.

He was right—the intensity of her prodding grew, "When? Where? How many died? When? Where?"

"Jasmine...Jasmine." Doc stood and walked around to the front of his desk and sat on the edge. "They were found on the beach at Galveston. Wednesday morning. There were...over 200."

"Wednesday! That's when I had the disconnect from Bee. That's when she started shutting me out—when I was sucked into that cold, dark...She knew. She sensed it. Two hundred? Bee knows humans caused this...why she wants out...back to the wild...that's why the darkness....the disconnect...the anger!"

Doc knew there was no stopping her sometimes--it was an almost trance-like state.

Jasmine continued, "Bee knew. I always felt the connection through Bee...the connection to their collective pod-consciousness. That's what was missing. That was shut off. *That* was Bee pulling back...away...from me...from other humans...the darkness of the stranding. It's our fault. Humans caused that stranding and Bee is telling me...telling me by shutting me out. I need to tell people...I need to let them know what she's doing. I..." Jasmine's voice faded into sobbing.

Powerful, passionate, and misdirected as she was, Doc knew Jasmine's resources were nearly unlimited and that she would follow through on anything she felt strongly.

Doc's tone became soft and calming calm. "We need to think of Bee's health and well-being at the moment." Doc sighed loudly. "I need to be here for at least another week to stabilize the six. Even then I could only come down for a day…two at most…"

He was interrupted by a subtle tone from his computer — new mail. "Uh…" Reminding himself to focus, Dr. Menke continued, "Make sure Bee stays isolated. No swimmers…nobody even walking in that area of Dolphin Towne. Have Adam monitor her natural feeding and if she isn't getting enough calories…I'll email him the caloric intake data he'll need…find a way to supplement with the typical frozen fish. But, keep her away from people. You…you keep away from her as well."

Doc fingered his mouse and glanced at the email. It was an encrypted message from Admiral Collins — flagged urgent. First, he had to finish with Jasmine. He focused and continued, "I will…I promise…I will talk to Randy and my team here and evaluate the soonest I can get to you. If things turned bad with Bee, I'm sure Randy could coordinate things here if need be." Dr. Randy Edwards was Menke's protégé and likely to succeed him as director at the rehab facility when he retired — he was more than qualified to handle the rehabilitating dolphins, but Doc knew that, in this case, he wanted to be in Texas.

"I understand, Doc. They..." And he knew she meant the dolphins, "...need you there--more at the moment. Heal them. I'll have arrangements for you on stand-by. Call me after you speak with Randy and the team."

Doc moved back to his chair and again woke up the computer. "I'll talk to them today and contact you later. Take care."

"And you as well."

"*Namaste.*" Doc didn't know if he was joking to himself, or serious. He had already hung up, put the phone off to the side and opened his email.

> *FREEHOLD*
> *MK6Chip transfer?*
> *ACRET*

Doc typed a quick reply.

> *SUCCESSFUL.*
> *FREEHOLD*

Standing to return to the rehabilitation tanks, Doc was brought back to his desk by another email alert.

> *FREEHOLD*
> *Virginia Beach covered. Tampa at issue. Dolphins massing, not stranding.*
> *Mobilizing MSOTs for Tampa.*
> *Stand by — you may be requested.*
> *ACRET*

"Shit!" Dr. Menke closed the laptop, folded his arms across the computer and buried his head. *He* wanted blackness, emptiness. What he got was anything but--images from the beach in Galveston jumbled with a high-speed replay of procedures, animals, charts, and sounds from the defense research project Admiral Collins had persuaded him to lead six years ago.

Chapter 35

Little Creek Amphibious Base, Virginia Beach, Virginia

"Admiral Collins, sir!" It was Saturday, but Lt. Commander Medlin was always available—his phone always handy. He grabbed his towel off the squat rack and wobbly-walked across the gym and into the hallway. "I trust you received my email yesterday with…"

"At ease, Lt. Commander. You did a fine job all around with my last request. And again, scanning for MK6Cs at the site was an insightful move, son…" The admiral was old enough and respected enough to call almost all active duty servicemen *son*. "…we have another dolphin situation in Florida." Collins paused for a reaction, got none, and continued, "I know this is similarly atypical. This isn't what the MSOTs were created for, but your skill set—your familiarity with the animals—your team is well-suited. You are also acquainted with the NMFS personnel who will ultimately coordinate the effort."

Medlin draped his towel around his neck and sat on a bench. He wondered exactly what the admiral could be wanting now—he knew there would be orders. What he didn't know was whether they would be legal—or ethical. "Sir? Our operational orders…?"

"Are on their way via encrypted email, via MSOTs Commander Kirk. Your access code is *truncatus*." Collins paused, and then continued, "You are deploying from Oceana today." Oceana Naval Air Station was the staging point for the MSOTs based at Little Creek. "The needed boats are already loaded on the C-5s and on their way. Your orders will detail other equipment needed specifically for this mission. The runways will be plowed by 1100. You and your men will rendezvous there for a noon departure."

"Boats, sir?" Medlin pulled the towel over his head like hood—unable to get a handle on the *why* of another domestic deployment. In his mind, this one could not be written off as either convenience or public safety. It seemed like an extraordinary effort— moving that many boats and men to Tampa Bay—for more dead or dying dolphins.

"The dolphins aren't dead--at least not yet. They've massed at the mouth of Tampa Bay—um...Egmont Key. We are sending you there to keep them from stranding and to assist the civil authorities— NMFS and FWC."

"Assist with what *exactly*, sir?"

"At this point...perimeter security...monitoring." The admiral noted Medlin's almost insubordinate tone, but simply repeated, "Monitoring, securing the perimeter..." He paused and added, "... also, acting as my eyes and ears."

"Well, admiral, sir, whatever the mission, the men certainly will be singing your praises for a Florida vacation after spending the last three days in..."

The admiral cut in with more important information, "Medlin--perimeter security and monitoring. I also want regular candid assessments—of the security situation, of what the other agencies are doing, of the status of the dolphins. In the not-too-distant future..." The admiral's pause allowed Medlin to finish in his mind what was implied — *assessment of whatever is required for national security.*

Collins continued, "When you arrive at Oceana a courier will meet you at your staging area. He will have a hard copy of your orders and an upgrade in your security clearances. The time may come when you'll be required to know more than even your current security clearances allow."

"Begging your pardon, admiral...sir...I don't understand why...the dolphins...are there MK6C dolphins there, sir? Still, I don't see how anyone could find the chips...or..." Medlin couldn't stop his cascading thoughts, "...or are the chips causing the strandings? Sir, it just doesn't makes sense, the chips were..."

"Commander! The time for analytical thinking may come. That time is not now. When you have the need to know, you will be informed of the necessary details. Now, have your men ready and on the plane at noon. When you land in Tampa, get those boats unloaded and on the water without delay. Continue to impress me. I will be in touch."

"Sir! Yes, sir!" The verbal salute was in vain. The admiral was gone. Medlin pulled the towel from over his head and headed for the locker room.

Chapter 36

The New House, Plettenberg Bay, South Africa

Robin had arrived late in the day—after routing the generous Dolphin Study Centre donor's private jet through Johannesburg, the eventual landing in Plettenberg, and a circuitous drive in the DSC van to drop his load of samples to the lab. He'd dropped Kora there as well—his old on-site apartment had been converted to graduate student and post-doc housing now that the new house was livable. The sun had set, but the orange glow rippled like glassy lava on the floor-to-ceiling windows that faced the water. After dropping his duffle of dirty clothes in the laundry, Robin moved to his home office and opened the sliding doors—letting the salty breeze pass through the house. Closing his eyes, he inhaled through his nose, filling his chest, holding briefly, and then exhaling slowly. He took in the view of the bay, his rack of kayaks and surf skis, the path to the water, the almost functional Jacuzzi. Thinking about Angela standing next to him—someday soon—he smiled.

Taking a step back from the sliding door, Robin collapsed into his reading chair and pulled the lever to raise his feet. He flopped his head to the right and looked at the stack of reading on the small table. *Shakespeare's Algorithm,* Arthur Will's latest thriller, sat on top of the 33 *Marine Mammal Science* manuscripts he had been neglecting. Privately, and sometimes not so privately, Robin loathed the poor writing skills of many of his fellow scientists. If not for the prestige of being a reviewer for *the* journal of international marine mammal research, he would've easily passed on the agony and eye strain of reading most of the papers. He switched on his reading lamp and set the book in his lap. After adjusting the angle of the light over his shoulder, Robin turned to the bookmarked page and briefly closed his eyes.

> *Professor Moorehouse and his "assistant" Lucy had just left the Royal Shakespeare Company's performance of "Othello" in Stratford-on-Avon and were buying some fish and chips from a street vendor. Mixed with the typical greasy newspaper wrapping was a page from an old manuscript. Uncharacteristically, mathematical equations mixed with lines of poetry…*

His mind clear of dolphins for the moment, Robin read.

John Sealy Hospital, Galveston, Texas

"Angela!" She was sitting in a wheel chair signing papers at the discharge desk. Turning, she flashed Kurt a manufactured smile and held up the wait-a-minute finger. After a moment the attendant wheeled her around and towards the exit.

"Thanks for coming. But, I'm sure someone else could have given me…"

He cut her off, "Doc is busy, one of the TT's took a downturn last night…Robin's an ocean away…my work is wrapping up…so you are stuck with me…"

"Thanks, Ben." She shook the wheel-chair attendant's hand after standing up outside the hospital.

Walking towards the car, Angela stopped and held Kurt's hands like a friend. "Thanks for calling Robin. I know that..."

Kurt let go of her hands, turned and kept walking. "It wasn't that hard." His next blink was a little prolonged. "It's been a long time. Too long."

"How did you even know that we still..."

Kurt stopped and spun around to look at her again. Pursing his lips and squinting a little with one eye, he struggled to get it out, "You glow a little every time you mention his name." She smiled and he immediately looked at the ground, turned and continued walking and talking, "Still, I confirmed it with Doc." Pausing, he thought about what to say next—"I'm happy for you." He knew that sounded contrived, so he just skipped onward, "It seemed the right thing to do. I like to do the right thing."

They stopped at the car. "Well. Thanks again for calling him." She paused and after he opened the door she just stood there. "Kurt." Angela's tone quickly changed from sincere to serious. "Do you really want to start spreading theories already? Robin...MARMAM. We really don't have any conclusive evidence for a cause, let alone a relationship. You just jump..."

"...right in without thinking. Passion first--plan later. Love is all you need!" Kurt was agitated and slammed the door. He walked around to the back of the car. "I suppose my credibility is shot after your hearings anyway. Might as well go down with a bang—better than the whimper I barely squeaked out when you left." One foot up on the bumper, he wobbled a little when he closed his eyes. "I...sorry.

I didn't mean to go there. I didn't..." Angela didn't say anything and the silent seconds dragged. Kurt continued, "I just think that when all is said and done—and it might not be said and done for years—that we are going to see some connection between Galveston and Virginia Beach, with the way it was handled, the Navy involvement, the missing chip...maybe even with Robin's stranding in Mozambique. It can't be coincidence...not these numbers...it can't."

After walking back to the passenger's side of the car, Kurt re-opened the door and Angela slowly climbed in. Looking her in the eye, he continued, "And, I think...yes, at this point I only think it...that someone is going to find a human cause—maybe not our missing chip, but a human mistake, something—for all of this." Kurt closed the door and very slowly moved around the back of the car.

Building G, NMFS Laboratory, Galveston, Texas

The short drive back to the NMFS lab was silent—no conversation, no music.

Angela clutched her bag as Kurt opened the door to the lab building. "You really don't need to walk me to my office. I'm perfectly capable." Though her head still throbbed, Angela was ready to get back on the job.

"I've got other things to wrap up here at the lab and it's on the way. I don't mind." Kurt closed the door behind them and followed her down the hall. "I need to see where the necropsy teams are at this point. They should be on the downhill side."

"Suit yourself." Angela opened the door and stepped into the over-sized office that, with the addition of a cot and some blankets, was her base of operations.

Kurt looked at the empty cans of Diet Coke and her haphazardly stuffed overnight suitcase. "You really should get a hotel room — especially after the concussion. I'd feel better if…"

"I'm fine." She closed her eyes hard, felt the strong, steady throb, reopened them and continued, "If I'm here I can get this wrapped up and be on my way to Tampa. Shit."

"Tampa?" Kurt stood in the doorway, arms crossed. "Something very wrong is going on here. Another stranding?" He could see the "yes" in her eyes. Pacing back and forth in front of the door, Kurt ranted, "Why didn't you tell me sooner? Another stranding? You could have told me at the hospital…during the ride from the hospital you…you…"

Angela sighed loud enough to interrupt. "I was surprised you didn't mention it to me — as plugged in as you appear to be." She let that hang for a few seconds before continuing, "They were doing a manatee aerial survey today. I got a call from an FWC biologist up in the plane over the mouth of Tampa Bay. She observed approximately 200 dolphins massing…" Her voice was unemotional, monotone. She held up a hand — *stop* — seeing that Kurt was ready to pounce. "They're swimming in a coordinated circle. The FWC observer…she's getting me a more accurate count, hopefully some photos. We've contacted FWC and NMFS assets in the area — I'll manage things remotely until I can fly to the site tomorrow. Director

Hamilton wants an all-out effort to prevent another stranding and to find out what the hell is going on." Angela let a little raw emotion creep into the last bit of the sentence. The emotion intensified as she continued, "What *is* going on? I should see a pattern! But, there is no pattern. What the fu..." The throbbing in her temples and the realization that Kurt was still there, stopped her cold.

Kurt stood silent.

Angela opened her laptop. She was a little perplexed—expecting Kurt to immediately go off. His silence was more than atypical. When he did speak, it was not what she expected.

"Robin." Kurt grinned and nodded. "You need Robin."

Angela's quizzical look and shake of the head said it all—*I don't understand.*

"You need Robin in Tampa. You need Robin in Tampa now." Kurt pulled an old wooden desk chair from against the wall and sat. He looked directly at Angela. It was *the look.* "Dr. Robin Nicely, your Robin, is the world's expert—expert—on wild dolphin societies. He's been studying some communities in South Africa since he was in high school. He knows more about their social structures...their relationships...than anyone alive. If you are going to try and save those dolphins *and* figure out what is going on, you need his help. And, you need it immediately."

Angela stared—*the voice.* The confidence, the clarity of vision—it had been a long time since a thought from Kurt had penetrated her this way. She nodded in agreement. "You're right."

That and a little smile were all she managed before she grabbed her cell phone, shoed Kurt into the hall, closed the door and dialed.

The New House, Plettenberg Bay, South Africa

Robin hadn't made it much further into the best-selling *Shakespeare's Algorithm* before the previous three days' fatigue caught up with his eyes—a testament to the limits of caffeine, the spell of a cool, gentle sea breeze, and the wiles of a chair that was probably a little too comfortable for reading.

Three hours into a drooling deep sleep, the spell was broken. Robin moaned—"Arrrgh!"--and rolled to the left—digging for the vibrating, ringing annoyance in his right pants pocket. Eyes still closed, he answered groggily, "Hello?"

"Robin! It's Angela!" Her headache gradually clearing, Angela managed to be a little bit perkier—maybe a little too perky for Robin.

"What do you want?" He shifted back to the right and his book fell to the floor. "Shit. What's up? It's late…I'm sleeping." Reaching for the book, he realized most of the manuscripts had been scattered on the floor by the breeze. The room spun and he was feeling the nausea of too little sleep and an abrupt wake-up call.

"Where are you?"

"At the house, I…" Robin moved quickly to cover the gaffe and not give away his secret about the new house. "What's up? You know what time it is here! I got back and passed out with a book…probably didn't get more than two pages…ahhh…good, drooling sleep, but I do need to get showered, get moving, what time is it there? Better yet, what time is it here?"

"I know you just got to Plettenberg. I know you want to supervise the testing at DSC. But, and I'm not asking this for myself, I need you here—now."

"Galveston? Now?" Robin slid his bookmark back into place and shuffled the manuscripts together. He placed the book on the reading table and walked the manuscripts to the desk on the other side of the room. "Are you okay? I mean your head, the...you want me...you need me?"

"I'm fine. *We* need you in Tampa..." Angela paused—the moment required a hint of drama.

But, Robin filled the silence with his own thoughts—noting that Angela had said "we," not "I." Her request was professional, not personal. He sighed.

Angela continued, "We need your expertise. Nearly 200 dolphins are massing in Tampa Bay—swimming a coordinated circle. I got a call from someone doing a manatee aerial survey and..."

"*Tursiops*? Do you know if they are *Tursiops*?" Robin circled around the desk and sat in his rolling chair.

"Unconfirmed. The information is still sketchy."

"Doesn't matter." His fingers thoughtfully rasped at the rough whiskers on his face. "Doesn't matter...200 inshore anything is...beyond..."

Angela interrupted, "We should have boats on the water within the hour to verify the species. Either way, you are the world's expert on wild dolphin societies. I need your help to save them and...or, at the very least, help us find out what is causing them to congregate like this. I..."

"I...I'm so tired right now. But, they're still alive? They could be dead by the time I get there. I'm tired, love. Sorry, not a proper excuse — not in paddling, not in anything. Suck it up — Derrick can properly supervise the testing. Kora's no slouch. I hope Vee is doing well. Uhg--no paddling...no surf ski tomorrow...can I borrow a boat in Tampa?" Robin talked through his wandering thoughts — his head still drifting in and out of the fog of interrupted sleep and distracted by the acid churning in his hollow stomach.

Angela let him ramble a bit and then continued, "I have Director Hamilton's okay and authorization for the airfare and expenses — all covered. First Class. You know *we* need answers."

Robin struggled to focus, but started sorting through the backpack on his desk — sorting through his work from Mozambique and inserting a couple new legal pads, his laptop, some pencils. He also scooped up a couple of the *Marine Mammal Science* manuscripts and hesitated — deciding to take them all for the long flight. "Right, I'll be on the road in an hour. What's going on now? What are you scheming?"

Angela filled him in on the specifics — the initial sighting, who was being contacted, and that he might just beat her there. When she was finished, Robin made sure to request whatever underwater monitoring equipment might be available — hydrophones, video cameras, anything that might help them look for anomalies or signals from the dolphins' behaviors.

Robin put all the manuscripts in his pack and started to move to the bedroom for fresh clothes. "Shit, love…I'm such an ass." Still groggy with sleep, Robin yawned, "How's the head?"

"No, not an ass—just a sleepy head. You asked me already and I told you--it's fine. The headache's mostly…" She closed her eyes, felt a dull, persistent throb and sighed, "…mostly gone."

"And, the tech? Her back?" Robin stared at the scattering of unpacked boxes and realized his duffel bag was still in the laundry. Changing direction, he headed downstairs.

Angela sighed and lowered her voice. "Likely paralyzed—at least from the waist down. She…uhg…stupid chip! Any luck with your chip reference?"

Dumping his laundry out of the duffel bag, Robin tried to visualize what he had upstairs in the way of clothing. Some of his wardrobe was still in storage at DSC—some was in boxes in the master bedroom. "Chip? I'm having a hard enough time figuring out what to pack and where it's at…what box…shit!" He realized that in his sleepy haze he was having a hard time not mentioning anything to do with the house. So, he went back to the chip, "Chip's probably nothing—an anomaly…marine debris. Kurt said it's missing anyway. Sorry I'm so irritable. I need to focus. Not enough sleep. I'll call or email from the airport—get you my flight details. Fly into…?"

"Tampa International Airport—TPA. I'll have someone waiting for you."

"I wish it were you. Or, better yet, no strandings and that you were on your way here. We could..."

"Come on back to reality Romeo — it suits you better. Now, get your gear together. Get to the airport. Think about the aggregation. If you have time, think about the chip."

"Will do, love. Bye." Robin sniffed the inside of the duffel bag — *not too bad* — and headed up the wood stairs.

"Love you." Angela hung up.

Chapter 37

Building G, NMFS Laboratory, Galveston, Texas

Kurt had wandered into the necropsy labs and then back to Angela's office. With her still on the phone, he quietly leaned against the wall outside the closed door. Knowing these stranding events were sure to be something big—something of a paradigm shift in how people thought about human-environment relationships—Kurt reviewed ways to inform and mobilize more people. He wanted real, honest answers. He wanted the marine mammal community to demand real, honest answers.

The door swung open, startled Kurt and interrupted his internal rant. Angela poked her head out, "I knew I heard someone out here." Stepping into the hallway and closing the door behind her, she continued, "Robin is re-packing and will be on his way within the hour. He'll probably beat me to Tampa. I hope he's in time to really help." Unexpectedly, Angela stepped forward, hugged Kurt briefly, and let go. "Thank you. Asking Robin to go to Tampa...that...that was a brilliant idea."

Kurt couldn't help but smile. "Thank you for the compliment. I hope he arrives in time to help. We don't have any idea if the other two groups exhibited a similar behavior...or, if they did, how long they may have massed before heading for the beach. Him coming here, the plan I'm sure you've already started...it could all be an exercise in futility."

"I'm hoping FWC or the NMFS folks in St. Petersburg will have boats on the water soon. Hmmm..." Angela took a small pad from her pocket, scribbled something, and continued, "...fishermen. That area gets a lot of recreational use — even this time of year." She knew the area fairly well from her time as the Southeast Regional Stranding Director. "...fishing guides, rec fishermen — we'll need to make sure that they are pumped for information. Maybe somebody saw them there sooner. That would help with the timeline."

As Angela shoved the notepad back into her pocket, she pulled out her now ringing cell phone and looked at the display — it was Director Hamilton. "Jake. Good news, I..." Angela paused, looked at Kurt and repeatedly shifted her eyes between him and the door to her office.

Kurt knew the look meant *I need to take this in private*. Nodding in understanding, he headed down the hall. Angela opened the door, stepped into the room and closed the door behind.

"Kurt is gone. Now, what's up? What couldn't we talk about with Kurt around?" Sitting again at the desk, Angela opened her laptop and looked for a message from Robin.

Director Hamilton was curt, "Have a pen? Call me back immediately at 301-555-1775."

Angela's foray into her email was short-lived — she dialed the new number.

"Thank you, Angela." There was a pause as Director Hamilton reevaluated his approach — a pause Angela had to fill.

"Jake? What's with the phone number? I'm trying to wrap up here, get Tampa organized and..."

Director Hamilton decided on the direct, authoritative approach, "Angela. It's a secure line. We're sending the Navy team from Virginia Beach to assist with the situation in Tampa."

"Aren't there Navy or Coast Guard assets in Florida we can use? Secure line, Jake? What's...? We *who*?

"Angela. The team from Virginia Beach, they weren't just sailors. They weren't just SEALs."

"I've heard the rumors, Jake. Are you telling me these guys are some black ops marine mammal team?"

"I'm not telling you that. What I am telling you is that the team has training beyond SEAL training—integrative training—and a certain familiarity with the species in question. It's a familiarity that Admiral Collins thinks can be useful."

Jake paused.

Angela ruminated.

Jake continued, "They did such a great job in the adverse conditions at Virginia Beach—exceptional, really. I'm sure the local authorities, the Coast Guard would do fine but under the circumstances...besides, the admiral said they were excited about the Florida weather—a nice reward. Can't blame them, it's still frigid here. And these guys are ours—they'll give us the assets to thoroughly control the situation. I like not having to depend on volunteers and a patchwork of local authorities for a situation like this. The Coast Guard will still assist, but they have other important duties to attend to as well. We need to keep the curious public away — keep them from disrupting our rescue efforts — just the air of authority of a Navy presence will help. I think this could make the difference."

"And, Robin?" Angela was scribbling on a new legal pad — outlining instructions for the necropsy crew in Galveston and thinking, *I've got to get to Tampa.*

"Now…of course, we still want Robin there….he could also make the difference…and we'll want Dr. Menke as well. The admiral definitely wants Menke….can you?"

"Doc? You know he has his hands full here. How about Randy? Um…Dr. Randy Edwards has been Doc's right hand, sometimes his left hand, for eight years. He doesn't get the credit being in Doc's shadow, but he's…"

"It has to be Menke. The admiral insists. He feels the situation requires the gravitas of Menke…and Nicely."

And, Clarke? But, she kept that slight to herself.

Director Hamilton continued, "In one way it's simple math — six versus 200. If we can save 200…hell, if we can save 25…if we can get any idea as to why this is happening…even if those six were to turn. Besides, if Dr. Edwards is so good he can stay with the dolphins in Texas. So, yes, we need Dr. Menke and Dr. Nicely…and you."

Relieved that she was finally mentioned, Angela conceded, "Yes, I suppose it's a logical way to proceed. I'm writing up my instructions for the necropsy team now — very detailed, very clear, very…"

"I wouldn't expect anything less, but…you still need to wait a day. Your head." Jake was adamant — his voice made that obvious. "Make sure you keep that appointment to have it checked tomorrow. I want you healthy. You'll need to be 100% to manage an event like this. Get clearance, fax it to me and I'll have a Gulfstream waiting for you at the airport."

Angela continued to scribble notes on here pad, "Understood, boss."

"And obviously the details about the Navy team are to be kept between you and me at the moment. When you speak to Doc…"

"I think he needs to know…he's…"

"He'll know when the time is right. Understood?"

"Understood."

"Well done. You are doing an excellent job." Director Hamilton paused to let her soak in the compliment. "Give me an update before you turn in this evening and…and, make sure you take care of that head."

"Thanks. Yes, Jake." Angela set the phone on her desk and wrote a few more lines on the legal pad. She re-opened the laptop and moved to her email. She didn't know when Robin would get it, but she needed to send him an email with the updated plan — with information about the Navy involvement. Snickering, she knew he'd eat up all that "hoo-yah" attitude being thrown around — like hanging with his macho surf ski buddies on the beach. She'd let him know about Doc as well. Smiling slyly, Angela thought, *And me? I'll let my trip to Tampa be a little surprise.* Angela started typing.

Chapter 38

MacDill Air Force Base, Tampa, Florida

"Florida baby!" Master Chief Petty Officer, Angel Samson, held his arms out wide as the back of the C-5 opened on the tarmac at MacDill Air Force Base. "The Sunshine State! Hoo-yah!" The sun was low on the horizon, turning the high, wispy clouds into orange flames. "Too bad we have too much work to do to enjoy the sunset while sitting on the beach with a beer and a few bikinis. Why couldn't we get *those* orders?"

Lt. Commander Medlin exited behind Samson and paused-- soaking up the 65-degree "heat". Opening his eyes, he looked at the two other C-5s on the tarmac before turning to his vocal Master Chief, "Be happy we are out of the snow, Samson. Now, let's get our little fleet rolling to the boat ramp." He handed Samson a gear checklist and added, "Besides, 65 degrees is a little cool for a bikini."

"I'm sure we could find a few, sir. Instead, we get to baby sit more fuckin' wild dolphins. At least they're not dead...yet."

Medlin had started to make his way towards his MacDill liaison when the comment from Samson had festered just long enough to register. He stopped and turned back, "Master Chief Samson!"

"Sir?"

It was a difficult line to walk with the men—especially since Medlin was relatively new to command. A few years ago he might have made the same type of comments, loosely thrown around the same bravado. Now, he had to rein that in — in himself and in the men who, like Samson, he believed could follow him into the ranks of leadership and develop a deeper relationship with their marine mammal partners. He stepped crisply and deliberately at Samson — stopping six inches from the Master Chief's face. Looking directly into Samson's eyes, Lt. Commander Medlin whispered, "Now, I don't necessarily give a shit about these wild dolphins. But, I do care about the reputation of the Navy and MSOTs. And…" He paused to allow the Master Chief a moment to absorb the importance of what he was saying. "And, *we* would not be here if this were not a matter of the utmost importance — requiring *our* specialized training. Every situation demands our best. Now is the time for some serious team focus. Understood?"

Samson responded in a volume appropriate for his commander's proximity, "Sir, yes, sir." They exchanged salutes and Medlin re-started his walk towards his MacDill liaison.

Chapter 39

Dolphin Towne, Tortola, BVI

"Adam?" Jasmine knocked lightly on the slightly open door to the network control room.

"C'mon in." He swiveled around to face the door as she walked in.

Jasmine sighed and swept one hand through the air, "I'm always overwhelmed by all this...artificial energy...it seems so...so removed, so distant, from the source...but, I know you love it and do good things with it...I know..." Sitting down in the other chair in the room she looked up at the monitors—her eyes searching for Bee. "I know you are doing a lot of interesting research. I just wanted to let you know that I'm glad you found a place here." She smiled—her head tilting ever so slightly, dreamily, to the side, "I really hope you'll always want to be here."

Adam was caught a little off guard—first by her admission of knowing about his research. Then, when she stood up and walked over—hugging him hard, pushing back slightly and kissing him. Adam sighed. Jasmine sighed.

Squatting beside his chair, she took his hands in hers and smiled again. "I'm sorry. I don't know why...after that time at Bomba's I...not too many things frighten me...I'm sorry it took so long for me to..."

Smiling, shaking his head, Adam sighed and whispered, "Worth the wait. Just promise me you won't do another romantic 180 on me--ever. I couldn't..."

Putting two fingers to his lips Jasmine stopped him. "I won't. It's grown too powerful."

Moment interrupted — the phone on Adam's desk started to ring. He ignored it. *Let it ring. Let it ring.*

But, Jasmine stood and looked at the caller ID.

"Doc!" She grabbed the phone and repeated her exclamation, "Doc!"

"Jasmine — good news. I'll be able to get down to see you tomorrow morning. Only for the day. I need to be out and in Tampa by the evening..."

"So short a stay, I think we might need..."

Doc's heavy sigh was repeated twice and Jasmine stopped. "I really need to be in Tampa tomorrow. I hate to burden your heart with this but..."

"Another stranding!" Jasmine collapsed back into the other chair — the color left her face and she started to tremble. "I knew it wasn't the end. I could feel the cold creeping in around me..."

"No!" Doc stopped her from spiraling too much. Adam, moved behind her chair and hugged. Doc continued, "Not a stranding, not yet anyway. There are 200 or so dolphins swimming together in Tampa Bay...circling. They just don't mass like that...anyway, they want me there. I don't know how long I'd be there...it could be weeks. I owe you, the aquarium owes you..."

Jasmine pulled Adam's arms tighter around her. "Doc, that's not why I created the endowment—not to keep you on a leash. I..."

"It's okay. It's okay. The director...the director of NMFS understands. He is sending me a government jet. I'll be at the airport at 6am. Please be there waiting."

"Okay. 6am. I'll be there waiting—Adam will have everything ready here. He'll keep the clients out of your way. Thank you. Thank you. Your heart is pure love—that's why you are such a healer. I can't imagine..."

"I can't imagine not helping our girl Bee. How is she?"

Jasmine glanced up at Bee's monitor and thought, *Beautiful, but troubled.* "Still eating free swimming fish. Adam..." She glanced up, touched his cheek and smiled, "Adam says she's eating enough—we haven't had to supplement. Still...still, I get this dark, hollow feeling—like my soul was drained out through my feet...I...I can't shake it."

"Tomorrow. I'll need help for the full exam. 6am, remember."

"We'll make it so, Doc. We'll make sure you can get back on the plane and to Tampa before the end of the day." Carefully, sliding out of Adam's arms and standing up, Jasmine stepped towards the desk. "Thank you."

Hanging up the phone, Jasmine turned to Adam.

He looked at her strongly—deep in her eyes. She found enough light in his presence and in herself to smile, "*That* might have to wait."

Nodding, Adam moved forward, "The pod…the clients in the retreat group—they did great today. If you go to the airport for Doc, I can brief them at breakfast and get them started on the day's encounters. Then I can help you and Doc. They have waterside yoga after lunch, so that will give us free time as well. We can make this work Jasmine. We can make it all work Jasmine."

Her look back said, *I know.* They both knew it meant something more as Jasmine took Adam's hand and led him out of the control room.

Chapter 40

Building G, NMFS Laboratory, Galveston, Texas

Angela reached under her blue NMFS polo shirt and undid her bra — deftly pulling it out her sleeve and tossing it to the floor. Her khakis were already in the same heap of dirty clothes in the corner. She felt a little guilty about going to sleep when she knew that students were still hard at work on the necropsies, but if she wanted to be on a plane to Tampa tomorrow, she knew she needed to rest. Grabbing her cell phone, she slipped under the wool blanket on her cot and dialed. Reaching out to the nearby desk, she turned out the lamp.

"Angela. How are you?"

"Tired, Jake. But, the head feels much better. I can close my eyes and there's no throbbing. I'm sure I'll be cleared to fly tomorrow." Rolling over on her belly, Angela slid the pillow under her chest and propped herself up slightly on her elbows.

"Excellent. I'm very glad you are doing better."

"Thanks." Angela kept the conversation moving so she could be sure to get some extra sleep. "I continue to be impressed by the necropsy teams — good, efficient, detail-oriented...I can't say enough. I'm confident they will be able to handle completing the 18 remaining necropsies and the distribution of the samples without my direct supervision. I'll be meeting again..."

Director Hamilton interrupted, "And Doc? How did he seem about going to Tampa? You know he's getting a junket to BVI out of us. Somehow he got the admiral to agree..."

"Admiral Collins authorized *that*? I still don't get it. BVI? Dolphin Towne? He asked the Admiral for *that*? Can't they get another marine mammal vet? I just don't get..."

Jake cut her off. "Doc's their vet. And, you know he and the admiral go way back—Viet Nam, the Navy dolphin program. Well, they're still very close. That must've been it."

"Of course." Angela wasn't sure if she was agreeing that she understood the relationship between the Admiral and Doc or maybe that the admiral wanted one of his own cronies close at hand for some other reason. Shoulders stiff, Angela shifted to her back and felt her body relax. *Relax*, she told herself, *You'll be there tomorrow night too.*

Jake continued, "He'll be down there, do his exam and to Tampa before the end of the day tomorrow. According to the flight information you sent me, Robin should be there in the morning."

"I know, I just wish one of us were on the scene now. I should be there now."

"Lt. Commander Medlin. His team is on the water now—ETA to Egmont Key is 15 minutes. They are in charge of perimeter security. The Coast Guard will assist with managing the curious public—outside the Navy perimeter and in the air. I'll email you Medlin's new contact information. Two agency boats are on-site— one from FWC and one from our St. Pete office. I didn't want to add any more boats than needed—I'm sure those animals are stressed enough."

"Yes. Yes. I talked to the director at FWC in St. Pete and our man on the NMFS boat about an hour ago. Good to keep the public out and our work boats to a minimum—for now." Angela paused. "Oh, and I've confirmed the species--*Tursiops*. More bottlenose...actually around 150—according to our spotter in the FWC plane. A few less than originally reported—but, still unprecedented group size and behavior." After rolling back onto her belly, Angela continued, "Anyway, we'll also have that FWC plane in the air again tomorrow. I'm glad Robin will be there. What...what kind of authority will he have?"

Jake sighed, "Advisory. He's not a citizen. He can only have an advisory role. Medlin will command the boats in the area when he gets on site. When you, hopefully, arrive tomorrow, you will be given on-site command. Medlin has authority to make time-sensitive decisions if necessary, but I hope he won't have to. Everything else is through you—so don't let your phone get out of reach. Remember, you are the one who is really in charge." Jake paused and his supportive, cheerleader tone kicked in, "This is a big multi-agency operation—Navy, FWC, NMFS, Coast Guard keeping the perimeter and the skies clear. Do this right...and, I know you will...and, people will notice."

Pleased with herself, Angela grinned and thought, *Then, I'll bring the gravitas! I'm so humble.* With Jake waiting for her response, she continued, "Okay. I'm glad any decisions are going through me—even now. I know Medlin is *familiar* with dolphins, but he does not have the same expertise as Dr. Nicely, Menke or myself. I don't want any mistakes—even if we can't save them...well, I'm hoping we'll learn something. We have to learn something. We'll talk in the morning after Robin lands. I'll call you then."

"Rest well. So far, well done."

Angela closed the phone and reached out to set it on the desk. Hesitating, she opened it back up and dialed Robin—voicemail, of course. "Robin. Angela. I have updates. Call me as soon as you can. Love you." Flipping the phone closed she snuggled into the saggy cot.

Day Five

Sunday, February 23, 2008

Chapter 41

South African Airways Flight 203, somewhere over the western Atlantic Ocean

Robin rolled to the right in his seat and his blanket slid into the aisle. The watchful first-class flight attendant carefully re-covered him, but the weight of the blanket was just enough to stir him from his six and a half hours of sleep. Robin looked up through sleep-caked slit eyes at the attendant, "Right, thank you." Seeing the apologies in her eyes he set her at ease, "No worries. I have some reading I need to do anyway." Easing the seat into a more upright position he sniffed the air, "Coffee?"

"Fresh brewed. We're about 90 minutes from New York …" His big smile must have caught her off guard. She smiled back and said, "I'll get you some."

Robin fished under the seat in front for his shoes — jammed somewhere with his pack full of manuscripts. Sliding into his clogs, he stood and walked to the bathroom. The coffee, a small fruit bowl and a croissant were waiting on his tray table when he returned. The second cup of black coffee stirred Robin enough to finally pull some manuscripts out of his pack. He'd left his book home for a reason — he needed to get through those papers.

Sighing heavily, Robin took a sip of his refilled cup of coffee, uncapped an ultra-fine, red Sharpie marker and started to read, *Hypomorphic Evolution of the Semi-Circular Canals and the Vestibular*

Sense in Delphinus Delphi. Dr. Oxf Johnans, Dr. Dieter Viernen, & Heidi Brult...

"Sir?" The flight attendant smiled. Robin tucked the manuscript he had been working on under his seat and turned his head toward the aisle. "We're starting our descent to New York. Would you like anything else?"

Robin smiled big again, "No thanks, love."

She handed him an immigration form and moved on to the next row. Robin returned to the stack of manuscripts. *Brainwave-Behavior Relationships in Tursiops truncatus: a micro-telemetry and video activity budget approach. Adam Reich, Dolphin Towne, B.V.I.*

Rogue was scrawled across the cover page in large letters — Robin had done a first read on this one before the strandings. *Rogue*, was his way of identifying the author — not a PhD, not a grad student, not affiliated with any recognized scientific institution. He worked at a swim-with program in the Caribbean--a *persona non grata* as far as the *serious* marine mammal community was concerned. Next to the scrawling of *rogue* was an equally large red smiley face. "Yes." Robin remembered--great thesis, well-written, interesting results. His thoughts moved his eyes from the paper to the window — the morning lights of New York were competing with the sun's glow to the east. He also remembered wanting to Google Reich — something he could now do on the layover in New York.

Moving back to the paper, Robin flipped to the abstract page. "Shit!" There it was--*micro-telemetry* — that was where he saw the reference to a subcutaneous transponder. "Shit! Shit! Shit!"

"Sir?" The concerned flight attendant shot him a confused look and leaned into his space—his exclamation was just a little too loud. "Is everything okay?"

"Sorry. It was a good *shit*. Fuck. That didn't sound..." He rolled his eyes, paused and looked her in the eye while he whispered. "I really am sorry. It was just a eureka moment." She stared blankly. He tried again, "A sudden realization. An epiphany." She nodded her understanding, moved her eyes from side to side as if to say, *think about the other passengers*, and then stood back up. Half-standing and lifting his head above the seats, Robin looked around, apologized to the rest of First Class and then, niceties aside, went back to the manuscript.

Turning to the discussion section, Robin's eyes skimmed and searched. He found what he was looking for near the end:

> *While initially invasive, the subcutaneous telemetry device will ultimately be less cumbersome and more reliable for the monitoring of captive animals then the current external transmitter. The battery and transmitting technology exists and I am currently in the process of constructing a prototype device.*

Slightly disappointed, Robin rocked back in his seat and ruminated on the paper, *Captive animals...building a prototype...still, this guy may have some insight.*

As the plane descended toward JFK, Robin stuffed the manuscripts into his backpack and made a list of things to do while in the airport— more snacks, check voicemail, check email, Google

Adam Reich. After moving his seatback into an upright position, he stuffed the backpack under the seat in front and closed his eyes. Daunting—he knew the task ahead was more than a little intimidating. While listening to the landing gear deploy, he thought, *What if I can't come up with anything in Tampa? Is Angela risking anything bringing me here? What am I risking?*

The descending plane popped his ears and he sighed heavily, *That's wimpy talk, Robin. Nothing risked, nothing gained—and, the potential for gain, for knowledge is great here.* Fingering the customs card, he reached for a pen. He closed his eyes and chuckled— knowing all he had was a lead on a chip that was likely inconsequential to the strandings.

Chapter 42

Building G, NMFS Laboratory, Galveston, Texas

"I'm sorry ma'am." Medlin's voice trailed off into an apologetic whisper.

Angela reached for the desk light, turned it on and looked at her watch—5:30am. "It's okay, Lt Commander, I'm usually up at..."

"No. Dr. Clarke. No, that's...not it. I'm sorry we...I'm really wondering why..." The hesitation and apprehension was obvious as his voice trailed off.

Wrapping the blanket around her shoulders Angela swung her legs over the edge of the cot, sat up and chuckled to herself, wondering if this special ops tough guy needed some stroking. "You did a fine job, an above and beyond the call of duty job, at Virginia Beach, the weather...well...it was a good call by the admiral and the director and we appreciate what you and your men did." There was no immediate response from the commander—just silence. Maybe the Lt. Commander didn't need stroking—still, Angela was interested as to why he was so apologetic—perhaps he didn't know that she was a least somewhat aware of his "special training."

Angela started thinking of other possibilities and continued, "Medlin, what's wrong?" Her tone turned anxious, "What's happened to the dolphins? Commander, what happened to the dolphins?" She paced the room wrapped in her blanket—waiting for an answer.

"Status quo with the dolphins, Dr. Clarke. No change." But, Medlin's voice had changed — the softness was gone, the surety of military formality was back. "We have five of our boats 100 meters from the group. There are two FWC boats and the one NMFS boat stationed at a similar distance. The Coast Guard is issuing a *Notice to Mariners* establishing an exclusion zone 1000 meters beyond our current perimeter. Unauthorized air traffic has also been excluded from the area. There are two planes, as per your request, flying overlapping shifts starting today. The first plane will be in the air at 0700. They'll be video recording as well as making their regular observations. I have a helicopter standing by to rendezvous with Dr. Nicely at TPA at 0900."

"Thank you." Angela sat in the old swivel chair and put her feet up on the desk. She noticed the sudden change in his voice — he was all business now. Trying to lighten things up and get to the reason for the change — or the real reason for the call — she moved on, "How's the weather there? A little warmer than Virginia this time of year?"

"Yes, ma'am. The men are grateful, happy to be here — looks to be mid 70s and sunny today." Medlin took an audibly deep breath and continued, "Dr. Clarke...do you have any idea what's causing these strandings? The numbers...I've worked with...uh...I've read a good bit about dolphins..." A hint of emotion crept back into his voice, "Do you have any idea what's going on?"

Angela had a little *aha* moment, and thought, *How close does this guy work with dolphins? He seems to care more than someone who has*

*gotten some supplemental intro to working with dolphins. How
"integrated" was the training that Jake had alluded to?*

While it was commonly accepted (but not necessarily
approved of) in the marine mammal research community, it was *not*
public knowledge that certain Navy SEAL teams were trained to
operate as needed with trained dolphins. But, what Director
Hamilton had suggested to Angela was that Medlin's team was not
simply a differently-trained SEAL team — they were something
separate and possibly something much more.

Angela pulled her feet off the desk and her knees to her chest.
"Yes, it's a lot of dolphins--three sites. You would think there would
be some common link. A similar number stranded in Mozambique
last week — there, it was an obvious *morbilivirus* event. No doubt
about it. With these…honestly…there's nothing at the moment."

Angela finished and the silence on the line again grew
uncomfortable. She felt a need to fill the space. "Dr. Nicely is *the*
expert on wild dolphin communities and behavior. He's probably
read more papers than anyone alive on dolphin research of all kinds.
He runs the stranding network in Africa and has shepherded the
career of that continent's best marine mammal pathologist. I'm
hoping he'll see something." Angela opened her laptop — wondering
if she had saved the email with Robin's flight information--and
continued. "Dr. Menke will also be there sometime this evening."

"Menke." Medlin finally spoke again. "Yes, Admiral Collins
mentioned Dr. Menke — his current work and his earlier affiliation

with the NMMP in San Diego. Yes, the admiral let me know that Dr. Menke was coming—a good thing, I suppose."

Angela opened her email—one from Robin. She skimmed the email and looked at the computer's clock—figuring he should already be at JFK. Her focus back to Medlin, she continued, "Yes, Dr. Menke getting there is a good thing—he'll be our pathology expert on scene."

"And you, Dr. Clarke? When should we expect you?"

It was the first time she had thought about her head since waking up. She closed her eyes--no throbbing. Angela smiled. "There was an accident here yesterday--an explosion near one of the labs. I had a bit of a concussion…"

"An explosion?" Medlin's concern was obvious.

"These NMFS buildings are ancient—1890s military. I was in the electronics lab in the basement with a NOAA tech examining something we found in one of the carcasses."

"An electronics tech?" There was a little surprise in Medlin's question.

Angela ignored him and plowed on, "…something exploded. I was in the hospital overnight--minor concussion. I have to get cleared by the doctors later today before I can fly. I'm hoping to be on a plane and in Tampa tonight." Pausing, she closed her eyes, took a deep breath and continued, "The headache seems to be gone, so I'm thinking I'll get the green light. Unfortunately, the tech didn't fare as well…" Looking at Robin's email, she never stopped talking, "In the meantime, Commander, make sure the observation boats maintain their 100m distance. Minimize engine use—hold stationary positions when possible. In no way do we want those animals to feel trapped. There should be at least two areas in your perimeter that never see boat traffic. We want to keep the voyeurs out while keeping the dolphins from feeling trapped. Okay—Dr. Nicely. When he arrives, make sure Dr. Nicely gets anything he needs to make the needed observations—there should be some equipment already on its way. Make sure he calls me with his first impressions. The same for Dr. Menke if he beats me there. Don't hesitate to call me immediately with any questions or any updates. Is that clear?"

"Uh…yes, ma'am."

Rocking back in her chair, Angela propped her feet on the desk and smiled. Satisfied that she had sufficiently overwhelmed the Commander, Angela moved to end the call. "I have another call I need to take, Commander." It was a lie, but she didn't give Medlin a chance to question—immediately hanging up. For a moment, she sat silent--wondering why Medlin had really called her. Shaking her head, realizing she didn't have an answer, Angela dialed Robin.

Egmont Key, Tampa Bay, Florida

Lt. Commander Medlin closed his cell phone, slid it back into the belt clip and climbed the tower on his "command ship"—a modified version of the new MK V.1 Special Operations Craft. The 81-foot carbon-fiber boat was the largest of the "portable" special operations craft—large enough to carry 16 team members, an operating crew of five, and four small inflatable boats. It had an enclosed control deck and forward compartment. This particular small ship was modified for MSOT operations — with sophisticated tracking and imaging gear, an in-deck travel tank for dolphins, and an eight-foot observation tower.

There was room for two on the tower, but Medlin was alone — the other conscious member of his team was busy starting a pot of coffee. The light breeze was enough to ripple the surface of the water, but not enough to wash out the sound of the repeated blows of tens of surfacing dolphins 100 meters away. His mind latched onto something Dr. Clarke had said, "Electronics lab," and his first thought was, *MK6Chip.* He shook his head and looked down tracking control station and at the above-the-surface dishes and antennas. He looked back out towards the dolphins. Medlin filled his chest with a deep breath, exhaled, and closed his eyes. Startled by a tap on his boot, he opened his eyes and didn't finish the thought.

"Coffee, Commander?" Master Chief Samson held a large no spill mug up towards the base of the tower platform.

"Thanks, Master Chief." Medlin sat on the edge of the platform and drank — looking at the brightening sky in the east. He shifted his stare to Samson. "Chief, I'm sorry I came down so hard on you on the runway yesterday…"

"Pardon me, sir, but you were right. It's not our job to question orders — doubly so if they are of special interest to someone like Admiral Collins." Samson looked out over the water. "And, I certainly meant no disregard for the wild dolphins, sir. We, of course, have a special bond with the dolphin members of our team and all feel the loss — and potential loss — of so many in the wild." He looked back at Medlin. "It's just a different type of mission than we are used to, sir."

Medlin smiled, "And still not as nice as bikinis on the beach."

Samson chuckled, "No, sir."

"Now, Master Chief," the tone turned serious again, "We have training and knowledge that is classified. We need to keep that in mind when interacting with the public. And, we'll all have much more civilian interaction real soon. Make that clear at this morning's briefing."

Samson nodded agreement.

Medlin took a long draw on his coffee and looked out at the mass of dolphins. "That classified training and knowledge might also help us save some of these dolphins. So, what are Lopez and the others thinking?"

Chapter 43

Terminal 4, JFK International Airport, New York

Robin immediately turned on his cell phone when the plane pulled into the gate. There were five messages—Vee, two from Angela, David and Kora. He could only imagine the number of emails. While retrieving his backpack and laptop from under the seat, he listened.

"Robin. Angela. I have updates. Call me as soon as you can. I love you." Smiling, he continued through the messages.

"Robin. Vee here. I hope your trip to the U.S. goes smoothly. All well here. We should finish the necropsies today. I'll send my current summary of the pathology, etc. in an email later today. I'll accompany the final samples back to DSC and can assist your team if you like. No need for me to be in Cape Town for another week. Please advise. Oh, and don't let all that ribbing go to waste—ask her. She loves you. Cheers!"

Robin pulled his earpiece from an outside pocket of his laptop bag, plugged it into the phone and wedged it in his ear—making it easier to carry his stuff and head through the jetway.

"Hey, it's me…Angela. I understood you were landing at 0600? Anyway…I figured I'd give a summary update here…Well, the dolphins at Tampa are status quo. *But*, our NOAA administrator, and retired Navy admiral, has seen fit to request the assistance of the same Navy team that was on site in Virginia. A Lt. Commander Medlin is our current on-site coordinator. Sounds like they've got the area well secured. Expect a Navy liaison to meet you at TPA for a helicopter ride to Egmont Key. Doc...Dr. Aldo Menke will be arriving sometime tonight—again at the admiral's request—following a quick trip to one of his benefactors in the British Virgin Islands. Nice deal for him. I'll try to call again shortly. I've also sent you an email. Covering my bases. If we don't talk sooner, call me when you get on site in Tampa Bay. I want your first impressions. Love you!"

Exiting the jetway, Robin looked for the signage directing him to Baggage Claim/U.S. Customs. While scanning, he noticed a uniformed woman conspicuously standing there--a sign in her hands with his name on it. He turned off his phone. Approaching him, she held out her hand, "Dr. Nicely, I'm Officer James, U.S. Customs Service, please follow me."

Robin's puzzled look, and inability to move, must've signaled that he needed a little more information.

"Dr. Nicely, nothing to worry about. We were notified that you were entering the country as a guest of the National Oceanic and Atmospheric Administration. As such a guest of our government we extend expedited customs processing. Your luggage will automatically be transferred to your connecting flight and, if you will follow me, I will process your passport and visa."

Officer James started walking and Robin joined her. "No lines?"

"No lines."

Robin smiled. "Excellent. Thank you for your assistance, Officer James."

The customs process went quickly, with Robin receiving a special diplomatic visa for his visit. Officer James extended the courtesy of using the secure diplomatic lounge and escorted him to domestic terminal. Showing his visa to the security guard at the door gained him entrance to the lounge and access to free food, drink, and wireless access. He sat in a comfortable recliner and powered up his laptop while getting back to his voicemail.

"Howzit, brah? David here—45kph out of the Southwest today. You missed some sick runs. Allen, Pieter, Huli and I worked a shuttle and did three 15k's downwind. One casualty on the second run—Allen pitch-polled his Mako and it snapped behind the bucket. Between the three of us we got him back to shore—only about 500 meters. We'll drive the shore tomorrow to see if we can recover the pieces. Afterwards we were going to party at the new house—just a few kegs....Well, wanted to let you know what you're missing Dolphin Boy. Cheers!"

"Bastards." Robin pulled his training log from his backpack and shook his head at the blank pages. "Bloody Wednesday. That was the last time I paddled. Shit!" Turning the pages, he crossed out workouts he had planned up until today. In his mind, he grumbled, "I've got to find a way to get in some workouts here. Flatwater, downwind, doesn't matter. I bet I can find someone on the paddling list serve or surfski.info message board to lend me a ski." Grabbing at a little fold in his belly, he sighed.

The repeating beep in his ear brought him back to the task at hand—it was Angela.

"Angela!"

"It's about time, mister! I don't know how I missed you the first time, but I tried three more times and your phone was off. What's up with that?"

"Customs. You can't be on the phone in customs. I just got to the lounge and..."

"Lounge? A little early for a beer, huh?"

"Funny girl! I was greeted by a U.S. Customs officer. Seems I'm a guest of the U.S. government and I get special treatment — luggage transfer, expedited, personal processing, diplomatic visa, and use of the diplomatic lounge. It's nice to know people." He smiled, knowing she could imagine him eating up the special treatment. "Free food, drink...wireless. Comfortable reclining chairs..."

"With all your gloating, I'm surprised your head made it through the door."

"It's a double door — they know their guests well." With his internet connection finally up and running, Robin moved to open his email.

"Did you...?"

"Yes, yes. I got your message when I landed."

"So, the Navy team, Doc...um...Dr. Menke. You got all that?"

"Of course, love." Robin opened her email — scanning it to refresh his memory. "Menke's going to the British Virgin Islands? To Dolphin Towne? Is he going to Dolphin Towne?"

"Yes, it's owned by Jasmine Summers—*Roland Summers Marine Mammal Rehabilitation Facility*? She paid to build the rehab facility, Doc's rehab facility, at the Caldwell Aquarium. He helped her rehab a *Tursiops* a few years back. She owns Dolphin Towne. She's...she's way out there. That place is *beyond* New Age. He worked a deal with the Admi..."

"That's it! That's the place with the chip! On the plane...even I can only sleep for so long. I finally got into my *Marine Mammal Science* manuscripts. Dreadful reading for the most part. That's beside the point. I came to one I had read before and it jumped out at me...well, I had written "rogue" across the cover page in three centimeter red letters—I also had...um...drawn a big, red smiley face. I remembered wanting to Google this guy and his facility and re-read the abstract—this guy is into some serious mircotelemetry. He might know something about your chip—or, the technology necessary to make it! And, now that Menke is headed there...sometimes you've got to love this inbred, incestuous marine mammal world..."

Angela took advantage of the thoughtful pause. Robin was about the only one who could command a conversation and overwhelm as well as she. "Not likely—way too touchy-feely for that. Beyond touchy-feely. There's nude swimming with the dolphins, mind-meld sessions...pretty much everything just short of interspecies copulation. You'll see when you go to the website. They're kooks who think that their dolphins speak for all the dolphins — or for an extraterrestrial intelligence. Kooks waiting for the mothership."

Starting a Google search, Robin continued, "I don't doubt your assessment love, but this paper is tops. Not only is it well-written, the science is sound and quite a good step forward in integrating modern technologies — telemetry, computers, video — with behavioral research. Whatever kind of flake Ms. Summers might be, this Adam...Adam Reich is a serious scientist."

"Well, I can't imagine..."

Robin cut her off, "Well, you had better. I'll email you some links, but the gist of it is that this Adam Reich was something of a prodigy. Was in Dr. Harvey Lykes' MIT-Woods Hole program and was responsible for some major advancements in the technology and software Lykes was using...I remember that paper from Dr. Lykes. What's this....hmmm....seems the emphasis is on *was* in the program. There are a couple of discussion group threads...wow, they are how old? Some threads talking about a kind of mental breakdown or meltdown. Seems he just up and left MIT the summer after his first year. Then, nothing--not a peep."

"And, you think he somehow ended up on Tortola?"

"Kids like that...prodigies...sometimes they can handle the pressure, sometimes they can't. Some excel and can get over the social awkwardness, the social inexperience, of being a few years younger than their academic peers. Others, well...I think Adam was one of the others. Sucks to have that exposed on the internet."

"And, the chip? You think he…" She didn't have a thought to finish.

"He was working on decreasing the size of his telemetry devices. Near the end of his discussion, he mentioned the next step — a subcutaneous microtelemetry device. My best guess…hmmm…and, it makes sense based on your assessment of Dolphin Towne…my best guess is that someone there…this Jasmine Summers or her clients…"

Angela interrupted with a mocking snicker, "Pod members. She calls them…"

"Whatever," Robin could sense Angela's distaste for the facility and its owner, but wanted to stay on track, "Someone associated with the facility is probably a bit of a Luddite — or, at least not comfortable with obtrusive technology in such a…um…soft environment. Makes sense given their clientele. They love their personal technology and the benefits it can provide in every aspect of their lives — but, their image of the species is clean and pure. This device would help maintain that angelic image."

While talking, Robin bookmarked several pages on Adam, and then typed in **www.dolphintowne.com**. "Wow." There was no exclamation, but the gravity in his voice, and the long pause, let Angela know that something had impressed him.

"*Wow* what?" It was obvious that Angela couldn't stand being left out of the loop — even for five seconds.

Robin didn't notice — or didn't care--continuing as if she hadn't said a word, "Dolphin Towne is an impressive place — from the website to the facility. Live video of dolphins not swimming with clients...beautiful natural lagoons...lush landscaping...off the grid. Organic meals...wow, those swim-with packages aren't cheap. Oh, I see the mind-meld you were talking about—theta waves. Hmmm...looks to me that Mr. Reich found the perfect low-stress environment to continue his interest in dolphins. Quite a state-of-the-art, integrated system—holistic in that it incorporates his technological prowess with her New Age experiences."

"So, you really think he's legit?"

"Well, he has the academic background and the brainpower. Seems from your assessment of Ms. Summers that he probably also has access to the..."

"Cash? Yes, Summers--Jasmine Summers. You have no idea?"

Angela took Robin's silence for a *no*.

"She's the *other* daughter—the *quiet* daughter--of Roland Summers of Summers Media fame."

Robin nodded to himself and chuckled, "And, her sister was the not-so-quiet, bad-girl star of that annoyingly crappy reality TV show you are always rushing to your laptop to watch." He sighed loud enough for the bar tender in the lounge to walk over and see if that was a signal that he wanted service. After shoeing him away, Robin continued, "Sorry, I could never understand how someone of your...um...intellect? No, someone so action-oriented...someone who really lives quite an exceptional life, could be attracted to..."

"Not now, Robin!" That conversation always irritated Angela, so she continued her train of thought. "So, yes, Reich would potentially have plenty of financial resources at his disposal. It's rumored she has quite a trust fund. He could afford the needed technology. And, it seems…and, you are more than a good judge of academic potential…it seems that he has the brainpower. So, what next?"

"I'm getting close to needing to make my connection. I'll send him an email immediately. I'll call him when I get to Tampa." Robin started typing furiously.

"Okay. I'm starting to wrap things up here and…"

"Damn! Love…how's the head?" Half in the email, half in the conversation, Robin tried not to botch either, "You're okay?"

"Better. Much better. Thanks for…thanks for asking."

"Sorry, love. You, of all people, know how I get caught up in a train of thought—how I get focused. Just like you."

"Believe me, I know." And, sometimes she loved it. "I'm feeling better, but the doctors will let me know how much better. I have an appointment for an exam, some tests at 11. I'll call you when I know more."

"Likewise, I'll call you with any new info on Reich and with my initial evaluation on site in Tampa. I'm hoping that I'll come up with something concrete enough to take our minds off your mysterious chip." He hit send, shut down his laptop, and shouldered his backpack.

"I think we're all hoping for that."

Walking out the lounge door and into the corridor, Robin finished up, "I can't promise miracles, but you know I will do all that I can. Bye, love."

"I know you will exhaust yourself in the effort—and, I *love* that about you. Bye."

Walking to his gate, Robin took the time to get to his last voicemail message.

Chapter 44

Dolphin Towne, Tortola, BVI

Adam looked at the clock in the lower right hand corner of his computer screen. It was 6:02am and Dr. Menke should be on the ground at the Beef Island Airport. He knew he had about 30 minutes.

At 5am, Adam and Jasmine had briefed the other two staff members who helped them manage the guests. While Adam would take all the clients through the daily orientation, they would complete the follow-up. The regular Eli House staff would see to their other needs. Adam and Jasmine would be free to assist Dr. Menke.

Following the pre-dawn staff briefing, Jasmine headed for the airport to pick up Dr. Menke. Adam was making sure the video, computers and telemetry units were functioning properly for the morning swim sessions. As the diagnostics were running, he turned to his email. "Nicely! Dr. Robin Nicely!" Adam punched his fist in the air and read.

> Mr. Reich,
>
> I am currently reviewing your manuscript submission to Marine Mammal Science. First, I wanted to let you know that it is one of the most well-written papers I have read during my five years on the journal's peer review board. I will strongly recommend to the editorial board that they accept it for publication. My hope is that my colleagues will do likewise.
>
> I know it is very atypical, and really a breach of our rules, to contact an author directly, but I had a question about a small portion of your

paper that may assist me in dealing with a developing stranding situation — on which I am consulting--in the United States. In your discussion section you mention the next phase of your microtelemetry development — the subcutaneous transponder. I was curious to know if you knew of anyone else who might have already developed or is in the process of developing a similar device. If not, I was wondering if you had any idea how long the technology needed to create such a device has been available.

Thank you for any input or suggestions.

Sincerely,
Dr. Robin Nicely
Assistant Director
Dolphin Study Center
Plettenberg Bay, South Africa

"Holy shit!" Adam stood up, paced two laps around the room while sporting a full-face smile. He laid his fingers back on the keyboard as he sat back down and began to type.

Dr. Nicely,
Thank you for your kind words regarding my manuscript. I only hope that your colleagues will view the work of an unaffiliated, non-PhD with your objectivity. For me, it would be a good first step back into the academic world I dearly miss.

My prototype subcutaneous telemetry transponder is complete and in use in Sammy — a bottlenose dolphin on site. I did an exhaustive review of current technologies prior to undertaking the project and honestly don't know of any researchers using similar telemetry devices.

*As for the availability of the constituent parts —
hardware and software — my best guess would be
five years for the military, two years for those in the
industry who know how and where to look. If
something similar has turned up in one of your
stranded animals, I would assume it is of military
origin.*

*I have attached the same schematic for the
subcutaneous transponder that is on its way to the
U.S. Patent Office. I'd also be happy to examine any
device you may have retrieved — the reverse
engineering would be a nice challenge.*

*Thank you for honoring me by including me in this
discussion.*

*Kind regards,
Adam Reich
Dolphin Towne, BVI*

Adam looked again at the clock — 6:14. Realizing that Doc
would be arriving soon, he headed out the door and up the
cobblestone walkway — time for coffee and a snack. On the way, he
couldn't help but grin.

Chapter 45

Admiral Collins' House, Fairhaven, Maryland

The vibration of his Blackberry on the nightstand sat Admiral Collins upright in bed. "What now?" he mumbled as he looked at the display that read — *Email: FEW.*

As Collins made his way from the bedroom, through his office and out on the snow and ice-caked deck that overlooked Chesapeake Bay, he scrolled through the message.

> *THE FEW*
> *Email intercept.*
> *Dr. Robin Nicely contact with expatriate Adam Reich of Dolphin Towne, BVI. Email regarding subcutaneous microtelemetry transponders. Reply from Reich noted technology potentially available to military for five years. Reich noted if such a device were retrieved from a stranded dolphin it was likely of military origin.*
> *Discuss options.*
> *BLADE*

The cold air was invigorating — biting at his face and bare legs. He reveled in the intrigue, but still doubted the chip's real relevance — the technology was well-tested over time. Pulling the open doors behind him he moved back into the office, set his Blackberry on the desk and woke up his computer. Walking over to the fireplace, he lit the rolled, paraffin-soaked newspaper that was already in place and stacked some kindling on top. Returning to the desk, he sat and typed a message to all the members.

THE FEW

    *As per the latest secure email message —
foreign national, Dr. Robin Nicely, and expatriate
US citizen, Adam Reich, have been informed of the
discovery of a metallic cylinder (i.e. "chip"). They
still do not know what they were looking at — the
MK6Chip was never opened or X-rayed. The device
is now secure. They really have nothing but a few
bad photos and speculation.*

    *MSOTS on site and in command in
Tampa.*

    *NMFS has no leads as to cause of three
strandings. Carcasses are yielding no verifiable
commonalities. Still, proximity to CONCH
activation zones must be regarded as suspicious
and we must be prepared to protect this valuable
defense system. The success — even a single kill — of
the project warrants our protection.*

    *Is it a feasible trade-off to direct NMFS
focus to the chip? Discuss.*

    *If not, suggest we act today in Tampa.
Discuss.*

ACRET

Admiral Collins looked at another photo of Doc on his desk. This one was more recent, taken while Doc was on leave from Caldwell and directing one final project, per the admiral's request, at the Navy Marine Mammal Program facility. The program involved 30 animals and a week of exposure. Reluctantly, Menke sacrificed six dolphins to more rigorously verify the results of the testing. Collins had wanted nothing like the problems associated with the Navy's controversial Low Frequency Active Sonar exercises. Responsible for several beaked whale deaths in the Bahamas and off of California, training with the system was temporarily suspended by a lengthy lawsuit that made it all the way to the Supreme Court. While the court had ruled in favor of the Navy—and not restricting training exercises—Congress and a new President had created a law seriously restricting current systems training and future sonar research.

Consequently, Doc put CONCH through the research ringer and his findings were solid enough that NMFS Director Jake Hamilton, sporting a temporary security upgrade, was to allow a very limited review of a redacted version of the report. Hamilton did not hesitate to give his approval. With that report in hand and suitably censored—and the support of Senator Hulme—the first phase of CONCH deployment was funded by Congress.

Walking over to the fireplace, the admiral squatted, grabbed his poker and stirred the embers. Lying two larger pieces of split cedar on the coals, he stared into the orange glow, inhaled the aroma and wondered if they had been thorough enough.

Fire growing, Collins walked back to the desk and his cell phone—a short message indicated that there was new information to share with the MSOTs in Tampa.

He dialed his on-site commander to share the news. "Lt. Commander Medlin, our satellite tracking indicates three MK6Cs near Egmont Key. I need immediate verification of MK6Cs in that group. I need a test of two-way interfacing."

"Yes, sir." *MK6* was the Navy's designation for dolphins trained to patrol coastal facilities such as ports, piers and moorings. The MK6C designation was something special—reserved for dolphins trained in coastal and offshore patrol and to blend in and interact with wild dolphins. A sophisticated subcutaneous chip facilitated the monitoring of the MK6C dolphins with satellites and specialized tracking equipment. It also allowed MSOT "handlers" to send a variety of commands to the trained dolphins.

"Medlin, make this discreet—I don't want the other agencies questioning what you are doing. Clear?"

"Yes, sir. Not a problem."

"I'll expect a report within the hour." Admiral Collins didn't wait for a response. He set the phone back on the desk and turned again to the now brightening waters of the bay—wondering what more sacrifices were going to have to be made.

Chapter 46

Dolphin Towne, Tortola, BVI

Adam was waiting on the Eli House veranda when Jasmine drove up with Dr. Menke. Bouncing down the steps he headed for the van door, but Doc was already on his way out.

"Adam! Great to see you." Doc smiled and stuck out his hand. They shook hands and as Doc broke the grip he put on a passive face and looked at Jasmine, "Of course, it would be nicer if it were under different circumstances."

"Of course, Doc. I understand." Adam moved to the back of the car and helped Jasmine with the Doc's small backpack and two large Pelican cases.

As they walked up the steps, Adam nodded toward two fresh mugs of coffee on the table where he had been sitting. Doc smiled, grabbed the coffee and put his nose over one mug, "Mmm...still favoring that Ethiopian Harrar." He looked at Jasmine, took a sip and followed Adam through the main hallway.

Jasmine smiled back, "I never imagined I'd become a creature of habit—oh-so-predictable. My sister would love that. Used to be..." Sighing she moved past her momentary, self-indulgent distraction, "Adam, Doc wants to start with a look at your videos and such."

"Makes sense." Turning left down the stone path, Adam led Doc to the Education Center and his control room. Inside, he set down the two Pelican cases and moved to his computer. When the screen woke up his email was still open. The email from Dr. Nicely was still open. Closing the email program he started accessing Bee's video activity log and syncing it with her other telemetry data. With the process started, he turned to Doc.

"It will take a few minutes to sync the data with the video of the feeding and vocalization activity." Moving to the edge of his seat, Adam looked at Jasmine, then at Doc. "A couple of months ago I submitted a manuscript to *Marine Mammal Science*—based on the synchronization of my telemetry data—specifically brain waves—with a video activity log." His involuntary smile took up most of his face. "This morning I received an email from a member of the peer review panel."

"They accepted *your* paper?" The surprise in Doc's voice was obvious—not because of any lack of scientific skill on Adam's part—he was very aware of Adam's background and abilities--but because they never accepted work by anyone with his lack of credentials. Doc re-started with an apology, "I'm sorry, Adam, that didn't sound right. I didn't mean it to come across…"

Adam stood up and circled around the back of his chair to again face Doc and Jasmine. "I understand. I'm not associated with a typical research facility or oceanarium. I don't have a PhD and I don't have any co-authors with those credentials. I figured I'd submit anyway—see if anyone on their review board could see past that and judge the merit of the study design and results." He held the back of the chair tightly, rocking himself slightly, "And, at least one reviewer has." Letting go of the chair, he crossed his arms and slouched. "But, it hasn't been accepted yet."

Jasmine was glowing, even fawning a little. "That's a big step. How wonderful."

Doc noticed and could see that their relationship had definitely changed since his last visit. "By all means, that is huge. Hopefully, this reviewer—who was it?"

"Robin Nicely. Dr. Robin Nicely from South Africa."

Doc's gaze drifted into a stare—lost in Adam's computer screen while he thought how it was a small world. It was a very small marine mammal research world.

But, Adam's excitement continued. "Oh! Oh! Not only did he email me about his favorable read of my manuscript, he asked me to consult on some type of telemetry chip…well, possible telemetry chip they found during the stranding in Texas. In my manuscript …"

Doc interrupted, "It's nothing—one piece of metal in over 200 animals. I'm surprised at you." Shaking his head, and sucking the emotional enthusiasm out of the discussion, Doc lectured, "Didn't Dr. Nicely tell you? They don't have any data to support the theory that the metallic cylinder they found is some kind of tracking or telemetry device. They are acting on the gut feeling—gut feeling—of one of my students who worked in at the Humane Society chipping dogs and cats last summer. Sure, it might *look* similar, but before they could examine the interior—if there even was an interior—the object was lost in an accident at the lab. They don't even have the object in question. This speculation is a waste of everyone's time. Nobody is using technology like this for dolphins anyway."

Adam bit his lip, but couldn't hide his grin.

Menke noticed Adam's reaction, stopped and knitted his brow.

Adam realized the obviousness of his facial gaffe and—hoping to divert Doc and Jasmine--backpedaled a little on his previous statement, "Well, I'm not saying that we know what the object is...er, was. But, if it were some type of telemetry device, I could say that today's technology—in the right hands—makes it possible." Noticing that Jasmine had lost interest, he turned to Doc.

Unable to read the look in Doc's eyes, Adam continued carefully, "From what I know of microtelemetry *theory* and the available resources—and I told Dr. Nicely this--I would say that the military had the potential to create a basic device at least five years ago." Adam looked at Doc again. "Based on the materials publicly available today, I've been able to draw plans for my own basic subcutaneous device." He turned and walked over to Jasmine, gently taking both her hands and looking her in the eyes. "I've not built it—don't worry. It was just an intellectual exercise—something to keep my mind stimulated."

There was a spark of understanding in Jasmine's eyes. Adam was not as convinced that he could so easily deceive Dr. Menke. When he turned to continue, Adam looked at the floor instead of into Doc's eyes. "At this point, I bet the Navy has got transponders that can supply all sorts of data and that they can track and access at a much greater range." Adam let his enthusiasm carry him one daring step further, "And, Doc, knowing your previous employer…well…you worked with the Navy dolphins…do they exist? Is the Navy using technology like this?"

Menke shook his head and looked patronizingly at Adam, "You know better than that. I can't talk about most of the work I did at NMMP—almost all of it is technically classified. It's only been the last five years that the NMMP has been…um…even somewhat publicly visible. And, I'm sure—being the intelligent young man that you are—you know that it was mainly a PR maneuver—highlighting the exemplary veterinary care, continuing additions to marine mammal science and only very cursory descriptions of designated programs. And, *that* is all I have to say about that."

The screen on Adam's computer changed, and Doc noticed what looked like two windows—one of video and the other of data.

"But that said, I am very impressed with Dr. Nicely's review and with your abilities. I'd be interested in coming back—after all this stranding mess is resolved—and really getting into what you have done." He looked over at Jasmine—she smiled and nodded approval. "Now, to the task at hand—Miss Bee."

"Okay. Miss Bee." Adam sat down and tapped a few commands into his computer—the video and telemetry data popped up on one of the larger high definition monitors. "Here we go."

Chapter 47

Egmont Key, Tampa Bay, Florida

Medlin climbed down from the tower where he had been nursing a second cup of Master Chief Samson's coffee. The rest of his men were awake — most milling around with coffee and munching on meal bars. Circling his finger in the air, he signaled Samson to rally the team.

"Better than waking up in the snow, gentlemen. But, no time for enjoying the tropical weather right now. Immediate orders. Verify location and number of MK6C dolphins in this group. Test two-way interface for each contact."

Samson looked his commander in the eye and smiled, "Well, no more guessing as to why we're here."

Ignoring the comment, Medlin continued, "You all know that MK6Cs are classified. We need to get this done discreetly and quickly. Do not attract the attention of our neighbors." Looking out at the FWC and NMFS boats, then back to the men, he ordered, "Now, move!"

Ramirez, the team's telemetry expert moved to the inside control station. The other men stood by for any needed manual adjustments to the external tracking equipment.

Amidships, Medlin stepped close to Samson, remembering his comment, "I think that is only part of it, Chief." He looked around and hushed his voice even more, "I'm thinking that our trained dolphin comrades might be causing this whole mess…"

Samson finished his commander's sentence, "...and we're here to cover that *malfunction*." He looked at the men adjusting one of the small parabolic tracking antennas. "And, in Virginia Beach? There were no MK6Cs, sir — we checked. I don't get the connection."

Medlin sighed, "Maybe there isn't one...or, maybe the only commonality is the level of security required." Pausing, he thought about the incinerators and Squires. "But, we were definitely covering *something* there too."

"Yes, sir. National security." Samson shrugged.

"Whatever." Medlin struggled with his conscience. "Mmmm...I just hope it's worth the sacrifice of all those dolphins. I can only hope that what I said earlier is true — that if we are here — if MSOTs is here — it must be very serious."

"Let's hope so, Lt. Commander."

Admiral Collins' House, Fairhaven, Maryland

It was as close as they had come to an all-inclusive meeting since just after 9/11. Six of the seven were accessing a new tool-- encrypted instant messaging. Six of the seven were digesting what Rear Admiral Lawrence Collins, US Navy (Retired) and Undersecretary of Commerce for Oceans and Atmosphere was proposing:

THE FEW

Three MK6C dolphins confirmed in Tampa Bay group. Two-way interfaces functioning.

Suggest authorizing commands immediately. Suggest simple turns to achieve an at-sea bearing. Then "swim." MSOT escort as needed.

ACRET

Encrypted or not, the admiral still preferred to allude to the necessary action. But, what was intended was clear to the others—the three MK6C dolphins would be instructed to lead the massing dolphins out to sea. The hope was also clear—that the animals were strong enough to get far from land, but that they would weaken enough to eventually die far from land.

Chapter 48

Dolphin Towne, Tortola, BVI

"Well that is very impressive. I can see why Dr. Nicely thought so highly of your work—the way you've blended things is very well done…well done." Dr. Menke, looked briefly over the telemetry print out from Adam to confirm his initial results. "Well, if your comparison to her baseline is sound…" He flipped through a few more pages of graphs, "…and you have three years of data to back that up—impressive. Well…" He stood up and walked over to Jasmine and put a hand on her shoulder, "…there have definitely been some changes."

Jasmine's head dropped to her chest, "I knew it."

Doc prompted Adam to analyze what he had found, "Looking at the data, what do you think?"

"Me?"

"You know the data better than anyone. You know Bee, well almost as well as Jasmine. What does the data tell you?"

"Well, first I compared the three years of baseline with the anomalies of Jasmine and Tommy's swims. The baseline was of other swim encounters—mind meld, basic package, etc. The differences were obvious. Bee exhibited increased respirations and heart rate during both swims. There was a slight increase in body temperature both times. There was a real change in brainwave activity. First, there was an amplitude shift–an increase in brainwave amplitude—similar to what happens in humans with depression. I saw this both times.

Jasmine's encounter ended with that amplitude change. During Tommy's swim, the amplitude shift was followed by another brainwave change—something akin to a seizure spike in humans. A sudden and involuntary reaction..."

"Yes, nice summary of the data. Now, what does it tell you?"

Adam looked at Bee's live camera and sighed heavily. "When I was at the Woods Hole lab I got to look at some of the telemetry data that they had collected the summer before I had arrived. Clunky contraptions they saddled those wild dolphins with—I'm certain they were obtrusive enough to affect the data collection..."

"Stay on track."

"Right. Sorry. The data were associated with observed behaviors—mating, hunting, traveling, socializing, etc. I don't recall behavioral data linked with the amplitude increase. But, there were data associated with defensive behavior."

"Defensive behavior?" Jasmine was visibly upset, "Who would attack a smiling dolphin? Did the researchers..." Her question trailed off as she turned sullen.

"Sharks, Jasmine. Sharks." Knowing how Jasmine over-felt everything, Doc tried again to console her with his hands on her shoulders.

"Right!" Adam was visibly excited, bouncing on his toes as he paced, "Bee's spike—an almost five times increase in brainwave amplitude--during her attack on Tommy was nearly identical to the data I remember from the shark encounter. She perceived Tommy, for whatever reason, as a similar threat."

Jasmine looked up in horror, tears welling in her eyes, "Texas, Virginia, Mozambique, Tampa. She perceived a threat because her wild friends told her about the strandings. Because humans have attacked her family. Because she's pissed about being locked away and not being able to do anything about it. Because it is a dark time for dolphins." Jumping from her chair, Jasmine ran frantically out of the control room. Dr. Menke and Adam looked at each other in stunned silence.

"Shit!" Adam headed for the door. "We'd better follow her!"

Doc and Adam trotted down the path towards Bee's lagoon. "You think she'll…"

Adam nodded as he ran, "…let Bee out? That would be my bet." Short-cutting behind the pump-building and through some shrubbery, they arrived at the south end of Bee's Plexiglas wall — the end with the gate that could open to Ballast Bay. Jasmine was not there. She was not anywhere to be seen. The gate was closed. A loud blow confirmed Bee was still in the lagoon.

Between deep breaths, bent over with his hands on his knees, Doc laughed, "I guess we don't know her as well as we thought. It would have been my guess too…even with all the pain it would cause…I assumed she would have set Bee free. She was *that* frantic."

No, in Jasmine's mind, that was still not an option. As she ran from the room, her mind was frantic but focused on one thing, *I need to tell my pod what is causing Bee this pain. I need to tell the world. That is what she would want. That is how she would want me to ease her pain. That is what Bee wants. I need to tell everyone.* Impassioned urgency hurtled her into the business office—where she locked the door and sat behind her computer with more eagerness than ever.

Editorial Offices, Summers Media, New York, New York

"Yes, Mr. Traubst. Our Information Services people have verified that the email is from Jasmine." Associate Editor Josh Lee swiveled his chair around to face the glass wall in his office and stretched out his long, skinny legs. Standing, he looked out into "the pit"—the main "news floor" of the vast Summers Media empire. It was the place where most of the information that went out on the websites, cable and broadcast TV channels, radio stations, newspapers and magazines originated, was synthesized, written and edited. Leaning on the glass wall, Josh listened to the company's CEO and Chairman of the Board.

"Yes, Mr. Traubst. I'll put people on the story right away." Josh turned and sat back at his computer, as Karl Traubst repeated his directive with increased fervor. "I *will* make it happen, sir." Hand on mouse, Josh scrolled through his email lists—struggling to focus while Traubst reiterated the immediacy of the order and the thoroughness he expected. Distracted and hoping to end the conversation, he replied again, "Yes, Mr. Traubst. By the time people go to bed tonight they will all be thinking *dolphins*. By the end of tomorrow, it is all they will be talking about." He paused for the final word from the company's all-powerful leader. "Understood, Mr. Traubst." Josh hung up and momentarily stared through his computer screen — thinking about the man and his power to set the world's news agenda.

Opening a new email message, Josh tapped a special "breaking news priority" option and started to type. Pausing, he reached over and nestled his phone on his shoulder. "Carlye. I need you in my office now."

By the time Josh had finished his email and hit send, Carlye Fairbanks, the weekend coordinator for affiliate news assignments was standing in the doorway eyeing an empty chair. Swiveling away from the desk, Josh shook his head. "You won't be here that long." Sighing and taking a deep breath he continued, "This comes from Traubst and I don't have time to get into the details at the moment. I need assets in Tampa…"

"WTBT."

He nodded. "I need a chopper in the air heading to…" Swiveling back to his screen to look at Jasmine's email, "…Egmont Key in Tampa Bay. There are more than 100 sick dolphins swimming around in a large group." Josh held up his hand when he saw Carlye roll her eyes. "I need a local investigative reporter to start digging with the involved government agencies on site — whatever they might be. I want images in 30 minutes and I want words soon after that."

Carlye nodded and turned to leave. Josh stood quickly enough to stop her, "And, I need you in the conference room in 10 minutes with contacts for Galveston, Virginia Beach and Mozambique."

Her knitted brow was looking for a little more background. Shaking his head, Josh just shoed her away, "Don't ask now. Do now. Go!"

Chapter 49

Tampa International Airport, Florida

"Dr. Nicely." It was obvious the uniformed man had no question as to whom he was greeting—a quick Google image search and the subsequent current photos had allowed easy and unquestioned identification. The Navy ensign held out his right hand, "Dr. Nicely, I'm Ensign Jefferson I'll be escorting you to baggage claim and then to the helipad, sir."

Continuing to enjoy his special treatment, Robin smiled. "Thank you, ensign—lead the way."

Robin's bags were waiting on a cart under the watchful eye of another sailor. There were no introductions, Jefferson just nodded at his comrade and he seamlessly joined their walk towards a secure exit. Once outside, they piled onto a waiting golf cart and zipped across the tarmac to a military helicopter.

Robin settled into his seat and started fumbling with the harness. Jefferson climbed into the troop area shaking his head, "I'll help you with that when the time comes, sir. Right now we are on hold. Seems the captain is getting bad fuel pump readings. He's running a diagnostic. We have a vehicle on the way for a back-up transport. Just relax."

Chapter 50

Editorial Conference Room, Summers Media

New York, New York

Karl Traubst, current CEO and Chairman of the Board, was such a non-journalist. An odd choice by the reckoning of most media types, Traubst was the hand-picked successor to Roland Summers. Best friend of the company's founder, Traubst had no media industry experience beyond the marketing he signed off on while CEO of Deutsches Financial Services. DFS was the Summers Media pension fund manager, and Traubst was Roland's personal financial manager. Through successful investments, Karl Traubst and his team had allowed Roland to leverage himself into one of the fifteen richest people in the world. When Roland stepped down in 2003 to focus more on his philanthropic work, his majority of shares allowed him to anoint Karl his successor—a move that was seen by many as a simple reward for DFS's work on his portfolio. While Summers recognized the need to have a financial genius at the head of his diverse empire, the journalists saw only a snub. Don Eider, the award-winning and much-loved Senior Editor of *Global Report Nightly* was passed over, and though Traubst rarely interfered in the day to day workings of the news departments, this was enough to earn him the loathing of most of the Summers news team. When Roland Summers died three months after his retirement and his two daughters took no interest in the company, the issue was magnified—no one in the news services liked Traubst.

Josh was confident that, going into the conference room, he could use this animosity to his advantage—as a motivator for his reporters.

"First, Carlye—update."

"WTBT's chopper is in the air, but there is restricted airspace over the area you requested—Coast Guard orders. They will get as close as possible. I have a camera team that should be on the water in 15 minutes. But, again, there is an exclusionary area and the Coast Guard will get antsier once more news crews get in the air."

Josh's scowl had obvious meaning.

"I know—not good enough. But..." Carlye just rocked back in her chair and smiled. "...I re-tasked SumSat4. I'll have high-res images of the dolphins ready for distribution in 10 minutes—less than 10 minutes."

"Brilliant!" Josh was glowing.

Three SumSat satellites were in geosynchronous orbits around the globe--their primary focus was as private weather and communications satellites. A gamble that was one of the last of Roland Summers' pet projects to liberate the media from government dependence, the satellites had proved a boon for the company and secured Summers' media holdings the top place among an increasingly demanding and technologically savvy public. Consequently, two other satellites were placed in asynchronous, low-earth orbit and included the latest in high resolution imaging. It was one of these low-earth satellites, SumSat4, which was now positioned in a sure-to-be-controversial geosynchronous orbit over Tampa.

Josh continued, "I want those images up on the web sites ASAP. I want something running on the Global Report Headlines ticker ASAP. As soon as we have a few more words, I want an international break-in—every news outlet we own. Monitor the situation while I get to the rest." Josh eyed Carlye's laptop and then the others gathered around the table.

His eyes stopped with Kelli--who was sitting shaking her head. Her mouth started to open, but Josh glared and held up his long finger.

"You all would not be here if this were not something that was important to someone. That someone is Karl Traubst. And, while most of you may be wondering why you never heard of Mr. Traubst's passionate interest in dolphins before, I can tell you that is because he has no passionate interest in dolphins. But, he does have a passionate, paternal interest-- and this never leaves this room—in supporting the dolphin-loving daughter of the man who was his best friend and the founder of this company. He is doing this at the request..." he paused for effect, "...at the request of Jasmine Summers."

Josh held up his finger again. To create a little extra drama in his enforced silence, he stood up and closed the conference room door. While he was skinny, his height was still significant enough to be imposing.

Eyeing everyone as he returned to his chair, Josh continued, "You know I don't like this kind of directive. I don't like someone re-prioritizing our editorial direction. I don't like the order to create news." He sat back down. "But, I do love my job. And, I do love managing the news resources that Summers Media has at its beck and call." He looked at Carlye again — giving her a visual kudo for utilizing those resources so well. The rest were chomping to ask questions, but Josh continued, "All of those resources will be at your disposal. Spare no expense."

Momentarily feeling the silent crush of all those more experienced eyes on him, Josh retreated to the plan he had sketched on his yellow legal pad.

Carlye's furious key tapping jumbled Josh's thoughts. She smiled, stood up and walked over to the big screen, high definition monitor on the wall. SumSat4 was in place and with the press of a button the image was on the conference room wall. The clarity was amazing — a real-time, moving image of a mass of dolphins and a small flotilla of boats. The room was silent. Back at her laptop, Carlye tapped again and the image changed slightly — a few words of text added to the bottom.

"It's now the home page lead on all of our news websites. It will be a news flash on WTBT in..." She looked at her screen, "45 seconds. It's going to all of our science websites, newsgroups and list serves."

Josh beamed, "Excellent — good start. Make sure WTBT is getting that extra content so we can start national break-ins." Turning back to the rest of the team, he continued to hand out assignments for Galveston, Virginia Beach and Mozambique.

There was one person left at the table without an assignment—science writer Becca Farnell. Josh turned to her, "Becca." He looked around the table. "I want Becca cc'd on everything you send me—everything. Becca, you are to check every scientific detail." Becca sucked in a big breath—ready to let out a huge yawn—when Josh held up his finger. With everyone focused on her, she managed to let the air out a little more subtly. "Becca, in addition to the fact checking, I want you to become our expert on these dolphins and the scientists who study them."

Josh stood up and paced at the head of the table. He looked at the live image on the monitor and then back to his team. "If we are going to be told to make news, I want us to make the best news that we possibly can. Hold nothing back. If there is a Pulitzer in this story, I want you to find it. If there isn't, I want you to exhaust the possibilities." Waving his hand towards the door, he shouted, "Go!"

Chapter 51

TEXMAM Office, Galveston, Texas

"Hello, this is Kurt."

"Kurt Braun?"

"Yes. How can I help you?" Kurt shifted in his chair—balancing the phone on his ear while he reached for his mug of tea.

"Mr. Braun, my name is Jackson. I'm a journalist with Summers Media and I'm on my way to Galveston to report on your stranding as part of a special report we are putting together on the recent string of dolphin events—yours, Virginia Beach, Mozambique, Tampa."

"Tampa? You know about Tampa. I haven't seen anything in the news yet."

"Well Mr. Braun, it is now the lead story on every Summers Media news outlet in the world—in the world. Turn on the television. Check the internet."

Kurt took a long draw on his tea, set the mug down and went to GlobalReport.com. "Holy shit!" The image of the dolphins in Tampa Bay was nearly full screen. "Look at that—holy shit!" Standing up and pacing the room, Kurt continued, "It's about time. It's about time that somebody in the media is taking a *real* interest in this…in this tragedy…this is unprecedented, Mr. Jackson. There has never been concurrent…"

"Jackson Dafoe. Jackson's my first name."

Stopping to scribble the name on a legal pad on his desk, Kurt apologized, "Sorry — Mr. Dafoe. But, like I was saying there has never been a concurrent stranding of this many dolphins of the same species…actually there has never been a single-day, single species stranding in one location of this magnitude. Unprecedented. *That* in itself deserves more attention…"

It was obvious to Jackson that Kurt's comment and the trailing off of his voice were meant to lead him beyond what already seemed unprecedented. He couldn't resist — besides, it was his job to bite at innuendoes like this. "But, something else deserves more attention?"

"Absolutely." Kurt paced circles around his desk. "Absolutely. Beyond the coincidence of these simultaneous — and, seemingly anomalous-- mass events, we have the involvement of Navy teams at two of the locations, a suspicious man-made object removed from a carcass here in Texas, an explosion and the subsequent disappearance of said man-made object, the arrival in Tampa of a South African dolphin expert who was present at the stranding in Mozambique, and the involvement of the world's leading marine mammal veterinarian who was at one time the head veterinarian at the Navy's secret marine mammal program." Out of breath, he sighed and sat on the edge of his desk.

"And, you think those connections are a factor?"

"Absolutely--no doubt."

"Okay. I'll be there late this afternoon. Any documentation you might be able to pass on would be helpful. Also, is there any way that I can sit down with you and…" Jackson consulted his laptop, "…this Dr. Angela Clarke?"

"I'll be here. Dr. Clarke…" Kurt tried to recall the time of her follow-up appointment at the hospital. "…Dr. Clarke will likely be on her way to Tampa by then."

"Okay. I'll have our Tampa team get with her there."

"Tampa team? You have a Tampa team?" Kurt stood and re-started his pacing.

"A Tampa team, a Virginia Beach team, a…well…let's just say that Summers Media *is* taking this very seriously. One of our board members has a special interest in what is happening. And, if any of what you are telling me is true, then there is much more to this than the glossing over the media seems to have given it. If there is more, I'll find it. It's what I do."

"Excellent. I'll be available…"

"Hang on…I've got your email from the TEXMAM website and will send you my cell number. Email me directions to your office. Also, those other players involved—the vet, the South African dolphin guy, anyone else you think is important—text or email me their names. I can get a jump on my research while I wait at the airport."

Kurt made his way back around the desk and sat at his computer. "I'll do that. I'll also send you the links to some of the public marine mammal discussion groups and websites that I think might be helpful." Another long drink and Kurt finished his tea. "Thank you for caring."

"Don't get me wrong when I say this, but it's the story I care about, not the dolphins."

Call ended, Kurt sat forward in his chair and immediately went back to **www.globalreport.com**. His eyes widened — the satellite image from Tampa Bay was like nothing he'd ever seen. Nodding his head in self-satisfaction, he sat back and smiled — knowing the world would have to take notice and take action.

Chapter 52

Admiral Collins' House, Fairhaven, Maryland

Admiral Collins swiveled in his chair to look out at the slowly melting snow — thinking, *How far do we take this? Can I risk exposing one program to protect another? Maybe one. Definitely not two. It's an easy decision, Larry.*

An audible email alert brought him back around to the desk.

> ACRET
> *Check out globalreport.com. Speculation is out of the bag — possible connections drawn between you and FREEHOLD and NMMP. Too late to neutralize the satellite and the news flow. Suggest joint Navy/Department of Homeland Security news conference. Suggest sacrificing MK6C to deflect any potential interest in CONCH.*
> BLADE

Collins could feel his heart rate climb as he typed the Global Report URL into the Internet Explorer address window.

"Fuck!" He yelled and pounded the desk with his fist. Sprawled across the front page was a video loop of the Tampa Bay dolphins and the headline, *Possible Navy Involvement in Mass Dolphin Deaths*. Scrolling down, Collins read further:

> *According to TEXMAM Executive Director Kurt Braun, the use of Navy assets — some teams of which are rumored to have special dolphin training — is "highly irregular and unprecedented." Navy teams were used to assist*

with a mass stranding near their facilities in Virginia Beach and are now providing perimeter security on the water where a group of live dolphins may be getting ready to beach in Tampa Bay, FL. Mr. Braun also pointed out that Dr. Aldo Menke, lead veterinarian on site for the Galveston mass stranding, and now on his way to the Tampa Bay event, is the former head veterinarian and research director of the top secret Navy Marine Mammal Program. It was further revealed that Dr. Menke has close ties with Admiral Lawrence Collins (US Navy Retired), the current Undersecretary of Commerce for Oceans and Atmosphere and the Administrator of the National Oceanic and Atmospheric Administration (NOAA). The National Marine Fisheries Service (NMFS), is a department within NOAA and is responsible for overseeing all mass strandings of marine mammals in the United States.

The admiral pushed away from his desk and roughly opened the doors to his deck. He stormed out—squishing through the melting snow—stopped at the railing, grabbed on hard and rocked. If the deck hadn't been so soundly constructed, he may have ripped the railing off. But, the light breeze on the water and the sound of the small waves hitting the shore seemed to soothe him. Closing his eyes, Collins turned his head into the warm sun for a moment, then turned and walked back into his office. Mind clear, he began to type.

BLADE
There is nothing in that report that points at MK6C or CONCH. There is no evidence of illegal activity. It makes connections that anyone could find with some persistent internet searching

or phone calls. Any foul play is all innuendo — nothing more.

Knee-jerk reactions can be very telling. Sacrificing any program at this point would only encourage more attention.

Suggest immediate recall of MK6C commands in Tampa.
Suggest we get FREEHOLD to Tampa sooner. Suggest he also review data from CONCH testing again. Suggest we also have current NMMP staff review same data.

As a fallback, suggest we prepare news conference materials to reveal MK6C link to strandings if necessary.

Suggest we have SBT 22 transported from Mississippi to MacDill to assist with perimeter security. There are also two of our assets available on that team.
ACRET

After hitting send, Collins sent a brief high priority message to Dr. Menke:

FREEHOLD
Tampa — Now. No more delays. Your plane is ready.
ACRET

In the time it took to write and send the email, Collins had CC'd the other members his message to BLADE. All had immediately replied in the affirmative. He was already dialing Lt. Commander Medlin. Satisfied with his leadership, phone to his ear, the admiral headed to his kitchen for a cup of coffee and some breakfast.

Egmont Key, Tampa Bay, Florida

"I said *abort*, Lt. Commander. Repeat. Abort!" The admiral yelled through the phone.

Medlin temporarily tucked the phone under his arm, rapped on the control room window and shouted, "Abort! Ramirez! Abort!"

Inside, another of the team members shook the telemetry expert's shoulders. Ramirez stood and took the headphones off his ears. "Commander?"

Marching into the control, Medlin repeated, "Abort! Don't send the command."

"Sir? I already sent two--to MK6C-12 and 9. I can send a recall com..."

"Yes, send it now! Send it now! Recall those animals!"

Ramirez refocused on his work station and Medlin stepped out of the command cabin. The Lt. Commander un-tucked the phone and returned to the admiral. "Sir. Two MK6Cs received the command. Several dolphins started moving west. We are..."

"Get them back, Commander. Recall those animals now!"

Medlin took the liberty of rebuking the admiral's interruption with what seemed like a long pause. "Ramirez is in the process of sending the recall commands, sir."

"Very well, Medlin. Authorize Dr. Nicely's transport to the site. I expect immediate notification of his arrival on site. I expect an immediate report on his initial observations. I expect to know immediately if anything starts to change. Understood?"

"Understood, sir." Medlin closed his phone and, while shaking his head, walked back into the control center.

Ramirez removed his headphones and nodded. "Recalls sent, sir." Biting his lip he squinted and shook his head. "I shouldn't ask you any questions, should I, sir?"

Medlin frowned, "Not at this point." Turning and looking out over the water, he dialed Ensign Jefferson at the airport.

Chapter 53

Egmont Key, Tampa Bay, Florida

The trip from the airport was quick. Once the helicopter was cleared, it was only seven minutes to the site at Egmont Key. They were to rendezvous with one of the three Rigid Inflatable Boats (RIBs) boats stationed approximately 100m from the established perimeter. Robin was to be lowered in a harness.

As they approached the waiting boat, Robin tapped Ensign Jefferson on the shoulder. The ensign acknowledged him, but Robin's shouting was unheard with all the helicopter noise. Jefferson tapped the switch on his helmet and mouthed *microphone*.

Robin nodded and pressed the button, "Before I go down, I'd love to get a view from the top. Can we make a couple of passes?"

"Roger, that would be fine, sir."

The pilot had been monitoring the conversation and turned his head back to look at Robin. Nodding his agreement, he took the helicopter over the mass of dolphins.

"Holy fuck." There was gravity, not volume, to Robin's comment.

"Sir?" Jefferson used the question to remind Robin that he was still being heard.

"Sorry, I..." Something caught Robin's eye and he stopped. "What the fu...sorry, look over there—quickly! Um...three o'clock. See those dolphins?"

Jefferson nodded. The pilot replied, "Yes, sir."

Excited, Robin shuffled closer to the window — fidgeting, but not really getting any better view. "They look like they've just joined the group...like they just swam in. Yes?"

"Looks that way, sir." Jefferson nodded as he spoke. The pilot agreed.

"Interesting. I wonder if the observation plane saw *that*? I'll have to talk to them once I get settled." Robin shifted back away from the window and nodded at Jefferson. "Alright, ensign, let's get me down there."

Ensign Jefferson gave him a thumbs-up and the pilot banked back towards the waiting pick-up boat.

Chapter 54

Dolphin Towne, Tortola, BVI

After several personal reassurances from Karl Traubst at Summers Media, Jasmine finally emerged from her office. Doc and Adam knew better than to pace outside her door — that would only drive her to stay isolated — instead, when she emerged Jasmine found them at the sand ramp entrance to Bee's lagoon. It was obvious they had just completed Bee's exam.

"Adam, Doc." Jasmine sauntered in the soft sand. She stopped and closed her eyes. "I'm sorry I ran out like that." Opening her eyes she walked up to where they were squatting around Doc's open equipment cases. "I had to take action." Her eyes drifted into unfocused space. "Once again, I had to use atypical means to save the dolphins."

Adam stood up and walked over to her. Holding her hands he asked, "You're okay?"

"Better." She smiled and kissed him lightly on the cheek.

Doc placed a vial of blood in the foam case and stood up. "What *atypical means*?"

Dropping Adam's hands she walked to the edge of the water. "When I built Dolphin Towne I had to use atypical means — my trust fund, my connections, the power of association, the power of my name." Bee surfaced and blew, catching her eye. "I had to use those connections again."

Doc fumbled the next vial and dropped it in the sand, "Shit!" The force of the expletive was stronger than his clumsiness required, but allowed him to vent some of the momentary rage he was feeling toward Jasmine as he wondered what she might have done. He struggled to hide his concern over her actions. "Why…what do you mean? What connections do you have to save the stranded dolphins? What could *you* do? How…"

Jasmine cut off Doc's rambling, "I called on the Summers Media empire. I called on Uncle Karl…on my father's friend, Karl Traubst."

Adam's grin grew wide in acceptance, "Way to go!" He grabbed her and hugged.

She returned the grin and the hug, and then stepped back. "They already have satellite footage of the Tampa Bay dolphins on TV and the web. He assures me that they are putting their best…"

"Satellite images?" It finally registered with Doc. "They can't show much…can they?"

Adam answered with nerdy glee, "Summers put several private satellites in orbit just before Roland…before Jasmine's dad retired. They not only had communication capabilities, but were equipped with the latest weather imaging. What wasn't widely publicized was that they were also equipped with the latest HR-HM cameras and software. Amazing stuff…" He saw their puzzled looks and clarified, "Sorry, I forgot I need to tone down the tech talk — High Resolution-High Magnification cameras. The things that can read your car's license plate. Awesome, just awesome."

Doc closed his case, turned and moved slowly towards the Eli House. "That's great. I need to run inside. My bag?"

She trotted up the sand and stopped him — looking deep into his eyes. "My Bee?"

Menke took a deep breath. "Adam and I did an exam while you were in the office alerting the world. We went through the typical commands and presentations for an exam — no problems. We got blood easily. I'll have to run that. But, all else looked good. No abnormalities. Physically, she looks great." He looked to Adam for affirmation.

Adam nodded.

Doc continued, "But, we still have the changes documented by Adam's video activity logging." His arms extended and he gently held her by the shoulders, "But even that is considered normal *wild* dolphin behavior. And..." Doc paused in thought, ...*and I know this isn't easy for you Jasmine — gentle, dolphin-loving soul that you are...* "And, even though she's been in captivity for five years, she's still a wild dolphin."

Adam crept up and took her in his arms. Dr. Menke, turned and walked toward Eli House.

Jasmine, broke Adam's hug, looked up and yelled after him, "We took your backpack and cases to Adam's control room before you came down here to do the exam, remember? What are you looking for?"

"My Blackberry. It was in my backpack. Yes, I left my Blackberry and my backpack in the Education Center when we brought the equipment cases to the lagoon. I'll be back in a minute."

"We're going to head up to the house and grab a quick snack. Meet us in the dining room?" Jasmine took Adam's hand.

"Yeah, okay." Doc turned, passed the couple and made his way to the Education Center and to Adam's control room.

"Damn it!" The buzzing from his backpack made it obvious that there were messages on his Blackberry. He dug into the outside pocket and pulled it out—there were priority messages from BLADE, ACRET and THE FEW. "Shit!"

He opened the messages, one after the other and again raged in his mind, *Privileged, New Age trust fund…* Doc fumed—pushing Adam's rolling chair hard and knocking over a CPU.

His stare was lost in the monitors—images of Bee swimming. Taking a few deep breaths, he walked over and up-righted the now-scratched CPU. "Okay." He whispered to himself and took a few more deep breaths.

Sitting in the rolling chair, he sent a message back to Collins.

ACRET
Understood. Contact plane and have them ready in one hour. I'll be there. While in flight I will re-examine the CONCH data—for you—yet again.
FREEHOLD

Menke would only succumb to a reexamination of his work for one man other than himself—his friend from Viet Nam, his mentor and his comrade in the fight to protect the homeland. Still, Doc's pulse pounded--agitated by the admiral's doubts. The research was sound; there were no commonalities within the strandings and no causal relationships. He looked to the monitors, to the dolphins, to calm himself again — but, he just sat there shaking his head. Then, in real time, he saw Bee catch and eat a fish — Doc smiled and relaxed. Jasmine was too gentle of a soul — and too clueless of geopolitics — to know the potential damage she had done.

Sliding the chair up to Adam's desk, Menke caught a glimpse of some papers off to the left — technical drawings of electronics peaked out from under a few pages of text. Grabbing the papers, he rocked back slightly and flipped the pages. What he found weren't schematics for Adam's current external transponder. Doc smiled. The drawings were for an electronics package that looked very similar to a prototype of the Navy's MK6Chip — Adam's supposed "intellectual exercise." Doc knew better — in the margins were notations pertaining to Sammy. Clipped to the schematics was a spreadsheet documenting the chip insertion and follow-up exams. Doc knew that Jasmine had no real knowledge of what Adam was doing with *her* dolphins. Thinking *that* might be useful information, he examined the plans more closely.

Doc carefully replaced the papers, got up and grabbed his backpack from the floor. Pausing he looked back at the papers on the desk and smiled--imagining what Adam could do working with the resources of Defense Advanced Research Projects Agency (DARPA) and under the influence of THE FEW.

The thought had him locked in place. Setting the backpack on another chair, Doc moved back to the desk and sat. He shuffled through the schematics again. While setting them down, he jostled Adam's computer mouse—lighting up his dormant computer screen. Doc looked at the running files. There was Bee's activity log and several files labeled *TWMM*. Doc opened *TWMM-1*. *Hmmm...Theta Wave Mediation Meld...Stacy Melrose and Torto — Lagoon 2*...There were three brain wave windows on the screen. The graphs labeled *Stacy* and *TortoB* showed almost identical wave forms—theta waves. The graph labeled *TortoA* looked nothing like the *Stacy* or *TortoB*. Quickly, he opened *TWMM-2*, *TWMM-3* and *TWMM-4* and smiled, "Same basic pattern--you sly son of a bitch."

Swiveling around in the chair, Dr. Menke took in the view — not of the dolphins, but of the state-of-the-art hardware. His mind was churning as he looked at the servers, the high definition monitors and the electronics work in progress on his work bench--Jasmine didn't know the half of what her beloved Adam was doing with her dolphins and her clients. Back facing Adam's computer, Doc found and read the email from Dr. Nicely that had Adam so excited. He'd have to ask Nicely about Adam's paper when he got to Tampa. The thoughts—Nicely in Tampa, Adam so excited about his paper, Adam's deception of Jasmine—now had him staring through the computer screen. Shifting in the chair, Doc reached into his pocket, pulled out the MK6Chip retrieved from Galveston and smiled.

Chapter 55

John Sealy Hospital, Galveston, Texas

"Dr. Clarke, you're a little early." The admitting nurse looked at her watch—10am.

Angela stuck Kurt's car keys into her briefcase and smiled her best fake-smile that didn't seem fake, "I know, but I was hoping I might be able to get started earlier. There's another dolphin situation in Tampa that I need to deal with. I need to get this done so I can get on my way. Now, is there any…"

The nurse held up her hand and Angela stopped. Angela almost never stopped-- but sometimes she knew when not to push someone who could exercise a tremendous amount of power over her if she came off as being too rude. She smiled again.

"Dr. Winters has nothing scheduled until your appointment." The nurse held up her hand again as she moved to another window on the computer. "And…it must be your lucky day--an MRI slot is available." She handed Angela a clipboard. "Fill these out completely. I'll page Winters. If he's here, we can get you going ahead of schedule."

As best as she could, Angela beamed, "Thank you. Anything helps."

Taking a seat next to the desk, Angela started to fill out her forms when her phone rang.

"Robin--finally. You're on the water?"

"Yeah, love, on the boat now. But, I took the liberty of having the helicopter make a pass over the group. Couldn't pass up seeing it from the air—amazing thing 200 dolphins in a mass…"

"147. I got a call from the plane 45 minutes ago. They put someone with dolphin aerial survey experience in the plane—it's different than counting manatees. Yes, well…they counted 147." Angela could see that the nurse was getting ready to call her up.

"Precise. Okay. Anyway, love, the queerest thing—it looked like maybe 12-15 just joining the group. I wouldn't have expected that at this point. But, then again we don't know what to expect…we don't know much…um…anything really, about pre-stranding behavior, so this is a new book being written as we…"

"Robin!" The nurse was summoning Angela and she couldn't delay after asking them to rush her in. "Robin, I need to get with the doctors now. I'll call when I get out of the MRI. Anything else? Quickly!"

"Adam Reich. I think we need to bring him here from BVI. I have a feeling he might be able to help us. His ability to collect field data, his critical and innovative thinking…"

"Reich? Tampa? He's not…I'll be right there, Dr. Winters." She sighed. "Let me think on that…we could have him fly back with Doc…you sure?"

"Dr. Clarke?!" Now, the nurse was doing the doctor's prodding.

Robin laughed, "I heard that. Go. Think on it. I'll come up with a more compelling argument to challenge you with. Go, love. Get well."

"Love yo..." Angela heard the phone disconnect and stopped. Looking up, she smiled uncomfortably and walked over to Dr. Winters.

Director's Office, NMFS, Silver Spring, Maryland

"Director Hamilton. I was hoping that our hearings last week would be the last we'd see or hear of our dolphin friends for a while. I was hoping I could bury those environmentalist fish-huggers for a while and keep the reauthorization language of the Marine Mammal Protection Act off the back of my constituents. Now, I turn on the TV or my computer and the damned porpoises are everywhere. I don't care about their fuc..." Senator Hulme sighed and started again, "I don't care about the conspiracy theories that are being bandied about—Navy dolphins causing them to strand and shit like that. I don't care that they're trying to turn that Dr. Menke into the dolphin Dr. Mengele. That's a load of crap and we know it. What I do care about is when they pull out all the environmental whackos that start blabbing about pollution from the Mississippi flowing into the Gulf, dead zones and red tide killing manatees, oil drilling and oil spills, and commercial fishing by-catch and sea turtle deaths. Even though none of this is causing 600 dolphins to go crazy and kill themselves, it still brings all these things prominently before the voting public. That's bad for my business."

Jake knew better than to fill the senator's dramatic pauses. He rocked back in his chair, put his feet up on the desk and sat quietly. It was never stated, but it was widely known that Hulme was instrumental in smoothing and expediting Jake Hamilton's appointment. What wasn't widely known was that Admiral Collins had prompted Senator Hulme.

"Now, Jake," Hulme got chummier and continued, "What I'm not hearing is anything from you — from National Marine Fisheries. No quotes, no reports, nothing. What's our girl doing in Texas? What's going on in Tampa? Virginia Beach? The media is all over this thing and you're saying nothing. There needs to be a reasonable *scientific* response."

Sitting upright, Jake rolled closer to his desk, "I'm sorry, senator. Dr. Clarke...she was in an accident, an explosion in Texas. She's okay, but was in the hospital overnight."

"I'm sorry. I didn't..." The senator's voice faded with sympathy.

"She's fine." He looked at his watch. "She's getting a follow-up MRI as we speak. But, amazingly, she's not only been coordinating the completion of things in Texas, but has been in close contact with the Navy team and local agencies on the ground...err...on the water, in Florida. She already has a preliminary rescue plan in place and is mobilizing..."

"Great. I'm glad to hear that she is okay. But, what has she found out? Anything?"

Director Hamilton sighed, "The preliminary findings are—and, you'll be relieved to hear this I'm sure—inconclusive."

Jake could almost hear the senator smiling through the phone, "Inconclusive. That's good. But, *the public* needs to hear that from an authority on our side—now." Senator Hulme let that sink in and continued, "That's only the preliminary findings?"

"Right. The on-site examinations, the visual exams during the necropsies, on-site blood work. While there were plenty of things wrong with these dolphins, there was no one thing...well, the preliminary results can't point to any one cause."

"And the next step?"

Reaching for his mouse, Jake started to scan his email while he answered. "Waiting for the results from the blood and tissue samples that have been sent out. We may have some results within a day—some take more than a week to process properly. And, we do want them processed properly, senator. In the mean time we can't..."

Senator Hulme finished Jake's sentence, "...you can't stick your necks out. I understand. But, I suggest that you say something about the preliminary results ASAP. Tell the country—tell the world—what you just told me. The dolphin media frenzy that suddenly seems to have popped up is counterproductive disinformation. There has not been a single word from NMFS—from our agency in charge. *That* is more than unacceptable. I can't believe that you...I can't believe that the admiral has not found that unacceptable. I highly suggest that..."

"...that I have Dr. Clarke make a public statement when she is through at the hospital." Jake continued, "I'll have her outline what we know, or don't know, so far. I'll have her reiterate the inconclusiveness — that should put the whackos in their place."

"Good plan. Now, any word on Virginia Beach?"

Jake sighed again and began composing an email to Angela while he was talking, "The same--inconclusive at this point. I'll have Dr. Clarke include that in her statement as well — of course."

"Very well. One more thing…"

"Tampa Bay?" Jake knew that was next.

"Yes. Of course I'm assuming we are doing everything we can to keep those animals from dying as well?"

Jake finished his email to Angela and hit *send* — knowing that it would go to her phone as well as her laptop.

"Jake?" The senator was a little agitated that Director Hamilton did not respond. "Director Hamilton?"

"Sorry, sir. We do have a unique opportunity in Tampa Bay. We know so little about pre-stranding behavior that — if all else fails--we'll at least end up adding to our knowledge base." Jake knew that was not enough for the senator. "Dr. Clarke is planning an all-out effort, sir. As I mentioned before, we have a Navy team assisting with security and monitoring. We are also coordinating with our local NMFS office and the Florida Fish and Wildlife office. We have two experts on their way — Dr. Robin Nicely, from the Dolphin Study Centre in South Africa should be on site…well…now. He's the world's foremost authority on dolphin social behavior. We also have

Dr. Menke….he'll be there late in the day. Dr. Clarke already has an outline of quite a multi-agency rescue plan. The hope is that Dr. Nicely and Dr. Menke will have some information to present to Dr. Clarke when she arrives late this evening. Then, she'll tweak her draft and start formulating a final rescue plan. When the time is appropriate, we'll put the plan into action."

"Impressive. I'm sure the admiral will be pleased with your work. Now, impress me and deal with the press."

"Yes, senator. I'll take care of it."

Jake hung up and immediately dialed Admiral Collins. "Sir, I just wanted to let you know that I've just spoken with Senator Hulme."

"Thank you for letting me know. What did the blowhard have to say?"

"He was concerned, considering the sudden increase in media coverage of the strandings—their linking it to everything from over-fishing to pollution--about our lack of news presence."

Collins interjected, "Concerned for his own constituencies…and, rightly so. He beat me to the punch. You were next on my list of calls to make for that very same reason. Did you put the senator's mind at ease?"

"Sir, Dr. Clarke is currently taking care of her follow-up at the hospital. I've left her a message to make a public statement as soon as she is available. I'm going start making arrangements for a press conference at the rehabilitation facility—a nice backdrop couldn't hurt." That idea had just popped into Jake's mind, so he immediately started an email to the director of the Caldwell Aquarium.

"Nice touch but will the senator be pleased with what our side has to say?"

"Of course sir—still nothing conclusive from Dr. Clarke. I would have informed you immediately if I heard otherwise-- certainly nothing involving any of the senator's interests. We *are* hoping that the tissue samples and blood..."

"Yes, yes—I'm sure good people are working on that all around." At least the admiral knew that the scientists at the Armed Forces Institute of Pathology were working diligently. "Thank you for keeping me informed. I'll look for the press conference later today."

With the phone finally silent, Jake composed and sent several emails—first, the one he had been writing to the director of the Caldwell Aquarium, then, to his Public Information director, to Kurt Braun at TEXMAM, and an additional one to Angela.

Chapter 56

Dolphin Towne, Tortola, BVI

Jasmine and Adam were sitting close, on the same side of the table, enjoying fresh coffee and some whole grain rolls, when Doc approached. Adam turned, "Find it?"

Doc smiled and held up his Blackberry. "At least 15 messages — one very important." He looked at Jasmine. "They want me in Tampa ASAP — as in now. Seems there's been some change in the swim pattern in the group and they think it may be a move towards stranding."

Adam sat up straight — serious. "Really? I didn't think anyone knew much...anything really...about pre-stranding behavior. Certainly, nothing about it in such a large group. Who's making *that* call?"

"Why *your* Dr. Nicely — that's who." He pulled out a chair and sat.

"How can Nicely make that call from..." Adam's eyes glazed over and he nodded, "Ohhhh...consulting. He told me he was consulting on a stranding in the states. I just assumed he was still...he's in the U.S., isn't he?"

"I knew you were a smart lad." Doc poured a cup of coffee and took a sip. "He's in Tampa Bay — out on the water observing."

Clunk! Jasmine loudly set her mug on the table, startling Adam and Doc. They both turned to her. She crossed her arms and stared back and forth, "And, Miss Bee? What about Bee?"

Doc looked at Adam. "You told her?"

Jasmine looked at Adam. He repeated most of what he had already gone over with her. "Yes…our observations were normal…that there really wasn't much else to do. That, yes, Bee is acting more like a normal wild dolphin. That, yes, she may no longer be amenable to swimming with humans — any humans." He frowned and looked down at the table top.

Looking at Doc, Jasmine forced a weak smile, "Thank you for coming down. I'm sorry it was a big trip for nothing — especially when you have more important things to do in the states."

Dr. Menke leaned into the table and reached across to Jasmine. She uncrossed her arms and gave him her hands to hold. "It was not for nothing. Bee is very important to you and you are very important to me. I wanted to be here for you." Still holding her hands, he looked at Adam, "I'll have the blood samples forwarded to Texas. Jasmine, Randy will call you with the results. But, now I must be going."

Gripping Doc's hands tightly, Jasmine nodded, "I know. I understand. If anyone can help save them — save that pod — it is you."

"Well…" Doc turned to look at Adam, "…I think we could use some other help."

Adam squinted and mouthed, "Me?"

Doc nodded. Jasmine took her hands back, "Adam? You already have Dr. Nicely. From what Adam says he's the best at…what is it?"

Adam smiled wider, "Social behavior...dolphin communities...behavioral ecology. *He* is the best." He looked back at Doc, "Why would you want someone like me?"

"*You* are a thinker and a doer. You have the critical and creative thinking skills that can make you a valuable member of the team. You have never been involved in strandings, so you might have a fresh perspective. I think, at this point, we need that...that, and you might just be able to help us with your technological prowess. The Navy has some barely-functioning proto-type dolphin monitoring equipment that could use some expert tweaking..." Doc made an "I don't know" gesture with his hands.

Shaking his head, Adam stood up and started pacing. "But, you're leaving...you're leaving now."

Doc stood as well. "As soon as I can gather my things and get to the car." Doc looked reassuringly at Jasmine, then back to Adam. "I know you could be a big help. And..." He looked back at Jasmine, "...we need all the help we can get if we are going to save those dolphins. Besides, you'll get to meet and work with Dr. Nicely."

Jasmine closed her eyes and nodded. "Yes." Opening her eyes she looked at Adam. He stopped pacing. Jasmine pulled him close. "You are brilliant. Go, help Doc save the dolphins. I'll be here for you when you're done." Her smile was just a little impish.

Doc sighed, "Then it's settled. How much time do you need?"

"If Jaz can pack me some clothes..." She nodded agreement and Adam continued, "...it will be cooler there...I can run down to the control room to pack my other things — my laptop....some video equipment...some of my tools..." Adam was caught in the flow of his thoughts, "I've got a couple transponders and some lightweight tracking gear..." There was another span of silence as he went through a checklist in his mind. "Oh...sorry...20 minutes."

"I'll head back down to the lagoon, gather my gear and meet you at the car."

Adam grabbed another roll from the basket on the table and left the room. Jasmine walked over to Doc, "Take good care of him. He's come a long way—more balanced, more at peace with his gifts. He's in a good place." Taking one of Doc's hands in both of hers, she continued, "Adam and I...*we're* in a good place. I know you can see how much I love him."

Doc moved one of her hands over his heart and paused, "His transformation is obvious. The power of your connection is obvious. That's why I think it's finally safe for him to venture out—to face the world again."

Pulling Doc into a hug, Jasmine said, "You are a great soul. Thank you." Breaking the hold, Jasmine moved to the hallway. "I'll get Adam's clothes packed and meet you both at the car out front."

Doc made his way to Bee's lagoon. After taking a moment to watch her swim—something about the beauty and grace of a dolphin gliding effortlessly through the water was still moving—he started packing his gear. When he finished, Doc walked over to the gate in the bay wall, set down his gear boxes and looked out over the clear, blue waters of Ballast Bay. In the distance, amidst the moored sailboats, he could see a wild dolphin surface and breathe. Doc looked back at Bee in the lagoon and ran his fingers lightly over the gate's hydraulic lever. Shaking his head, Doc picked up his gear and headed for the car.

Chapter 57

Egmont Key, Tampa Bay, Florida

Once settled on board the Navy command boat, Dr. Nicely contacted what he assumed was the FWC observation plane he had seen from the helicopter.

Emily Havens, Florida's most experienced dolphin aerial survey observer filled him in on her observations, "I noticed the small group moving to the larger group as well. I have some video and a few photos. But, what I saw was different—more complete. These weren't new dolphins joining the group. They were dolphins that left the group, traveled about a quarter mile west and then returned. In fact, it almost looked as if the entire group was making a move to follow. Then they turned around and the group went back to the same old, compact pattern of movement."

"Thanks. That's very helpful. I don't necessarily know what it means, but it's definitely significant." Robin shifted his weight as the wake from a large yacht rolled under the hull. He shook his head—the media coverage was attracting more and more sightseers. "Again, well done, Emily. And, let me know immediately if you see any deviation from that standard pattern of movement again. Understood?"

"Yes. Understood."

"Thank you." After hanging up, Robin looked at his watch—Angela was probably still in the hospital.

"Whoa!" The South African scientist was tossed up against Lt. Commander Medlin. He straightened himself up and apologized, "Sorry, I haven't quite got my sea legs...oh hell...can't we do something about the sudden increase in sight seers? Widen your perimeter?"

Medlin leaned against the boat tower. "You're right. With the exponential increase in media coverage and the sure-to-be more curious public, I think it's time. Our current assets are stretched as thin as we can be and maintain the current perimeter. I'll have to contact the admiral to authorize coordination with other local authorities."

Dr. Nicely looked out away from the dolphins and at the flotilla of media boats and private yachts that had taken up station outside the ring of official boats. "I know I have no real authority here, Commander, but I think it's time for you to make that call. We need to minimize the chance of any unintentional — or intentional for that matter — public disturbance. We need to give these dolphins the best chance we can."

"Believe it or not, I've read a few of your books. Don't ask me why." He looked hard at Robin and held up his hand, "Seriously, don't ask me why. But, they were well done and enough for me to — after meeting you in person — give you a certain amount of authority in this matter."

"Thank you." Robin climbed the tower while Lt. Commander Medlin went inside the command cabin and hit his new speed dial one — Admiral Collins.

John Sealy Hospital, Galveston, Texas

Following the MRI, Angela sat in a small room waiting for Dr. Winters. She looked up from her legal pad when he entered.

Smiling back at her, he nodded, "You are good to go. The MRI showed no problems." He handed her a slip of paper. "You told me you needed this."

She looked it over. It was a medical clearance to fly — and smiled. "Thank you. I appreciate you accommodating my amended schedule. Very helpful, but…"

"…but now you must run." He held up his wait-a-minute finger. "I wanted to let you know that Ms. Singh…well…she is out of ICU and conscious…doing very well. But, I'm not at liberty to discuss her complications."

Angela stood and shook Dr. Winters' hand, "Yes, thank you." She turned and walked out — she'd have someone from NOAA send flowers and a card.

The unique beep from her cell phone let her know she had an email. She frowned — it was Jake's message about the news conference. She frowned again when she noticed no message from Robin.

At the car she paused to make a call. "Kurt. I'm cleared to go."

"Great news. Are you…"

"I don't have time. Director Hamilton wants me to do a news conference before I fly to Tampa. So…I don't have time." She fidgeted with the key in his temperamental lock. "Here's the plan. I'm going directly to my office in Building G—cleaning things out and packing up. Then, to the necropsy team. Then, to the rehab facility. Then, to your office to review the plan and your action items. Then, back to the rehab tanks for the news conference. Then, I'm on my way to the airport and to Tampa."

"So, you'll be leaving…" He was fishing for a time.

"2pm. I hope to be in the air by 2:30." She sighed. "Okay, I just now got your damn car door open. Have you tried replacing the batteries? Why don't you just get the remote fixed or replaced? Hey, gotta go."

It was a short drive, but Angela had time for one more call—to Director Hamilton. "Jake, I'm cleared—all is well. I'll fax you the note from my doctor when I get to my office here."

"That's great to hear. I'm glad you'll be clear-headed for the news conference."

"Right—thanks for all the advanced notice. Just have that NOAA plane ready to roll by 2pm."

"2pm? The news conference is scheduled for 1pm. You have to meet with everyone else—Kurt, Randy--to get them straight before you leave. You're going to fit all that in and be on the plane by 2pm?"

Angela smiled and her confidence was reflected in her voice, "You know me better than that. Of course I'll get it done."

"Fine. Make sure you emphasize the inconclusive nature of what we know already. There has been too much speculation in the media—let them know it is not warranted. When you're finished, I'll have a plane waiting for you. I'll let everyone know you're coming."

"Thanks. I'll send you any updates from the plane."

Admiral Collins' House, Fairhaven, Maryland

"Lt. Commander Medlin. Good to hear from you. I'm assuming Dr. Nicely is on board?" Collins was back at the desk in his home office.

"Yes, sir. He arrived about an hour ago…and…and, just a minute, sir."

"And you're moving so that he can't hear you?"

"Affirmative…okay. While still in the helicopter, Dr. Nicely managed to get the pilot to fly over the dolphin group. He saw the recalled two MK6Cs and some other dolphins returning to the group."

Collins walked outside on his deck. Most of the snow had melted through the cracks in the planking. "And…"

"Well, sir, at first he thought they were dolphins just joining the group—newcomers. But, sir…that FWC aircraft was already in the air and he called them once he was on board. Sir…admiral, the woman in the aircraft saw the animals leave and return."

The winter air was warming enough for the admiral to unzip his fleece jacket. "Relax. They'll make no connection with the movement and anything we did…with anything your team did."

"You are right, sir—absolutely."

There was a pause, but Collins could tell that the Lt. Commander was thinking—processing something.

"Honestly, sir, they don't have a clue. Dr. Nicely says they know virtually nothing about the pre-stranding behavior of any marine mammals—let alone the behavior of atypically large bottlenose dolphin groups like this. I...I just thought you should know that he made the observation, sir."

"Anything else?"

"Sir, there's been an exponential increase in the number of private boats just outside the secure perimeter. I understand that the media has been flooded with the stranding stories and images in the last few hours, sir. I'd expect the crowd to only get larger. I recommend that, for the safety of the animals and to better serve the goals of our mission, that we enlarge the perimeter. I wanted your authorization to enlist help from the Coast Guard, local marine police units and to request more aid from state Fish and Wildlife officers."

"Request denied—for the local assistance anyway. Have them patrol and inform at local boat ramps and marinas—preemptive work. For the perimeter, Lt. Commander, SBT 22 is in-route to MacDill now. They'll have five of their own SOC-Rs and we're sending them three more RIBs from Little Creek. When they arrive, they will deploy and assist with enlarging the perimeter under your command." SBT 22 was a Special Boat Team trained in riverine operations and based in Mississippi. The SOC-R—Special Operations Craft-Riverine—was their specialized high speed boat.

"Understood, sir, but until they arrive..."

"Until they arrive, you hold tight. I will have the Coast Guard in St. Petersburg issue an updated notice to mariners detailing the expanded perimeter and no-fly zone. You have a chart there, Medlin?"

"Yes, sir."

"How large an area can we secure without interfering with commercial shipping?"

"Well sir...the dolphins are about a quarter of a mile east-northeast of the south tip of Egmont Key. Most of the commercial traffic into Tampa goes through a channel 1.5 miles to the north. The north tip of Anna Maria Island — a residential area — is about 1.5 miles south. There is some commercial traffic that goes between us and Anna Maria into the Manatee River, but that is negligible. So..."

"...so let's go with two miles. Let the Coast Guard notify that commercial ships in the commercial channel will be our only exception to that exclusionary zone. No press, no public."

"Sir, even with SBT 22 and their boats...well...that would be stretching things mighty thin. I don't think we could effectively patrol that much..."

"Yes. We can have the Coast Guard's helicopters and small boats patrol the edge of the two-mile perimeter. I'll have the folks at MacDill round us up some more small patrol boats. Then we'll assign two-man teams to each. We'll keep them circulating between your current position and the two-mile limit. The activity will keep them sharper than sitting at anchor."

"Agreed, sir. I'll coordinate with Lt. Commander Warner when he arrives."

"Excellent. You will retain overall command authority."

"Thank you, sir."

"You've earned it, son. Keep up the good work." Collins closed the doors to the deck as he walked back to his desk. "Two more items. I've recalled Dr. Menke from the BVI—he should be landing at MacDill around 1400 hours. Treat him as you would treat me."

"Understood, sir. I'll have the helicopter waiting."

"Finally, Dr. Clarke has been cleared to fly. Her ETA at MacDill is 1800 hours."

"I'll have the helicopter waiting for her, sir."

"I'll expect a report shortly after they both arrive." The admiral hung up and rested his head on his arms on his desk.

Chapter 58

TEXMAM Office, Galveston, Texas

Angela walked into Kurt's office with a huge box of necropsy files. She dropped the box on his desk — on top of his tattered copy of the *Odyssey*. "Still have *that* old thing?"

Kurt moved the box to the floor. "I didn't think you had time to belittle me, but if you want to get into it…"

"You're right, I don't have the time." Sitting down, she pulled a legal pad from her laptop case and looked at the box. "Those are the up-to-date necropsy files. They need to be entered into the data base ASAP and emailed to Director Hamilton, Dr. Menke, Dr. Nicely and myself. That's your priority."

"Yes, sir." Kurt saluted and smiled.

"Asshole. I don't have time for sarcasm." Angela referred back to her notes. "Director Hamilton will make the database available to the Armed Forces Institute of Pathology and Patel Pathology Associates. That authorization and distribution must go through the director."

Kurt was writing while she was speaking, "Okay. Next?"

"The necropsy teams have 17 more carcasses to go. They've done amazing work. Anyway, I want you to circulate down there every hour to check on things — answer any questions, put out any fires, get the completed files back up here quickly. Keep an eye on their quality control — even though they are getting a little more rest, they are getting tired. Make sure the samples are packaged and sent properly." Angela waited for him to finish writing—and, for acknowledgement.

He put his pen down sharply--sarcastically. "Next?"

"That's it. Other than the live animals—and, Randy has that covered—we're almost done here. News conference in 10 minutes and I'm on my way to Tampa."

"Your official statement?"

"Nothing conclusive—here, Virginia Beach."

"And Tampa, what are you going to say about that?"

Angela stood up and walked to Kurt's desk. She picked up the *Odyssey* and flipped through the frail pages. Shaking her head, she tossed it back down. "Only what most people now already know—and, that we have one of the best teams of marine mammal experts in the world on the job." Angela could see Kurt looking at the old book. "And you? Other than the tasks I've assigned, what's up for you?"

Relaxing, Kurt leaned back slightly in his chair. "Summers Media is responsible for the sudden media frenzy surrounding the strandings. Jasmine Summers—Dolphin Towne."

"I know. I also know you've fed them some facts and some theoretical connections of your own."

"And, I'll be feeding them more. Jackson Dafoe, the youngest winner of a Pulitzer Prize for investigative journalism, is on his way here from the Summers Media headquarters in New York. He won't be here in time for your staid press conference, so I'll give him a summary and my interpretation."

"Really?" Angela moved toward the door—five minutes to one and she needed to get over to the rehab facility. "Seems like a wasted trip to me. All he'll get here is more unsubstantiated theory and stories about how I broke your heart. Remember to spice it all up with that."

"Why would you...?"

Halfway through the door, she stopped, "For my money, the story is in Tampa—that's where we'll get real answers. That's where they should be sending reporters."

Then, she was gone. Kurt sat up, rolled in closer to the desk and rested his head in his hands. His left hand dropped to the Odyssey and thumbed the crumbling edge of the pages. His right hand moved to the computer mouse and he clicked on a file labeled *Marine Mammal Mythology (working V7)*. From the desk drawer he pulled a large box of note cards and grabbed a stack labeled "Chapter 47."

Chapter 59

NOAA, GS-3, Somewhere Between Tortola and Tampa

Sitting uncomfortably, even in the wide seats of a government jet, Doc wondered if he first should have cleared his invitation to Adam with the others. Tired of fidgeting, Doc unbuckled his seatbelt, got up and walked back to the toilet.

Necessities completed, Doc sat in the seat opposite, but facing Adam's. He shifted and reached in his pocket, concealing the MK6Chip in his hand. Smiling at Adam, he said, "Put out your hand."

Doc put his closed fist over Adam's hand and opened it. The chip dropped dramatically into his palm. Adam was bug-eyed and speechless.

"Look it over. Give me your evaluation. Take your time."

Adam held it close to his eye and rolled it over and over. He glanced at Doc and then reached down to one of his bags. Pulling out a small magnifying eye piece he examined the object more closely. He looked at Doc and shook his head.

Doc held out his hand and Adam returned the chip. Doc was waiting, "So?"

"I can't open it, can I?" It was a question with the tone of a statement.

Doc shrugged his shoulders and handed the chip back to Adam. "I don't know, can you?"

Adam's eyes widened and he dug threw his bag for a few tools. "Regardless...if it is what I really think it is...I'd say it's well beyond where I thought they'd be."

"Oh, it is. It most certainly is."

As he carefully manipulated the chip and worked at the seal, Adam could feel that Doc still wanted specifics. When the seal popped, he slid the works out of the shell like he was at the world championships for the old board game "Operation." Holding the delicate electronics package up to his eyepiece, he smiled. *"Well* beyond where I estimated the military would be — although the use of a titanium shell as the main receiver/transmitter is what I've done with mine. Amazing similarities, but this looks like it might be satellite trackable with a radio transmitter *and* receiver. Shit--that means they could give remote commands to trained dolphins. Remote signals to trained dolphins! Doc?" He looked up at Menke.

There was no reaction from the vet, so Adam continued, "Imagine what they'll be able to do in a year or two. Imagine what they'll eventually be doing with nanotechnology." Again, he looked up at Doc.

Menke smiled and nodded his head. "Imagine where *you* could take it with access to that real cutting edge technology."

Still manipulating the innards of the chip, Adam replied, "Oh, believe me. In the minute I've been looking...well, I already imagined where I could go — real time satellite tracking, communication and upload. With the right power source, I could have it completely satellite capable. Of course, that would just be an intermediate step…the breakthrough will come with the integration of nano…"

Doc tapped him on the knee and held out his hand. Adam frowned, slipped the electronic innards back into the shell and dropped the chip into Menke's hand. Doc slipped the chip back in his pocket.

Even without the chip in front of him, Adam excitedly rambled on—his enthusiastic chatter about the technical possibilities turning into a background drone as Doc sat thinking.

Finally, Doc interrupted, "You know in Tampa we'll get to work directly with Dr. Nicely."

"You mentioned that earlier today--yes. I'm very excited!"

"I was truly impressed that he had such high regard for you and your research. He is one of the most well-respected marine mammal researchers in the world."

"I know—he's the best. That's why the email from him meant so much."

Doc held up his hand. "I can imagine--especially after all that you went through at MIT and Woods Hole. A good scientific reputation is a difficult thing to regain—but, you've made a good first step…but, only a first step."

Adam looked sadly puzzled. Doc continued, "Dr. Nicely is extremely well-respected, but he is also a bit of an academic rebel. You probably didn't know that he worked in building construction for five years before he finally focused his intellect enough to even start college." Adam shook his head, *No.* "Even then, he only decided to study marine mammals because he kept a high school dolphin observation project going with anecdotal reports of his study area taken during his kayak training. Because his academic path was non-traditional he is always on the lookout for rogue academics — albeit rogues with rigorous methodologies — to groom and support. As tough as he can appear physically, he does have that soft spot." Doc looked down at his hands folded in his lap. "Unfortunately, there aren't many others in the marine mammal community — especially those on the stuffy editorial board of *Marine Mammal Science* — who think the same way."

He gave Adam a fatherly look and continued, "What I'm trying to say is that Dr. Nicely's support may not be enough to get you published or to earn back your scientific credibility — no matter what your abilities." Sighing and tapping his fingertips together, Doc moved on, "Many in the marine mammal world are aware of the breakdown that you had at MIT. In fact, Dr Lykes still makes an example of you at his graduate student orientation. They all have a good macabre laugh — and at least one student usually drops out the following day. There are still a few old Adam Reich meltdown discussion threads floating around cyberspace."

Silence. Adam's mouth tightened and he closed his moist eyes.

A serious smile took over Doc's face as he reached out to Adam. Adam's eyes opened, and Doc continued, "But, I have an offer for you that, in addition to Dr. Nicely's support, is sure to put you back in favor — to put you at the top of your field."

Adam just nodded.

"Okay. First, what I am about to tell you cannot leave this plane."

Adam nodded again.

Doc sunk back into his seat. "Some of this will sound unbelievable — but, I assure you, it is all true. What I just showed you is called an MK6Chip — a...well...let's just say beyond top secret, telemetry device designed for the Navy Marine Mammal Program. Nine years ago the Biosonar program started with a clunky external device...BMT — Biosonar Measurement Tool. At the time they were only looking to record emitted clicks and whistles and returning clicks and whistles. Within two years, they realized the true potential and moved way beyond that simple device." Doc dug the MK6Chip out of his pocket again. "This is the latest generation — it can monitor heart rate, body temperature, brain waves and acoustics. It is a *huge* leap forward in monitoring "wild" dolphins. It has a limited satellite interface — limited because of the power requirements and current technologies. Typically, in their current deployment, they are programmed to interface once a week. Most of the data is transmitted via radio — to mobile tracking gear or via..." Hesitant to mention the recent link to CONCH, Doc got less specific, "...another type of tracking network. The device is also capable — as you surmised--of receiving signals. MK6C dolphins have been trained to receive and interpret those signals as commands and then to respond to those commands."

Adam swallowed hard and fought the dryness in his mouth. "Is that…" He pointed at Dr. Menke's hand. "Is that the chip that Dr. Nicely mentioned? The chip that was found in one of the stranded animals in Texas? Did the MK6Chip cause that mass stranding? You worked for the Navy. Did you help develop it? Test it?" He shook his head and looked at his feet. "I can't be a part…Jasmine wouldn't…"

Doc stopped Adam with a not-so-fatherly glare. "What I've already told you makes you a part of this." He smiled, "Now, to answer your questions. Yes, it is the chip that Nicely mentioned — the chip found in one of the Texas animals. No, I don't believe that chip led to the mass stranding."

Squirming a little in his seat, Adam obviously had more questions. Doc held up his hand again — but this time it was a vibration from his Blackberry — it was Admiral Collins.

> *FREEHOLD*
> *Dr. Nicely requesting Adam Reich's assistance with Tampa. Dr. Clarke reluctant, but seems willing to defer. Your take?*
> *ACRET*

"Give me a minute Adam." Doc fingered the keys.

> *ACRET*
> *Reich already in transit to Tampa. Accompanying me. Believe he is ripe to assist us. Briefing on MK6Chip now. Await further communication.*
> *FREEHOLD*

Doc continued, "Dr Nicely's support is essential to your comeback. But work with me on this and I will give you the full backing, the full gravitas of my own scientific reputation, the Navy Marine Mammal Program and, let's just say, some very important people in Washington."

"I don't understand. I'm already on my way to work with you on…"

Doc's Blackberry vibrated again. "I'm sorr. Hang on."

FREEHOLD
You saw earlier communication. MK6Chip is not currently an issue.
I know you are aware that Reich does have a history of emotional instability — that can work in our favor, or against us. YOU are trusting him with very privileged and potentially damaging information. Your strategy may be sound, but the boy may not be. Exercise caution. It is your ass on the line. I will hold communicating this to the rest until you have his commitment and outline a detailed action plan. I will be looking for another communication before you land.
ACRET

Doc stood, walked his Blackberry back to his backpack and then returned to the seat across from Adam.

"A very important person in Washington?" Adam joked while fidgeting with his fingers.

"I actually think he's in Maryland right now." Doc reached across and steadied Adam's hands. "Relax — I'm here to help you."

"And, to help yourself and your friends — the military."

Nodding, Dr. Menke sat back in the seat. "Our interests are only with the security of the nation. It's nothing personal. The ends are not power or money for their own sake. It's about the protection and the preservation of our country — of our way of life."

Adam sneered, just a little, "At any cost."

"No," Doc was firm, "There are definite limits. But, there are also acceptable sacrifices that can be, must be, made. You live in the BVI Adam, but I'm sure you are familiar with the increasing threats facing the United States. With the increasing commitment of traditional military assets abroad, we've had to develop other means of protecting our borders."

"MK6Cs?"

"Among other programs, yes."

"Why me? Why do you need *me* at this point in time?"

"Because of the work you did at MIT and Woods Hole — your synthesis of high technology with a sophisticated, integrated approach to high-end dolphin brain functions and acoustics. That work was well beyond where your older peers, even beyond where Dr. Lykes was going. Because of where you've taken it — monitoring even more body parameters with outdated, civilian technology — even with your limited resources at Dolphin Towne. Because of the sudden credibility you have with Dr. Nicely."

"You know the stress of my work at MIT drove me into the ground — into a nervous breakdown. My work at Dolphin Towne has flourished because of the atmosphere — because of Jasmine..."

"...and Jasmine's money." Doc moved to the edge of his seat. "She still doesn't get the Theta Wave Meditation Meld, does she?"

Adam's eyes widened and he said, "*You* know?"

Nodding, Doc's voice grew soft, but serious, "It's a clever technological ruse—very clever. But, way beyond the ethics of a serious researcher—of someone wanting to publish in *Marine Mammal Science*...way beyond the ethics of someone Jasmine Summers could continue to love." Sitting back again, Doc continued, "But, it's a ruse that could prove very useful to us. It's a ruse that Jasmine will never have to know about."

"I don't understand why you are doing this to me." Adam rocked back and forth in his seat--shaking. Doc didn't answer.

Adam forced the words out, "Go on."

"Dr. Nicely requested some sophisticated equipment—sensing equipment that can help monitor vital signs, heart rate, brain wave activity, communication...something that could focus on and monitor individual animals in the group."

"And the Navy...they have something like that—the prototypes you mentioned?"

"Oh no. We have no such equipment. We have people working on the design for the precursors, the pieces. We have some components, but no finished, functional product. We told Nicely we'd do our best."

"And that's where I come in."

"Initially we were going to send him the current technology—advanced hydrophones mostly—knowing that wouldn't do any of what he really wanted. Then, I got a close up look of what you've accomplished at Dolphin Towne...put that together with how blindly enthusiastic Dr. Nicely is to support your dream, then add the precursors, pieces and resources from the Navy Marine Mammal Program's development team..."

"And I create some cool-looking phony telemetry gear and some phony readings? You don't need me for that."

Doc shook his head, "Phony gear--no." Then, he nodded, "Phony readings? Maybe...*yes*—a potentially brilliant idea. Well, whichever it ends up being, we *do* need *you* for that. We need you precisely because Dr. Nicely wants so strongly to believe in you. I expect he will be blinded by his enthusiasm for you."

Adam took a deep breath and focused on the technical challenge, "That's a little more interesting, but I think it's manageable. If I have the right pieces I can at least create a sort of parabolic focusing device...I have some of my own transponders that I can cannibalize..." He bent over and started fumbling through one of his bags—taking a quick inventory. Sitting back up, he had more questions for Doc. "Obviously, if you want genuine gear, you want the genuine readings—real data from the dolphins and the environment."

"Yes--very perceptive." Doc smiled, "I think this just might work out."

"I *will* need to know what I'm covering—*and*, I'll need to know what you want him to see."

Rocking back again, Doc put his finger tips together, "You see, that's the quandary. *We* don't even know what we are covering. Some of my associates have an idea....but, I don't necessarily agree with their theory. So..." He looked up and directly into Adam's eyes, "So, I don't want to bias you with their speculation. I'm hoping your fresh eyes will discover what we need to cover." After a brief pause, Doc answered the second part of Adam's question, "As for what I want him to see...anything that is not uniform. I don't want any serious commonalities within the group--nothing that could point to a specific, causal relationship."

Adam's smile was weak, "I could do that, but..." He sat there looking at Dr. Menke—who was expecting more. Shaking his head slightly, Adam sat in silence. Doc waited.

Tears welled in Adam's eyes. As one slid down his cheek, he continued, "I...I can't...If ...if anyone...if anyone ever found out—if Jasmine...the dolphins...what's to happen to them? Will we save them or are they one of your acceptable sacrifices? Oh, shit...if Jasmine found out...Jasmine..." His voice faded and he closed his eyes.

Doc moved the edge of his seat—putting his face close to Adam. There was no one else in the passenger cabin, so his whisper was intended only for effect, "If Jasmine finds out you've actually created that subcutaneous chip...that you've inserted it into one of *her* dolphins...that you've lied about that *and* your farcical Meditation Meld..." Adam looked up with his red, wet eyes and Doc continued, "...you won't be welcome in her arms, in her bed, in

Dolphin Towne or anywhere in the marine mammal community again."

Sliding back into his seat, Doc asked again, "So? Will you do what I'm asking? Do we have a deal?"

Adam ran his fingers through his sweat-dampened hair, took a quick, shallow breath and nodded.

"Fine--it's settled. We'll have a lab set up for you at MacDill Air Force Base. All the equipment we have in development is already on its way. Make me a list of what else you might need. If there's something that you don't think exists yet, ask for it anyway. Once you get further along, you'll have full access to a helicopter and a boat—whatever you need--for testing."

"And..." There was serious stress—serious fear--in Adam's eyes.

"...and," Doc paused, "...and, if we can somehow save some of those dolphins in the process...well, that's a nice side benefit...something else to add to your resume."

Adam closed his eyes, "Something else to add to my stress."

"Yes, given the nature of the event, you will, of course, be under a time crunch—enormous stress to perform. *Enormous stress.* The difference is that this time, you will be generously rewarded...by all means we want to make it well worth your while."

Crossing his arms, Adam gave Dr. Menke a look that said, *Go on...*

"I think we can arrange a triumphant return to Jasmine and Dolphin Towne—albeit with special privileges and duties. You'll have access to advanced computing and the latest hardware and materials. You'll have a very liberal supplementary budget. In return, you will be expected to do some work for us—say, developing the next generation MK6Chip for example. You'll also be expected to work with our development people on special projects."

Doc fell silent for a moment, but feeling the emotional surge of being on a roll—of all the pieces seeming to fall into place—he continued, "Of course, you will be expected to maintain the façade of scientific advancement via Jasmine's funding—continuing the reasonable real-world development of your telemetry tools and behavioral studies. You will publish in peer-reviewed journals. You'll be free to pursue any avenues you want—as long as you do our work when requested."

"And no one...no one will know what I've really done in Tampa or what I'll really be working on at Dolphin Towne?"

"She'll never know. I promise." Doc knew Adam was most concerned about Jasmine.

Adam reached next to the seat and pulled out his laptop and a legal pad. He looked at Dr. Menke and then across the plane to Doc's other seat. "I have to get started."

Content and excited to have Adam's commitment to his plan, Aldo Menke shuffled back to his seat and his Blackberry and started sending a series of high priority messages.

Chapter 60

Roland Summers Marine Mammal Rehabilitation Facility
Galveston, Texas

At one minute to one, Angela walked up behind the bank of microphones carefully placed to highlight the rehabilitation tanks and the teams working on the live dolphins. It was quite a show, with all the major networks—including Summers Media's Global Report—and cameras and microphones set up to capture what was going on in the tanks as well as what was happening up front.

Angela walked up to the director of the Caldwell Aquarium. "Hi, Angela. I'll do a very quick introduction and then let you make your statement."

Nodding, Angela stepped to the side and took it all in. She grinned—knowing full well they'd all be disappointed.

Angela looked at her watch—1:08. Dr. Hendriks was being anything but brief. He bragged about the Caldwell Aquarium and their leadership as a marine mammal rehabilitation facility and droned on and on about the generous endowment of the Summers Foundation that made the construction and continuing operation possible. Impatient, she looked over the edge of the closest tank. She spotted Shari and Bryan in the tank working with Pirate. Angela smiled—pleased with herself for remembering their names. A heavy tap on the shoulder brought her back to the press conference.

"Dr. Angela Clarke, National Director of Marine Mammal Health and Stranding."

Stepping to the podium, Angela nodded to the director, "Thank you, Dr. Hendriks. And, thank you, members of the press for taking the time to be here." Placing her notes on the lectern, she continued, "I'm going to make a statement and then I will have a limited time…" She looked at her watch, "…ten minutes, to take your questions. Please hold your questions until I have completed my statement."

"The Office of Protected Resources, National Marine Fisheries Service, is currently managing two mass strandings of *Tursiops truncatus* — bottlenose dolphins — one in Virginia Beach, Virginia and the one here in Galveston, Texas.

"First, let me be very clear--mass strandings of this nature are unprecedented. Typical mass stranding events take place over several days — sometimes weeks — and involve far fewer animals. These two events are unique in that the animals beached on a single day and, in that the numbers are extraordinarily high.

"Now, Virginia Beach…" Emphasizing the severity of the winter storm and its impact on the management of the event, Angela outlined the exemplary work of the Navy team and the status of the carcasses at the Virginia Aquarium. Her presentation was cut and dry — simple facts, no emotion, and no speculation.

"Because of my more direct, on-site involvement here in Galveston, and because we managed to examine almost all of the beached carcasses, I can give you a few more details. But, first the basics…" Angela reviewed the numbers, the progress on the necropsies, and the status of the live animals.

"At this point in our investigation we have no strong leads as to what may have caused these unusual mortality events. The hope is that the pathological examination of the blood and tissue samples will reveal something that will help." Again, she presented simple facts, no emotion, and no speculation.

"We currently have no evidence of any connection between the two events. We have no evidence of a connection between these events and what is currently going on in Tampa Bay."

Angela could see the restless chatter erupt amongst the reporters. She held up her hand, "Please…please let me continue."

The crowd quieted and she went on.

"Tampa. We were alerted yesterday morning…" Everyone had now seen the Summers Media video footage and read the theories based on Kurt's speculation, but Angela stuck to her "script"—noting the high-profile researchers—Dr. Menke and Dr. Nicely—that were involved, the help of the Navy, Coast Guard and the Florida Fish and Wildlife Conservation Commission. She outlined her action plan and what was currently happening on the water. "Believe me when I say, we are doing everything humanly possible to save those animals. I have already put a preliminary plan in place. That will be modified based on information from our experts now arriving on the scene. And, following this press conference, I will be flying to Tampa to manage the operation myself."

Angela folded the sheets of legal paper with her notes in half and held them behind her back. "Finally, the National Marine Fisheries Service wants to thank all of those that have contributed to our efforts in Galveston, Virginia Beach, and now in Tampa—we could not manage these events without the help of local agencies and volunteers."

Looking at her watch, Angela took a deep breath, "Okay…10 minutes only—questions?"

Egmont Key, Tampa Bay, FL

Dr. Robin Nicely sat inside the Navy command vessel with his laptop open and tapped into the boat's satellite antenna. Lt. Commander Medlin, Master Chief Samson, Ensign Ramirez and Seaman Cuello also stood looking at the screen. They were watching Angela's press conference—live from Galveston.

Bored by Angela's dry and unemotional delivery, Seaman Cuello just had to comment, "Serious…a serious ice queen."

Puffed up by all the *hoo-yah* on board, Robin stood up and walked the two steps towards Cuello. Moving three inches from the SEAL's face, Robin spoke softly, firmly, "I assure you Cuello, she is no fucking ice queen."

The sailor took a step back and apologized, "No offense intended, Dr. Nicely, sir. I didn't know…"

Robin finished the seaman's sentence, "…that she was my fiancée?" Sternly, Robin stuck out his hand to shake—Cuello reciprocated and they clasped for an uncomfortably long time. Robin smiled and, while still holding the ensign's hand tightly, continued, "Professional, seaman. Let's just call her professional. Outside of her job, she is very *different*. Let's leave it at that." After another hard look in the eye, Cuello nodded and Robin let go. Turning to Medlin, he asked, "Now, what did I miss?"

"Seems Dr. Clarke's on her way here after the press conference. Dr. Nicely, maybe you should wait to defend her honor in person."

The team—excluding Cuello—laughed hard. Robin pouted. Medlin walked over and put his hand on the civilian's shoulder. "C'mon, we wouldn't rib you if we didn't think you could take it—if we didn't like you."

Robin regained his posture, laughed and moved to watch the screen again. But, he was actually staring through the monitor and thinking—that was the first time he had called Angela his fiancée.

At the press conference, Angela deftly answered a reporter trying to give credence to Kurt's conspiratorial connections between the admiral, Dr. Menke, Dr. Hamilton, the SEALs and the, now lost, metallic cylinder. "I can assure you that Rear Admiral Collins, Dr. Aldo Menke, Dr. Jake Hamilton and SEAL Team 4 are only connected in their quest to go above and beyond—to do everything possible—to find any answers with regard to the strandings in Texas and Virginia Beach…and, to do everything humanly possible to save the lives of those dolphins in Tampa. As for the world's leading expert on dolphin social ecology, Dr. Robin Nicely, and myself…" The camera zoomed in on Angela's sly, almost playful smile, "…well…after dealing with his own mass stranding in Mozambique over the last two days, an exhausted Dr. Nicely flew to Tampa on a moment's notice and is now evaluating the situation. So...our personal relationship has its advantages."

Laughter spread across the press conference and the deck of the Navy boat.

When the laughter subsided, Angela had the final word, "Thank you all for coming. I will have another briefing in Tampa once I assess the situation. Thank you for coming." Smiling, she walked away from the podium.

Each member of the MSOT passed Dr. Nicely and patted him on the back. Robin closed the laptop, tucked it back in its waterproof case and climbed up the boat's tower with Lt. Commander Medlin. Medlin caught Nicely's eye, raised his chin and nodded to the northeast—the first boats from small boat team were arriving to enforce the expanded the perimeter.

Chapter 61

NOAA GS-5, Somewhere Between Tortola and Tampa

Adam sat with his laptop, completing a list of equipment and materials he would need to do as Dr. Menke asked. He had some electronic equipment with him, but would need access to things he could only imagine the military would have. Creating his own names for these things—and describing them in detail—Adam completed the list. Using a FEW-modified version of a Navy encryption program that Doc had provided, he emailed the list to his new "handler." He felt the littlest of thrills at being involved in something secret, something big—until he thought about Jasmine. Looking over at Dr. Menke, Adam closed his laptop.

The vibration in his Blackberry brought Dr. Menke's head up from a brief nap. Still a little groggy, he looked quizzically at the email alert—it was Adam's list. After quickly scrolling through the items, Doc forwarded the list to Admiral Collins. Then, he grabbed a thick file from his backpack and walked over to Adam.

"Thank you for the list. I've sent it on. Most of it should be there by the time we arrive. Eventually, you'll get everything you've asked for."

Adam sighed—puffing up his cheeks and blowing the breath out pursed lips. He looked down at his closed laptop and answered, "So will you."

Stroking the brown folder in his lap, Doc sat in momentary silence. He closed his eyes.

In the silence, Adam looked up—his eyes moved to the file. "Doc?"

With a sigh, Doc opened his eyes and forced a smile. He dropped the file in Adam's lap. Stuck to the outside of the file were several stickers. One said "top secret;" the second said "DARPA"—the acronym for the Defense Advanced Research Projects Administration. The other obvious sticker was from the Navy Marine Mammal Program. "Don't open it just yet." Looking at his watch, Doc continued, "We don't have much time before we land…and you won't have much spare time once we get there…" Doc's grin was still forced and uncomfortable, "…but, look this over when your brain needs a little breather from the task at hand. It's a good faith gesture on my part…to…to show you the type of project you'll be working on in the future. Just check it out when you get the chance."

Adam nodded. Doc looked away, got up and moved back to his own seat.

Even in his somewhat weakened emotional state, Adam sensed Dr. Menke's discomfort—the world-renowned marine mammal veteran wouldn't quite look him in the eye. Wondering if there was something more to the file labeled "Wendall" sitting in his lap, he made a mental note to at least skim it before they landed.

NOAA GS-3, Somewhere Between Galveston and Tampa

"Thanks for having the jet ready. You're support has always made my job easier." Angela looked out window at the grey winter waters of the Gulf of Mexico and sighed through her cell phone.

Jake heard the sigh, "Tired? Dr. Angela Clarke is tired?"

She sighed again, but couldn't leave it at that, "Not now. This is all too serious for teasing now...now that the press is hounding us. I always sympathized with alleged criminals when they were tried in the media before they ever got to court for a fair trial. Now, I can empathize instead. I feel like we are on trial before the whole world."

"We *are*...but I know you can handle it. That is why you are where you are—*National Director of Marine Mammal Health and Stranding*. You can handle it."

Angela closed the window shade and pulled out her legal pad. "I know...now, you called me remember? Or, was this just a pep-talk? I appreciate it, but..."

"Dr. Menke is on his way to Tampa. We thought it best he get there ASAP—no delay, no matter how big his benefactor..."

"That's good, but it seems like there's something else you want to tell me." Angela retraced and darkened the numbers for the action items on her legal pad—waiting for an answer.

"Menke is bringing Adam Reich with him. He believes he can be of some..."

Shit! Angela, surprised at not being consulted on the final decision, interrupted, "Doc is bringing Adam Reich with him? Dr. Menke is already bringing Adam Reich? I know I mentioned the idea to you—Robin wanted him--but this guy hasn't done any serious research since he had some kind of nervous breakdown at MIT...what, five or six years ago? He left his professor without even a phone call—uncalled for...unreliable and unprofessional."

"Honestly, I'm with you. I don't know what they both see in this kid. The information I have on him...well...I agree with your assessment—emotionally unstable and an unconventional scientist at best."

Angela sighed, "Scientist? *Scientist* is a word I'd use very loosely."

"Yet, two men we both respect seem to think he can be an important part of this. Doc thinks he can magically create the kind of gear that your Dr. Nicely wants to monitor the dolphins. Doc thinks he might offer some fresh perspectives—some creative problem solving—since he's never worked a stranding. So, I'm going to defer to them and support their decision."

"I suppose I'll have something to say..."

"While you were at the press conference I also ran this quickly by Admiral Collins. He agreed that Menke and Nicely—Robin— might be on to something...that...he agreed that maybe some outside thinking...some fresh eyes..."

Angela doodled in the margins of her pad—writing the word *admiral* with a flourish. "Seems I'm outranked and outnumbered. I suppose Robin and...shit!" That one came out for Jake to hear.

"You haven't called him, have you?" Jake knew how focused Angela could be when she was working—how everything personal took a back seat to the task at hand. "You haven't called him since the hospital or the press conference, have you?"

"I'm nodding. Yes and yes." Then, she shook her head in disbelief and lost herself in her thoughts, *How could I neglect...someone who barely calls me? Someone I only see every couple of months? Someone who moves me like no other?* Angela smiled.

The director brought her out of it, "Go. Call me when you are on site and have been briefed."

"Thank you."

"Go."

Angela hung up and dialed Robin. She rolled the idea of Adam Reich around in her mind until the phone stopped ringing.

"Hello."

"Robin! I just got off the phone with Director Hamilton and he said that Doc is bringing Adam Reich from Dolphin Towne…that you agreed he might be helpful…I didn't think we were…"

He was rarely rude to Angela, but Robin interrupted, "Right, love. I'm guessing that head check-up went your way." Angela could tell that he was pissed. "Fucking nice of you to let me know." She could hear him move the phone away from his mouth and could faintly hear "Shit! Dumbkop." Robin moved the phone back to his mouth. "I'm so sorry, love. I know you had a lot to squeeze into your last few hours in Texas. But, you could have at least sent a text or something to the man who loves you."

"I love you too!" Angela was beaming, but realized she needed to get down to business as well. "Now, Adam Reich?"

"What can I say, love? He has the technological skills and the background in acoustics, communication and brainwaves that is somewhat lacking in our other assets—Dr. Menke…me…you."

"But, he has no advanced degree, hasn't worked with anyone reputable in years and is likely an emotional mess. How can you…?"

Robin didn't wait for her to finish, "Call it a hunch. Call it convenience. But, from what I've read about him…well…"

"Well, I think you are a sentimental softy — a romantic. But, I assumed you would have pictured yourself as the knight in shining armor and not some has-been or never-was."

"I really think he can contribute. Dr. Menke thinks he can contribute. For this situation, we need all the critical and creative thinking we can get. Trust me on this — I've read about him. I've read his manuscript. I'd rather have him than the holier-than-thou Dr. Harvey Lykes any day. And, to extend your analogy…I think this effort is going to require the entire Round Table, not just your favorite knight."

Momentarily distracted by strong talk from the man that she loved, Angela eventually focused on and digested what he had to say and not how he was saying it. "Okay. I suppose Doc has a plan for our prodigy?"

"They're setting up a lab at the air force base in Tampa as we speak. Dr. Menke thinks Adam can have something functional — some sort of parabolic directional receiver that will be able to provide a variety of information in a day — maybe less. Supposedly, the parts and equipment are already arriving."

"I hope we have a day."

"Me too. So, are you okay with this? Okay with Adam?"

"Two men I respect...two scientists I respect...more than just about anyone... and Admiral Collins concurs as well...Director Hamilton was reluctant, but deferred to the admiral...I guess I'm okay with it." Angela relaxed enough to recline her seat and kick off her shoes.

"Good. Now, let's move on. I want your permission to take a boat into the group. The Navy just deployed a new rigid inflatable with a nearly silent electric motor. It's no dinghy, but again, it is silent running. I just want a closer look—see if there are any patterns...circulation within the larger group, groups within the group, obvious dominant animals...get an idea of the speed of the general movement—stuff we can't pull out of the aerial videos. I'll be careful. I really feel like I just need to get in the mix."

"You're the expert. If you think you can get close—into the group—without sending them all into the beach somewhere, by all means do it."

Robin sighed heavily, "Honestly...I don't know anything about a behavior like this. I don't know how they'll react. But, I just can't sit here on my hands anymore."

Angela didn't like the despondent Robin, so she helped him through, "By all means, get out there. Maybe you'll see something. If not, maybe bringing in Adam Reich will open our eyes and ears to what's happening." Chuckling to herself, she realized he was right about Adam, "Thanks for convincing me, ever so subtly, that it was a good idea to have him here."

"No problem, love. See you in..."

"Two hours, I hope. See you soon."

Angela reclined her seat more—wondering if they should have brought in a few more well-respected experts. After tucking a blanket around her legs—she composed a generic email and included Dr. Lykes from Woods Hole, Murray Ostend from the University of California at Santa Cruz and Tamara Karlstaad from the Scandinavian Oceans Project in Oslo on the "to" list. But, before she hit "send," second thoughts danced in her mind. Instead, she hit "delete," closed her laptop and her eyes.

Chapter 62

TEXMAM Office, Galveston, Texas

A head poked through the half-open door, "Mr. Braun?"

"Yes, Kurt. You call me..." Kurt hesitated; Dafoe looked much younger than his reported 26 years. "You must be Jackson Dafoe."

"Yes, I really am 26 years old. I've been with Summers Media for four years—ever since getting my Master's at Columbia. Thank you for seeing me. I know you must be very busy."

Kurt smiled apologetically and motioned for his guest to sit. "Busy, but always time to help get the story out—to get this story out. I'm wrapping up most of my involvement in this anyway. The necropsies are almost done. The live animal rehab is out of my hands...the data analysis is out of my hands."

"And, the data?" The question from Dafoe was meant to be leading.

Sliding a box from his desk into his lap, Kurt paused—uncertain whether his motive was vengeance or truth. Deciding what really mattered were the dolphins, he picked up the box and put it into Jackson's outstretched arms. "Copies of the data are now in your hands. Make sure it gets to the right people."

Dafoe sat with the box now in his lap. "You have Dr. Clarke's permission to make this material public?"

"Let's just say it came from 'an anonymous source at TEXMAM and get it into the hands of some top scientists — Harvey Lykes at Woods Hole, Murray Ostend at UC Santa Cruz — anyone."

Dafoe agreed, "I will. I'll make sure..." But before he could finish there was a knock on the door frame.

"Kurt?" Shari and Brian appeared in the doorway and saw Jackson. "Sorry, we don't want to interrupt any..."

Smiling, Kurt waved them both in. "Nonsense. Shari and Brian, meet Mr. Jackson Dafoe."

The three shook hands while Kurt continued, "Mr. Dafoe is a Pulitzer Prize-winning journalist from Summers Media in New York. He's here to find out more about our stranding — about all the strandings."

"It's an honor, Mr. Dafoe." Shari was a little awed. Brian stood just behind her and to the side — he was still shy around new people.

"Jackson, Shari and Brian were the first of my volunteers on the beach last week and are now intimately involved in the rehab of TT18 — *Pirate*."

Jackson looked at Shari, "200 dolphins — that must have been pretty overwhelming."

"207 dolphins, and..." She reached back and Brian grabbed her hand. "...and, we managed--good training."

Looking at Brian, Jackson asked, "How are Pirate and his friends doing today?"

Brian took a step forward and smiled. "Pirate is doing much better, sir--especially better since he opened his bad eye on Thursday night. He's now taking all the food and fluids and..."

Shari put her hands firmly on her son's shoulders, stopping him in mid-sentence, "Brian, let's let Kurt and Mr. Dafoe get back to work." Looking over at Kurt, she continued, "Sorry to disturb you again. We just wanted to let you know that we'll be in for our usual office shift tomorrow."

"Thanks. I can certainly use the help with data entry."

"Nice to have met you, Mr. Dafoe. I hope you can help the dolphins." Shari and Brian turned and walked out.

Jackson looked at Kurt.

Kurt understood the unstated question and answered, "Single mom and her son—two of my best volunteers. They did an exemplary job on the beach that morning. Great mom—great kid."

"Nice human interest, but that's not my gig. But, is it okay if you give me her contact info and I have someone else from Summers follow up?" Kurt nodded and Dafoe looked down at the box of files and rifled through the data sheets. "Ummm...this is nothing I can make sense of—anything outstanding? Any common links between the animals?"

Kurt sighed, "They stranded on the same stretch of beach in a single mass at the same time—unprecedented for their species. Um...and this was very consciously omitted from the press conference--there were only three mature males in the animals here— some male calves. Mostly, sexually mature females and female calves. Devastating to the population." Kurt closed his eyes. "That's really all we have."

"Not much to go on." Jackson frowned, "Do you have anything more than what you told me over the phone? Any hard evidence of a cause?" The reporter was unhappy.

"I'm not a scientist. I can't…"

"No, I believe your degree is in the History of Science — specializing in science and mythology. *Mythology.* I hope there is something more to your theory--to your tenuous connections — to *this* myth *you've* created, Mr. Braun."

"There is…and, I assumed you would…" Kurt closed his eyes, and his voice weakened and faded.

Jackson Dafoe stood up quickly and tucked the box under his arm, "I can see why your credibility is constantly in question."

"Just make sure the data…"

Turning on his way out the door, Dafoe cut him off for the last word, "I'll make sure someone else sees the data. I'm also on my way to talk to Dr. Edwards at the aquarium's rehab center. I have to get something out of this trip."

Kurt pulled his legs up to his chest as he swiveled his chair back to the desk. He tucked his head down, closed his eyes to block out the world and rocked.

Chapter 63

MacDill Air Force Base, Tampa, Florida

"Dr. Menke. Mr. Reich. Welcome to MacDill Air Force Base — home of the Southern Command. This way please." Ensign Jefferson motioned towards a waiting black SUV.

"Mr. Reich, Dr. Menke requested that I get you to your new laboratory ASAP. So, we'll stop there first. Dr. Menke, after we get Mr. Reich settled I'll get you a helicopter ride to the site."

Doc closed Adam's door and climbed into the front seat. "Thank you, Ensign Jefferson, we appreciate your help."

The vehicle approached a small complex of single story buildings surrounded by a double row of high razor wire-topped fencing. Jefferson stopped at a gate manned by two marines — there he passed one his ID while the other used a portable device for a retina scan. Dr. Menke did the same. "Ensign Jefferson and Dr. Menke, you are clear to proceed with Mr. Reich to the security office. He is your responsibility until he is scanned, finger printed and badged. Thank you."

Jefferson rolled up the window and looked over at Doc, "They just don't let anyone in here, fellas — at the security office you'll get finger printed, photographed, have a retinal scan and get issued an ID badge. Then we'll get Mr. Reich to his new digs."

Following the security necessities, Jefferson led Adam and Dr. Menke to the laboratory in Building 6. Their ID badges got them through two more guards and the first door. A retinal scan got them into Adam's laboratory.

Adam walked in and he stammered, "Doc..." His mouth dropped open and he shook his head. Trotting over to the table he picked up something that looked like a battery. He moved to the left and picked up the tools for doing micro-soldering. Everything he requested had been delivered. "I didn't think it was possible..."

Doc held up his hand and looked at Jefferson, "Ensign, would you mind leaving us for a moment?" Jefferson, nodded, exited the laboratory and Doc continued, "Everything is possible. Getting this equipment here while we were still in the air wasn't easy — but the people with whom I'm associated thrive on doing what is not easy. You have the best in the world — in the world — at your disposal."

Adam sat on the rolling work stool. Doc came over and put his hand on Adam's shoulder, "You have a lot of work to do. I know you've already got something worked up in your head..." Adam nodded. "...I don't need to remind you of the time frame we're working with...we need top work and we need it more than fast. The timeframe..."

"Immediately. Now. As soon as possible. I understand the gravity of the situation." Adam moved Doc's hand from his shoulder. "If I need anything..."

"Here is a list of numbers and emails — mine, Lt. Commander Medlin — the head of the Navy teams on site — and Ensign Jefferson. We're to be your only contacts for now. Understood?"

"Yes, sir."

"Good. Now, I'll have Jefferson come back in to take your orders for food and drink. You...you make me not regret bringing you here. Impress me. Impress Dr. Nicely. Impress the world...and do it quickly."

Adam didn't respond. After Doc left the room, Adam opened his laptop bag—pulling out his computer and his notepad. He compared the sketch on his pad with the computer-aided rendering on the screen and nodded—ready to get to work.

Chapter 64

Editorial Conference Room, Summers Media
New York, New York

Josh had temporarily moved into the Editorial Conference Room — the multiple high-definition screens made monitoring the output of his news division a little easier than sitting at his desk.

The big screen still held the satellite image of Tampa Bay. The screens to the left displayed a sampling of Summers' TV stations — Global Report 24/7, the Tampa Bay affiliate, New York, and Los Angeles. Two other stations were up — Classic TV was showing re-runs of *Flipper* and GEOTV — their science station--was cranking up a hastily scheduled "Dolphin Week". The screens to the right held images of six Summers websites — four news sites and two science sites.

Josh was pleased with the initial response of his team — the world was alerted. Now, he wanted to get at the meat of the story and looked down the table at his staff. "Carlye? Becca? What are we finding?"

Becca was preoccupied with the fax machine, but Carlye sat next to Josh and looked up at him, "Nothing much, yet — but, everyone is digging hard. We've had a few setbacks even — there are still no flights into the Virginia Beach area and apparently Dolphin Towne has stopped taking new guests for the moment."

Josh drifted off in thought for a moment and then came back with a sigh. "Reservation or not — accepting guests or not — get a reporter to Tortola now. I want her poking around the island — asking questions and ready to go if we get her in." Josh got up and walked to the head of the table. "How about Mozambique?"

"Case closed. The talk on the professional message boards is about a..." She looked quickly at her notes, "...*morbillivirus* epidemic — seems it was pretty obvious from the start. It was a mess, but no rumors of conspiratorial links to what is happening in the states."

"And..." Josh searched his mind for a name, "...and, that Dr. Nicely — the one who was in charge there and is now on his way to Tampa?"

Carlye laughed, "Well, it wouldn't even make a bad tabloid story."

"Yes? What?"

"Okay — Dr. Nicely and Dr. Angela Clarke have a long-term, long-distance relationship."

"Right — not even a bad tabloid story. What else in Tampa?"

"Obviously, we still have our video feed."

"That's going to get stale fast — already has."

"I know." Carlye sighed. "What I don't know is how long the FCC or NASA or the Pentagon will tolerate that low of a geosynchronous orbit — it's not normal procedure. But, it's what gets us the best image." Following a momentary blank stare, Carlye continued, "We have assets in Tampa, but nobody's talking — not at the federal, state or local agencies. They are all deferring...well...to Dr. Clarke..."

"And..." Josh drummed his fingers on the table.

"And, Dr. Clarke is in route to Tampa—in the air and unavailable at the moment. Not that it matters—her news conference this afternoon was..."

"I saw it. She's protecting her bureaucratic ass—someone else's ass...doesn't matter. I think politicians are pulling her strings." Josh finished, got up and started to circle the table. Carlye just watched. When he got close to the fax, Becca held up her hand. Josh stopped.

"I just received this from Dafoe." Becca shoved a handful of papers in his face. "Over the last 20 minutes...600...at least 600 pages of data sheets from the Galveston stranding. He also mentioned something about most of the Texas dolphins being females and calves. Seems this was all he could squeeze out of his anonymous source--Kurt Braun."

"Kurt Braun!" Carlye jumped out of her chair and walked over to Josh and Becca. "Braun and Dr. Clarke...it was some time ago..." She looked at her notes, "...seven years ago they were a couple. They weren't married, but they lived together. Apparently, when Nicely came into the picture, they split up." Shrugging her shoulders, she laughed and looked at Josh, "Makes it a better tabloid story, no?"

Josh put up a wait-a-minute finger and turned back to Becca. "Data sheets...got some experts you can get them to?" Becca nodded. Josh smiled. "Okay, make it so. Make sure they also know about the females and calves—and, make it urgent."

Chapter 65

Egmont Key, Tampa Bay, Florida

"Dr. Menke, sir. It's an honor to welcome aboard such a distinguished colleague of Admiral Collins."

"Thank you, Lt. Commander. I've heard great things about you and your team—um…both for your work here and in Virginia Beach. Enjoying the warmer weather?"

"Yes, sir." Medlin looked to Dr. Nicely on his right.

Dr. Menke smiled. "Ahh…Dr. Nicely, it's been some time—you look well."

"Quite the ride in, eh Dr. Menke…?" Robin looked up at the departing helicopter.

"Aldo or Doc—Dr. Menke sounds too formal for someone who knows Angela so well."

Robin tried to hold back his smile, "As you wish--Doc. It has been a while, but I'm glad that you are here—and, that you managed to coerce Adam Reich to join us."

"Coerce? Once I mentioned your name, the lad was after *me* to tag along. Seriously, though…it had been more than a year since I had been to Dolphin Towne and…well, the work he's been doing there is quite amazing. I don't doubt that the work he'll do here will impress you even more than that *Marine Mammal Science* manuscript of his you've been reading."

"When is Adam coming out…?"

Menke shook his head and put up his hand, "I figured it best to get him started on the equipment we'll need to pull information from that group." Doc looked over toward the swimming dolphins. "We've managed to get most of what was on his list of materials and some things that weren't--it's nice having some friends in high military places. No one wants this event to end like the others—no one."

"I'm with you there. I've seen too much dolphin death this week. But, do you think he'll be able to put something together that quickly?"

"I'm betting on it. He already has a schematic rendered on his computer. I'm betting that with the data he can collect for us, we'll be able to solve this thing and save those animals—hopefully without Angela's rescue plan."

"A storybook ending? I think we'll still need her plan." Looking perplexed, Robin continued, "I was out there...amongst them...for an hour earlier today. It's like nothing I've seen before— nothing. There's definitely a mass circulation pattern. All of them are moving counter clockwise at roughly the same slow speed—about five kilometers an hour...pitiful for them."

Doc closed his eyes, paused, and then reopened them. "Anything else?"

"Yes, there seem to be smaller sub groups—10-15 animals in each. It's not something that just anyone would pick up—it's very, very subtle." Robin looked out towards the group of dolphins. "I've spent significant time observing long-beaked common dolphins off the South African coast. They travel in pods from 50....well, up to 1000 animals, but also have distinct smaller groups. The groupings here aren't that distinct, but that training helped me know what to look for..." His mind obviously drifted for a moment—then he turned and looked directly at Dr. Menke. "About a third of the animals looked to be calves. That may have been the most stunning thing—many of the animals looked less than...maybe two years old."

Doc shook his head. "I wonder if the adults were mostly female? All but three of the sexually mature animals at Galveston were female—the rest were calves..." This time *he* looked out over the water, "I haven't really had time to think about that and whether it could be significant. Angela was going to..."

Robin cut in, "She never mentioned that to me—never mentioned the preponderance of females and calves. But, if there are that many calves in this group, I'd assume—she'd hate me doing that—that most of the adults are female. Shit, that could be..."

"Significant—yes. She was going to do a literature search and then there was the accident and then the call from Tampa."

"And then the press conference." Dr. Nicely just stood there perplexed, "Literature search? I'm the expert on dolphin social ecology—on dolphin communities."

Doc turned back and looked Robin in the eye. "So, now you know. And...?"

Robin's stare returned to the group of dolphins. "Devastating for the *Tursiops* population in Texas." He shook his head. "Nothing comes to mind immediately. I just don't get it. I've never..."

Reassuringly, Doc grabbed Robin's shoulder and gave a little shake, "You're tired. We're overwhelmed. *But*, we have some of the best marine mammal minds in the world working together now."

Robin smiled, "And, one more on the way."

Funny, Doc mused to himself, *I never thought of Angela in quite that way*. But, so as to not offend Robin, he agreed, "Of course, when she arrives the team will be complete."

Medlin cleared his throat, turned and pointed to the RIB pulling alongside. "As per your request, Dr. Menke — a boat for you and Mr. Reich." Medlin looked at three members of his team. "Ramirez, Taylor, and Lopez, will be at your service."

"Thank you again, Lt. Commander. Very efficient. Everything the admiral has said about you is true. You set a fine example — your father would be proud. Keep up the excellent work."

To hide his mild snickering at all the smoke being blown up his ass by Dr. Menke, Medlin turned around to face his men and answered with a hearty, "Yes, sir!" He moved to help his men transfer their gear bags and bins and wondered why the admiral and Dr. Menke felt it was so important to keep bringing his long-dead father into this.

Dr. Menke turned back to Robin. "You and Angela will still be based here — with the radios and phones we can stay in constant contact." Doc looked at his watch. "Hmm…she shouldn't be too far behind me." He smiled and whispered, "Give her a hug for me, Robin." With that, Doc climbed aboard the other boat and they slowly pulled away — taking up station at the west end of the group.

Chapter 66

Egmont Key, Tampa Bay, Florida

Lt. Commander Medlin looked up at the woman being lowered from the hovering helicopter and laughed. He shouted over the sound of the rotors, "Man, Dr. Nicely, it's not every guy that gets an angel special delivered via the US Navy."

Robin just shook his head.

Up on the boat's tower, Seaman Suarez guided Angela to the deck.

With the harness and helmet finally removed, Angela took a loving couple of steps towards Robin and then stopped cold. He had taken a couple of steps back. Angela gave him a little sneer, wondering if all the testosterone being thrown around on the boat was what cheated her out of even a stiff hug and a little kiss.

Ignoring the sneer, he introduced Angela to Medlin, "Lt. Commander Richard Medlin, I'd like you to meet Dr. Angela Clarke." Medlin stuck out his hand and Angela reciprocated for a quick shake.

"Nice to finally meet you, Dr. Clarke." Medlin smiled.

"Likewise, Lt. Commander — after all the telephone conversations, it's nice to put the voice with a face."

Robin nodded and continued updating Angela, "Dr. Menke is on one of the other larger boats — one of the RIBs...uh, rigid inflatables. He'll be over shortly so that we can talk face to face. I figured you'd want an update and to modify your action plan accordingly."

Angela sighed, but figured he was just being professional. She looked at her watch, "When?"

Robin pointed out from the port side, "Here he comes now."

Adam's Lab, MacDill Air Force Base, Tampa

"Thanks, Jefferson!" Adam had been working since he and Dr. Menke had arrived. He was hungry and thirsty.

"Not a problem." The ensign loaded the refrigerator with a variety of subs, wraps and cookies from Subway, some fruit, a six-pack of Mountain Dew and a four-pack of Red Bull. He brought a cold can of the energy drink and a bag of tortilla chips to Adam at the work table.

"Awesome." Adam chugged half the Red Bull. "New 12 ounce cans? I can handle that...I haven't had one of these in more than three years—imagine—but I can handle that now. Work, work, work!"

"Okay, kid. I'll leave you to it..." Jefferson glanced over Adam's shoulder at a large metallic dish, "...whatever *it* is."

"Top secret, ensign—top secret!" Adam saluted and laughed.

Jefferson shot him a serious scowl. "This is serious stuff. Our MSOT wouldn't be here if this was not something with national security implications. So, I suggest you get your brain and your fingers back to work. I'm sure Admiral Collins brought you here because you have some special skill that he needs. Now, get..."

Jefferson stopped when Adam stood and asked, "Admiral Collins? Who the hell is Admiral Collins? And, what's an *emsot*?"

"Just get back to work. Let me know if you need anything else—food, drink, whatever." Jefferson headed for the door.

"How about information about this Admiral Collins?"

Jefferson shook his head and just kept walking out the door.

Day Six

Monday, February 24, 2008

Chapter 67

Operations Center, National Counterterrorism Center

Virginia

"Jenna!" Jenna Damne, the UEAR team leader, was sleeping — head down on her desk. Chuck Millard got up from his desk, thumped her on the back, and strongly whispered, "Jenna! Get up!"

"What the...?" But, as her eyes cleared and she could see the large monitor on the wall, she stopped the question and replaced it with an exclamation, "Shit! Holy shit!"

Millard smiled broadly, "Yes! Yes! That's what — CONCH is at it again! Off Maryland — heading for the mouth of Chesapeake Bay."

Jenna took a swig of cold coffee and frowned, "Okay, team — you know the drill. Only... it's not a drill. Confirm and communicate — start the process now! We need the appropriate operational assets in motion now!"

The team jumped at her commands. She had been right about the commendations from the President for their execution of the operational plan for the Texas intercept — they had made the team even more diligent and motivated. Looking at her watch — 0107 hours — she swallowed and dialed her secure line to the Director for National Intelligence.

"Director Shaw, I'm sorry about the hour--this is Jenna Damne from the National Counterterrorism..."

"Ms. Damne, I remember who you are and it is my job to be woken up in the middle of the night. Now, report."

Jenna sat back down at her desk, "Sir, I wanted to inform you that at 0107 hours—approximately one minute ago—the UEAR team commenced execution of an operational plan and intercept based on a CONCH verified threat—approximately 75 miles from the mouth of the Chesapeake Bay." She looked over her desk and tapped loudly—making a *what's up* gesture to Millard. He shot back a thumbs up and Damne continued, "Sir, we have assets moving into the area as we speak."

"Once again, well done. Pass my kudos to your team. Email me the preliminary data and operational plan. I'll brief the White House. Keep me informed. And, Ms. Damne, *never* mind the hour."

"Yes, sir."

With the operation in action, Jenna called the team to a quick meeting. She shared the director's compliment and added her own, before getting back to being serious, "Now that's two CONCH alerts within the last three days, people. I'd say we are likely within the window of imminent danger." Looking at the original Intelligence Estimate, she erred on the side of caution, "According to the IE, the hostiles have a minimum of three and a maximum of four similar vessels—so, it's likely that our job is not yet over. Stay the course..." picking up her coffee mug and holding it up for all to see, Jenna concluded, "...stay awake."

Chapter 68

Adam's Lab, MacDill Air Force Base, Tampa, Florida

Adam rolled back from the work table, pushed his safety goggles to the top of his head and stood. He nodded and strutted a circle around the table. A crooked smile took over half of his mouth and his eyes focused on the three pieces of hardware he had just completed. Nodding again—satisfied--he sat back on the stool and took out his cell phone.

"Adam? It's 6:30am, what can be…?"

"Doc! Doc! It went smoother than I ever could have imagined. Actually, it went just as I had visualized it would while sitting and sketching on the plane. It's amazing what you can do when you have the right tools, the right equipment, the right materials…"

"It's amazing what you'll continue to do with those resources. Well done. Now, I guess we need to get you a lift out here to do some tests."

"Easy. I need a couple more hours to weather-proof the gear. I can't afford to lose all this…to lose the time or the equipment to the salt water." Walking over to the refrigerator, Adam grabbed a 12-ounce Red Bull and a tofu scramble wrap. The tofu scramble wrap was a special request—Adam was beginning to miss Dolphin Towne's healthy, organic meals.

"When? When can we get you out here?"

There was a pause as Adam finished chugging his Red Bull and Doc got a little impatient, "Come on. When?"

Adam crushed the can and tossed it into a recycle bin, "Have my ride here at 11:30 — I'll be ready."

"11:30. Jefferson will be waiting for you. And, of course…again…very well done."

Hanging up and walking back to his work table, Adam sat fidgeting on his stool — caught in the buzz of his first success and a little too much caffeine. He was certain he'd impress Dr. Nicely with what he'd created. He was certain he could figure out what was causing the dolphins' abnormal behavior. He was certain that his hands were starting to shake, "Shit." But, he knew it was more than just the caffeine — it was Jasmine. He was beginning to realize that even if this all worked out and he triumphantly returned to Dolphin Towne, that he would never be able to look into Jasmine's gentle eyes the same way again. Dry-sobbing, he lowered his head into his hands.

Chapter 69

Little Island Park, Virginia Beach, Virginia

"Sun's up, surf's up—let's go! Time to get out of the car, dudes!"

Sitting in their full wetsuits, tucked under a down comforter, and looking at the snow still piled in the parking lot, Jesse and Lance failed to share Peter's enthusiasm for catching some waves. "No way. Let's go get some IHOP and then come back—it's only 34 degrees, man. It's going up to 50 later. Let's get outta here."

Peter ignored his friends and opened the door—the cold, damp air whacked him in the face, "Shit!" He jumped back in to the laughter of Lance and Jesse.

"Hardcore, Pete—hardcore." Lance laughed some more. "Hey, let's get some breakfast."

Stifling his laughter, Jesse expanded the argument, "Coffee, pancakes, let's hit the IHOP and come back when we're done. Turn this thing around and let's go. That storm is still churning offshore— the waves will be here."

Reluctantly, Pete agreed and started the car. While there were areas of the parking lot where the snow was obviously compacted by some kind of heavy vehicles, the plowed section of the parking lot was small—so, Pete had to pull forward and back several times to avoid the snow piles and maneuver the car back towards the entrance. Unfortunately, the fogged windows made it hard for him to see and he backed hard into one pile. "Shit! Car won't move! Now, we have to get out—let's go!"

The car had slipped over the edge of the parking lot—dropping one tire slightly into some soft snow at the base of a huge snow pile. Lance drove his feet deep into the pile to get a better footing to push the car.

"Whoa! There's something in the snow!" He pulled his legs out of the snow and started digging. "Shit! It's a body." Continuing to dig, he revealed a bit more. "It's a humongous fish tail!"

"That's no fish tail, dumb-ass—that's a dolphin tail. Holy shit!" Pete reached to the roof of the car, unstrapped his board and drove it into the soft snow around the tail—digging. The others were reluctant to use their boards that way, but helped with their gloved hands—now oblivious to the cold.

It warmed up as they dug, and the sun helped melt away some of the snow. In fifteen minutes of digging, the surfers had uncovered three dolphin carcasses. "Bad ass storm, huh?"

"I'll say. Way cool. Should we call someone? The aquarium?"

Jesse grabbed Pete's board and re-strapped it to the roof. "Let's look in the phone book at the IHOP. Let's go!"

Virginia Aquarium and Marine Science Center, Virginia Beach

Dr. Ed Bordon, Curator of Marine Mammals, couldn't believe what he was hearing. "What are you boys doing outside now? Surfing? The roads are barely passable and the temperature...you're nuts!"

"The waves were supposed to be eight to 12...shit...sorry...I mean, what about the dolphins?"

Bordon mouthed instructions to his veterinarian and then walked out of the room. "I'm just about to get started with necropsies on nine dolphins that came from that same site over the weekend…"

"From Little Island? Over the weekend? You're nuts! You were out here in that storm?"

"No way. Listen, there was a stranding. It wasn't made public because we didn't want anyone venturing out in the storm to catch a peek — too dangerous. We didn't even send our volunteers. The Navy brought the animals in for us. I guess they missed a couple…"

"Three. We dug up three. There might be more. But, we were cold and beat from digging in the snow. We're…okay, yeah table for three…we're at IHOP now, man. We just wanted to let someone know."

"Thanks. I'll…" Dr. Ed Bordon stopped — the call had ended — and walked back to the necropsy room. "Dr. Caruso, I'll have to excuse myself for a few more minutes — it seems three more carcasses have showed up under the melting snow at Little Island State Park. I shouldn't be too long."

"Anything for you to get out of cutting, Ed, I know."

"Absolutely." Bordon went to his office, made some calls and put his a much scaled-down version of his original recovery plan in motion. Slumping into his desk chair, he reluctantly made another call, "Dr. Clarke, I have some news."

Office of Admiral Collins, NOAA
Silver Spring, Maryland

Rear Admiral Collins paced around his desk and leaned on his large window — absorbing the chill and digesting the latest email from Dr. Menke. Menke wasted no time passing along information from Dr. Clarke about the three additional carcasses in Virginia Beach. He started planning for their recovery, but his thoughts were interrupted by his cell phone.

Back at his desk, Collins looked at the caller ID and answered, "Director Hamilton, good morning. It is a good morning, isn't it?"

"I just got a call from Dr. Clarke, sir. I have an update on the Virginia Beach stranding. It seems that some surfers discovered three new carcasses at the stranding site."

"New strandings?" The admiral feigned any new knowledge of the situation.

"No...no, sir. Apparently, they were under some big piles of snow — I know the Navy team plowed an area for their vehicles and a work area...maybe they inadvertently covered a few...in the near white out conditions it would have been... Anyway, a team from the aquarium is on its way to recover..."

"No! We need to..." The admiral didn't finish — instead, wandering briefly into his thoughts, he remembered that Medlin's team scanned for MK6C animals. There was no need to panic--the scan was negative. His team was careful and thorough — at least on that count. Regaining his composure, Collins continued, "Sorry. I had to take a moment to think it through. That sounds fine — I'm glad to see the Virginia Aquarium folks are on the ball. They can get through the snow okay? I mean, the roads are good?"

"Sir, they have a four wheel drive vehicle. I'm assuming the roads are like here — passable, but not good. I'm sure it will be some time before they..."

"Yes. Roads were marginal on my way to the office this morning as well--damn nasty driving. Anyway, let's plan a face-to-face for 5pm today — I'd like a complete update of where we are at in all of these strandings. If Dr. Clarke can join us via conference call, which would be a bonus."

"I'll make it happen, sir. Your office at 5pm."

Chapter 70

Egmont Key, Tampa Bay, Florida

"Amazing." Angela stood shaking her head. "I've never seen..."

"Not in *Tursiops truncatus* you haven't." Robin had persuaded Angela to break away from her rescue-planning phone calls to accompany him on another exploratory excursion in the electric powered inflatable. They were now sitting in the middle of the circling group of bottlenose dolphins.

"I'm sorry I didn't tell you about the preponderance of females in the Galveston animals. I wasn't..."

"...supposed to share. Doc alluded to that. It's okay." He pointed to a smaller, gray shape in the water. "With the number of calves, I can only speculate that most of the adult-size animals are females."

At hearing the word "speculate," Angela scrunched up her nose.

"Yes, yes—how much you *love* speculation. But, it's going to be tough to get a look at their genital slits and anuses in this mess." The proximity of the genital slit to the anus and the umbilicus is one of the main ways of determining the sex of a dolphin. Males have even spacing between all three. In females, the anus is closer to the genital slit.

As the boat drifted, Dr. Nicely took notes and measured the speed of the dolphins. Typically, dolphin speed is measured using a power boat pacing alongside the swimming animals. That method is good for measuring mostly linear movement and when there is no concern about the pace boat influencing other observable behavioral factors. But, Dr. Nicely had found that procedure inadequate for measuring the speed of movements that were less linear and in situations when a moving boat might influence behavior he was trying to observe. To address the problem, he worked with a manufacturer to design, build and test a radar gun for increased accuracy at low speeds—zero to 50 miles per hour—and to have minimal impact on the dolphins own sophisticated sonar system. It was *that* instrument that he brought from South Africa and was using now. Angela just stood on the bow in silence--watching the slow-swimming dolphins.

"Angela?" She still stood there mesmerized. "I have something to share. Angela!"

He rarely called her *Angela*, so that brought her out of her trance. "I'm sorry. What's up?" She took a few steps closer to him.

"They seem to be moving about a three-quarters of a kilometer an hour slower than when I was out here before. I don't know if it's significant—just an observation...a change. Damn!" He wrinkled his face and shook his head, "I hate this. I've no clue what's going on. No fucking clue!"

Robin's outburst pulled her completely out of her lingering daze, "They're starving. You said you didn't observe any feeding behavior. I certainly haven't seen any. They're starving. They're slowing down. They're dying. I'm afraid we're too late."

"Short of some kind of miracle..."

"We don't believe in miracles." She stepped right into his face and continued, "We're scientists. What we'd need would be an outpouring of men and materials large enough to create a temporary rehabilitation facility to house all of these animals. We'd need boats and crews to capture and transfer them and vets and volunteers to treat them. I've got people mobilizing, but in the time we may have left...the kind of effort we need...that's not going to happen..."

"...no matter how much people love their smile?" Robin took a step back — away from Angela.

"Not going to happen in the time that we have left — no matter how much people love their silly dolphin smile." Angela fell silent again. They were feeding off of each other's negativity. "I just don't think I can mobilize sufficient resources in time...if they spiral anytime soon...well...at best we might be able to get three or four out of the water and to a facility."

Robin turned and looked to the east — towards MacDill Air Force Base and a fast RIB heading towards Dr. Menke's boat. He could see the transfer of a passenger and a few large cases of equipment. A look through his binoculars confirmed his assumption. Tapping Angela's shoulder he pointed in the direction of Doc's boat. "Adam Reich."

Angela shrugged and Robin's phone vibrated softly. "Hello. Yes. Okay. I'm done here anyway. See you in a minute, Doc." Turning to Angela, Robin filled her in, "It seems Adam has already created some new monitoring equipment." He smiled wide, "I knew this kid was special — super smart, newly motivated. Anyway, Doc wants to use the electric boat to test the equipment and wants us to bring it over to transfer Adam and the gear."

"So, we finally get to meet this prodigy of yours. Maybe he'll at least be able to tell us why they are dying..." Her voice trailed off as she again looked out over the dolphins.

Robin stepped up close and gently touched her cheek—she turned her head. He looked into her eyes—serious, "Maybe there is still hope. Maybe Adam..."

Abruptly pulling away, Angela shook her head. "It's not some surf ski race where you take an unexpected swim and then battle yourself back into contention. That's something you've prepared for—trained for. We haven't trained for this. No one has trained for this!"

"I still think he can help." Robin turned and nodded to the crewman at the throttle and the electric boat crept out of the mass of dolphins and towards Dr. Menke's craft. Angela sat on a small seat in the bow—silent. Moving up behind her, Robin whispered, "I still think you can help. You are *very persuasive* when you need to be." After giving her a light kiss on the neck, he continued, "I still think you can motivate and mobilize and organize the rescue help we need, love. It's one of the things you are more than good at. So, stop sulking and make it happen. I can't imagine *you* taking 'no' for an answer."

As the electric boat drew closer, Robin could see Dr. Menke waving and nodding in Adam's direction. Nicely waved back as the pulled alongside. "Doc!"

"Robin, Angela—how goes it out there?"

Angela stood up and nodded acknowledgement, but only Robin waved again and then fended off the larger boat. Two MSOT members on Dr. Menke's boat held the electric boat steady as Robin passed up his gear bin and back pack. Angela climbed up—Robin followed.

Doc repeated his question, "So, Robin, Angela—how goes it out there?"

Robin nodded in Adam's direction.

"You're right, Robin--introductions first." Adam moved closer and Doc waved his hand in the young man's direction. "Adam Reich, meet Dr. Robin Nicely and Dr. Angela Clarke."

Adam enthusiastically grabbed Robin's extended hand, "It's an honor, sir. I'm very excited...more than excited to have the honor of..." Robin shifted his eyes to Angela and back, cutting Adam off in mid-sentence. Correcting his enthusiastic oversight, Adam reached out to shake Angela's hand, "Dr. Clarke it is also an honor to meet and work with you." Stepping back, he glanced out at the mass of dolphins and confidently continued, "Now, if I can be so bold as to ask Dr. Menke's question again? How are things out there?"

"Not good, they seem to have slowed down--moving about three-quarters of a kilometer an hour slower." Robin's vacant eyes and very subtle side-to-side head shake bared his feeling of helplessness. "Not that I know if that really means anything."

Adam noticed Nicely's despair and realized that even the mighty need some stroking from time to time. "Used that radar gun you developed I bet. That was a well-done project—good application to this situation." Adam lifted his head in the direction of the equipment cases now being transferred to the electric boat. "I'm confident *that* will tell us more, sir. I should be able to safely target individuals—locking onto unique signature whistles--and record body temperatures, heart rate, sonar and other acoustic activity, brainwaves…" He drifted in silence for a moment, "But, I have some calibration to do first—making sure that I can filter out the background…boat sounds, water sounds, water temperature…well, whatever might corrupt my readings."

Doc patted Adam on the back.

Robin smiled, "I think we were smart to bring you here." Looking to Angela for confirmation, he got folded arms and raised eyebrows instead. He knew what that meant—*we'll see.*

Prodding Adam towards the electric boat, Doc moved things along, "Yes, I think you're right, Robin. Now, we've got to get Adam out there ASAP—he still has a lot of work to do." Looking at Angela, Doc continued, "I'll call you with an update once he's got everything up and running."

Angela nodded and the rest of Doc's crew climbed aboard the electric boat. Refocused, she pulled out her phone and started making more calls.

Chapter 71

Office of the Director of National Intelligence
Washington, D.C.

Director Shaw paced laps around his desk--waiting. Three hours earlier, the *USS Mercer* had destroyed the target that had been closing on the Chesapeake Bay. But, even though the kill was confirmed, the results of the *Mercer's* initial survey of the scene had Shaw more than concerned--high levels of radiation were detected in the area of the wreckage.

Luckily, the intercept was 37 miles from shore--minimizing any serious health or environmental threats. Still, Director Shaw was worried about the device that produced that radiation. Once the detection had been made, another team was quickly dispatched to the area to search the wreckage and determine if the radiation was from a radiological dispersal device — RDD/dirty bomb--or a true nuclear weapon. Two robotic mini-subs would survey the wreck site.

Sitting back at his desk, Shaw's mind drifted back to the Texas coast, *That sub...that sub was a decoy...conventional weapons...possible self-destruct. It was meant to draw out attention away for this strike. No, they wouldn't waste any assets that way — that's not smart. And, they are smart. Still, this sub was the real deal...the real deal and we stopped it.* He allowed himself a smile and rocked back in his chair. A ring of his phone brought him forward again.

"Director Shaw.

"News, Ms. Damne?"

"Yes, sir. Amazingly, a large portion of the sub's bow was intact. Amazing, because the whole sub was basically an explosive, sir. From what we can tell, it was likely meant to surface and then detonate—dispersing radiation into the air. A dirty bomb. Fortunately, there must have been a fault in their wiring or something, sir, so the entire ship did not detonate and disintegrate when the *Mercer* attacked."

"And, the radiation."

"Plenty. Every nook and cranny was crammed with caesium-137. The crew—parts of two bodies were recovered—showed severe signs of radiation sickness." There was a pause on the line, "Sir, we know that dirty bombs are mostly ineffective, but this one was big enough to cause health problems, civil disruption and certainly create some serious post-event paranoia."

Shaw stood and paced again. He knew it was his job to be paranoid—not the people's. After another second of silence, he continued, "One sub—this sub—might have a goal of paranoia. But, I can't believe with two subs..."

Jenna Damne interrupted, "Remember, sir...CIA estimated three to five subs were constructed, sir. Sorry, sir."

"That's alright—I've got a lot of information to track. But, that assessment just reinforces what I'm thinking. I can't believe that with up to five subs the ultimate goal was to make America more paranoid. That's not how this group operates. They want a show. They always want a show."

"Sir, that is our feeling as well. We ...."

Director Shaw finished her sentence, "...need to continue our current monitoring status with CONCH. Please put that gut feeling of yours into an updated assessment that you will email me within the hour."

After hanging up, Shaw sat and closed his eyes. He snorted quietly and smiled—remembering the exemplary job Collins had done of getting CONCH put in place. Opening his eyes, Director Shaw sat up and laid his fingers on his computer keyboard—he was sure the admiral would do a similar job making sure it remained in place and functioning.

Chapter 72

Egmont Key, Tampa Bay, Florida

Adam was deep into calibrating his equipment — sitting in the stern of the boat with his laptop and Ensign Ramirez.

Doc was sitting amidships — near the steering console-- watching, when his Blackberry vibrated. It was news from Collins about the CONCH detection and subsequent kill near the Chesapeake Bay. He continued reading — he filled his lungs to sigh, but restrained himself — confident that he had properly vetted the detection system. Instead, his pulse throbbed as he replayed his initial communications with the admiral — and the admiral's initial insinuation that CONCH might be at fault.

Anger led to impatience--Doc stood up and moved over to where Adam was huddled with Ramirez. Lightly, he placed his hand on Adam's shoulder, "How's it going?"

Adam looked up and moved aside the large headphones so he could hear. Ramirez kept working.

Doc looked at his watch — 2:36pm--and repeated the question, "How's it going?"

"I'm still working on the filtering out the background — the calibration. It's taking longer than I expected — just more out there than you think of back in the lab. It's tedious and time-consuming, but necessary."

Nodding, Doc replied, "I understand — but, time is one thing we have less and less of. If we are going to understand what is causing…" Menke stopped as Adam looked hard into his eyes. Nodding again, Doc turned and went back to his earlier seat.

Putting his headphones back on, Adam went back to work and back to his own thoughts. *Doc doesn't care anything about what is causing this. He's just protecting somebody's ass — maybe his own. What's that? Wow, schools of fish generate lots of noise. Different then working a mostly closed system…there…okay — filtered that. I don't understand what he's worried about. I skimmed over his research. Short of the duration of the study period — I didn't see any flaws. That was minor. I didn't see anything that an extended study period would have amplified or revealed. One more filter — wow, I just can't believe the noise.*

Adam slipped his headphones back again and tapped Ramirez. The MSOTs tracking expert removed his headphones as well. "The filters for audible sound are finished. Now, we need to look at the stuff that you and I can't hear." Tapping on the keyboard, Adam pulled up a different window. It showed all the other sound in the area — a mass of waves for him to sort through.

Ramirez smiled and shook his head, "This is some amazing shit. Amazing."

"I knew you'd like it, now…" Adam motioned to his laptop and they both put their headphones back on.

Chapter 73

TEXMAM Office, Galveston, Texas

"Kurt? Kurt?" Shari and Bryan had just arrived at the TEXMAM office for their regular Monday afternoon office work — but, Kurt was nowhere to be found. The offices were empty. Kurt's office door was open and the light was on — but, no one was inside. Shari went inside — sitting on the desk was an envelope with Shari's name scrawled in three inch letters. Before Bryan could follow, she turned--blocking the door--and said, "Bryan, go get the computers booted up."

"Okay."

Shari looked at the envelope on the desk. The desk looked very clean--too clean. She looked around the room. Things were missing — Kurt's things. Grabbing a letter opener, she slit the envelope and pulled out the single, folded page. Hesitating, she turned the page over and over in her hand. Finally, Shari slowly unfolded the paper--it was hand-written:

> *Dearest Shari,*
>> *Despite what you may think, I'm no longer fit — I'm no longer able — to carry on my duties at TEXMAM. I'm can't a part of this anymore-- yelling in deaf ears. I'm sending my letter of resignation to the board of directors later today.*
>> *Please, continue the good work you and Bryan are doing. Good hearts like yours may change how people approach these events — maybe.*
> *All the best,*
> *Kurt*

Her legs shook like they had when she had first seen the dolphins beached at Galveston. Slouching and leaning back on the desk, Shari's thoughts got angry. *That bitch — that Angela bitch — drove him away.* She carefully refolded the letter and put it back in the envelope.

"Mom? Mom?" Bryan was getting antsy — poking his head in the door, "The computers are up — let's go."

Folding the envelope, Shari stuffed it securely in her jeans pocket. "Bryan, Kurt has been called away…"

"To Tampa? I bet they want him in Tampa to save those dolphins. Kurt is a great one for…"

"Yes." She didn't confirm or deny his speculation, she just moved on. "Now, let's get to those data sheets and photos. Make Kurt proud--keep your eyes open for anything unusual — okay?"

"Okay!" Bryan moved over to the desk next to Shari's work station — she would be entering the data sheets while Bryan downloaded photos to attach to each animal's file.

An hour later, Shari was churning through the data entry when Bryan tugged at her arm. "Mom?"

"We only have 30 more minutes before we need to head home. I want to get as much done as…" He tugged again.

"Mom!"

"I'm sorry, baby. What?"

"Did I ever really explain to you why they called Pirate, *Pirate*?"

"C'mon. I really don't…"

"Mom, look at these photos." Bryan had arranged eight split-photos on the computer screen—one showing each side of a different dolphin's head. "They called him Pirate because he had one bad eye—one eye closed—like a pirate would cover with a patch. These other dolphins...well, all the dolphin pictures I've entered...they all have one eye closed."

Shari moved closer. "You're sure? Show me more." Bryan scrolled through the all the headshots he had entered.

"See?" Bryan smiled.

"We need to tell Kurt..." Shari started for Kurt's office, remembered he wasn't there and stopped cold. After a long moment, she turned back around to face her son. "I need to get this information to that woman at NMFS." He nodded enthusiastically and she continued, "You stay here and keep working. I'm going to go into...into Kurt's office to make a couple of phone calls."

Back in Kurt's office, Shari was again startled by how clean it looked—like he took everything of value—like he was leaving for good. There were no knick-knacks, no notepads, no rolodex—nothing that had phone numbers or emails—nothing that was Kurt. Shari kept looking—opening each of the desk drawers.

In the large bottom drawer, she found a stash of things she never thought he'd leave behind--his copy of the *Odyssey*, a book manuscript—dated from the previous day-- book research files, and several legal pads of book notes. Shari left the office and headed for the large closet they used as a mailroom.

"Mom? Did you get anyone? Dr. Clarke?"

"Not yet. Keep at the photos. You're doing a great job."

Shari retrieved a medium-sized box and some packing tape and went back into Kurt's office. Carefully, she removed the book materials from the drawer and placed them in the box. On one of his note pads, scrawled on the side — and obviously traced over a number of times with more and more ink — was *Angela*. Under her name, in similar dark characters, was written *Dr. Robin Nicely* and a strange-looking phone number. Shari wrote the information on a blank piece of paper and placed the notepad in the box. After closing the door quietly, she dialed.

"Hello." The accent was unfamiliar to Shari, but the man sounded nice enough.

"Dr. Nicely, we've never met before — my name is Shari Casseine and I'm a volunteer with TEXMAM. I worked for Kurt Braun. Kurt…um…Kurt is unavailable right now, but I was…that is my son and I were entering data and photos from the stranding …um…I guess I should be asking…I found your name next to Dr. Clarke's on one of Kurt's notepads…I …"

"Ms. Casseine — Shari. Relax. Slow down. Take a deep breath and focus." Robin nudged Angela and put the phone on speaker. "Dr. Clarke is here with me — I've got you on speaker phone. Now, from the beginning…"

Shari filled them in — the photos of all 201 dolphin carcasses showed the same anomaly. One eye was closed.

There was a moment of silence on the Tampa end of the line, then Robin's brain started working overtime, "So, it could be some kind of eye infection, fungus, virus, bacteria…something causing error stimuli in the optic nerve…causing a spatial disorientation and the circular swim pattern…the proximity to each other…it still doesn't make sense! We'll need to magnify the photos, then go back and sample the eyes of each of those animals, and check those in Virginia Beach and….."

It was obvious to Shari, that Dr. Clarke had put a stop to Dr. Nicely's speculation. "Shari," Dr. Clarke's voice was gentle and patronizing, "Thank you for sharing this information, but where is Mr. Braun? Why isn't he calling me? Too busy working on his book?"

Shari stood and paced around Kurt's desk keeping her expletives to herself. "With all due respect Dr. Clarke — and at this moment, I'm not sure how much respect is due — I don't know where Kurt is. All I do know is that he has resigned from TEXMAM and cleaned out his office. The last time I saw him was yesterday afternoon while he was talking with Mr. Dafoe from…" Shari paused. "Forget about Kurt, Dr. Clarke. I'm sure he'd rather you focus on the photos than on whatever whim he is following now."

"Shari, Dr. Nicely here again. This may be something important — high marks to your boy for recognizing this — well done. Now, can you email me those files? My address is **rnicely@dsc.org.za**. Keep it to five or six photos per email. I know it's cumbersome, but I can't let my inbox get overwhelmed. Keep them coming in small batches and I can get them downloaded quickly. Understand?"

"Yes, I'll do that for you. Thank you for listening. I hope what we found will help. Please let Dr. Clarke know that I'll also pass along anything I hear about Kurt."

Shari hung up and sat quietly for a minute. After taping up Kurt's box, she walked back to Bryan, smiling. "Well done.. Now, we have to get those photos emailed to our new friend, Dr. Nicely." After that, she'd think about finding Kurt.

Egmont Key, Tampa Bay, Florida

Robin's brain was still reeling—going through all the potential pathogens that could cause such a wide-spread eye infection. Angela tapped him on the shoulder--nothing. She tapped harder and glared.

He scowled. "What?"

Angela stepped back and looked around. The men on the boat were all watching. She raised her eyebrows and stared at Robin.

"What?" Narrowing his eyes, he looked hard back at her—she just continued staring.

After a long minute of silence, Robin shook his head, "You're not worried about Kurt are you?"

Knowing she had won, Angela smiled on the inside. "I just think it's odd that he's suddenly disappeared. He's flaky—flighty even—but, I can't imagine him leaving like that. It's not responsible—this is too big a deal to him."

"You still care about him." Robin put on a poorly-faked pout.

Angela closed her eyes in obvious disgust, "No—I care about the strandings...about the data...about unsupervised volunteers...no, unsupervised children of volunteers offering up seemingly important data."

Robin smiled, "Right—the data. I'm sure that's first in your mind—but, I'm sure you're at least curious..."

"Only because it's now impacting our data, and...and, because I just have a feeling he is up to something...something."

"Well, if it's any consolation, I think that even with the good job he did on the initial stranding...well, I think his reputation—his credibility—is still questionable." His look was serious.

"Yes, thanks to me. Yes, I understand that's what your look means. Anyway...I hope those photos come to you soon. At least then we'll be able to see if his disappearance is negatively impacting that data."

Robin looked around—the Navy men were no longer watching. He inched closer to Angela and whispered, "Oh, you know how I love when you speak of data like that..."

Angela pushed him away, "Not here. Not now." Her voice wasn't loud, but her tone was firm and serious—her arms were crossed.

Robin knew better than to push back. Instead he continued the original conversation, "Do you think we should tell Doc about Kurt?"

Relaxing again, Angela moved back closer to Robin, "No need. I'm sure he's got his hands full right now." She looked at her watch—4pm—and at the sun getting lower in the west. "I thought we would have heard from him by now. What's up with your boy wonder?"

"These things take..." And, then Robin realized his gaffe, "Yes, I know—we don't have time. Shouldn't Doc have also updated us by now—especially with that conference call coming at five? In this case I think that no news is..."

Angela shook her head, "...bad news. He's not getting us anything and I don't know what else to do. I don't have the resources to..."

"I know. I know. You don't have the resources to set up a rehab facility for all these animals, to capture these animals. I don't have the knowledge—the expertise—to know what's going on. We think this is pre-stranding behavior. But, do we really fucking know? No! It's frustrating because we know that most of these animals—75, 100, 125, 150 *more* dolphins—are going to die and there doesn't seem to be a fucking thing we can do about it! Not you, not me, not anyone."

She'd never seen Robin that frazzled, that frustrated—it helped her focus for the moment. "Well, we need to try and save some. I'm going to plan some captures. You think about how we might be able to safely separate some from the group. I'm going to make more phone calls. I have made *some* progress at moving people into position faster. If the dolphins haven't hit the beach by tomorrow morning, we are going to get some to temporary rehab tanks somewhere—Eckerd College maybe." Angela smiled at the idea—the campus was on the water, only a few miles away, had boat access and one of the nation's larger marine science programs. The students were ready-made volunteers. "I'm going to continue making calls and I am going to make this rescue happen." Angela took out her phone and turned to move to the bow of the boat.

Staring at nothing, Robin still continued to ramble in frustration, "Why can't I do something? Why can't I think of something to do? Why..."

Angela stopped and turned back. It was her turn to be the strong one in the relationship — to bolster his ego, his self-confidence and not let him cower in the company of such other manly men. Walking back to Robin, she put a hand firmly on each shoulder and forced him to make eye contact. He stopped rambling and she spoke quietly, confidently, "You can do something--call Vee. He's the one you've groomed to be the pathology expert. Call Vee and forward him the photos..."

An instant, face-wide smile knocked the blankness from Robin's face, "Right! I can have him review the photos, do an exhaustive literature review and...and, I don't know if this was your intention or not, but I can have him review the photos of the carcasses from the Bazarutu stranding. I had him save two intact carcasses in the icehouse in Mozambique — shit, he's in Plettenberg now. Well, I'm sure he can get Dr. Lindelo to biopsy the eyes of those carcasses. Maybe there is a link after all." Pausing and wrinkling his brow, Robin took one of Angela's hands off his shoulder and held it softly in both of his hands. Through his pursed lips he whispered, "Sorry — thank you."

Angela just nodded and smiled — happy that her man was back. With that, Angela moved to the stern of the boat, opened up her cell phone and went into action.

Chapter 74

Egmont Key, Tampa Bay, Florida

Adam tapped Ramirez on the shoulder, pointed to a particular sound wave on his screen and questioningly shrugged his shoulders. Ramirez moved a little closer to the screen then sat back and shrugged his own shoulders. Adam looked at Ramirez again. The ensign shook his head, "It's nothing I've seen before."

"And, you're..."

"Yes, the best." Prior to joining the MSOT, Ramirez had SEAL electronics specialist. Prior to that he had worked sonar on a nuclear missile sub. Because he was so good at what he did, it took three requests and the intervention of some higher authorities within the Navy before he was finally allowed to even apply for SEAL training. His particular role on the SEAL team allowed him to use and maintain those skills, and draw the attention of MSOT commanders.

"Nothing like this?"

"Never. You?"

"Vaguely." Adam closed his eyes. He snickered to himself in amusement, *Theta Wave Meditation Meld*. Smiling, he continued, "No—nothing I can clearly recall. But, something about it is very interesting. I just can't...I just can't place why it means something to me." Adam didn't have a photographic memory, but he knew he'd seen the wave pattern someplace. "Can you use your computer to record an extended sample? I want to check its consistency and direction." Ramirez nodded.

Adam continued, "In the meantime, I'll filter it out and move on."

While Adam worked, Ramirez tapped at his workstation, targeted the sound and started collecting an extended sample. Convinced that Adam was again absorbed in his work, the ensign tapped on his keyboard and captured a quick sample of the pattern — convinced that if Adam found it "very interesting," it might also be of interest to someone else. After attaching the file to a short email, the ensign hit "send."

Chapter 75

TEXMAM Office, Galveston, Texas

"I'm sorry, Mr. Dafoe—Kurt Braun isn't here." Passing the phone to her other ear, Shari walked toward the office door.

Shari didn't know how much she should say. She didn't want to get dragged into a long conversation—it was time to get Bryan back home and ready for his next day at school.

Looking out the door of Kurt's office to make sure Bryan was still in the bathroom, she continued, "For some reason Kurt has resigned as Executive Director of TEXMAM. He turned in his resignation at the end of the day today—the news is on the web site already. I really don't know anything else—I haven't seen him since…well, since you were here yesterday. Nobody's seen him since yesterday. It's not like him to disappear like this."

"Interesting—very interesting. Ms. Casseine, thank you for the information. It may prove important…you…you were working there unsupervised today?"

"We were trained well. Kurt was a great teacher—very thorough, very patient. We have an enormous amount of data to enter and hundreds of photos to download and catalog—we're still committed to getting it done."

"Anything interesting in the data or photos? If you don't mind me asking…"

"I don't mind. I think Kurt already told you that all the animals were mostly females and juveniles…"

"Yes. We've known that for a while now--anything else?"

Shari hesitated, but thought this might be the only way for Kurt to hear about Bryan's discovery. She was sure Dr. Clarke would never tell him. "Yes. The photos...the photos showed all the animals with one eye closed for some reason. Of course, we don't..."

"...know the reason. Great, another dead end."

"No, no. I also passed the information to Dr. Nicely and Dr. Clarke in Tampa. They might come up with something—talking about parasites and viruses and..."

"You don't sound too confident."

"Sorry, I started thinking about Kurt again—wondering...whether I should try his cell phone..." But, she remembered seeing his TEXMAM phone left on the desk. "No, that won't work. He left his phone here."

"I'll let you know if I hear anything about him. Thank you again for your confidence and the information."

"Thank you." Shari hung up. Bryan was standing in the doorway to the office with his backpack over one shoulder.

"What were you wondering about Kurt, mom?"

"Let's get going. We need to get you home and ready for school tomorrow."

Chapter 76

Office of Admiral Collins, NOAA

Silver Spring, Maryland

"Admiral Collins, sir." It was 4:50pm — NMFS Director, Jake Hamilton was early for the meeting with his boss.

Collins shook his head at the graphic on the screen and forwarded the file to an asset on the NMMP research team. After closing the file and the original email, he closed his laptop, looked at Jake, and walked over to greet him. "Nice to do this in person when we can. I'm assuming Dr. Clarke will be joining us on the phone."

"Menke and Nicely as well. If that is okay, sir?"

"Yes, absolutely --well done." The admiral closed the door and motioned Director Hamilton to sit.

"Thank you, sir." Jake was visibly stiff and uncomfortable in the chair.

"You've got something on your mind."

It was a statement, but Jake answered like it was a question. "Yes, sir." In his discomfort, he continued to fidget. He hesitated to elaborate.

The admiral repositioned his desk phone so it would be easier for them to hear the speaker and then turned to lean on the edge of the desk facing Director Hamilton. Looking at his watch — 4:52pm — he realized he had a few minutes. "I know you are wondering about my...um...let's just say *unusual* interest in these dolphin strandings — wondering why I've taken such a personal interest and have been so hands-on."

Jake said nothing — did nothing. The admiral continued, "Very well. As I mentioned the other day after the hearing, most of all, I am looking out for the security of our country. I'm also looking out for both of us. Actually, for you, me and Dr. Menke. A few years ago, you were given special security clearance to review a redacted report on the potential environmental impact of a new defensive sonar system — something designed to protect the nation's ports and coasts."

Director Hamilton nodded — he remembered the security clearance and the review.

Admiral Collins walked over to another chair, pulled it close to and in front of Jake, and sat. "After some initial delays, the system has been in place and functioning in its first three locations for about four months. This past week, the system was responsible for identifying and helping neutralize two threats to the homeland. While the entire U.S. is not yet covered, the sonar net has been deployed in coastal areas surrounding approaches to the Chesapeake Bay, Tampa Bay and Galveston."

"So, coastal Virginia and Maryland, Galveston, and Tampa Bay?" Jake shook his head.

"Yes — eventually, all our major ports will be protected. The approaches to New York City are due to come online by the end of the month. But, our Chesapeake Bay, Galveston and Tampa Bay networks went online four months ago." Collins stood up and returned the chair to the side of his office. After walking around his desk and pausing momentarily he sat. The desk clock said 4:57pm.

"So, you think that this sonar net…that there's a chance…"

"There's always a chance we missed something—Dr. Menke missed something, you missed something. I'm not blaming you, of course. The data you reviewed—even with your temporary security upgrade—were very limited. I'm not concerned with placing blame at this point. I'm not even concerned if that actually is the cause." Admiral Collins paused. "What I am concerned with is anything—anyone—that may compromise a system that has successfully, repeatedly, protected this country. Because of that, I plan for all the possibilities."

"But, sir…the dolphins…nearly 600 dolphins…the environmental impact…" A usually stoic and calm man, Jake looked down in his lap and fiddled with his wedding ring—turning it repeatedly. "…all those females and calves, sir."

"The dolphins may be a sacrifice we need to make to protect this country--regrettable, but necessary. *Now*, I'm sure you understand why I've taken such a personal interest in this case. And, I'm sure that you recognize the amount of trust I am placing in you as well. At this point…at this point, the country cannot afford even the whiff of a tenuous connection between that system and the strandings—whether there is one or not. And, I know I can count on you. I know it."

Jake realized it was too late to second guess himself. He stopped fidgeting with his fingers, sat up straight and looked with confidence across the desk at Collins, "Yes, sir."

The admiral had timed his disclosure well — his assistant just buzzing in with Dr. Menke, Dr. Clarke and Dr. Nicely on the phone. With the line open, he started, "I wish this were under better circumstances and with everyone in person, but welcome to all of you. This is Admiral Collins. Director Hamilton has joined me in my office. I've had dribs and drabs of updates from most of you, but I'd like a nice succinct review of what we know to date. Dr. Clarke?"

"I'm afraid, sir, that little has changed. With regards to the two mass strandings, we have no conclusive pathological commonalities at this time. The commonality we do have is that the vast majority of dead animals were females — sexually mature females and calves. There were a number of male calves. Of course, we do not know if that holds true for Tampa. Field identification of a dolphin's sex and age are difficult under ideal conditions — especially tough given the circumstances in Tampa."

"Pardon me, admiral." Everyone could hear Angela taking a drink "There is one other commonality we are currently investigating, sir. Many of the animals, carcasses sir, in the Texas stranding appear to have had one eye closed for some reason — I've ordered re-sampling of whatever carcasses are still available and sampling of the live animals being rehabbed. The few Virginia Beach animals will also be examined and sampled. Unfortunately, by the time this discovery was communicated to us from Texas, the waning light made it impossible to examine the live animals in Tampa, sir. That observation—and trying to survey the animals' sex--is on the agenda for tomorrow. But, to say that those field observations are challenging would be a gross understatement, sir." Angela drank again. "In the meantime, Dr. Nicely is conducting a review of the literature on all manner of eye problems in dolphins."

"That's all we have on that. I know it's not much and the likelihood that something will turn up that will help us save the 150 or so dolphins in Tampa is near zero, but it's all we have. Because of that, sir, I've come up with a plan to capture and attempt the rehabilitation of a limited number of dolphins starting tomorrow. We have to try, sir. I've also activated a much more comprehensive rescue effort—something to have ready if the initial rescues are successful. I've got more fishermen lined up, help from Mote, Clearwater, Sea World and above-ground pools being assembled at Eckerd College as makeshift rehab tanks. We'll be ready." Angela paused for acknowledgement, or a response.

The admiral didn't comment on Angela's plan. Instead, he grumbled, "The most studied dolphin species on the planet and we still can't figure out what the hell is going on? Mind-boggling."

"Maddening—frustrating beyond belief, sir."

"Dr. Nicely?" Collins assumed who it was since the accent was one he didn't recognize. "Just do your best to make the American people's investment in your time here worthwhile, doctor."

"Yes, sir. My apologies."

The admiral looked at Director Hamilton, shook his head and rolled his eyes. "Thank you again Dr. Clarke—thorough, honest update. Now, Doc...Dr. Menke, how are things progressing with Mr. Reich?"

"Sir, he did an amazing job building equipment overnight. The kid is a whiz. Unfortunately, the calibration and the filtering of the background noi..."

"Doc, please—progress?"

"One moment—I'll see where he is at." After a long pause, Dr. Menke returned, "He has completed the calibration and filtering and is testing the ability to target and reacquire individual animals, sir. He anticipates actual data collection beginning within the hour, sir."

"Very well. Keep us all in the loop."

Silent for the call so far, Director Hamilton felt left out, but had to say something, "Well done, everyone. It seems you've teased out what meager leads there are and have put a plan in place to further explore them. In the meantime, Angela, what exactly do you have planned for tomorrow's limited rescue effort?"

Keen to hear, the admiral leaned closer to the phone.

"Well, there are three commercial fishermen in the area that have been trained to assist with live captures and enough NMFS and FWC marine mammal folks with experience enough to..."

"Dr. Clarke." The admiral forcefully interrupted and Angela stopped. "I'm sorry. I've been thinking on this limited effort. I'm sure you've put a number of hours into coordinating your limited rescue effort, but I think that something of this nature might disrupt the group and send the rest on to a beach somewhere. Dr. Menke? Dr. Nicely?"

Menke answered first, "I like the idea of saving animals. But at this point I do think the disruption might not only send the other animals to shore, but keep us from using Adam's equipment to collect data on a truly unique event...an event that may have high scientific value. If I had a vote, sir, it would have to be *no*."

Smiling, Collins asked again, "Dr. Nicely?"

There was a long pause—Director Hamilton shrugged at the admiral, smiled—he really expected Nicely to stand up to Angela Clarke.

His tone professional, his voice clipped, Robin finally answered, "I would agree with Dr. Menke. I'd recommend we put any rescue on hold until Adam has had a chance to collect and analyze a day's worth of data. We can't risk disrupting the group and the potential for learning something that could potentially save another large group, for a handful of animals. Let's collect more data. Let's have Angela's more comprehensive plan in place—ready to go at a moment's notice."

The silent pause was deafening--uncomfortable. No one expected Angela to respond—and she didn't. But, they all expected someone to move on. Finally, the admiral took charge, "Well, with the director's consent..." He looked over at Jake.

"Yes, sir—I agree."

"With the director's consent," Collins continued, "let's give Reich his day. Make sure he understands we want some analysis — *analysis*--within 24 hours — *24 hours*. Quicker, if possible."

"Yes, admiral." Jake fidgeted in his chair — it was just a little too small to comfortably handle his large frame.

"Dr. Clarke. I commend your effort to take action — it is usually exactly what I am looking for…and, in the very near future it might be the right action. Take the time to gather the troops as it were — hone the details of your more comprehensive effort and be ready to go if Mr. Reich doesn't turn up something extremely useful."

Confident in her plan and the people she already had moving into stand-by positions, Angela finally managed to speak, "Yes, sir. Be assured the effort will be monumental."

"Very well. Despite what you all may think, you are doing an extraordinary job with an unprecedented situation. I trust you all will do what it takes. Good luck and good night."

With the call complete, Director Hamilton made a move to get up from his uncomfortable chair, but the admiral signaled him to stay seated. "The next 24 hours are going to be difficult for Dr. Clarke. She is a doer, not a waiter. I understand that she is going to do everything she can to mobilize the largest dolphin rescue in history — probably already has. I'm sure she'll be ready if Reich fails to provide some insight and a solution."

Jake stood, "I'm sure she'll be more than ready, sir."

"At this point, I'm not sure how this will play out — there are many variables under consideration. We are covering all of our bases."

"Whatever you deem necessary…it's a matter of national security…then whatever must be done."

Collins nodded, but doubted the director's sincerity. Turning his back, he walked to look out the window at the leftover snow glistening as the city's lights came on. Jake stood and showed himself out.

Chapter 77

Beef Island Airport, Tortola, BVI

Near the small airport's taxi stand, something—someone vaguely familiar—caught Rachel Remmy's eye.

Rachel walked up to the man and stuck out her hand, "Mr. Braun? Kurt Braun? My name is Rachel Remmy. I'm with Summers Media."

The man stepped back and nearly tumbled over his rolling suitcase. Rachel apologized, "I'm sorry, I didn't mean to startle you, it's just that…"

Kurt had regained his footing, grabbed his roller and started to walk away. Rachel pursued him—clomping along in her Birkenstocks. "I'm sorry; I was just surprised to see you. I'm working on the dolphin story, checking out Dolphin Towne and I was just surprised to see you here."

Stopping, he turned to face her. She stood silent and he looked over her granola-girl, hippy chick cliché of an outfit—from the toe rings and sandals to the calf-length, gauzy, white skirt and the tie-dyed halter top—but didn't say a word.

"You…you…" It suddenly hit her that he was here—not in Texas managing the stranding, "You're not in Texas, Mr. Braun. You're here in the BVI…"

He stepped closer and finally spoke, "I'm no longer the executive director of TEXMAM. I officially resigned earlier today. I'm here…" Coming closer, he whispered, "I'm here to get away from all of that—to get away from the death and the bureaucracy and the politics...the lies...the uncaring people..." Feeling himself getting agitated, Kurt stopped and closed his eyes. "I was heading to Dolphin Towne to relax. I hoped *that* environment would..."

Rachel reached out and gently touched his shoulder, "They aren't taking any new clients. I'm not sure why. The official line is that the dolphins are in an extended *Off-Cycle*—a sort of regenerative period away from human contact. We think it's because the owner, Jasmine Summers, is too busy whipping up the media frenzy about the strandings to deal with her clients. I've tried several times to get in—to get a reservation—no luck." Seeing Kurt's disappointment, she tried to console him, "But, this is an amazing island—not many people, little stress and plenty of other secluded places to unwind...to decompress and forget."

Kurt shook his head and smiled weakly, "I bet she'll take me. Once I tell *my* story, how could she turn me down? Who better to let in? Who better to help heal?" Confidence regained, he pulled his suitcase towards a waiting taxi and climbed inside.

Dolphin Towne, Tortola, BVI

Before Jasmine could get out the door, the cab driver deposited Kurt's luggage and drove away. Kurt stood in the weak light—backpack over one shoulder and the extended handle of his red rolling suitcase in his other hand.

Jasmine stopped on the bottom step—clothed only in a knee-length, gauzy linen night shirt--and held up her hand, "I'm very sorry, sir, but we're not taking any more guests. Now, I can call you a cab and can recommend some great cottages just down the road and up the hill..."

For a moment, Kurt was paralyzed and captivated by her radiance—the light shining through her clothing and creating an aura around the curves of her body. *Angelic*, he thought.

Taking a step forward, Kurt interrupted and explained, "Ms. Summers. I hate to intrude, but this is the only place I could think of to turn for peace. I'm...my name is..." She could see the pain take over his face and stepped down and forward to hold both of his hands in hers.

"Go on." Her voice was soft, caring, "Tell me."

"My name is Kurt Braun. I was...I *was* the stranding coordinator in Galveston...in Texas. I had to...over 200 animals and no one would listen...they're not doing justice to...I had to..."

His tearful wandering was cut short when Jasmine pulled him into a hug—strong and sincere. She whispered, "I've been to that cold, dark place. For you—after all you've been through--I have room in my lodge and in my heart."

Still wrapped in the hug, he whispered back, "Thank you."

Jasmine whispered softly, "Follow me" and then broke the hug. "I have a nice room with a balcony overlooking the bay...let's head up and get you settled."

Chapter 78

Egmont Key, Tampa Bay, Florida

Conference call complete, Dr. Menke returned to the electric boat to track Adam's progress. "Adam. How is that individual targeting going?" Tapping Adam hard on the shoulder, Doc seemed to jolt him out of a little nap. "How's the individual targeting going?"

After a big yawn, Adam answered, "It's going well— amazingly well. I'm able to isolate individuals and record data in files sorted by signature whistle. I can't believe I wrote this software in so little time...must've been in the back of my mind for years...anyway..." He yawned again, "...anyway, I'm also able to reacquire, on a limited basis, by searching for signature whistles. Right now, I'm recording snippets—30 second data shots—of each animal. So, we'll need to keep the boat moving slowly around the group, and then we'll have to run transects, slowly, through the group. The equipment is essentially on autopilot—that's why I nodded off a little."

Adam started to put his headphones back on when Doc stopped him. "You've been at this a long time with no sleep. I need you 100%. No amount of caffeine is going to keep you sharp now. There's some gear to starboard—see the bivy bag, foam pad and sleeping bag? Get some real sleep."

"But, I need..."

Doc put up his hand and nodded at Ensign Ramirez curled up and sleeping wedged between two of the equipment boxes, "You need to drag his ass over here and brief him. He can monitor while we run your transects."

Adam hesitated, then jostled an unhappy Ramirez-- happy that Doc insisted he get some real sleep.

Back on Angela and Robin's boat the atmosphere was much less restful. Lt. Commander Medlin had returned to the tower and the other members of his team had moved away from the couple.

Seeing the move, Angela pulled Robin into the forward compartment for a confrontation. "How could you contradict me like that in front of everyone? You were the one that inspired the two-step plan — what with your despair, your frustration at not being able to figure this out! You had nothing but ranting gloom and doom. I came up with a plan! I have people moving boats, tanks and trucks into place." Angela paced and seethed.

"Sorry, I'm human — I gave in to a little despair for once in my life...for once." In Angela's eyes he looked for some sympathy, or empathy, and found nothing. Turning from her to fiddle with his sleeping bag, Robin continued, "But, I've recovered my senses. Doc is right to want to give Adam more time. Doc is right that we may lose all of these animals, but in so doing we may save a similar group in the future. It's what makes the most sense. Even with the delay, I think we'll be able to execute your plan and bring some of these animals back if we need to." His voice was calm, reassuring. "I know you put a lot into your more comprehensive plan. It's a great plan — a better plan. It's also a good way of coping. You focused on something and saved yourself the embarrassment of temporarily turning into a drooling, dithering idiot like me." Robin faked a pathetic face and Angela broke into a small smile.

"Cute--barely." She smiled a little larger, "Now, let's get some sleep. In the morning I'm going to have everything ready to roll and you are going to do all you can to prod Mr. Reich to move faster — work your magic." Grabbing Robin's hand she pulled him towards the fluffed sleeping bags. Her smile turned a little saucy and she playfully raised her eyebrows up and down.

Inside the cramped compartment, Robin smiled at her sudden playfulness, shook his head, and shimmied into his sleeping bag. In less than a minute, they were both fast asleep.

Day Seven

Tuesday, February 25, 2008

Chapter 79

Office of Admiral Collins, NOAA
Silver Spring, Maryland

The admiral had stayed the night—sleeping on the convertible sofa in his office—after a flurry of emails with other members of The Few left him looking at a clock reading 11:30pm.

Now, with the sun just starting to brighten the remaining snow and his office, he sat and reviewed the exchanges from the previous evening. After the initial discussion of the facts—and the forwarding of Adam's "very interesting" wave pattern snippet to the rest of The FEW and to an analyst at the Navy Marine Mammal Program--the remainder of the evening was spent coordinating the necessary response, authorizing the consequent orders and activating their few deep-cover assets.

In the admiral's hands, was that well-worn photo from the corner of the larger 9/11 photo on his desk—that well-worn photo of his son, Wendall.

Following distinguished naval service in the Gulf War, and an honorable discharge, Wendall Collins took a research and development management position with Raytheon's New York office—based on the 91st floor of the World Trade Center's South Tower. As a leader within the company's Integrated Defense Systems division, Wendall helped spearhead the creation of software to process the complex data stream coming from Raytheon-designed radar systems and send accurate targeting commands to Raytheon-designed missiles. It was during this development phase — and the concurrent, Raytheon-led upgrade of the nation's defensive radar emplacements — that Wendall first conceived the idea of a national, defensive sonar net.

Collins remembered chuckling as he told his son, "No technology will ever replace the dedicated men and woman of our Navy and Coast Guard." He also remembered his son's deadpan answer, "Old school, sir — very old school." Convinced the sonar net was the better use of the country's limited financial resources, Wendall sketched out a preliminary proposal between other projects at Raytheon.

The admiral rubbed the face of the small photo with his thumb. Wendall was lost on September 11. His preliminary designs for a defensive sonar plan were not. The creation and implementation of CONCH was as much of a memorial to his beloved son as it was an integral part of the nation's defensive security. The project's final name (the original files were simply labeled "Wendall") recalled the memory of a long-ago family weekend on the beach in Key West. A pre-pubescent Wendall had found a large conch shell while walking the beach with his dad. The admiral remembered telling him, "Pick it up, son. Put it to your ear and you'll hear the ocean." Dutifully, Wendall put it up to his ear, but after a moment looked up at his dad and shook his head, "Not the ocean, sir — ambient noise amplified by the whorls of the shell. I read about it in one of my science books." But, Collins was stubborn — even after 30 years--and thought the name *CONCH* a great way to describe a sonar system that allowed them to "hear the ocean."

There was moisture in his eyes, but the admiral wouldn't cry. He stopped crying a long time ago. While he had been a member of The FEW since its inception, Wendall's death was what pushed him into his current leadership role.

Carefully, Collins placed the photo into the corner of the frame of the larger picture. He would do everything he could to keep his son's legacy alive.

Chapter 80

Egmont Key, Tampa Bay, Florida

"Adam." Ramirez shook what he believed was Adam's shoulder. "Wake up."

From inside the bivy sack Ramirez heard a muffled, "What time is it?"

"Time to get up." He poked harder, sharper at Adam's back, "It's 0645. You slept all night while I did all your work. Get up, genius."

Adam's head poked out of the sack, "You ran all the transects?"

Ramirez was smirking, "Yes."

"And, the dolphins didn't scatter?"

"No—as far as I could tell the group stayed intact."

Adam nodded and rubbed at his crusty eyes. "Is it...is the Parabolic Acquisition Device still running?"

"Yes."

"And, is it..." Adam pulled his upper body out and slipped on his fleece jacket.

"...reacquiring automatically? Yes. I wasn't joking when I called you *genius*. The equipment is working."

"We don't need you feeding his ego, Ramirez." Doc had overheard the rustling and conversation. He looked at Adam, "Nice nap?"

"I needed that." Adam was up and Doc handed him a mug of coffee.

"You deserved it. You got that equipment functioning faster than I could have imagined—great work. Now, we need that refreshed mind to start analyzing what was collected overnight. We'll be moving you back to the lab."

Adam took the coffee over to his laptop and sat examining his handiwork. It was still running smoothly. He tapped a few keys—checking different data windows. Looking up at Doc, he asked, "When? When are you moving me back to the lab?"

"ASAP. Another RIB is on its way."

Adam stood up and looked Dr. Menke in the eye. "I understand the need to get this data analyzed quickly." He moved closer and lowered his voice, "I understand your needs." Stepping away from Doc, Adam's voiced returned to normal volume. "But, let's not lose the chance to keep collecting data. I can download the program to Ramirez's computer workstation and he can continue to collect data. In an hour I can have it downloaded and running the PAD."

Doc furrowed his brow and asked, "*PAD?*"

"Parabolic Acquisition Device. I never was very good with naming this stuff." Adam glanced, again, over at Ramirez. "An hour—tops. Okay?"

Doc nodded, "Then, we get you back to MacDill."

"Excellent." Adam lifted his head in Ramirez's direction and the ensign moved the six feet to his workstation. While Ramirez woke up his system, Adam sat tapping at his computer—first shutting down the data collection program, then opening a network connection via the satellite modem in his laptop. He turned his head—Ramirez was still fiddling with his gear. Highlighting three files, Adam clicked and dragged. He turned his head again—Ramirez was looking his way – and carefully closed the lid on the laptop so as not to disrupt the transmission of all the overnight data to the Dolphin Towne servers.

Adam shuffled over to the workstation and Ramirez quipped, "Ready, genius?"

Adam just handed him a thumb drive and nodded.

Office of Admiral Collins,
NOAA, Silver Spring, Maryland

"Shit." There was no one in the office to hear Admiral Collins. He pounded his fist on the desk and yelled louder, "Shit!" Getting up abruptly, he did one lap around his desk—while opening and closing his fingers on the hand with which he had pounded the desk. He sat back down. "This kid is playing us? Playing us?" Collins hit the desk again.

There was a weak knock on his door and a feeble inquiry from his assistant, "Admiral?"

"Not now!" The admiral's voice boomed. Turning back to the email he was trying to digest, he sat seething, wondering—why hadn't Menke or Ramirez noticed this?

ACRET
Data upload from Adam Reich via SumSat.
Destination Dolphin Towne servers. Transmission
disrupted before completion. Estimate 28% of the
data successfully uploaded.
Data analysis in process via our NMMP
asset in San Diego. Dolphin Towne operational
plan design has commenced — anticipate complete
data-wipe.
BLADE

The admiral picked up his secure phone and dialed Menke.

"Admiral...I just saw the email. I..."

Collins did not let him finish, "You need to keep a closer eye on Reich. We cannot afford a breach like this again. We also cannot afford to expose ourselves with too many field operations. Find a way to keep the boy genius in check." Agitated and antsy, the admiral again got up and circled the desk with the phone to his ear.

"Yes, admiral, sir." Rebuffed, Doc's lost all emotion. "Sir, I believe this gives us more leverage with him. I'll make the most of it. Letting him know we know will make him more paranoid and much less likely to try something else. I'll make sure the electronic security officer at the MacDill complex shields his lab. There will be no unauthorized, outgoing transmissions with an electromagnetic barrier in place."

"Absolutely. Now, get Reich..."

This time Dr. Menke interrupted, "...to the lab, analyzing the data...figuring out what is really going on and then... and then creating a plausible, though false explanation for what is happening."

"Yes." Collins stroked his chin, "And, we'll make sure the data he did upload gets destroyed before anyone knows it's there. Get the job done. Let's get this over and done with."

"I'll…"

"Just get it done. We need to close the book on this." With that, the admiral hung up and shook his head. He looked again at the old photo of Menke, CC and himself in Vietnam — knowing that more sacrifices might be imminent.

Chapter 81

Casseine Residence, Galveston, Texas

"Mom." Bryan looked at his mom over the cereal he was eating. "Mom?"

Shari didn't respond. She just kept piecing together a sandwich for his lunch.

After finishing his cereal, Bryan took the empty bowl to the sink and walked over to his mother. She was putting his lunch in a brown bag. He tugged on her sweater, "Mom!"

Shari turned and hugged him. She could tell something was not right with Bryan, but said nothing.

"Kurt is gone, isn't he? He went to save those dolphins in Tampa, didn't he? He'll save them. I know he'll save them. He'll find a way to wake them up."

"Wake them up? What are you talking about?" Loosening the hug, she looked down into his eyes.

"I thought I remembered it—so I looked it up in one of my books this morning. Dolphins sleep with one eye closed. I figured they must all have forgotten how to wake up."

"Great research, my little genius, but I'm sure they thought of that..." Shari smiled, stepped out of Bryan's embrace and picked up his lunch. "Now, here's your lunch. You've got to get to the bus stop."

After taking the brown bag, Bryan took a step closer to his mother and stared up into her eyes. "Kurt is gone, isn't he?" Her momentary strength was gone.

Shari broke—leaning back on the counter as her knees weakened and her eyes moistened. "Yes" She took a long deep breath. "Yes, he is gone. He resigned from TEXMAM and has moved out of his office. I think he felt that he had done all he could do there…that nobody was listening to him anymore…that Dr. Clarke …she was really hard on him…I think he had to go somewhere else to help the dolphins…Tampa, maybe…somewhere. I just don't know."

Smiling, Bryan walked over to a chair and retrieved his backpack full of books. "I thought so." He shouldered the backpack and headed for the door. Stopping for a moment, he turned back and looked seriously at his mother, "We should help him, mom. We should find out where he is and help him wake the dolphins up." With that, Bryan pushed through the door and headed to school.

Sliding to the floor, Shari put her head in her hands. She knew Bryan was right—Kurt had helped them through the toughest time in their lives. Because of him, because of his faith in them, they had a second chance at being a family. Feeling a little stronger, Shari stood back up and wondered--*could they really be sleeping?* She couldn't recall anyone else mentioning that—or even joking about the possibility. Still, she thought there was some real strength to the innocent conviction in her son's voice. She stopped mid-thought and grabbed her own lunch out of the refrigerator.

Shari walked over to turn off the television—*Global Good Morning* was on. The Summers Media morning news show was what they were watching because of its relentless coverage of the dolphin strandings. Seeing the Summers Media logo in the lower right corner, Shari stopped and stared through the screen. Looking at her watch, she confirmed her plan--just enough time to make the extra bus connection needed. She could find Jackson Dafoe's number at TEXMAM and still have time to get to work.

Chapter 82

Adam's Lab, MacDill Air Force Base, Tampa, Florida

"Jefferson, can you re-stock the fridge with similar items for me? It's going to be another long day." Adam had just finished some vegan potato salad and the last Red Bull.

Dr. Menke nodded at Jefferson. The ensign nodded at Adam, "I'll get what you need. Be back in about 45 minutes."

With Jefferson gone, Doc moved closer to where Adam had started to set up his laptop. He was plugging it into four larger monitors—the better to view the multiple data streams with which he'd be working. When Adam was finished, and seated, Doc moved behind him and clasped Adam's shoulders hard.

Adam fidgeted, but Doc was strong—holding him in place. "Don't move. And don't ever try anything like that data transmission stunt again. Something like that could cost you your precious Dolphin Towne, those dolphins their lives…or more. This building is shielded—any attempted transmission will be blocked and I will be notified." Adam nodded and Doc loosened his grip, but did not let go. "Now, on to the task at hand."

Finally, managing to slide free, Adam stood and walked around to the other side of the work table. "The task at hand—yes. If there is an answer in my data, I'll find it. You can bet on that."

While he had begun walking toward the door, Doc stopped and turned to face Adam again, "I am betting on that. I am. Others, well, let's just say they may be making alternate plans."

"I'll let you know as soon as I find it. If I need to consult on what I'm finding…"

"You'll go through me or the call or email will not go through." Menke smiled and rotated his head to take in the entire room. "One of the benefits of being in such a highly controlled environment, my boy. Now, to work."

With that, Adam walked over to the refrigerator — forgetting that it was empty. "Shit."

"He'll have what you need shortly. Now get to work." Doc turned and walked through the secure door.

Adam clamped his mouth shut. The scream he wouldn't let out for Doc to hear was forced into the rest of his body. Eyes popping, the muscles in his face, shoulders and arms tightened and trembled. Sleep-deprived and depleted, his body found nothing in his stomach but acidic bile and convulsed into a series of painful dry heaves.

"Shit! Fucking shit you dumbass!" Sure Doc was out of earshot — out of the building — Adam let it out and slid his now rubbery body to the floor. Leaning against the empty refrigerator, rivulets of cold sweat ran down his back. He drew his knees to his chest and, sitting in that semi-fetal position, wondered how he ever let a chance to rebuild his reputation — his intellectual egotism-- sucker him into this mess. Eyes closed and body slowly rocking, Adam fell asleep.

"Adam!" He felt a firm hand on his shoulder. "Get a hold of yourself." It was Ensign Jefferson. "You know Doc won't be happy if you don't get this shi…if you don't get this project done ASAP."

Adam looked at his phone for the time—it was 2100 hours. He'd slept for about 40 minutes. Struggling to get his jelly legs to work, the ensign offered him a hand up.

"Thanks."

The ensign could see Adam shaking and walked over to the grocery bags on the counter to his left, "You need to eat. You need to eat so you can get this work done ASAP. There's salads, wraps, bottled water and..." Pulling something out of the bag to show Adam, "...another four-pack of Red Bull. Mind if I grab one?"

"Take one. One less for me."

"Thanks." Jefferson ripped the cardboard pack open and pulled out a can. "You?"

"Yeah. You're right. I've got to crack this thing now."

Jefferson handed him a can and turned for the door. "I'll leave you to it then. Make sure you eat something too."

"Thanks again."

The ensign stopped short of the door and turned, "Can you save those dolphins?"

Adam opened his can and swallowed a gulp. "I'm doing my best. The data we just...um, that we collected out on the water—I'm hoping it will tell me something. I'm going to do my best." He set the can down and started rummaging through the grocery bags. "But, honestly—they could be so far gone that I don't know if anyone can..."

Jefferson nodded, turned, and left Adam to his work. Under his breath Adam finished his thought, "...or, if anyone wants to."

Cradling the Red Bull, a salad and a chicken Caesar wrap in his arms, Adam shuffled over to his laptop and sat. A few taps on the keyboard and he had initiated his complex data sorting program. It would take 10-15 minutes for the initial sorting to be completed — longer for the more complex variables — so he opened up the salad container and started to eat.

Time to think — it wasn't really what he wanted. Losing Dr. Nicely's budding respect — it wasn't really what he wanted. *Losing Jasmine* — with that thought, he put down his fork and walked back to the grocery bags. He set aside a bag of blue corn chips and stowed the rest of the food in the refrigerator. Grabbing the chips, he sat back next to his laptop — four minutes thirty seconds until the initial sort would be complete.

Adam spun on the stool and munched on some chips — staring through the blank beige wall opposite the monitors. *Losing Jasmine* — the thought continued to pound through his mind like a haunting, thousand-monk mantra. Spinning back to his laptop, Adam did a quick look at the sorting update window — less than two minutes. Feeling the food and the caffeine recharging his body, Adam ripped into the chicken wrap and more chips — trying to drown out the thoughts with his chewing and crunching.

Microsoft's old-fashioned "ta-dah" sound brought his eyes quickly back to the monitor — *initial sorting complete*. It had been years since Adam had worked with anyone, but he still liked to verbalize his thoughts — to talk things out. "Okay, file by file..." The initial sorting took data associated with individual animals and grouped it according to pre-set categories like "vocalizations" or "heart rate." Adam checked each category to make sure that no data from other categories had been misfiled. While he was doing that, the higher level algorithms of his program were sorting for commonalities within the file categories.

Adam looked in the corner of his monitor for the time—2145. He tapped the keyboard and moved to the last file—brainwaves. A quick glance and everything looked normal, so he gathered his trash and walked it to the garbage can. At the refrigerator, he grabbed another Red Bull and moved back to his workstation. Before setting down the can, or sitting down, he walked to the door. For two minutes, he paced—door to desk and back again. The thought was back; the thousand-monk mantra was back pounding in his mind—*losing Jasmine, losing Jasmine, losing Jasmine.* He wondered what she was doing right then. He wondered if she would ever forgive him. His eyes moistened as he whispered to himself, "Only if I do the noble thing—only if I do what is right."

Adam knew the right thing—the noble thing—was to do whatever was in his power to save the dolphins—Dr. Menke be damned. So, his pacing ended at his workstation—where he sat and refreshed the screen. The data sorting program was still running smoothly and had begun to tease some commonalities out of the data.

"Commonalities. Let's see. Blah, blah, blah. Low heart rates. Duh. Low respirations. Blah, blah, blah. They're exhausted--that's to be expected. Acoustics...lots of signature whistle repeats—wow! Panicked answers to calls of...who's out there? What else? Lots of similar whistle and click patterns—wish I knew what those meant…someday. Still, let's see that up closer. Hmmm…not a lot of variation. Repetition…repetition. In their stressed state…that makes sense. Okay, that's at least somewhat interesting—mark it." He tapped at the keyboard and moved on to the next file— "thermoregulation."

"Nothing outstanding here. Good data. A good research paper—a ground-breaking research paper--but nothing of note. Damn it! This won't do…not for me…not for Doc…This won't do!" He pounded the table, stood up and did a lap around the room— stopping and sitting again. "This isn't what Doc wants. Doc wants the answer. I want the answer. I *need* that answer."

Chapter 83

Virginia Beach Aquarium, Virginia

"Dr. Clarke, good morning."

"Good morning, Ed. Nice to hear from you so early — work through the night?"

Director Ed Bordon heard the sarcastic tone of her question, ignored it, and answered, "No. But, I did get here early today to sort through photos and…"

"…and, what did you see."

"Lots of dead bottlenose dolphins. Sorry, nothing conclusive. Most of the animals appeared to have both eyes closed. Even the live animals had their eyes closed — must've been the cold and the snow. Maybe what they saw in the Texas photos was an anomaly."

"Don't assume."

"I didn't. That's why I changed the necropsy protocol to make sure we swab the eyes and get a sample of the tissues surrounding the eyes — sent to the appropriate labs per your direction of course."

"Thank you for taking the initiative. How are the other necropsies going?"

"The teams got started about 10 minutes ago. I brought in some volunteer vet techs we've trained to help speed things up. We should be able to crank through the rest of the carcasses — even the new ones — by the end of the day today."

"Thanks for the update. I'm glad to see you have things well in hand. I'll…"

Bordon's concerned voice interrupted, "How are things in Tampa? That's a lot of animals to lose—especially after Galveston and here."

"It's not good." There was a long silence.

"That's it? Not good?"

"That's the short answer—the only answer really--but that's not what you want. That's not what we want either. We have a tech on site who has managed to collect all sorts of data on the animals—heart rates, brainwaves, respirations, vocalizations, body temps. I have my doubts. Dr. Nicely is exploring the eye pathology hypothesis with one of his graduate student protégés. I'm making plans to rescue and rehab should nothing come of any of this..." Angela's voice trailed off.

"But, you're not confident you'll get your chance. You think they'll die before then."

"Maybe it's that—maybe I'm feeling something else--but, definitely feeling that my plan might not get played out." The slight tremor in her voice was faint, but noticeable. "I've got to go. Keep up the great work. Let me know if you find anything else."

Chapter 84

Dolphin Towne, Tortola, BVI

After a long, deep sleep, and a wonderful organic breakfast, Kurt was anxious to get a little exercise — something he hadn't done for days. Jasmine loaned him one of the resort's mountain bikes and a road map and he planned a ride toward Mt. Sage and then to the NW

Coast—with stops to hike up Mt. Sage and Mt. Healthy and a ride to enjoy the view at Shark Island National Park.

Though the steep hills along his return route—through Brewer's and Cane Garden Bays—were leg and lung-burners, Kurt returned to Dolphin Towne refreshed. The pure physical exhaustion was a welcome change from the mental and emotional trauma of the Galveston stranding—of dealing with Angela.

After returning the bike to the storage shed, Kurt walked to the dining room—looking forward to refueling with a fresh fruit smoothie and some whole grain pasta. At the door to the dining room, he stopped. Sitting with Jasmine, and enjoying a huge green salad, was Rachel Remmy—the reporter from Summers Media. He watched in silence until Jasmine noticed him—only then did he walk towards the table.

Jasmine beamed as he came up to the table, "How was your ride?"

Kurt closed his eyes, took a deep breath—slowly in and out—and smiled. Opening his eyes, he said, "Physically, I'm exhausted. Mentally...well...I'm getting there." He moved his eyes from Jasmine to Rachel and back to Jasmine.

"Oh, I'm sorry. I thought you might recognize Rachel."

Rachel looked at Kurt and smiled, "There were a lot of volunteers at the stranding, Jasmine--some were trained, regulars. I wasn't. I had been staying nearby and just had to help. Of course, I didn't know it would have this kind of an impact on my soul." She reached out for Jasmine's comforting hand.

Kurt pulled out a chair and sat. He fidgeted for a few seconds. He frowned and closed his eyes. A touch on his hands opened them. It was Rachel and her cat-like green eyes. With the reporter's red hair and freckled complexion she could have been Jasmine's younger sister.

Rachel continued with the charade and whispered softly, "I don't expect you to remember me — there were so many people and so many dolphins."

Kurt closed his eyes again — ignoring her, but not the scene at Galveston replaying in his mind--*So many people...so many dolphins.* The seriousness of the thought tightened his face.

But, another gentle touch to his hands opened his eyes again — Jasmine was closer now. "You are in a safe place — a healing place. I think having Rachel here — having anyone here who has been through something like this — well, it can help all of you heal."

Slow-sliding her hands away, she sat back in her chair and continued, "So, I want to put something on our web site — something to welcome other stranding participants to Dolphin Towne to restore themselves. All they need to do is get to my doorstep." Jasmine shook her head and then moved a little closer to Kurt. "With Adam gone...well, I don't know anything about web sites. Can you...do you? I..."

Kurt smiled, "I've helped maintain our TEXMAM site. If it's a simple addition, I should be able to figure it out. Sure, I think I can do that."

Jasmine sat back. "Wonderful. Get something to eat—nourish your body. Then, we'll head over to Adam's control room and try to make sense of things." Trotting to the kitchen, Jasmine disappeared—but a server came out to take Kurt's order. Rachel continued to work on her salad.

After Kurt ordered a strawberry-banana smoothie and a plate of whole wheat penne with sun-dried tomatoes, the server returned to the kitchen. Rachel put down her fork and scooted her chair closer to the table—closer to Kurt. Leaning forward, she whispered, "Thank you. It was the only way I could think of to get in. I…"

Kurt put up his hand and she stopped, "I understand. It's an important story. I'm not sure what's here to interest you—the strandings are all stateside. And, I'm not sure you are being quite *ethical*." Then, he smiled, "But, I don't mind having you here."

She continued whispering while checking over her shoulder from time to time, "Thank you. I'm here because my editor, a stickler for balanced reporting, sent me here. Jasmine has fired up such a storm at Summers Media that he wanted to have someone looking into things here. It may end up being simple human interest on the woman who drew attention to the catastrophe. It may end up being more. At this point…" Picking up her fork, she stabbed a few leaves of spinach, "…all I know is that this is the best fresh green salad I've ever had and that Jasmine Summers is one gracious—and I mean that with an emphasis on *grace* in its purest form—hostess."

Kurt's smoothie and pasta arrived and he ate. A few minutes later, Jasmine came back into the dining room. She smiled and moved her eyes from Rachel to Kurt and back. Her smile morphed into a bit of a smirk, but she said nothing about the vibe she picked up between the two guests. Instead, she looked at Kurt's nearly empty plate, "There's plenty more, if you…"

Holding up the last fork of penne, Kurt nodded, "It's excellent. I'll get more after your message is up on the web site." He put the last bite in his mouth and chewed while he stood up. After swallowing, he nodded to Rachel, "My pleasure, and thank you for the fine work in Galveston."

Jasmine linked her arm through his and gently pulled him away. She looked back to Rachel and winked, "The hammocks on the bay are a great place to unwind, Rachel. Maybe we'll see you there later."

Leaving the Eli House, Kurt marveled at the design of the grounds, "You really put thought into every detail—Dolphin Towne has an amazingly natural sense of place."

"It was a challenge; believe me—to create a synthetic environment that did not feel like an architectural leisure suit. Fortunately, I had a benefactor who was very understanding of my needs." They had walked into the Education Center and were standing at the closed door to Adam's control room. Jasmine pushed open the door and flipped on a light, "Here it is."

Kurt started in but in passing Jasmine noticed her face squinch up and her eyes welling with tears. He stopped and turned to her, "Are you…?"

Falling into his arms, he held her tight. She cried and mumbled, "I miss him. I miss Adam. I haven't been in here since he left. I…" Kurt just hugged.

After a minute, Jasmine stopped and Kurt relaxed his hug—she wriggled out and leaned against the door frame. Reaching across the space, he pulled the tear-matted red hair from her face and tucked it behind her ears. Leaning back on a desk just inside the door, he asked, "Where did he go? Where did Adam go?"

"I didn't tell you? I thought I told you. I know I told you about my Adam—maybe not this part? So much has happened—it's hard to keep track of it all. Adam…Adam went with Dr. Menke to…"

Kurt stood quickly and his eyes widened, "Menke? He left with Menke? Where'd they…Tampa…of course they went to Tampa! Why Adam? What's so special about Adam that Menke would fly him to Tampa? Holy shit! Why would Doc take Adam?"

Jasmine struggled with Kurt's sudden, aggressive questioning. Her body bucked as she held in the sobbing. Closing her moist, bloodshot eyes, she took five long, deep breaths. Opening her eyes, she was calm and controlled. Motioning to two chairs, she said, "Sit."

Her breathing exercise had not only calmed herself, but helped to moderate Kurt's frantic plunge.

With both of them seated, she explained in more detail. Jasmine told Kurt of Adam's work and breakdown at MIT, his sailing to Tortola and his help in building Dolphin Towne into what it is today. Of course, he was particularly interested in her explanation—

however rudimentary—of his extensive monitoring system, computer network and transponders. Even more interesting, was Dr. Nicely's personal recognition of Adam and of Doc's use of that carrot to entice him to Tampa. When Jasmine finished, Adam swallowed his thoughts and just smiled. He reached across the void and held her hands softly.

Jasmine's eyes closed and her chin dropped to her chest. "But I haven't heard a word from him—not an email or…"

"Sounds to me like he's the kind of young man who gets easily absorbed in his work. Most men of his quality—of his intellectual power—work that way. I'm sure he's thought of you, but I'm sure that he feels like the best thing he can do to honor you is to work tirelessly to save those dolphins."

Jasmine nodded and stood. "Yes. Yes, that sounds like Adam. He moves into a very intense flow-state." Pointing at what was obviously the main computer workstation, her voice suddenly turned business-like, "His login is *AREICH*—all caps. His password is *BombaShack*—one word with an upper case *b* and *s*."

She pulled a piece of paper from her pocket and handed it to Kurt, "This is the gist of what I want on the website. Do what you can." She turned for the door but stopped and flipped her hair as she looked back. "Thank you. Thanks for being here."

Kurt was alone—only the sound of the humming servers and his own conspiratorial mind-ramblings were left. He was sure there was a link between Doc, Adam and the chip from Galveston.

Rolling the chair over to the computer, he woke up the monitor and entered the user name and password. The screens that came to life were mind-boggling. There were—Kurt counted—17 different windows open and running. Kurt worked his way through what was open.

"Holy shit!" Kurt had stumbled on the partial upload sent by Adam from Tampa—*TampaData.1*.

"Holy shit, what?" Rachel's slim silhouette was visible in the doorway.

Holding up his finger, Kurt said, "Wait. Give me a couple of minutes. I need to get Jasmine's announcement up first."

"You've been here all this time and you haven't…" There was an impatient tone to her voice—but, she stepped out of the shadows and her grin let him know that she wasn't really annoyed.

The finger went up again, "Wait." Kurt was focused on the web site. It took a couple of tries, but after about 10 minutes he had Jasmine's message—her invitation up—it was on the front page as well in the discussion forum that Adam had started about the strandings. "I should post this invitation on MARMAM—seal my fate as a flake."

Rachel had settled into a chair and had pulled it up close to Kurt while he worked. "Now besides me walking in the room--what got you so riled up 10 minutes ago?"

Clicking the mouse a couple of times, he opened another window, "This."

"*TampaData.1?*"

"*TampaData.1*. Or 28% of it anyway. It's an upload that came from Adam's laptop. An upload of data on the animals..." Kurt finally had a chance to scroll through the variables, "...heart rate, brain waves, vocalizations...amazing...this guy is amazing. I don't know how he is collecting this data, but whatever he's using is revolutionary."

"Why only 28%? How'd you open any of it? Why didn't the file finish loading?"

Tapping the keys and moving the mouse, Kurt moved deliberately through the drop-down menu and sifted through different options. Finally, he answered, "That is really what is exciting—only 28% came through. Adam's got partial file recovery software—that saved whatever got through...but, look at this. There are these options—stopped at source, stopped at destination, power interruption, pathway interruption, other." It was *other* that was checked.

Rachel sat up, "That could be anything."

"Anything other than the other four. Or..." He started Googling frantically—nodding his head as he moved along. "Or, it could be any of the other four, but masked so as not to be recognized—see." Pointing at the explanation on the software company's web site he sat back and turned to Rachel.

She shook her head. "I think you're making a big leap here. You're thinking someone—in their best Big Brother fashion—recognized this upload and stopped it."

Kurt just nodded.

"That's not much to build a conspiracy theory on."

Rachel winked, but Kurt had turned and focused on the monitor. A warm, caressing hand on his shoulder broke the spell and his chin dropped to his chest.

Putting the other hand on his other shoulder, Rachel continued, "I think we need to get this data to Summers. Then, they can get it to the experts. I have secure access to the SumSat network, we can email it and…"

Her hands slipped off his shoulders as he swiveled his chair to face her. "That will draw attention here. If someone really blocked this — they must deem it valuable for some reason. If they know that some data got through…that won't be acceptable. The data isn't safe here. We may not be safe here."

"Kurt, what are you talking about? Getting a little paranoid? Who is going to such great lengths to…?"

"…to cover up the cause of three majorly anomalous mortality events. Strandings like this — deaths like this--don't happen — period."

"You think…Mozambique?" Rachel was puzzled.

"Yet to be determined. Supposedly, the strandings were spread out over a couple of days--supposedly. Still, even if that isn't linked, the three unprecedented U.S. catastrophes are a cause for major concern. The play your media outlets are giving it…well, that's the kind of coverage a tragedy like this deserves."

Rachel held up her hand and nodded. "We still need to need proof. In the meantime, I have some ideas. Let me contact my IT people—using *my* laptop—and let them know that I am sending the data file and have them prepared to try and trace any disruption of the transfer. Before we do that, let's burn the data onto DVDs and express mail them—or, whatever equivalent they have on the island—to a variety of people. We could mail them to Summers, to Dr. Clarke, to..."

"I'll come up with a list. Great idea!" Kurt sealed his approval with a quick kiss and moved his head back just enough to see her reaction, but still close enough to feel her sighing breath on his face. She leaned into him and they kissed again.

Rachel stopped and caught her breath, "Okay. Let's get those DVDs burned and in envelopes." Her hand was still in his and he stroked it with his thumb. Kurt smiled, "Okay--lots to do."

Chapter 85

Galveston, Texas

Breaks were different for Shari in her new job. Used to be, she would have a drink, a smoke and maybe some French fries. Now, she had neither the alcohol nor the cigarettes — and, the French fries were not on her new diet. Instead, she would typically sit in the office lunch room and read while sipping a cup of coffee and eating a turkey breast sandwich from home. Sometimes, she'd proofread a school report for Bryan. Today, she pulled out her phone and the slip of paper with Jackson Dafoe's number.

"Ms. Casseine — good to hear from you. You've got more for me from Galveston?"

"Actually, I was hoping you might have something for me. Do you have anything on Kurt's whereabouts? I'd like to contact him."

"I have a good source — one of our people actually--that puts him at Dolphin Towne on Tortola in the British Virgin Islands."

"He's in the Caribbean? British Virgin Islands? I don't understand. I thought he'd be in Tampa. I thought he'd be there trying to help. What is he doing on...Tortola?"

"Yes--Tortola. The best I can tell is that he really went there to get away from it all — to put the strandings behind him. Dolphin Towne is sort of a New Age swim-with-the-dolphins resort — supposedly, very laid back but very...well...out there. My contact there said Kurt was frustrated to the point of inaction—that he needed to get away."

"Kurt ran away? I don't believe it—he's not a quitter."

"Well, if it is any consolation...if he originally went there to drop out—to quit...I don't think he's sticking to that plan..."

"Why? Is he on his way to Tampa now?"

"No, at the moment he's not going anywhere. But, he is sending us some kind of information from Tampa that he thinks might help break this thing wide open. I'm doubtful. His reputation for accuracy is not good, while his reputation for outlandish theories is...well...fairly well known—sorry. But, Rachel—our contact there—she thinks he might be onto something...something big."

Shari could hear the questioning tone in his voice, "And you? What do you think?"

"I think your friend Kurt can be pretty persuasive when he gets deep into something—I think Rachel—our reporter there—I think she might have been swayed by the power of his argument. His passion. Either way, I won't pass judgment until we get the information and pass it through our experts."

Wanting to defend Kurt, Shari could barely hold her tongue. But, she did manage to restrain herself and finish the conversation cordially, "Thank you. Thank you for the information."

After hanging up and putting her leftover snack back in the refrigerator, Shari walked back to her desk. There, she made sure no one was looking over her shoulder and did a rare personal internet search. "Wow," was all that came out of her mouth when she finally arrived at the Dolphin Towne website and began scrolling through the 360-degree photos of the rooms, profiles of the individual dolphins and the pricey swim-with packages. Under "Contact Us," she found an email address the phone number. After jotting down the phone number, Shari started to type.

> *For Kurt Braun, Formerly of TEXMAM:*
> *Dearest Kurt,*
> *Your note was a big surprise. You know none of this was your fault and that you handled the stranding with great expertise. Anyone who thinks otherwise is mistaken. We are deeply saddened that you left — but we understand how hard this has been on you. We hope that you are recovering well at Dolphin Towne.*
> *Are you continuing to get the word out about what might be going on? Bryan is convinced we should find and help you. He's convinced that you are in Tampa trying to wake those dolphins up. He's a smart kid — good at making connections. He thinks their one eye was closed because they were all asleep. I told him it was a good thought, but that I'm sure Dr. Nicely or Dr. Clarke already thought of that.*
> *Anyway, Bryan is convinced you need our help. I'm at a loss for what to do. You've always been there to help guide me, I'd appreciate any suggestions.*
> *Your loyal volunteer,*
> *Shari*

Shari hit "send" and started working on the pile of paperwork on the corner of her desk.

Dolphin Towne, Tortola, BVI

Rachel returned to the control room with her laptop case in hand. "I called my editor and the IT department. I emailed them the data file as well. I thought we'd want as many records of this as possible—especially since the email to Dr. Clarke *did not* go through."

Kurt beamed when she came in the room—there was something about her energy that moved him. But, his momentary elation was tempered by Rachel's failure to get the data through to Angela. "Shit. You tried more than once, right?"

"Of course." She narrowed her eyes and shook her head.

"Right—you're a professional. I get it. Well... I've got the DVDs packaged and labeled. Here's the DHL number for pick-ups...I figured you should call. I don't think it's safe to use the land lines—I'm assuming they are all being watched. Your personal phone might be our best bet."

Rachel smiled and stepped out temporarily. Kurt turned his attention to the piles of notes on Adam's desk. There was a copy of the email from Dr. Nicely and the sketches of his subcutaneous transponder. Again, he pondered a working relationship between Doc, Adam and the U.S. Navy.

The thoughts were interrupted when Rachel sauntered back into the room and announced, "Done. They've got a pickup van coming within 30 minutes--at least some things on this island move faster."

Kurt still beamed, but in his mind he was questioning his attraction—there were other more pressing matters at hand. He sighed and his smile disappeared. Rachel shrugged, but Kurt just shook his head and waved her over. "Look—schematics of a chip transponder. It looks almost exactly like the object found imbedded in an animal in Texas. Odds are this Adam character was in on this from the beginning—hooked up with Dr. Menke when he was here for a routine check on the dolphins. Or, Menke recognized his disgruntled genius and courted him over a number of visits over the years. Who knows? But, something in his damn chip—the damn chip he built for the fucking military--malfunctioned and caused these animals to strand. Doc brought him to Tampa to troubleshoot."

Rachel moved behind him and planted a light kiss near his ear, "So, why send the data here if he's in cahoots with Dr. Menke?"

"Second thoughts. He needs a way out? He needs a way to let Jasmine know he's trying to do the right thing?"

"Devious. Your mind is devious." Another kiss landed and lingered on his neck.

Kurt looked up and into her eyes, "Distracted. My mind is distracted."

"Distracted?" Jasmine sauntered into the room. Rachel stood and stumbled on one of the chair's caster wheels—taking two awkward steps back from Kurt. Jasmine giggled, but as her face relaxed she said, "It's wonderful. If the feeling is right, don't deny it." Smiling at Kurt, Jasmine unfolded a piece of paper and held it out for him. "For you."

On his second reading through, Kurt drifted into thought. He folded the piece of paper in half—and then in half again--wondering if Angela or Nicely had any inkling of a long-term link between Adam and Doc. He decided to use Bryan's theory — that the dolphins were sleeping — to regain a little of his credibility. Then, he'd suggest the connection between Doc, Adam and the chip. After folding the e-mail in half one more time, Kurt nodded at Rachel's cell phone sitting on the desk. "Can I make a call?" Rachel said, "Of course." Kurt walked out and dialed.

Egmont Key, Tampa Bay, Florida

"Kurt? We're trying to get some work done here. We all can't just drop everything and drop out--go to some tropical paradise and lay in a hammock while..."

"Just listen. Please."

She was quiet long enough that Kurt continued, "I got an email from one of my volunteers — Shari Casseine. She mentioned something about the dolphins having one-eye closed. What's up with that?"

"Okay. Her boy was downloading and sorting the stranding photos..."

"Bryan? Awesome!"

"Can I continue?" She didn't wait for an answer — his silence was confirmation enough. "We looked at them ourselves. Sure enough — all of the animals have one eye closed. Robin is working with Vee — with one of his protégés — to survey any type of pathogen that might cause that type of reaction. We're getting eye biopsies of the carcasses that haven't been taken away. We've forwarded the photos and we're…"

Kurt interrupted, "…possibly over-complicating the whole thing--imagine *that*. Angela, it may be simpler. The dolphins might just be asleep."

Grumpy-faced at being interrupted, Angela nodded and a small smile spread her lips out of her frown.

"What?" Robin could see her disposition change. "What?"

She held up the wait-a-minute finger and put her phone on speaker. "Kurt, Robin is here now too. Tell him what you just told me."

"The dolphins might just be asleep."

Robin laughed, his face tightened and he shook his head. "Dumbkop!"

Kurt responded, "I'm sorry, but I think…"

"No, no—not you Kurt." Robin cut him off, "Me--dumbkop. How did I get so caught up in thinking it was something so much more complex. Fuck!" Even cloaked in a thick accent, the profanity was obvious. "They're fucking sleeping! The fucking dolphins are sleeping!" Robin quick-stepped around the boat, thinking—shaking his head. "Sorry. It might bloody fit…"

For an animal that must consciously surface to breathe, true sleep—mental and physical shutdown—would lead to deadly drowning. Instead, dolphins allow each side of their brains to go into a rest state for a certain period of time. During this rest, electrical activity decreases, physical activity decreases, heart rate and respirations drop and the eye controlled by the resting hemisphere closes. Some species pair up — safety in numbers — and swim regular, circular patterns.

Angela chimed in, "It *may* fit. But, I have a hard time believing we're witnessing some massive dolphin slumber party! It may very well still be something much more complex."

"Dolphin slumber party." Robin chuckled, then got serious, "Even if we can confirm that they're asleep — and, that's only a hypothesis at this point — that doesn't mean we know what triggered it...Something had to cause it. *That* might be the complicated part."

Kurt's voice was serious — even in tone, "I might be able to help with that — at least with the knowing whether or not they are really asleep."

Robin spoke up again, "Adam should be able to help with that — the data he's collecting..."

"...might never be seen by your eyes, Dr. Nicely." Pausing, Kurt sighed heavily enough to be heard — even on the speaker phone. "There's a lot to this, but I'll try to keep it brief. I'll try to keep it believable."

Angela rolled her eyes and looked at Robin — he shrugged. Kurt continued, "Please don't interrupt until I'm done — it'll be easier that way. I'm sure you know by now that I left TEXMAM. For whatever reason, I ended up at Dolphin Towne on Tortola. The owner wanted something posted on their web site. With Adam gone, no one else knew how to do it. I volunteered. He had other programs running on his computer and I was nosy. Long story short — there was an incomplete data file that was there. The file was labeled *TampaData.1* and sent *this morning* from Adam's laptop. I did some digging in the application and online and determined that there is a probability that an outside source stopped the data transmission. I think Adam may have been having second thoughts because the chip he designed for Doc — for the Navy--was malfunctioning and causing the strandings. I saw the schematics and…"

"I'm sorry to interrupt." Robin — true to his nature--was sincere. He could see Angela was chaffing and ready to pounce on Kurt's conspiracy theory, but motioned for her to stay quiet. Reluctantly, she nodded and he continued, "Sorry, I know you said not to, but I have to. Plausible — all very plausible and even probable — except for the bit at the end. Adam's been working on transponders of various kinds for years — he even mentioned the subcutaneous chip in the *Marine Mammal Science* paper of his that I reviewed. I don't think he'd do that if he were designing chips for the Navy. I think his motives were purely scientific."

Robin's even tone and reasoned argument were not enough for Angela. She had to react. "C'mon, Kurt! We don't have time for more tenuous conspiracy theories…maybe he was just backing up his data and lost his connection."

There was a 30-second silence and when Kurt continued his voice had lost some of its frantic, conspiratorial passion, "Okay…okay — can't imagine a genius like Adam with access to all that military hardware losing his connection…but…I guess that's remotely possible. Backing up his data…yes. Not working for

Menke…yes. Possible—but, I don't buy it. Regardless, he sent data that was only partially transmitted—the rest was blocked. I have that data—you don't. I can get you that data."

"Or, we can get it from Doc—or Adam." Angela's tone was more than a little haughty.

"No! I mean…shit. You shouldn't count on that. I'm not going to count on that. We tried emailing you the data and the message bounced back—right after we successfully sent the message to Summers Media. Somebody is watching us…watching Summers…watching you. I'm not going to risk another email from here or from Summers. I'm sending the data via DHL to you—and, to Robin—through the NMFS St. Pete office. Keep your eyes open tomorrow."

Robin could see Angela tensing to strike again. Holding up his hand and shaking his head, he managed to keep her at bay. "We appreciate your concerns and your help. We'll approach the subject with Doc and Adam. How should I say this? We'll approach it delicately. I'm sure we'll get access to the full data file and to Adam's analysis."

"Delicate or not—you won't get the answer you want. You'll only get what they want you to know—some kernel of plausibility. You won't get the real truth--at least not until it's too late." After a brief pause, Kurt said, "Keep your eyes open for the data. I'll find some way to get it to you." Then, the line went dead.

Robin looked at Angela. A shuffling noise from the boat tower turned both of their heads up. Medlin walked away and to the side of the tower--looking out over the dolphins and shaking his head.

Chapter 86
Office of Admiral Collins, NOAA

Silver Spring, Maryland

The admiral's fist was too sore to pound on the desk again. He had just received notification of yet another data-sensitive email transmission — this time from a Summers Media laptop at Dolphin Towne via one of the Summers Media satellites to their New York City offices and to Dr. Clarke in Tampa. Obviously, someone at Dolphin Towne had noticed the partial download and thought it important enough to try and pass it along. He couldn't imagine anyone at Dolphin Towne — Jasmine Summers especially — who would recognize the importance of the file. There had to be a reporter or some other prying, new and potentially dangerous player at Dolphin Towne.

Standing, Collins paced laps around his desk. While the data file had gotten through to Summers, the transmission to Dr. Clarke had been blocked. His mind raced. While a quick preliminary review of the data revealed nothing likely to be sensitive or damning on its own, he still thought the time had come to act — to deal with Summers Media and with the data that had made its way to Dolphin Towne. Pausing at the window, he noticed his pulse pounding in his ears and beads of cold sweat on his forehead. After several long, deep breaths and a wipe with his handkerchief, Admiral Collins moved back to his desk.

THE FEW

> *FCC and NORAD contacts need to order immediate SumSat4 repositioning. While move is in process, arrange for creative electromagnetic disabling of SumSat4.*
>
> *Dolphin Towne operational plan update? Suggest commencing data wipe operation ASAP.*
>
> *Summers Media data operation clearly not feasible.*
>
> *Preliminary analysis of transmitted data shows nothing likely to be sensitive or damning on its own. NMMP asset's analysis of earlier "very interesting" acoustic profile noted and filtered by Reich in Tampa is positive match. Detailed analysis of transmitted data and its potential relationship to CONCH is continuing at NMMP*
>
> *Update Tampa: Awaiting Reich's detailed data analysis. Operational assets in place and activated. Disruption of any further data transmission is primary objective.*
> *ACRET*

The admiral's calm focus was momentary. As he thought about Tampa he became increasingly frustrated. Again, he stood, paced and ranted out loud, "Where is Menke with some answers? We know Reich detected, and noted, but didn't recognize CONCH. We need something to move on before this has to get more complicated…" He got quiet, "…or someone gets sloppy." An email alert brought him back to his desk. While still standing, he opened the message.

ACRET
Dolphin Towne Update. Operational assets in place. Virus launch imminent. On-site operation will commence sometime after 2200 hours.
BLADE

Collins walked to the window — he knew he could count on Shaw.

Chapter 87

Dolphin Towne, Tortola, BVI

Kurt returned to find Rachel and Jasmine still sitting in the control room—chatting softly while rifling through more of Adam's papers.

"I had to call Tampa and let them know."

They both turned as he came in. Jasmine's eyes were red and swollen—they had discovered Adam's notes on the subcutaneous chip in Sammy and on the workings of the Theta Wave Meditation Meld. Jasmine's look was imploring him to say more—more about what information he had passed to Tampa and more about what of Adam's they had found.

Rachel saw Jasmine's look and tried to keep Kurt from going too far and further upsetting her. Her eyes implored him to tread carefully as she asked, "Let them know what?" Rachel and Jasmine looked at him intently.

He pulled the paper Jasmine had given him out of his pocket. "The e-mail...it was from one of my top volunteers. First volunteer at the stranding, actually. They...she and her son...they also do data entry for me. I left them a note—just saying thanks and good-bye. The kid...Bryan...smart kid...very smart kid. Well, he made some kind of a connection. He noticed that all the dolphins had one eye closed. He figured out I was gone. He thought that I went to Tampa to help wake the dolphins up--to wake them up."

Jasmine and Rachel shook their heads—they didn't understand.

Kurt continued, "Dolphins don't sleep like us. They need to surface to breathe—and that takes conscious action on their part. They shut down one side of their brain—and the eye that relates to that side gets closed. They become much less active. Typically, they don't eat. Anyway, I had to tell...I had to tell Dr. Clarke and Dr. Nicely that the dolphins in Tampa might just be asleep."

Jasmine couldn't hold back any more. She threw the papers she had in her hand to the floor and bawled, "Adam put them to sleep! Adam put them all to sleep! Why? My Adam? To sleep...a cold, lightless sleep. He did that...he..." The intensity of her questioning tapered to a mumbling murmur as Rachel closed in with a strong hug.

For the moment, Kurt seemed immune to the emotions flooding the room. In silence he picked Adam's schematics off the floor and put them back in order. Then he faced the two women, "We need to get these to the media and to some other marine mammal experts. I need to look at Adam's data. We need to get the chip information scanned and emailed to our list of scientists. We need those DVDs and copies of these papers in DHL's hands. We need to do this now." The intensity of his voice—*the voice*—picked up as he spoke—as he focused.

Kurt continued, "Rachel." She was still hugging a now calmer Jasmine. "Rachel." She broke the hug, looked at him and stood. He closed, then opened his eyes, "Copy the chip papers, take that box of envelopes of DVDs and carefully unseal them—add the copies and reseal them. Then get the envelopes to the front of the house and wait for DHL. Call them and see where that pick-up is--quickly."

Rachel grabbed the papers and moved to the copier.

Kurt walked over and squatted in front of Jasmine. He took her hands in his. "Jasmine. I don't know if Adam — or how much Adam — may be involved in this. Honest."

She quickly pulled her hands away and pulled her legs into a fetal position on the chair. Her voice was a weak whisper, "I don't understand all of this — all of his notes and projects…there is so much…all of this machinery. There's a lot I don't know about my Adam. But I do know his soul." Gently putting her legs to the floor, she stood gracefully and walked out of the room.

Rachel's eyes followed her out and then tracked back to the task at the copier. Kurt grabbed the original papers and scanned them. "I'll save them on this flash drive and then email using your laptop…" He sighed.

"Right." Rachel had moved to re-stuffing the DHL envelopes, but shook her head as Kurt stood there with her laptop bag in his hand.

Lowering his head, he joined in the head shaking, "Right, yourself--that email bounced back — one of those crappy nondescript mailer daemon replies. I wonder how many of the millions of those people see every day are generated by our interventionist government."

Standing up with the box in her arms, Rachel said, "The DHL truck should be here any minute. After getting these off, we can take the car and head down the road—someone has to have a computer we can use to get around the system..."

"But if Summers is being watched..." Kurt's stare was not focused.

Rachel smiled, "I have personal emails for almost everyone that matters at Summers. In fact, we could email it to anyone and everyone in my address book...even use some of the email addresses you've got floating around in your head—using someone else's computer of course."

"Brilliant. I hope someone can get it in the right hands." Kurt slung the laptop bag back over his shoulder and nodded at Rachel, "I've got my own copies of the file on a DVD and a thumb drive--let's go."

Editorial Conference Room, Summers Media
New York, New York

"Shit!" Josh pushed away from the table and ran to the conference room door. He shouted across the newsroom floor, "Carlye!" Almost everyone stood—but didn't look at him. Their gaze was fixed to the "snow" on the big screens set around the news floor—snow that now took the place of the image from Tampa Bay.

Carlye came jogging to the door and pulled him inside the conference room. "I just got notice from SumSpaceTech. They're the subsidiary that manages SumSat operations."

Josh paced in front of the blank big screen. "Notice? Notice of what?"

"SumSat4 was in a geosynchronous orbit at only 250 miles altitude — where it needed to be to have that high magnification, high resolution image of Tampa Bay. That's not a typical orbital profile for a communications satellite or a commercial imaging satellite. That's typically where you find military satellites. NORAD decided we had overstayed our welcome. They *strongly requested* that the FCC order us to move. The FCC did just that — SumSpaceTech started pulling back out to 1,000 miles while still focusing on Tampa."

Josh walked right into Carlye's space, "And?"

"And then we lost the image--electromagnetic disturbances according to SumSpaceTech. Josh, the satellite is fried. There won't be any more images. But..." She walked around the table, opened up her laptop and started typing.

"But what?"

"But, we *do* have a data file that was sent by Rachel Remmy on behalf of one Kurt Braun, formerly of TEXMAM..."

"And, data are so much more exciting than live images." He flopped back into his chair at the head of the table.

"Well, maybe not at first sight. But, these data were, according to Rachel, important enough for someone to interrupt and block most of its transmission to Dolphin Towne."

"Important to the same people who asked to have SumSat4 removed?"

"Of course, any connection is yet to be determined. I have our IT folks sniffing around to see if anyone is monitoring us — it is delicate business...but we have plenty of IT people who've worked in countries with sophisticated internet surveillance systems." Carlye sat in the chair next to the associate editor, "The data…well…We're not going to risk sending it anywhere else. Becca is already flying in some dolphin experts to check it out."

A flash of light turned their heads back to the big screen. The image was a fuzzy night vision view of the scene in Tampa from water level — from their camera crew out on the water.

Josh turned back to Carlye. "Well, at least that's something. Let me know what Becca gets out of those experts. Let me know if you hear anything else from Rachel. And…" he sat up straight and smiled, "…make sure the public knows *why* we lost our killer satellite image."

Chapter 88

Egmont Key, Tampa Bay, Florida

"Thanks for joining us." Robin gave Dr. Menke a hand up as he came aboard the command boat.

Doc nodded, "Robin, Angela...Commander." Medlin stood just behind the two scientists who had been under his watch.

Angela went right to work, "What is the word from Adam? What has he found?"

Medlin handed Doc a dry cushion and he sat. "Word is that as of his last update—which was on my way here—word is that he's only found expected commonalities. Things like low heart rates and respiration rates. He said the acoustic patterns were a little more interesting—repetitive, very repetitive. But, that he didn't think that was a sign of anything more than dealing with the stress and conserving energy."

"We've almost lost another entire day, Doc." Angela fidgeted with her cuticles, not sure she wanted to confront Doc. "I could have had at least a couple animals out of the water and in rehab by now. We need something from someone now or I'm putting my mother of all rescue plans into action. I can't sit by and..." Angela felt a familiar hand on her shoulder—and a slight squeeze.

"My man in Plettenberg...in South Africa...he hasn't come up with any pathological reason for the eye closure in the Texas dolphins." Robin let go of Angela and stepped to the side, "Right now, our only possible explanation..."

Angela turned to Robin and glared. She wasn't ready to share that speculation.

Shaking off Angela's disapproval, Robin continued, "Right now, our only plausible explanation comes from a 12-year old boy."

Menke's grin took up most of his face, "And, what explanation might that be?"

Angela shook her head at Robin. This time, the South African didn't answer Doc.

"Dr. Nicely?"

Neither Robin nor Angela answered. But their thoughts on how to respond were cut short by a voice behind them. "That they are asleep, sir. The boy suggested that the dolphins were asleep."

Robin spun and looked at Medlin. "Commander?"

Lt. Commander Medlin stepped forward — he had overheard the phone conversation with Kurt. "Regardless of who is involved in this event for what reasons, I think we need to share this information."

While Angela and Robin stared at Medlin, Doc, out of their view, sternly shook his head at the MSOT commander. In the momentary silence, they all shifted into a tighter circle. Then, Robin spoke, "It makes sense based on the photos. It makes sense based on the behavior patterns we see in this group. It's possible that they have been in some kind of prolonged sleep state — essentially asleep for a month, maybe two months. No eating, little activity. We..."

Angela cut him off, "...we need to verify that they are asleep. We need Adam's data for that — to see the brainwave patterns."

"Yes, Adam should have that data." Robin agreed. Medlin nodded as well.

Doc glanced through the side of his eyes at Medlin, then looked out into the darkness and scratched at his chin. "Prolonged sleep...I suppose it's possible. But, could they have slept long enough to create the emaciation we saw in Texas and still survive? Some..." He pulled out his Blackberry and headed for the inside command center. "Give me a few minutes. I'll raise the boy genius."

Chapter 89

Dolphin Towne, Tortola, BVI

"Jasmine! Kurt and I...Jasmine?" Rachel yelled as they passed through the main hallway of the Eli House—on their way toward Dolphin Towne's front gate. With a hand on her shoulder, Kurt stopped the reporter and they both stared at Jasmine—she was fixated on the wide screen television in the lounge.

Jasmine sensed their presence, but a whispered, monotone reply was her only acknowledgement, "The hope has left this world. Have you seen the TV?"

They both looked at the owner of Dolphin Towne, but Kurt tilted his head and asked the question, "What?" His first thought was that the dolphins in Tampa had finally beached, but Jasmine spoke up before he got to probe deeper.

"No, the dolphins in Tampa haven't stranded..." She had sensed his concern, "...at least as far as I can tell. The TV—the image from Tampa Bay is gone. Well, the up-close satellite image anyway. Apparently, the...FC...the Federal Communications Commission ordered Summers to move the satellite into a higher orbit."

"FCC? Come on..." Kurt shook his head, "My bet is on the Pentagon. I think someone in the Department of Defense has a lot invested in what is causing this."

"I've got to see this." Rachel set the box of DHL envelopes on a small table and walked next to Jasmine—leaving Kurt in the doorway. "Summers knew it was risky moving the satellite into that orbit. It was a stretch—they wondered how long they might be allowed to linger in that space. So, definitely not unexpected. Certainly a plausible request from the FCC—whether the order originated with them or not...a smart move on someone's part if they are trying to blind us to their next move."

Kurt turned and smiled, "Now you're thinking—putting pieces together."

"Enough thinking. We need to get the information we have out to Summers--out to the rest of the world. We need other people to start making those connections—and backing them up with the hard evidence we don't have."

Jasmine shuddered, sobbed and slumped to the floor. "Why would Adam do this? To the dolphins...to me...he can't have..."

Touching the Dolphin Towne owner's shoulder, Rachel crouched down and whispered, "At this point, any evidence of his involvement is circumstantial—*circumstantial*." She glared back at Kurt—the look said, *hold your tongue*—and then continued whispering to Jasmine, "If we get it to Summers in New York there is a chance they might prove a connection to Adam. But..."

Sniffling, Jasmine whispered, "...but, there is a chance they might prove there is not."

"Exactly!" Kurt was a little too enthusiastic and the recipient of another hard stare from Rachel.

Shifting to the floor in front of Jasmine, Rachel slid her hands down to hold those of her hostess, "There is always that hope. But, first, we need to get the information out. We think that someone might be monitoring the Dolphin Towne servers and emails *and* any transmissions to or from servers and phones linked to Summers Media. We need to find another computer to send the information from…"

Kurt had realized the importance of a little patience, calmed down and also moved to the floor next to Jasmine. "Do you know of anyone close to Dolphin Towne with a computer and a good internet connection—a fast connection?"

"I…I…Adam would know…" Jasmine sobbed again, caught her breath and continued, "…but, I know he's not here." She sighed, "Give me a minute."

Rachel looked at Kurt rolling his eyes and again narrowed hers at him.

Sitting up straight, Jasmine started to think out loud, "There's Teresa and Frits—met them when I sailed to the Bay Islands off Honduras in 2001. They live on a sailboat moored at the north end side of Cane Garden Bay…they used to come here more often to swim…Adam said they used to email their encounter logs. He was all agog about their computer system and satellite uploads and…damn—they sailed for St. Maarten six days ago." She sat silent for about thirty seconds and then stood up and walked to the television. Turning off the power, she turned and looked right at Kurt, "Malcom Knaggs. He's British—lived in Singapore before moving here…the manager at Hillside Cottages….go out the drive, make a right then…make your third left…it's uphill past the cottages to his house. His house is yellow — the cottages are eggshell blue. I'll get you the keys to the Prius…"

"Okay, Jasmine, but it's 9:45."

Kurt was stopped by Jasmine's smile — it was the first he'd seen in a while. "Malcom's a dear friend, Kurt. The first Wednesday of most months he brings over a bottle of wine or two and some other Brits staying at the cottages or moored in one of the bays. We drink and talk world politics. He's got a huge network of wanderers he stays in touch with. I guess that's why he's got the big computer set-up at his house. I'll call him…"

"No!" Kurt caught Jasmine's shoulder as she reached for the phone. "Sorry. I'd recommend that you not make any calls or send any emails until we get this out. Just write a note — an introduction-- on one of your cards."

"I understand. He's very welcoming. Once he sees my car and my card…well, you'll be his best friend." Jasmine walked out of the room and down the hallway toward the foyer. Rachel and Kurt followed with the box of envelopes.

"Here's my card. Here are the keys." Jasmine gave them to Kurt and closed her hands over his. Sighing she said, "Do what you have to, Kurt — the dolphins are more important than Adam."

Rachel looked at the box of envelopes Kurt had set on a chair in the foyer, "DHL could be here any minute…can you…?"

Jasmine nodded and Kurt and Rachel headed for the door.

Chapter 90

Adam's Lab, MacDill Air Force Base, Tampa, Florida

"Asleep? Dr. Nicely thinks they're asleep? I don't…well…hmm…the repeating acoustical patterns…the group swimming…the…"

"We don't have time for an extended dialogue!" Doc was agitated.

Adam's acoustical analysis was nearly complete and he didn't want to stop—he continued to type furiously on the keyboard. He'd meant to get to the brainwaves earlier, but he got caught up in his analysis of the acoustics. "There's a great deal of data and…well…I just have to finish up this…"

"Now, Adam! Stop what you are doing and focus. Focus on the brainwaves--now!"

Adam stood and stretched—arching his back. He had been hunched over the keyboard for hours. He cracked his neck. "Okay, Doc—okay. I'll start the analysis now. Stay on the line. I should be able to tell you something fairly soon."

The phone line was open, but Adam worked in silence—navigating through a layer of files and opening the brainwave imaging file for the first dolphin. "Holy shit!"

"Adam?

"Hang on, Doc." Adam typed furiously at the keys—pulling up data from 12 dolphins at a time. Quickly, he pulled up a file of "standard" dolphin brainwaves for comparison. "That's it—delta waves. Delta waves, Doc—they're asleep. Well, half their brain is anyway. Yeah, but you know how that works in dolphins—unihemispheric sleep. The other hemisphere varies from individual to individual—most are beta waves some are...are much more interesting."

There was a pause as Adam again typed quickly.

"What, Adam? What is more interesting?"

"Hang on, Doc." Adam sat staring at the monitors wondering what to tell Doc. He wondered if any of this information would make it back to Dr. Nicely or Dr. Clarke. Knowing the answer to that, he started to scheme a way—a long-shot way—to eventually pass the data along to one of them.

Doc grew uncomfortable with the silence, "Adam, don't do anything stupid."

"I know the drill." After a brief moment to gather himself, Adam continued, "Yes, they are asleep—all have delta wave patterns in one hemisphere. But...but that might not be the most interesting—or the most serious--thing. I did a quick time-lapse look at a sampling of other individuals...of their other non-sleeping hemisphere. Over the time we were collecting the data about...let's see..." He did some quick calculations. "Over that time, approximately 30% of the subjects moved rapidly from beta to alpha to theta waves. What I haven't seen...this is the bad news...what I haven't seen is the usual increase of activity in the other side of the brain—no preceding move through the entire wave sequence until they get to beta waves and are alert. If both hemispheres go to sleep...well..."

"They drown. They no longer can make the decision to surface and breathe. They drown. *Or,* they put themselves in a situation—on a beach—where they can't drown." Doc sighed—Adam could hear it through the phone. "Then, this mess might be over."

Adam walked over to his cot and flopped flat. He said nothing.

"Adam?"

The silence remained.

"Adam!"

He pulled his knees to his chest and rocked slightly on the squeaky cot, "What are you going to tell Dr. Nicely and Dr. Clarke?"

"That's none of your..."

"I'm sure they're asking. I'm sure they want to know what I'm seeing in the data. They know I have data. They know I'm not an idiot. They know I've got to have something to say." Adam had jumped off the cot and was pacing around the room. He stopped at the refrigerator and grabbed his last Red Bull.

"Yes, you're right—they are already asking. I'm with them now—on the command boat. They're watching me through the windows right now."

"If you don't tell them, you'll get nothing out of me—nothing."

"If you give me nothing, the dolphins are sure to die. If you give me nothing then you are ruined. You'll never be able to go back to Dolphin Towne. It's that simple. Doing nothing is not an option for you." Doc didn't wait for Adam's response. He knew there was none coming. "Now, they're asleep. Almost a third of them are slipping towards sleep in the other half of their brain. Something...something is causing this. That is what I want out of you, Adam. *That* is your next step — and quickly."

Doc hung up and Adam found himself sitting on the cot with an open can in his hand. He got up to go check the garbage can, but noticed several open cans sitting in various places throughout the lab. He sat back down, sipped the Red Bull and thought out loud, "What puts dolphins to sleep? What could have put them to sleep...a month...maybe two months ago? And...damn it...what's still out there and shutting down the other half of their brain?"

Egmont Key, Tampa Bay, Florida

Doc walked slowly towards Angela, Robin, and Medlin.

"Adam confirms it — they're asleep. Delta waves in one hemisphere in every animal. Who would've thought...?"

Robin smiled, "A 12-year old boy — that's who." Doc just shook his head. Robin continued, "You know, I was thinking about this while you were on the phone — thinking about sleep behavior in dolphins. It's really quite an extraordinary and appropriate system. The other half of the brain stays fairly alert, but they often team up with a buddy to find safety in numbers — at least that's the theory."

Angela smirked, "No safety in these numbers."

Ignoring her, Robin went on, "It's certainly possible that as the sleep became prolonged, the buddy pairs buddied up and so on and so on—until we had a mass like this."

Medlin chimed in, "That makes sense, Dr. Nicely. Does that relate to the number of females and calves in the group?"

"Possibly, commander. Since females and calves may be part of small groups already...it's conceivable that an aggregation like this could happen faster. Calves and females and sleep..." Robin drifted into a blank stare.

Doc sat and listened—he saw no need to expand on Adam's findings. His colleagues seemed quite content to stare and wait for the ruminating Dr. Nicely.

After a minute-long silence, Robin nodded and continued, "I'd need to do a search to confirm this, but the most recent research I've seen actually suggests that females and calves can go up to a month without *any* sleep. Speculation is that they do this to keep moving in colder, wilder water—for energy conservation and defense. It's been observed in orcas and common dolphins, but never documented in bottlenose." Robin was caught in the flow of his thoughts, "Personally, I think that might make them more susceptible—since they may already have a sleep deficit--and more likely to form protective..."

Finally, Doc rudely interrupted to address the elephant on the boat, "Thanks for bringing us up to speed on the latest in dolphin sleep research, but the big question remains—what caused these animals to go to sleep, for one, two, maybe three months?"

Nicely nodded, but did not answer. He didn't have an answer.

Angela broke the silence, "Robin, Doc…my question is — how do we wake them up? How do we wake them up and get them healthy?" With her hand up, she paused and then continued, "*My* answer is that we get them out of this environment and into rehab tanks ASAP." Again the hand went up — silence. "Doc, any word from Randy on how the dolphins at Caldwell are responding?"

Doc stuttered, "I've…I've been so focused since we arrived…I…I haven't…"

"We need that information." She turned to Robin, "If it's environmental, isolating them and getting them nutrition and fluids might help. If it's viral or bacterial, that might show as well. So, my rescue plan will be put into action at sunrise and…"

This time, Medlin stepped closer and firmly interrupted, "Only pending the approval of Admiral Collins." His chin dropped to his chest and he looked at his feet.

"Medlin!" Doc marched forward — then stopped. He reacted without thinking and Angela and Robin were now staring hard.

Medlin lifted his head — his face expressionless--and turned to the two other team members that had moved closer to the conversation. He nodded and they quickly walked toward Doc — taking up station to his right and left. "We can't let this go on any longer, Dr. Menke. I can't. I can't let you or the admiral kill more dolphins. I can't let the Navy and MSOTs be tainted by killing more dolphins." The two MSOT men moved in and restrained Doc firmly. Robin and Angela still stood speechless.

Doc knew better than to speak without thinking again. His stare was straight ahead and into nothingness--detached. He didn't dare look at Angela or Robin.

"Your Blackberry, Doc. Give me your phone—now." Medlin stepped closer and reached out.

Doc's eyes narrowed and he struggled not to blurt out what he was thinking—how the commander was foolishly risking his career and the security of the nation. Holding his tongue, Doc reached into his pocket for the Blackberry—his hand lingering long enough to inconspicuously tap his speed dial 1. Message sent, he pulled it out and handed it, with a dramatic flourish, to the Lt. Commander.

Office of Admiral Collins, NOAA
Silver Spring, Maryland

Admiral Collins did not want to leave his office—he knew that the next 24 hours would be crucial to resolving the dolphin crisis in Tampa Bay and covering any doubts about CONCH. And even with today's modern electronics and their ability to keep him in touch 24/7, he still felt that being in his office added something—an air of legitimacy—to his unofficial command. His most recent operational plan-- the disruption of SumSat 4 video transmissions--had been successful. Now, Collins waited for what he hoped would be a devastating two-pronged attack on the Dolphin Towne computer network and for Doc and his wonder boy to solve this mystery and make it go away — or, at least, to come up with a plausible public explanation. If they didn't, he would take definitive action. Assets were activated and standing by in Tampa. He was pleased, but not satisfied.

A groan echoed in his hollow stomach and he moved from the desk to the table where his assistant had left an assortment of food from the NOAA cafeteria. The baked ziti smelled the best, so he peeled back the foil cover and stuck a fork in the pasta. A buzz reverberated on his desk and he hustled back without his food.

It was a simple pre-set message from Menke:

Compromised.
FREEHOLD

"Shit!" He wanted to throw his Blackberry against the wall, but managed — barely — to keep his rage under control. "Fuck!" The tension ran from the admiral's clenched fists, through his arms and shoulders to the bulging veins in his neck and face. The acid in his empty stomach churned. Heart pounding, Collins placed his two shaking hands on the edge of the desk and took three slow, deep breaths — cold sweat beaded up on his forehead. He took three slower, deeper breaths, but the calmness brought clarity and the clarity allowed him to again focus on the situation — that message meant that Doc was no longer in control of the situation in Tampa Bay. The failure of his old friend and trusted colleague fueled his rage and he gripped the edge of the desk tightly and lifted —just enough to send his Blackberry sliding, and his body slumping, to the floor.

Day Eight

Wednesday, February 26, 2008

Chapter 91

Adam's Lab, MacDill Air Force Base, Tampa, Florida

"Adam, this is Lt. Commander Medlin. I'm in command of the naval assets assigned to secure this situation. I know it is late, but...but, there has been a change in the command structure of this mission. You are no longer taking orders from Dr. Menke—you are taking orders from me..."

"Commander, I don't understand, what has happened to Doc?"

"I don't have time to get into details...let's just say, he was not looking out for the best interests of the dolphins...or you. Understand?"

"Perfectly." Adam pushed his swivel chair back from the table and did a celebratory twirl.

"Good. Now listen...we're going to put Dr. Clarke's comprehensive rescue plan into motion. At sunrise we'll have all the resources in place and..."

Abruptly stopping the spinning chair, Adam interrupted, "...and they'll scatter—using the last of their energy. Then, they'll start to expire. Some will make it to the beach. Some won't. Some will make it into the nets—but won't last long. A handful might survive. Many of them are already on their way out. Did Doc tell you what I found?"

"The delta waves—sleep. He said you verified that."

"Dr. Clarke and Dr. Nicely there?"

"Yes, they're right here. Dr. Clarke is on the phone, but Dr…"

"Get her now! Put me on speaker phone. And get me immediate transportation out to the site. Now, Commander! We don't have much time."

Medlin pulled Angela from the phone and they all huddled in close. "We're here, Adam — all three of us."

"Okay. Okay. I knew Doc wouldn't give you all of my data. Shit, no one has all of my data…I haven't even seen all of my data…well…anyway…yes, one hemisphere showed typical sleep waves — delta waves. But, in 30% of the other dolphins the time-lapse data showed the other hemisphere slowly moving toward the same — a slow progression from beta to alpha to theta waves that could mean…"

"…the other half of the brain is going to sleep." It was Dr. Nicely. "Doc mentioned nothing about that!"

"Yes! But the kicker is…the *big* problem is that the hemisphere that is already sleeping…" Adam's voiced trailed off as he shook his head and paced in tight neurotic circles. "Shit! The problem is *that* hemisphere is not responding to the transition of the other half of the brain — by moving out of sleep mode. There are no indications of the currently sleeping hemisphere moving into an alert and awake state. If both hemispheres go to sleep…"

"…they drown." This time it was Lt. Commander Medlin — he had just rejoined the conversation after stepping away to arrange Adam's transportation. "They can't consciously surface to breathe and they drown."

"Right. *Or,* they try and prevent that drowning." Adam was already stuffing all the gear he could think of into a large duffel bag and a waterproof Pelican case.

Medlin nodded, "They beach."

"Correct." Adam confirmed and continued, "Dr. Clarke, you need to get that plan of yours ready. It may be the only way to save some of them—very few…but at least some of them. Maybe getting them out of that environment and into a tank…have the dolphins rehabbing in Texas shown any signs of…? You can find that out for me easily enough. Well, either way…the rescue…yes…yes, I think it's worth the risk to save a few."

"Believe me, Adam—I'm on it."

"Yes, I'm sure you are, Dr. Clarke. But you can't move the animals in the dark. I still have…"

"About six hours. We'll be ready to roll at sunrise."

"I'm already packed. Give me that time…get me out on that boat with Ramirez again….*now*…with his help maybe I can figure this out…I have to figure this…" Jefferson walked through the door and interrupted. The ensign smiled and nodded. Adam started walking towards the door. "I'm on my way."

Medlin chimed in, "Yes. Jefferson will see you to us safely."

At the door, Adam stopped and scanned the room. Next to his workstation he noticed his backpack and wondered if there was anything in it that he needed. As he walked back, he went through its contents in his mind—assorted pens and pencils, his toiletries, the manuscript from his Marine Mammal Science submission and

Wendall. At the thought of *Wendall*--the top secret file Menke had passed him on the plane—he hustled over to the workstation and rifled through its contents. Why had Doc, knowing time was of the essence, even suggested he spend some of it reviewing that file? Adam grabbed the file and stuffed it into his duffel.

As he passed the refrigerator, he grabbed a couple Mountain Dews and stuffed them in as well. Ensign Jefferson just laughed, "Let's go."

Egmont Key, Tampa Bay, Florida

The Rigid Inflatable Boat had a top speed of 40 knots and Adam was back on Medlin's command boat with the rest of the team within 20 minutes. Slowly, the larger boat moved toward the edge of the dolphins and the stealthy electric RIB where Ramirez had been continuing to collect data. The electric boat was crowded with equipment, but in addition to Adam, they transferred Dr. Nicely, Seaman Taylor and an M4A1 rifle for Ramirez.

When he saw the weapon, Ramirez looked for an answer in Medlin's face. The Commander frowned and nodded. "Get the job done—help them find the answer, Ramirez. And, help …help protect our friends—Dr. Nicely and Mr. Reich—if need be."

Ramirez snapped to attention. "Sir, yes, sir!" After stowing his weapon, the ensign started transferring Adam's gear.

Medlin then turned his look to Adam and whispered, "I've risked my job—the only life I've *ever* wanted—for this. No matter how it turns out, my days in the Navy are over. Make that sacrifice worthwhile." With that, he turned and climbed back aboard his command boat and up its specially fitted tower.

Robin looked at Angela—clad in her Navy-issue life jacket-- and nodded as the command boat slowly pulled away. Across the water, in the dim lights of the boat, she mouthed, "Stay safe. I love you." Angela's boat was turned before he could reply—they would take up station just 50 meters away.

Robin's spell was broken by Adam's voice, "Sorry, Dr. Nicely—can you take a couple steps back and take my gear bag? If you don't mind handing me stuff if I ask for it..."

Smiling, Robin agreed, "Not a problem—happy to assist."

Adam moved to the computer workstation and huddled with Ramirez. The ensign whispered into his ear, "Dr. Menke?"

"You know. You probably know more than I do."

"I know what the commander told me...maybe a few other things--other things that..." Ramirez looked away from Adam and at the workstation monitor he had just refreshed—he didn't have confidence that he could look Adam in the eye and be convincing, "...well, there are some things that make helping you a non-issue. Now..."

Adam cut in and stated their new mission, "Now, in all that clatter we filtered out earlier, we need to find a dolphin lullaby."

Chapter 92

Hillside Cottages, Tortola, BVI

Small yellow lights lined the cracked concrete driveway that led steeply uphill—past the rental cottages and to a small flat spot outside a larger, yellow house. Kurt moved the Prius back and forth three times to squeeze it next to the gold Jaguar that took up most of the small parking area. It would have been hard for anyone in the house not to notice all the maneuvering and movement of the headlights. A bright outside light popped on just as Kurt put the car in "park."

Rachel turned to him, "Well, obviously someone knows we're here—let's go." She grabbed the briefcase at her feet.

As they exited the car, a tall, thin man in boxer shorts ambled down the steps from the house to the car park. "Who the bloody hell taught you to park a car and…" He noticed it was the Dolphin Towne Prius, rubbed some of the sleep out of his eyes and asked, "What are you doing with Jasmine's car? She okay? Adam? It's bloody late to be looking for a cottage and I didn't think they were full anyway…I guess I should let you explain…sorry."

Kurt and Rachel looked at each other and then back to the man now leaning on the hood of the Jaguar.

Kurt ventured, "Mr. Knaggs?"

He stuck out the right hand at the end of a gangly, hairy arm, "I'm Knaggs—Malcom Knaggs, yes."

Kurt shook his hand and continued while Rachel did the same, "Mr. Knaggs, Jasmine sent..."

Malcom stood, walked a foot away from Kurt and looked down into his eyes, "Your names?"

"Right," Kurt fidgeted in the small space between him and the taller, older man. "Kurt Braun and this is Rachel Remmy. We're staying at Dolphin Towne and..." He looked at Rachel for help — not knowing how much to tell Mr. Knaggs.

She stepped closer and took over the conversation, "Mr. Knaggs..."

"Malcom, dear — call me Malcom."

Sighing, she continued, "Malcom, I'm a reporter with Summers Media — based out of New York City. Kurt is formerly director of the marine mammal stranding network in Texas. There have been several mass stranding — dolphin-beaching — incidents in the US over the last few days. There is another potential stranding in Tampa, Florida. Adam flew to Tampa to help. Now, for some reason, *someone* is monitoring and disrupting outgoing and incoming communications from Dolphin Towne and Summers. We have information — data — that we think is important to preventing the stranding and/or exposing the people who might be causing it. We're looking for a computer-savvy third party who might be able to help us get our message and information out to people who will know what to do with it."

Knaggs snickered and turned toward the house, "Come inside...quite a story...don't get much intrigue here on Tortola. Came here to get away from that—mostly…" Stopping at the top of the second step he looked back—neither of them had budged. "Well, come on. I'm not MI6, CIA or DIS or friends with the Smoking Man—at least not anymore."

Kurt and Rachel followed Knaggs up the two steps and through the door—not so sure that the shadowy Brit wasn't in league with some government agency, a drug cartel or the real world equivalent of the *X-Files* antagonist. The large open room had walls lined with a variety of artwork—batik wildlife paintings from Africa, Maori carvings from New Zealand, bark paintings from Kakadu in Australia, and a couple of wooden canoe paddles from Tahiti. "This way, please." The lanky Brit motioned them through a dark doorway.

The darkness stopped them—until Knaggs flipped a switch and the light revealed a room stuffed with technology. On the right side of the room were several servers and a long desk with three individual workstations—keyboards, CPUs, webcams, Bose headphones and large flat screen monitors. On the left side of the room was a long, low metal file cabinet topped with a Bose stereo system and what looked like an old short-wave or Ham radio. Along the ceiling at the far end of the room were six flat screen monitors—obviously linked to security cameras throughout the Hillside Cottages property. Below the security monitors, hung a pistol in a black leather holster. In the corner, leaned a shotgun with a wooden stock.

"Wow." Kurt looked at Rachel—she looked back at him. They both looked at Knaggs.

He smiled and nodded, "There are things you don't want—and don't need—to tell me…and there are things I don't want—and don't need—to tell you. Suffice to say, that if Jasmine has put us together, that is all the information we need to establish mutual respect and trust."

"Okay." Rachel looked at Kurt—he nodded and she continued. "Okay, let's get to it. We need to compose a message and attach some files. Some of the files are word documents, some are scanned documents. I'll be sending them to a fairly extensive list of recipients. If there is any way that we might be able to…to…um, mask the origin of the message…"

Knaggs pointed to the farthest keyboard and monitor. "Use this one. The CPU is under the desk. You can plug your…"

"…thumb drive…" Rachel filled in the blank.

"…yes, plug in your thumb drive there. Type your message in MS Word. I suggest you keep it concise. I'll be back momentarily—I think I should at least put on a t-shirt."

Kurt looked at Rachel, "You're the journalist. You're the one who has some credibility. You're the one with the email list."

She sat at the keyboard and bounced her fingers on the home keys without typing anything. She bounced a few more times and then started typing. Kurt read over her shoulder. Malcom had returned in a threadbare, blackish Sex Pistols t-shirt and read over her shoulder.

"Never did think much of the military use of dolphins. But Adam? I can't imagine the kid involved…now, Doc…I shared a few bottles of good New Zealand wine…Oyster Bay Merlot and an Australian Pinot Noir…" The Brit scratched the unruly patch of brown hair on the top of his large head, and continued, "…can't remember that name…bollocks…did some political sparring with Menke. He was all in for that Iraqi invasion in '03 — bit of a hawk…seemed to know a few too many details about…well… I could easily see…Oh, right…sorry, you've obviously got your own speculations. Now…finished?"

"Yes." Rachel pushed the chair back from the desk and stood.

Knaggs sat down. "I have several different email programs, addresses and aliases. I'm thinking we'll send your message and files in various combinations and formats — that should help it get through to someone, somewhere. Savvy?"

"Yes — absolutely." Kurt pulled up a chair on one side of Knaggs. Rachel pulled a chair up on the other. The Brit's long fingers danced on the keyboard — creating address lists, attaching files, and, finally, hitting "send."

Editorial Conference Room, Summers Media, New York

"Josh?" Carlye had trotted from her desk to the editorial conference room — Josh had his head down on the table. "Josh!"

"What is it?" He slumped back into the leather chair and stretched his arms over his head. Carlye waited. "Well?"

"Have you checked…no, of course you haven't — you've been sleeping. Anyway, when you check your personal email — Rachel has your personal email, right? Of course…anyway, you are likely to have an email message with attached files from Rachel Remmy and Kurt Braun. It seems that almost everyone Rachel knows here at Summers has gotten the message in some form with some combination of attached files sent to their personal emails."

The associate editor stood up and looked at the big screen — just a distant, blurry green night vision image from Tampa. He turned back to Carlye, "Something relevant?"

During the moment he had looked at the screen, his science editor, Becca had come in and was standing next to Carlye. It was Becca who replied, "I have Dr. Lykes examining the data we received earlier and looking over the files we just received from Rachel. I have an electronics specialist on his way — should be here in 10 — to examine the schematics of the chip…"

"Chip?" Josh looked at Carlye and then back to Becca, "Chip?"

"I figured Carlye had…" She looked at Carlye shaking her head and continued, "There were schematics for some type of tracking…well… maybe a communications chip…something that could be implanted under the dolphin's skin and transmit data…the schematics were found next to Adam Reich's computer at Dolphin Towne. Adam Reich is now in Tampa with Dr. Aldo Menke, Dr. Robin Nicely — the South African — and Dr. Clarke."

"There seems to be another connection between all these players..." Josh's voice trailed off in thought.

Becca continued, "And there was also a manuscript for a scientific paper that was submitted by Reich to Marine Mammal Science. Clipped to that hard copy was an email from Nicely bubbling with praise for Reich's work..." A vibration from the phone in her pocket stopped her—she pulled it out and answered, "Dr. Lykes? Sleeping? Yes, ask Rob to lead you to the Editorial Conference Room. We all need to hear this...thank you."

Josh had retaken his seat at the head of the table—albeit with a cup of fresh coffee. After a quick sip, he asked, "Sleep? For what we're paying him, Lykes shouldn't be..."

Sitting next to him on the tabletop, Becca interrupted, "Not Lykes, Josh—the dolphins. Lykes is convinced the dolphins are sleeping--something about brainwaves and such. But he said he had something bigger than that...he's on his way..." She looked through the glass walls into the newsroom and toward her section, "here he comes."

Lykes hobbled into the room using a cane.

Josh stood and held out his hand, "Dr. Lykes—Josh Lee. It's a pleasure to meet you. Please take my chair."

"Thank you, Josh." Lykes hooked his cane on the chair's arm and sat. "Becca did you tell them..."

Everyone else took a seat close to Lykes. Becca answered, "I told them about the sleep. I wanted you to explain the real issue with that sleep."

"Well, okay. I'll try and put this in terms you can understand. The brainwaves that Reich has recorded—brilliant work by the way...a shame the boy couldn't handle the stresses of...well, that's a story for another..." He took a deep breath and continued with a summary of how dolphins sleep. When he stopped, Josh shrugged.

Lykes sighed. "The issue with the dolphins in Tampa is that the other half of their brains—the currently conscious half—seems to be slipping slowly into a sleep state...while, at the same time, the currently sleeping half shows no sign—exhibits none of the brainwave pattern changes—indicating the transition to a state of consciousness. It won't be long until both sides of the dolphins' brains are asleep and..."

With a blank expression on her face, Carlye stood, "...and the dolphins stop breathing—shit!"

Josh stood and walked around the front of the table, "And that chip we have schematics for—what Kurt Braun says is a dead ringer for the chip he and Dr. Clarke recovered from one of the dolphins in Galveston...is that chip Reich created...well, may have created for the Navy...could that have caused this?"

Lykes shifted in the chair and rotated it to look at Josh, "I don't know. It certainly isn't a science fiction stretch to think that if you can monitor brainwaves that you might be able to alter them—purposefully or not....But, at this point, that we know of, only one chip has been discovered. I can't see one chip having the power or range to put them all to sleep unless that is what it was designed to do. There's some value to getting the data out, but I can't understand why the NMFS team hasn't made it public—they must have their reasons."

"Okay—noted." Josh moved back to the table. "Carlye, Becca—we still need to get Dr. Lykes on the air with his interpretation of the data. We need to do that ASAP. We need this information out ASAP. I want graphics of the actual brainwave files—anything visual that can help people understand...background featurettes on dolphin sleep, what we know about the Navy Marine Mammal Program..."

"The chip?" Becca asked.

"I know this is a stretch, but...I want Kurt Braun's speculative connection reported ASAP. Of course, emphasize the *speculation*, but get the idea out there—get people's reactions. I want the schematics of that chip on the screen and on the web ASAP. I want the analysis of our on-the-way electronics expert on the air as soon as his work is complete. Now..." He looked up at the wall of clocks from the different major cities in the world, "...now, I want the first of this out within 15 minutes—so move it!"

Chapter 93

Office of Admiral Collins, NOAA

Silver Spring, Maryland

Admiral Collins slowly rolled his limp body over and leaned his back against the side of the desk—his shirt and his head were drenched. His breathing was still quick and shallow. He looked at his watch— 20 minutes. He'd been out of it for over 20 minutes. Knowing it wasn't his heart, he felt around the front of his desk and opened the middle drawer—fumbling for the ever-present gummy bears. After popping a few in his mouth to bring up his blood sugar, Collins stretched for the Blackberry that had slid off the desk. There was nothing--no new messages. He sucked on a handful of the chewy candy and whispered to himself, "Okay—now, get your ass off the floor." Collins pulled himself up and flopped into his chair--weak, dizzy, and shaking. After finishing off the gummy bears, he managed a little smile.

While the admiral knew he'd have to get some real food shortly or there was the potential for another hypoglycemic crash, he also was coherent enough to know he had to attend to an imminent crisis. He scrolled through the covert operatives on his Blackberry— knowing he had to put new operational plans in place immediately. The admiral hesitated—questioning his commitment to taking full responsibility and acting without the consent of THE FEW.

Dimming the lights, he grabbed the uneaten ziti, sat and rotated his chair—in the dark he could now see out the huge window.

The lights glistened hypnotically on the damp parking lot, streets, and the patchy piles of still melting snow. He got a chill and realized he was still sitting in his wet shirt. Turning and standing, he set the ziti on his desk, walked over to the credenza and stripped out of his tie, shirt and t-shirt—replacing it from the drawers with a simple grey sweatshirt that said "Navy" in blue block letters. Back at his desk he sat, picked up the ziti and again rotated to look out the window. He ate and stared into the night.

After finishing the pasta, he turned back to the desk. Everything had slid slightly out of place and after taking a minute to re-order his things—including his photos—Collins pulled out the keyboard and woke up his monitor. He nodded, "Time to end this."

> *THE FEW*
> *Freehold's site command compromised. Elements of MSOT on site likely compromised. Immediate action required. Request permission for our asset to signalMK6C dolphins to move from site.*
> *ACRET*

After hitting "send", the admiral sat in his chair waiting for what he thought would be an instantaneous reply. Six minutes had passed and he was fidgeting in his normally comfortable desk chair. The admiral marched over to the spread of food and brought two pieces of garlic bread back to his desk. He sopped up the sauce from the ziti and ate—wondering how he could have misjudged Lt. Commander Medlin's commitment. For some reason, he knew that Medlin had been the one to compromise Doc's authority—he was the only one on the team who had that kind of power and took that kind of initiative.

Pushing back from the desk, Collins stood and looked at his watch—10 minutes had passed. Feeling physically better, he did three laps around the desk and paused to move his mouse and refresh the computer screen--nothing. Grabbing his Blackberry, the admiral walked over to and leaned against his cold window. He again pulled up the number for Ensign Ramirez—and then hesitated. Ramirez had worked unquestioningly with Collins up to this point— providing snippets of information he wasn't getting from Medlin or Reich. Ramirez was eager for the assignment and the praise he hoped would move him quickly up the MSOTs hierarchy. Certain the ambitious MSOT specialist was not compromised as well, the admiral sent a quick text message: *Stand by.*

Back at the desk, he set down the Blackberry and again refreshed the monitor. "Come on!" He screamed—unhappy with the glacial decision-making he thought THE FEW was created to bypass.

Two email alerts—the triple beep of his computer and the triple vibration of his handheld indicating he had received a priority message—stopped his rage.

ACRET
    Breaking news on all Summers Media stations and websites. Data fragment analysis by experts confirms that dolphins are currently in unihemispheric sleep, but slipping into total sleep. Their prediction: large scale mortality imminent if no cause found or if not rescued. Press questioning

why this data/information has not been released by NMFS.

Summers also aggressively promoting speculative link between Dr. Menke, the NMMP and a subcutaneous chip transponder designed by Adam Reich. Speculating that Reich was working with Menke and for the Navy. Schematics of said chip are online now. Press speculating that Reich is in Tampa to troubleshoot that chip.

Suggest immediate – IMMEDIATE – SPAWAR press conference confirming the link between Dr. Menke, NMMP, and a subcutaneous chip designed by Reich. Announce immediate standing down of MK6C – or whatever we want to call it – program. Express regret for losses. Announce rigorous review of research and approval process for new projects – and, subsequent implementation of new guidelines. Contacting SPAWAR Commander now. West coast press conference likely to be less attended...

Throw the weight of the Navy and all government agencies involved behind the rescue plan that will begin at sunrise.

Coordinating statement and press conference with the Navy Press office. NMFS will also need to make a statement via Director Hamilton.

Stand by for further instructions regarding Tampa.
BLADE

"Damn it!" *Stand by? Me?* Collins stood and paced around the table. At least his compatriots were smart enough to keep the press conference out of Washington. SPAWARSYSCOM—the Space and Naval Warfare Systems Command--was located in San Diego and oversaw the Navy Marine Mammal Program. A little calmer, and back sitting at his desk, Admiral Collins tapped out a reply to the group.

> BLADE
> Understood. I will contact Director Hamilton and coordinate press release to coincide with and mirror that presented by SPAWARSYSCOM. I've attached a copy of the press release I drafted as per an earlier email – feel free to borrow ideas or disregard.
> Reich still best positioned to search for possible CONCH link. Suggest he continue his investigation with time remaining before rescue operations commence. We need to know – sooner is better than later.
> Suggest after NMFS statement that Director Hamilton contact Dr. Clarke in Tampa. Full support of comprehensive rescue. Hamilton will order Reich's work to continue until rescue commences. Our asset has orders to communicate any of Reich's results directly to me and to suppress the transfer of Reich's results to anyone else.
> ACRET

Closing his eyes, Collins rocked back in his chair and paused. Rocking forward and opening his eyes, he reached for his Blackberry and sent a more detailed text message to Ensign Ramirez.

> Press Reich to find cause. Report any results to me immediately. Under no circumstances allow Reich to communicate any findings with anyone but you – this is of the greatest importance. Suppress any attempt by Reich to transfer classified information to anyone besides you. As noted earlier, one asset on SBT-22 positioned nearby to assist if needed. He will respond to your signals as

indicated earlier. Narrowly targeted, non-lethal force authorized if necessary.

Text message complete, Collins dialed Jake Hamilton, *his* Director of the National Marine Fisheries Service.

Chapter 94

Dolphin Towne, Tortola, BVI

It was nearly 1:00am on Wednesday when Rachel and Kurt returned, exhausted, to Dolphin Towne. The Eli House was dark—the entire property was dark. Continuing up the front steps, Kurt stopped at the open doorway and sniffed.

"Something's burning." He continued walking through the long, wide central hallway turning his head as he passed each of the side halls.

"Burning or *burned*?" Rachel caught up and asked.

"Good point." Kurt reached the back porch and sniffed again. "Electrical, I think. It's got that…"

"Yes, metallic…crispy wires…"

"Like a massive power surge fried everything." He turned to Rachel and looked her in the eyes. "Did you notice any lack of lighting on the drive back? Were other houses lit?"

She shook her head and he stepped farther out on the porch—leaning on the railing and scanning the grounds. His head stopped at the faint light coming from the Education Center.

There, in the hissing glow of a Coleman lantern, they found Jasmine sitting at Adam's desk and staring at a dark, cracked monitor. Her face was covered with sooty wet streaks. Her hair was pulled back—frazzled pieces stuck out like red straw.

"Jasmine?" She didn't answer, so Rachel walked closer and tried a forceful whisper. "Jasmine."

Trying to shake herself out of her daze, Jasmine looked at Rachel, "Oh." She looked over at Kurt trying in vain to wake up one of the computers with a melted mouse and keyboard--her eyes looked through him, "You got the word out?"

He nodded and she responded, "Well done." Jasmine resumed her stare at the darkened monitor.

"What happened to the computers? To the lights? Was there a power surge? Everything smells..." Kurt sniffed again at the strong burnt electronics odor that dominated the room, and continued, "...burned." Scanning the room as his eyes adjusted to the dim light, he noticed the real extent of the damage. Burned or singed papers were strewn everywhere among the still smoking servers and half-opened file cabinets. Bad — but it could have been worse.

"Dark. Everything went dark..." Wide-eyed, Jasmine looked up at Kurt. "There was a helicopter...hovering...warm air...*hot* air...and everything went black. Just like with Bee — the light left this place. Just darkness. Confusion, then darkness."

Kurt and Rachel turned Jasmine's chair and kneeled in front of her. Kurt whispered, "Darkness? Confusion? Helicopter? Try and focus — exactly what happened while we were gone?"

Jasmine shuffled trough some of the charred papers on the desk and shook her head, "you were gone a long time...I was checking on the Summers websites to see if they were getting out what you sent. They hadn't but...but all of a sudden the screen scrambled up and then went blue. I got calls from two of the guests who were connected to the internet through our system — their computers crashed as well."

She sobbed, stopped and stared into Kurt's eyes. "How is Malcom? Helpful? You got the information out?"

He nodded again, "Yes, he was able to help us confirm that the information got through to multiple sources. He's very...um...resourceful for a British ex-pat looking to avoid any intrigue...Now, what happened after the computers crashed?"

She sighed and stuttered — her throat still dry from crying. "I went to the Education Center. Not that I would know what to do — but that seemed like the place to go. On the way...that's when I heard the helicopter. That's when...there was a nice breeze — did you notice the nice breeze off the bay? That's when the air got hot--heavy. That's when the darkness came again — lights out. Except for the sparks...flames..." She stared down at the fire extinguisher next to the desk.

As Kurt stood, he asked, "And, the helicopter? You saw it?"

"Heard it. Then, it was gone."

Rachel looked at Jasmine and grabbed one of her hands. "Let's get you up to the house, get you showered and get you some water and food." Pulling the Dolphin Towne owner up, she tugged her out the door. Kurt scanned the dead control room one more time and then followed with the lantern.

Chapter 95

Egmont Key, Tampa Bay, Florida

Adam scrolled through the several snippets of interesting background "noise" he and Ramirez had filtered out before starting the data collection. Ramirez was working on the other half of the file on his workstation. They'd been at it about 25 minutes and both of them were starting to close and rub their eyes more frequently.

Lost in the isolation of his headphones, Adam thought, *Okay...I've seen this before...the other day...yes, when I saved it. When else? Doesn't look...natural.* He carried his laptop the four steps to Ramirez's workstation — noticing that the ensign had just set down his cell phone. He tapped and pointed at the wave patterns on the screen. "Ramirez? Found in nature?"

Ramirez shook his head. "When I was on the *USS*...well...when I was on the sub I went..." He sighed, reluctant to give out detailed information about his time on a nuclear missile submarine, "...all over the world. Recorded all kinds of sounds — man-made, naturals — whales, fish, beach waves, turtles, volcanic vents...Didn't you ask me about that same wave-form...who knows? So much sound. Anyway, no in all of my sonar time I didn't record anything like that — especially the same sound from multiple sources."

"Thanks for the short answer." Adam paused — fixed on Ramirez's last thought. "Multiple sources?"

"Yeah, you asked me to run a directional correlation on it...yesterday?" The ensign shook his head. "I don't know what day it is...anyway, the day you first recognized it I did a directional correlation. There are eight stationary sources...I can give you the coordinates..."

"Eight stationary sources?"

"You need to figure this out, genius." Ramirez looked at his watch, "Time is running out."

Adam got quiet, walked back to where he had been and nestled into the fluffy sleeping bag on the deck. Computer in his lap, he again retreated into his mind and whispered out loud to himself, "Okay...a regular pulse that seems so innocuous...and then...wham! A more intense pulse at...yes...a specific, regular interval...both from the same multiple sources? Seen before? Yes...but, no...not exactly..."

"Dr. Nicely," The scientist had been straining, unsuccessfully, first to see what Adam was showing Ramirez and then to hear what Adam was whispering to himself, "...in my bag...?" Adam turned while he asked and saw Robin scurrying back towards the gear pile and nodding. "What did you find, Adam? What's up?"

"In my duffel there is a large file labeled *Wendall*—can you get it out and skim through it for me? Can you open it? I'm looking for...?

Adam was cut off by Nicely shining a bright flashlight on the file he was holding in the air, "This one?" *Top Secret* was stamped in red across the file. The seals of DARPA—the Defense Advanced Research Agency—the Space and Naval Warfare Systems Command,

and the Navy Marine Mammal Program were also prominently displayed.

"Yeah, that's the one. Can you open it and look for…"

This time, Adam was stopped mid-question by Ramirez—who, seeing the designations on the file, rushed to snatch it from the South African, Dr. Nicely. He stopped between Adam and Robin. He was shorter than the two civilians, but he had broad shoulders and moved with the air of a man trained to use confidence to keep himself and his teammates alive. "I'm sorry Dr. Nicely—even in this situation I don't believe you have the clearance necessary to be seeing this file…you're a foreign citizen and it just wouldn't be acceptable…sir." Robin handed him the file, moved back to the bench near Adam's gear bag and sat down. The scientist said nothing.

Ramirez, file in hand, walked into Adam's space. Adam took two steps back—stopping when he felt the bulk of a waterproof gear box behind him. Taking one more step, Ramirez whispered, "It's not proper—top secret. I…"

"I…I understand." Regaining his composure, Adam nodded at the file and moved them both away from Dr. Nicely. "Now, find me wave diagrams. I seem to remember some familiar wave patterns."

While Ramirez sorted through the file, Adam stared over the side of the boat and into the darkness. He scanned his mind and began to recall what he had skimmed on the plane. *The research design and the data collection looked sound – solid even – but…* Turning back to Ramirez, Adam grabbed the thick file and started to flip through the pages himself—graphs, charts, raw data—so much detail. "Yes!" His whole body jumped. He showed the wave patterns to Ramirez and they both looked at what he had isolated on the laptop screen.

Ramirez smiled and whispered, "Makes sense now—barely a wave—barely a pulse—something that is always on…defensive. Just enough to sense…something…without providing much information and possibly without offending sensitive sea life... Yes! This is a defensive system. Shit! This is a defensive system—the passive pulse wave is always on…sort of listening to the ocean with one ear. The intense pulse…" The ensign pointed to a second diagram, but Adam was again staring into the dark. "Hmm…the intense pulse is…aggressive and active, but still not like any of the sonar waves that I've seen—not the low or moderate frequency sonars that were supposed to be responsible for killing those beaked whales in the Caribbean a few years ago. The multiple sources overlap and create a 'net' that can cover a fairly large coastal area…"

Adam sighed, "Like Tampa Bay…or Galveston."

Ignoring Adam's speculation, Ramirez continued, "This is something innovative…something you turn on when you have a credible threat. This is seriously cutting-edge stuff. I'd better secure this file properly."

Ramirez didn't wait for Adam's consent—he walked over to the horizontal locker where his own gear was stowed. There he placed the file in a locking case, the case in a duffel, grabbed his phone and looked over his shoulder at Adam. The genius was busy tapping on his laptop, so he hurried back—he couldn't risk Adam attempting to transmit another data file.

Adam looked up on the ensign's return and then stared at the screen.

"What are you thinking, genius?"

"That I need that file back."

Ramirez sighed. He looked over at Dr. Nicely—who was sitting with his arms crossed looking out over the dolphins.

"I've skimmed it once already. I need to see if the waves in the study...see if the waves were overlapped during the exposure cycles...or..." He stood and followed Ramirez to the gear locker— noting the cell phone now on the deck next to the locker. "...or, whether—as I suspect--whether the exposure was exclusive to each wave. I also need to see if the test animals were subject to exposure from multiple sources. "

Ramirez retrieved the file, closed the locker and they both sat on the lid. Adam flipped through the pages. He flipped back a few pages, closed the file and stood. "I knew it!"

Nicely's head turned and the South African began to stand. Ramirez shook his head and shouted, "Sorry, Dr. Nicely." He put his strong hand on Adam's shoulder and the excited genius sat down.

Adam whispered, "I was right. The dolphins were only exposed to one wave at a time—never to both at once." He flipped through a few more pages. "And they were never exposed to waves from multiple sources. I can't believe that Doc would have been so pressed for time — what an oversight in the research design. It's not like him to…"

Ramirez tried to get him back to the point, "You think the compound effects might have…"

"…put them to sleep? Yes. That could be it. They tried to create a signal that was so unobtrusive, but instead the wave pattern of the sonar must somehow initiate and maintain dolphin sleep…if I overlay these patterns like they are actually transmitted in active mode…" Adam was doing the work in his head. "…they were using brainwave scans to create…what did they call it? *Brainmusic*…yes, that's it…synthesized custom sound waves to put people…"

"…to sleep. I get it. But…" Ramirez took the file, stood up and pulled on the locker lid — forcing Adam to stand. He put the file back into the locking case and into his bag — then he closed the locker and continued his thought. "It puts them to sleep. Is that the only plausible explanation?"

Adam didn't answer. He had moved back to his laptop and started to type. Knowing he couldn't send the information over the Internet without it being noticed or intercepted, he finished a quick file with a summary of what he knew and saved it on a thumb drive. He looked up — Ramirez had his back turned and was fiddling with something in his hands. Adam was sure the ensign was texting someone — he shook his head and whispered, "Trust no one." From his small pile of stuff, he retrieved two Ziploc bags, wrote "Nicely" on one and sealed the small storage device inside. With Ramirez still occupied, he sealed the first bag in the second.

Adam looked over at Dr. Nicely and his marine mammal hero lifted his chin and whispered, "Well?"

Finished with his phone, Ramirez had joined them and sighed at the question.

Adam nodded at Ramirez, and floated a question to Dr. Nicely, "Based on your observations and your past experience, have you seen anything that might have caused the dolphins to go into such a sleep state?"

Nicely understood--they weren't going to tell him anything — *need to know*. He was familiar with the phrase from all of the spy novels he churned through over the years. But, it was rare that he was not in the know; that he was left out of any conversation — especially a scientific one--especially one he'd been flown halfway around the world for — and he closed his mouth tightly in protest.

"Dr. Nicely," It was Ramirez, "You've already seen things you're not supposed to — I'm fairly certain there will at least be a minor debriefing before you are allowed to leave the U.S. But, I also know a man like you can infer a great deal from...well, in this case from a quick glance at the cover of a file."

Adam nodded enthusiasticlly and drew a harsh stare from Ramirez.

Robin had indeed figured that whatever was in the top secret file labeled *Wendall* was what they were discussing — that it might be linked to the cause. He also had glimpsed the wave patterns on Adam's laptop and inferred that Wendall had something to do with sound — likely some type of sonar. He hadn't seen the contents of their top secret file, but he'd spent almost half his life immersed in science and making connections. A small, lopsided grin loosened his lips--he had to answer, "I haven't seen anything in the physical environment that could have caused them to sleep. I've never heard of any pathogen, organic or inorganic compound...anything...that would induce sleep on such a scale. Angela...Dr. Clarke hasn't teased any serious commonalities out of the other two strandings — nothing as blatant as my *morbillivirus* event in Mozambique."

Adam was getting antsy, fidgeting with something in his pocket. "So?"

Crossing his arms and sighing, Nicely answered, "Process of elimination...we still don't have any direct evidence of a causal link...so if you have something plausible that might lead to a course of action..."

Adam pivoted toward Ramirez and marched them away from Robin. He looked back at a frustrated, again tight-lipped Dr. Nicely and then to the ensign and whispered, "Obviously, this *Wendall* has been deployed and we need to get it turned off — turned off now. My guess is that it is deployed...well, major strategic ports maybe? Test areas? Like Texas to protect oil refineries? And...and somewhere off Virginia Beach to protect...shit...D.C. and Norfolk. I know this information is classified, but we need to get it to Dr. Clarke — if we can get them out of the water...she was right...get them out of that environment we might save some. We...somebody...this sonar needs to be shut down now."

Ramirez shepherded Adam to the bow of the small boat-- farther from Robin--and looked into his eyes, "This *is* a classified defense system. My guess is that if it is turned on — if both pulses are active — that we are facing a credible threat to national security...a potential attack on the United States." Ramirez's harsh whisper bordered on being loud enough for Dr. Nicely to overhear, so the ensign took a deep, calming breath and continued in a less passionate tone, "We need to go through proper channels. Let me contact Lt. Commander Medlin and have him relay what we have through our chain of command. At least that way we keep it close." He looked over his shoulder at Dr. Nicely and then back to Adam. "I'll do it quickly and quietly."

"Okay, Ramirez. Then we'll *immediately* inform Dr. Clarke that her rescue is the best medicine for this group. Even with *Wendall* shut down, they're too weak to recover on their own."

Ramirez nodded. "I'll contact Lt. Commander Medlin — now."

Moving towards his laptop, Adam looked back at Ramirez--who was quickly sending a text message with his back turned. With the ensign occupied, Adam looked wide-eyed and directly at Dr. Nicely.

Robin knitted his brow — a silent question — *what?*

Adam pulled a small bag from his pocket, tossed it to Nicely and sat back at his laptop in serious silence.

"In the process, genius." Ramirez sat on the sleeping bag next to Adam. "We'll have word shortly." Adam had been lost in thought — lost in thinking about the unique new sonar the Navy had developed, lost in thinking about how they could have imagined it having a minimal impact on marine wildlife, and lost in thinking about how devastating it had really been. There was no response to the ensign's comment, so Ramirez tried again, "Lt. Commander Medlin is going to…"

Adam held up a finger and shook his head. A minute passed, and he whispered in the ensign's ear, "I can fix *Wendall*…yes…I can picture it…"

"Okaaaaaay." Patting Adam on the back and nodding, Ramirez started to stand. Adam put his hand on the ensign's shoulder and held him down in a squat.

"I'm serious—I can see it. Of course, *Wendall* will have to be shut down for some time…but…" Adam paused again in a blank stare. "I *can* see it."

Ramirez stood, tilted his head toward Adam and whispered, "I'll pass that on to Lt. Commander Medlin. I'm sure that will be useful information to relay to the powers that be." He pulled out his phone and walked toward the bow—sending a third high priority message to Admiral Collins.

Chapter 96

Public Affairs Office, Space and Naval Warfare Systems Command (SPAWARSYSCOM)
San Diego, California

"Thank you for coming. I know this is an odd hour to hold a press conference, but given the situation, we wanted to make a statement as soon as possible."

Rear Admiral Gregory Hancock, SPAWAR Commander, looked out over the dozen or so reporters that had managed to pull themselves out of bed on short notice and at three in the morning—more than one was yawning repeatedly. He fought off the yawn he could feel starting and continued, "Ladies and gentlemen, I'm going to read my prepared statement. Following that we will have five minutes for questions—five minutes only."

Shuffling the papers on the podium, Hancock began,

"As many of you know, there have been two strandings, two beachings of bottlenose dolphins—one at Galveston, Texas, and one at Virginia Beach, Virginia. The number of dolphin mortalities in both cases is unprecedented.

"Currently, another large number of bottlenose dolphins have massed in Tampa Bay, Florida. A joint task force of National Marine Fisheries Service, Florida Fish and Wildlife Conservation Commission, U.S. Coast Guard, U.S. Navy personnel and select marine mammal scientists--have been working tirelessly to ascertain the cause of this occurrence with the hope of averting another mass mortality event.

"While the involvement of Navy at this location and in Virginia Beach was originally reported as being 'logistical assistance,' the truth of the matter is that, in addition to providing logistical assistance, the Navy teams are on site to help maintain the security of what until this time were top secret assets. One of our Navy Marine Mammal Program projects here in San Diego was the creation and implementation of MK6C—bottlenose dolphins implanted with a chip that can transmit data and receive signals. The goal of the program was two-fold—to be able to monitor dolphin bioperameters, acoustics and sonar and to train the dolphins to respond to transmitted signals that would allow them to fulfill certain national security tasks. The success of the testing led to implementation— dolphins were chipped and deployed to port and coastal areas of particular importance. I've been authorized to disclose that those locations included coastal Virginia, Galveston Bay, and Tampa Bay."

The near comatose press corps started to murmur, but Hancock continued,

"The lead developers of the chip, Dr. Aldo Menke and Adam Reich, are on site in Tampa and have some evidence that they think may link prolonged use of said chips and repeated transmissions of certain signals with an unusual onset of a prolonged sleep state in bottlenose dolphins.

"As of 0300 hours Eastern Standard Time, today, all MK6C dolphins are being recalled. Following the recall and immediate recapture, the chips will be deactivated and removed. The recall, capture and deactivation in Tampa will be coordinated with NMFS so as not to disrupt the larger rescue and rehabilitation operation."

"The Navy deeply regrets...*deeply regrets* the unprecedented dolphin mortalities in Galveston and Virginia Beach. While a definitive link to the MK6C program has not been established, the program, as stated earlier, will be suspended pending the vigorous review of an appropriately independent, but properly security-credentialed, board of scientists. In addition, the scientific panel will vigorously review all NMMP research and testing guidelines. The NMMP, under my directive, will be responsible for implementing the panel's suggestions.

At sunrise, the Navy and the other government agencies involved will fully support the Tampa rescue plan designed by Dr. Angela Clarke from the National Marine Fisheries Service. We know that while the rescue in Tampa will save some dolphins, there are likely to be more dolphin mortalities at that location. Of course, we regret any role our programs may have played in those mortalities."

Rear Admiral Hancock's tongue slipped out and licked his lips, looking up from his papers he said, "Thank you for coming here at such an odd hour. We now have five minutes for questions."

Chapter 97

Director's Office, NMFS, Silver Spring, Maryland

"Thank you for getting those out for me, Sarah. I'm sorry about calling you in at this ungodly hour of the morning. But, with the way things are compartmentalized these days, I just don't have the press contacts and...well, the last time I sent anything out all by myself the press releases were stuffed in an envelope and mailed...I've never even..."

"I'm happy to help, Director Hamilton. It's my job." Sarah Meehan, the Director of the NMFS Office of Public Affairs, smiled, yawned and stepped through the doorway. Turning back, she prompted the baggy-eyed director, "We're sure to get more questions once this hits the news...once the rescue starts...we'll need to be ready for a real press conference tomorrow."

Jake leaned back on the front edge of his desk and yawned. "Yes...yes, we'll have to have something more official. I think you and I deserve a trip to Florida."

Meehan nodded and smiled with one side of her mouth. "The least the service could do for calling us in at this hour, sir."

"Yes...well, I'll have Travel and Transportation get us a jet for...9am?"

"Just enough time to get home, get a quick nap, pack my bathing suit and meet you at Andrews." She lingered in the doorway as Director Hamilton circled around the desk to his chair.

Raising his eyebrows and shaking his head, he grumbled, "That'll be all."

On cue, she left and closed the door. Jake sat at his desk — dropping his head into his hands. He was not looking forward to calling Angela in Tampa. A snoring snort jolted him upright and he shook his head. "Shit!" He picked up and judged the volume of his covered Dunkin Donuts coffee cup — it was still half full. After draining the cup, he picked up his phone and dialed.

"Angela, it's Jake. I have news."

"I was trying to get some sleep — got the rescue in the morning…so many boats coming…feel guilty napping — so many people working through the night for me." She yawned. "News about what? What news?"

The old, strong coffee had hardened the director's resolve and he continued, "I'm going to paraphrase a statement that was just made at a press conference by the SPAWAR Commander, Rear Admiral Gregory Hancock, regarding the Navy Marine Mammal Program and its possible involvement in the current dolphin strandings. Do not interrupt me. I will take your questions when I'm done. Understood?"

Angela had perked up some, but was still just a little too drowsy to disagree. "Understood. But, SPAWAR? What's…?"

"Angela!" She stopped talking and Jake outlined the highpoints of the press statement. Taking a deep breath, he paused and Angela knew now to respect the silence--the pause was for her to digest what he said before he moved on. After almost 40 seconds,

Director Hamilton continued, "We are to move forward with your rescue plan as soon as the daylight makes it safe for the rescue teams. Take note that the MK6C--the chipped dolphins I mentioned--will need to be directed to capture boats with naval oversight—specifically with Medlin's team on board--please make that adjustment in your plan accordingly. Coordinate with Lt. Commander Medlin. Understood?"

"Yes..." her voice trailed off—looking for the director's approval to ask questions.

"Now, I know you have questions..."

Angela pounced. "Adam and Menke have some kind of evidence linking those chips to all this? To the dolphin sleep? When did they find this out? Neither Adam nor Doc even hinted..." Angela hesitated—she didn't know if Director Hamilton was privy to the current command situation on the water in Tampa. Did he know that Dr. Menke had been taken out of the loop and placed under guard?

Her thoughts were interrupted by Jake's answer, "According to the press statement from Rear Admiral Hancock, *yes*." The director hoped that the statement was plausible enough...

Angela started at Jake again, "Adam was working with Menke on the development of this chip? That was never mentioned...they never...I can't imagine Doc...I certainly can't imagine Adam working with the military...they never shared any thoughts about the chips with us...it was never bandied about even as a possibility...Doc knew about the foreign object we found in Galveston. He wrote it off. We *all* wrote it off hours...days ago."

"The media has posted chip schematics found at Reich's Dolphin Towne lab on Tortola. That was one of the things that prompted the Navy to admit the links between Dr. Menke, Adam Reich, the chip and the strandings. The Navy has stated that there is preliminary evidence. I don't know why Adam or Menke might be keeping this from you...well, yes, I suppose I can--to protect themselves and what—well, up until the press conference anyway...what had been a top secret project."

"And now I need to amend my plan to make sure their Navy dolphins are captured and secured."

Jake sat upright in his chair. "That is what I'm directing you to do—with all your usual vigor and thoroughness. I'm sure Lt. Commander Medlin will cooperate. I'm sure he'll be receiving his own corresponding orders momentarily."

"I'll need to juggle some boats and people around..." Angela was already moving people in her head. "...Of course I can make it work."

"I know you will." Director Hamilton skooched his chair a little closer to the desk. "Now, obviously there is going to be more press reaction to the potential Navy involvement once the rest of the country and the world wake up. So, Sarah Meehan and I will be heading your way to set up and participate in a press conference. We're leaving Andrews at 9am and should be in Tampa by 11:30am. We'll have something organized at the NMFS St. Pete office for 1:30pm. I'll expect you to be there as well."

"Um, the rescue..."

He cut her off. "…the rescue will be in full swing and you can obviously remain in contact with them by cell phone. This has become too big for you to duck the press. You *will* be there."

"Okaaay. I'll be there."

"And, you'll be prepared with an update on the progress of the rescue."

"Of course."

"And, I'm sure they'll be looking for your reaction to the Navy involvement."

"Yes—I'm sure they'll be looking for my reaction, for your reaction, for how we—NMFS—could have let a project like this proceed without proper oversight or review…I'm sure there will be lots of questions. I'm sure I'll have lots of questions."

"And answers."

"I'll be prepared—I always am. But, answers? I think they're being fed to us by the Navy."

"Very well—you just be prepared." He ignored her jab at the Navy and continued, "I need to get things together for the trip. You need to modify your plan. Of course, I'll want your update once the actual rescue begins. I won't be in the office, so use my cell number."

"Understood…Director Hamilton."

Jake's chest rose and fell with a deep sigh as he placed his desk phone back in the cradle. He knew Angela was pissed—she rarely used his title *and* last name—but, he was too tired to care. Taking another deep breath, his tired body slumped back into his chair and he closed his eyes.

Egmont Key, Tampa Bay, Florida

Angela sat for a moment, trying to convince herself of the legitimacy of the information just relayed by Jake.

She still couldn't buy the connection between Adam Reich, Dr. Menke, a top secret chip and a more clandestine collaboration. Maybe she could see a link with Dr. Menke and the chip—Doc had worked many years for the Navy Marine Mammal Program. But, with Adam's background at Dolphin Towne? She just wasn't completely sold on the connection—she wasn't sold on something that so closely coincided with what came from Kurt Braun's conspiratorial mind. Still, it was all she had at the moment and allowed her to focus on the logistics of the rescue.

Angela scanned the boat for Medlin. He was on the tower and just pocketing his phone. She caught his eye and shrugged her shoulders. Nodding, he motioned her over with his head.

Medlin sat and hung his legs over the tower's platform. "I'll have a team list for you in a few minutes. How many boats can you spare?"

"Commander." She just stared into his eyes.

Looking away from her and towards the dolphins, Medlin repeated, "How many boats can you spare?"

"How many chipped dolphins do we have to capture?"

"That information is..."

"*Classified*. Yes—I get that. I'll have two boats for you. And, honestly, whether your chips are the cause or not, at least we'll be getting dolphins out of what is likely some kind of hostile environment. At least we'll have the chance to save a few."

"The captains of those vessels, their crew, they should not be privy…"

"Understood. I will only tell them that your teams are their crew of volunteers. I wonder…"

The Lt. Commander held up his hand and shook his head.

"Commander, I…"

"I won't go there." Medlin stood back up tall on the tower and Angela walked back to the forward cabin.

Taking a few nose-wrinkling gulps from a thermos of coffee — she hated coffee, but it was warm and caffeinated--she pulled out her phone and looked at the time. It was 4:30am — sunrise in less than two hours. With a couple of tries, she managed to get through to one of the two capture boat captains she wanted to task with rendezvousing with the command boat, taking on a Navy security detail and netting the chipped dolphins.

The chipped dolphins? Angela couldn't get it out of her head — she couldn't quite swallow the Navy fessing up to a project like that — to a project like that causing an episode like this. "Or Galveston…or Virginia Beach…" She whispered so that only she could hear and slid her phone out of her coat pocket.

"Ed…so sorry. I hate to wake you at this awful hour." She didn't really, but figured she was expected to sound apologetic.

"Angela? What…that's okay…it's important?" Ed Bordon stumbled on his words.

"I'm calling you at four in the morning! Of course, it's important!" Angela looked around—no one had heard her raise her voice. She continued a little softer, "The Navy had a news conference from San Diego at O-dark-thirty this morning—blaming some top secret tracking chip they implanted in bottlenose dolphins for the strandings. They also implicated Doc—Dr. Aldo Menke—and Adam Reich as the developers of the chip."

"And this has to do with me, why?"

"We found a chip in one of the dolphins in Galveston. It *disappeared* in an explosion in a lab there. They're claiming there are chipped dolphins in Tampa Bay—I've even been ordered to create Navy-led capture teams to collect them. I may never see these dolphins, or their chips, myself..." She paused and again looked around the command boat. Medlin was now sitting across from the driver who was dozing while standing up. "...something just doesn't add up to me. They're giving away this program too easily—they just don't do that if there isn't a bigger fish to fry...if there isn't something else causing this."

"And, you...you want my opinion? Surely, you've got experts more..."

"What I want ..." She cut him off, "...what I want is for you to get yourself and your necropsy team out of bed—now. I want you to do a finely targeted examination of all of your carcasses—even the completed ones. I want you to look about four centimeters anterior and to the right of the blowhole. I want you to explore that section of the melon. I want you to look for a cylindrical, metallic chip. There may or may not be any scar."

"It's *that* important?"

"It's *that* important. So, four centimeters anterior and to the right of the blowhole. Write it down. I have a news conference at 1:30pm today. If I can give evidence of a chip from the Virginia Beach stranding, I'll feel much more confident in supporting the Navy statement. If not, well…well, at least I can report on the rescue progress."

"You'll save what you can — I'm sure. And that will be better than nothing. Okay, I'll get my vet on the phone and my team in the lab. We'll get through all the animals before your press conference and I'll let you know one way or the other."

"I *really* appreciate the help."

"Good luck with the rescue."

"I'll take it." She hung up and laughed to herself. It wasn't often that she felt she needed luck — her operations were usually thoroughly planned and exquisitely executed. But, with the number of untrained capture volunteers on their way, with the makeshift rehab tanks and students standing by at Eckerd College, and with nearly 200 dolphins to try and rescue, Angela was happily resigned to accepting any well wishes. With luck in mind, she decided to try and reach and re-task the second capture boat captain — she needed one more to work with Medlin's team and the MK6C dolphins.

Chapter 98

Office of Admiral Collins, NOAA
Silver Spring, Maryland

Following the web cast of the SPAWAR press conference, the successful neutralization of the computer and communications network at Dolphin Towne and new orders issued to Lt. Commander Medlin, Admiral Collins had stretched out onto his cushy office sofa—hoping to nap. But, an urgent text message from Ensign Ramirez kept the dozing admiral from falling into a deep sleep.

The message was an affirmation that Reich's suspicions were similar to his own.

> *Reich detected Wendall sonar waves. Noted flaws in testing. Possibly causing dolphin sleep and strandings.*

Collins had managed to put his head back down and close his eyes—it was nothing earth shattering. There still was no hard evidence and no consensus. He still hoped that Reich would find something in quick order, but realized that if he didn't, the team working on the same connection at the NMMP would likely come up with something—some kind of hard evidence—albeit in their own time.

Just as the admiral's breathing started to slow, a second message alert sent his heart rate up and opened his eyes. This message from Ramirez was longer:

*Nicely not privy to Wendall — but he rules out bio,
chem, other physical causes. Reich certain Wendall
is cause--certain. Anxious for immediate shut
down. He agreed with suggestion/ruse to go
through proper channels — i.e. Medlin.*

With that second message, Collins sat himself upright on the sofa — maybe Reich had something more conclusive after all. He was happy that Ramirez was turning into such a quick-thinking asset — his brain power being useful for something other than tech work and sonar analysis. Getting Reich to agree to proceeding through proper channels because of the top secret nature of the project was brilliant — even though he was sure the ensign had said nothing to the commander. But, he was sure the deception would not last for long and that Reich would again look for a way to communicate his data to someone on the outside. The admiral typed out a brief message to The FEW on his Blackberry:

*Reich data supports CONCH link to dolphins.
Data uncompromised. Chip diversion prescient.*

A third message from Ramirez interrupted his typing:

*Reich sure he can fix Wendall. Reich can fix
Wendall.*

Collins deleted the message to The FEW he had started to compose, stood and walked to his desk. He needed to send something more comprehensive now and didn't want to spend the time pecking slowly at the Blackberry's miniature keyboard.

> THE FEW
>
> Reich's data supports CONCH link to dolphin sleep and strandings. That data is currently uncompromised. Reich requested immediate deactivation of CONCH. My asset on site suggested "proper channels" due to the top secret nature of the project. Reich agreed and asset contacted me.
>
> Reich also claims ability to fix – TO FIX – CONCH. This avenue must be pursued. The system has proven itself invaluable and must be saved.
>
> Reich's emotional stability is still questionable...
>
> Suggest extraction and relocation of Reich to a secure facility as soon as feasible.
> ACRET

The admiral rocked back in his chair, spun 180 degrees and looked out the window. He was tired and tired of waiting. Spinning back to face his monitor, he rocked forward just as new email arrived. He was impressed with the quick reply.

> ACRET,
> CG helicopters available for move to MacDill. Orders from the appropriate office will outline the sensitive and valuable nature of the potential human cargo. Appropriate personnel will take custody at MacDill. Proceed ASAP.
> BLADE

Collins sighed—at least no "special orders" would be required for the evacuation. It was not uncommon for individuals—military or civilian—with sensitive knowledge or certain security clearances to be extracted, moved, or detained by whatever branch of the military was at hand. He was happy Reich could be moved without the danger of exposing their valuable human assets in the Coast Guard.

Tapping on his keyboard to Ramirez, he wrote:

Disable Reich as discussed earlier — non-lethal force. ASAP — as soon as practical. Recovery and relocation plan will be in place. CG has orders for secure transport to MacDill. Medlin already informed of current backstory — MK6Chips are the cause.
ACRET

Chapter 99

Egmont Key, Tampa Bay, Florida

"What? Lt. Commander, sir?" Ramirez stood as he continued to listen to Medlin. Looking at, but not seeing Adam, he said, "I didn't think there was any pre-existing relationship..." Turning and walking toward the bow, the ensign listened. After hanging up and stuffing the phone back into his pocket he turned back toward the now curious Adam and Dr. Nicely.

"Apparently, SPAWAR San Diego just made a public statement...a statement linking our MK6C dolphins—our top secret, chipped dolphins--with the strandings and with this..." He looked out over the water toward the dolphins. "...event."

Ramirez could see Adam starting to shake his head and stopped it with his finger in the air and his words, "There's more. The Rear Admiral making the statement said that *you* and Dr. Menke worked together developing the top secret project. There are schematics and spreadsheets online—papers found at Dolphin Towne." Ramirez paused and stared into Adam's eyes. "There was also the typical U.S. Navy regrets the losses...blah blah blah...something about an independent scientific review...anyway, we're to cooperate with Dr. Clarke's rescue and immediately recall, secure and deactivate the MK6C dolphins. Makes sense to me..."

Adam's head shaking started again and he snorted out, "That's not true—not true! We all...Doc discounted the possible chip from Texas early on—we all agreed it was inconsequential." The frenzied genius looked at Dr. Nicely frowning and shaking his head. "I never—*never*--worked with Doc or the Navy on that...with Bee...with Bee...I worked with Doc on Bee...my chip...I built *one* for research...I developed it on my own...tested it on Sammy...I never..." He turned to Dr. Nicely who was standing and leaning his way. "I would never..."

Dr. Nicely was now the one shaking his head. "But, you came here with Dr Menke. Why would Dr. Menke really invite you here if you weren't an expert on what he suspected was in play? Fuck...that makes perfect sense—doesn't it?"

Pacing in a tight circle Adam's mouth moved but nothing came out.

In the commotion, Ramirez took a few steps back—toward the RIB's control console—the boat was anchored and the operator was sleeping. He pulled something that looked like a small flashlight out of his pocket. "Calm down, genius—calm down!" He glanced at Dr. Nicely—who was staring at Adam from the starboard side of the boat—and casually aimed the device at Adam—bathing him in invisible, infrared light. Adam closed his mouth tightly, turned to take a step towards his laptop and Ramirez yelled, "Adam. Don't do anything stu...!"

Adam stopped and turned—not knowing that he was now a "target acquired." Two whistles followed by loud thuds filled the air and Adam was thrown backwards, over the side of the inflatable boat and into the water.

Robin reached for a throw ring, but Ramirez, keeping low, pounced and held him down on the deck. "No! Stay down!" Ramirez whispered, "Shit!" The ensign held his breath and listened. "That was sound suppressed weapons fire, sir — an Mk 11 Mod 0 — a sniper rifle."

"You certainly know your sounds, Ramirez."

The ensign did know his sounds. But he wasn't going to share what he really knew about the sound — that the whistle was not from the ammo typically used in the Mk 11, but from small beanbags. Instead, he acknowledged the compliment, "It's my job to know sounds, sir."

"Why is your team firing at us? Why is someone firing at us?" Robin fidgeted, "Can you hear Adam? Can you hear him thrashing?"

Ramirez ignored the question and the splashing, "Who fired that weapon? Not any of my team, sir. My guess is that someone on the small boat team received special orders. My guess is that they didn't hear about the press conference — that their orders were not recalled."

"Regardless...regardless of what Adam may have done, he's still the only one who knows..." Robin thought about the thumb drive Adam had passed him and stopped himself. "He may still have information valuable to the rescue and rehab effort." Robin started to crawl toward the port side of the boat — Adam's side of the boat. "We can't let Adam drown."

But, Ramirez blocked his path, "Stay down! No heroics. We don't need two casualties." The ensign pulled out his phone and dialed. "Commander. We've taken sound suppressed fire…Reich is overboard. Can you secure the area and confirm origin of attack, sir?"

Robin squirmed. The phone slid off Ramirez's ear and he put his hand on the scientist's shoulder. "Stay still! The Commander saw nothing, but they are reconnoitering, contacting the rest of our team and the small boat team…then, heading our way." Robin pulled his legs up underneath his body and Ramirez squeezed his shoulder harder, "We really don't need two casualties."

But, as the splashing over the port side stopped, Robin couldn't just lay there—he tensed the muscles in his legs. Quickly sliding from under the Ramirez's arm, Nicely exploded upright--like a 100 meter sprinter from the blocks. Dashing the few feet towards Adam's side of the boat, the scientist launched himself into the water.

The sound of Robin going over the port side pontoon was drowned out by the diesel engines of Medlin's command boat and the Lt. Commander on the loud speaker, "Ramirez, Nicely, Adam! The area is secu…" Medlin stopped mid-sentence--seeing a shadowy figure jump over the far side of the inflatable boat. In the bright spot light, Angela recognized the body shape, "Robin!"

She pointed and yelled again, "Robin!" Medlin signaled his boat to come around while he manned the spotlight on the tower.

With the other boat occupied, Ramirez snatched up Adam's laptop and secured it in his gear bag in the locker. He also disassembled and carefully packed Adam's Parabolic Acquisition Device—a model of methodical military efficiency.

As soon as he hit the water, Robin had shed his heavy winter jacket and started diving—again and again and again—for Adam. The February water temperature in Florida had nothing on even the summer temperatures in South Africa—he'd taken plenty of swims on his surf ski while riding big waves and was usually at home in cold water. Still, the repeated dives—on top of the week's general lack of sleep and food—wore even his uber-fit body down after a few minutes. Clutching at the life ring that Master Chief Samson had tossed from the command boat, Robin looked back at the sailor and gasped, "Nothing!" But, not one to give up, after a moments rest, he took another deep breath and dove again—and again. Robin was relentless.

Samson was just stripping off his own heavy coat and boots to assist with the search when Robin pulled Adam's limp body to the surface and muscled it up onto the life ring.

"Robin!" Angela was close enough to see his uncontrollable shaking and to be heard under normal circumstances—but, he didn't hear her. He didn't see Master Chief Samson hit the water with more floatation. He didn't hear or see the closing Coast Guard helicopters—even in the brightening sky—and the rescue divers that dropped into the water next to him.

Chapter 100

Dolphin Towne, Tortola, BVI

While Rachel had taken it upon herself to get Jasmine cleaned up and fed, Kurt bounced between internet sites on the reporter's smartphone—sorting through the latest updates from Tampa. His one break was to let Jasmine and Rachel know that he had been right—that Adam and Dr. Menke were in cahoots and that the chip they designed for the military had caused the strandings and the event in Tampa. Jasmine had started sobbing at the news and he left Rachel to deal with her while he returned to the lounge.

After calming Jasmine down and sending her to the kitchen for some cold chamomile tea, Rachel walked into the lounge and stared at the sofa where Kurt had dozed off with her phone tucked in his arm. Sliding the phone out without waking him, she looked at the video loop playing on the screen.

"Kurt! What's going on? What are those helicopters doing over the site? Where did all those other boats come from? What's happening?"

Sitting up, Kurt fumbled with the lantern and turned up the light. He grabbed the phone and un-muted the volume as the cameras moved from the helicopters to a flotilla of small boats moving rapidly across the sunrise-orange-tinged water. The reporter's voiceover announced, "We're riding along with Captain Harry Dbronik, a commercial fisherman who works with the marine mammal stranding response team of Mote Marine Laboratory in

Sarasota. The boats beside us began moving toward the site about 20 minutes before sunrise—part of a massive effort involving federal, state and local government agencies, private marine laboratories and even the U.S. Navy."

The cameras panned back to the hovering Coast Guard helicopters and the reporter continued, "We did receive reports of Coast Guard rescue divers jumping into the water and…"

Jasmine had whooshed into the lounge, set down her tea, grabbed the phone from Kurt and hit "mute." She held one finger up to her lips.

Silence assured for the moment, she long-blinked and then whispered, "It's Adam—I can feel it. He's helped the dolphins, but…" Jasmine looked at Kurt—there was no response. She looked at Rachel—no response. Her body went limp and she flopped into one of the lounge's hemp-covered cushy chairs and closed her eyes. Frowning and opening her moist eyes, Jasmine looked at the helicopters on the phone screen and continued, "He's hurt…he helped the dolphins…but, but he's hurt…the helicopters are for him…"

"Jasmine, we don't know what's really…"

Kurt was cut off—first, by Jasmine as she bolted upright from the chair, "I know! Sometimes, I really just know!" Then, he was stopped by Rachel's firm hand on his shoulder.

Pulling out from Rachel's hand, Kurt stepped toward the door. "The rescue plan is being executed. I'm sure some of the dolphins will be saved. Bottlenose dolphins…well, they're very resilient. If Adam helped facilitate that in any way…he's only trying to redeem himself."

Rachel walked into a hug with Jasmine, tucked the Dolphin Towne owner's head into her shoulder and stroked her hair. Jasmine whispered, "I know he helped. I know Adam helped. *I know* Adam helped." Rachel's eyes moved to Kurt and begged him to stay quiet--to stop speculating.

Crying stopped, Jasmine continued her trance-like whispering, "I know Adam. I know Adam helped. I know Adam. I…" She closed her eyes again, "…I can see light being restored to the world-pod…the cosmic dolphin consciousness…I can…they're calling… " Suddenly, Jasmine wriggled from the hug and stood. Eyes bright, she said, "Follow me. Follow me." She held out her hands. Kurt and Rachel looked at each other, but grabbed one hand each and labored to move their legs. Jasmine smiled, gave a little tug and let go—skipping down the path towards the dolphin lagoons.

Jasmine led them the along the path that weaved through the seven natural dolphin lagoons. As they walked, all the three of them heard were the eerie and repeated blows of the resident dolphins surfacing to breathe. Finally, in the warm glow of the morning sun, they stood at the edge of Bee's lagoon. Bee swam slowly along the uneven edges of the natural-looking pool.

"Beautiful." Rachel was the first one to break the silence.

Jasmine sob-sighed, "Soul…soul mate—one of my…one of the world-pod." Rachel stopped her with a hug, but with a gentle squeeze Jasmine signaled that she was okay. She stepped aside and signaled them to follow. "Careful, it can be slippery." Jasmine led them along the top of the acrylic bay wall and sat — their feet dangling in the water of Bee's lagoon.

The rhythm of the dolphin blows, and their blank, tired stares were broken with a splash as Jasmine slid off the wall and into Bee's lagoon. "Jasmine!" Kurt stood and yelled — preparing to jump in after her. But he didn't — Rachel tugged on his shorts and shook her head. He sat back down.

While underwater Jasmine stripped out of her clothes. At the surface, she tipped her head and floated on her back — her breasts small islands and her red hair spread and floating lightly. An orgasmic sigh of pleasure melted into one of relief and her body drifted slowly into a vertical position. Entranced, Kurt and Rachel felt like voyeurs.

Bee accelerated--turning quicker and quicker laps around the lagoon and around Jasmine. Kurt and Rachel stood. "Didn't...?" Rachel hesitated in her question.

"Yes, Bee rammed one of Jasmine's regular...um...clients. Sent him to the hospital." Bee turned and accelerated toward Jasmine. "Shit!" Kurt hit the water. But it was unnecessary — Bee slowed and nuzzled Jasmine's belly.

"Bee! Jasmine loves Bee!" Jasmine rubbed Bee's beak.

Kurt stopped and was treading water. Rachel moved around the lagoon towards the small beach.

Jasmine giggled and grabbed Bee's dorsal fin. "She's fine now, Kurt — radiant. Her universal luminescence has returned. She knows." The dolphin cackled and towed her around the lagoon. After three laps, Bee slowed near the gate in the wall—almost coming to a halt—and Jasmine slid off.

"Jasmine!" Kurt looked to Rachel for direction and she signaled him to stay put.

The gate hadn't been open to the bay in some time, but Adam had been diligent about maintaining everything at Dolphin Towne—including the gate's manual hydraulic controls. Jasmine had no problem opening the lagoon to the open water. After swimming through the opening, she slapped the water gently with her hand. In seconds, Bee passed through and jetted by Jasmine. There was no hesitation, there was no other good-bye, and there was no sight of her in the bay. Bee was gone.

There were no words from Rachel or Kurt—their eyes moved back and forth from Jasmine to the bay. There was no emotion from Jasmine and no sign of Bee.

After swimming back into the lagoon, Jasmine shut the gate and made for the lagoon's sandy beach. Exiting the water, she headed up the path to the Eli House.

Kurt pulled himself out of the water and sat back down on the lagoon's wall—shaking his head. Rachel circled around and stood on the wall. With the gentle touch of Kurt's hand behind her knee, Rachel side-stepped away and sighed, "Sort of a storybook ending here—at least for Bee. That's not likely in Tampa Bay, is it?"

While standing, he shook his head, "No—even with what is probably the best organized dolphin rescue ever...even with all we know about bottlenose dolphin rehabilitation…that'll be messy." He stepped toward Rachel and she took another step away. Kurt stopped and looked at his feet.

Rachel looked out over the water—there was no focus in her eyes. "Kurt, I…I'm sorry…I really like you but…I live in New York…you, well…you have some things to work out on your own." She looked down at her clothing. "And this isn't really me…I just don't…" A couple more steps took her to where the wall met the rocks and stone walkway. From there, Rachel walked silently toward the Eli House.

Chapter 101

Egmont Key, Tampa Bay, Florida

Adam's lifeless body was lifted onto the electric RIB he had been using for his data collection. Ramirez stood by and stared at the young man's pale blue face as the Coast Guard rescue divers stripped off his heavy, wet clothes. Two hand-sized, red bruises were splotched across his lumpy, deformed chest and abdomen.

Taking a step closer, Ramirez stammered, "Is he…is he…?"

"He's breathing — shallow, weak. But, he's breathing." The diver looked up at Ramirez, "Step back, we need to get him packaged and to MacDill for treatment."

Working quickly, the team of three divers wrapped Adam in heavy blankets and slid him into a foil-lined sack that looked like a sleeping bag for astronauts. After lifting him into a litter, two men worked on securing a web of straps to hold him in place. The third put a Res-Q-Air mask over Adam's face — the inhalation rewarming unit would increase the oxygen getting to his lungs and help heat his core. Once the mask was in place and the oxygen flowing, the diver secured the unit to the litter.

Packing complete, Adam was carefully winched up to the waiting Coast Guard helicopter.

Ramirez tapped one of the rescue divers on the shoulder and pointed at the helicopter. "What do you think?"

"They'll know more when they get him to MacDill."

The ensign remained persistent and tapped again. "What do you think?"

Standing up from where he was packing his gear, the diver stared hard at the sailor. "I think he took two non-lethal rounds to the chest."

Ramirez shook his head—that still wasn't the evaluation he wanted.

"Yeah, I didn't think so. We get it…our orders made it clear he is someone important to national security." He squatted down to finish packing and continued, "The biggest concern is the chest wall deformity and if there is any damage to the lungs or other internal organs…any salt water in his lungs—that is never good…his vitals were weak, but not weakening."

Looking at the helicopter now speeding to the east, Ramirez asked, "And Dr. Nicely?"

"Nicely? Oh, the other one. I didn't hear. He's Bravo Team's responsibility." The rescue diver gestured over his shoulder with his thumb. The Bravo Team helicopter was now moving low towards the command boat where Robin was being treated.

Robin had been pulled aboard the larger command boat by Master Chief Samson and the rescue divers. He had stopped shivering—making the dangerous transition from mild to severe hypothermia. Samson helped the divers strip off his wet, heavy clothes. While the divers packaged Robin and hooked up another Res-Q-Air unit, Samson stuffed the clothes in a plastic bag, and passed them to Angela.

She squinted and looked at the bag. "What am I supposed…?"

The Master Chief smiled and shrugged. "Clean and press?"

Angela scowled. "Do you know me?" She walked towards the bow and stuffed the plastic bag in Robin's duffle. By the time she turned around, Robin's litter was hovering just off the port side — one of the rescue divers was harnessed and hanging with him. She scampered up the tower and shouted over at the diver, "Take good care of him!"

One of the Coast Guard divers on deck touched her foot and she looked down. He pointed at one of his ears, shook his head and she understood — they couldn't hear her over the roar of the helicopter. Robin couldn't hear her. But, the diver motioned her to bend over and shouted over the engine noise, "St. Anthony's Hospital. They're taking him to St. Anthony's hospital in St. Petersburg."

When she straightened up, and looked up again, Angela could see Robin's litter being shifted into the helicopter and the aircraft tipping it's blades towards St. Petersburg. As it moved away, her eyes moved to the rescue flotilla — boats large and small — lit up in the bright sunrise and moving into the area. Now, it was time for her to get to work. Cell phone to her ear, fingers pointing and hands slashing through the air — Angela started to direct the chaotic orchestra that was to play her marine mammal rescue symphony.

Commercial fishermen from all over the west coast of Florida — some trained, some getting on-the-job training — and rescue workers from state and federal agencies, Sea World, Mote Marine Laboratory, Lowry Park Zoo, and Clearwater Marine Science Center began to encircle and capture the sleeping dolphins. Two capture boats, with men from Medlin's team on board, would be responsible for the MK6C dolphins. Those animals would be taken to MacDill. The rest of the animals would be scattered throughout the state — those with the best chances would be taken to the more traditional facilities like Sea World or Clearwater Marine Science Center. Others would be taken to the makeshift tanks Angela had students and faculty assembling at Eckerd College.

With the rescued men on their way to get medical treatment and Dr. Clarke engrossed in an animated cell phone conversation standing on the tower, Lt. Commander Medlin walked to the side of the command boat and caught the attention of Ensign Ramirez — who's RIB was now tied alongside.

"Ramirez!" The ensign hustled over to starboard side — close enough to have a real conversation. "Ramirez, take that RIB and Reich's equipment back to MacDill ASAP. I want everything secured on base."

Ramirez, his mouth partially open, stared at his commander — the same commander that had usurped the authority of those looking out for the best interests — the national security interests — of the country. "Sir?"

"I'm sure there is sensitive information there, ensign. I'm sure it wouldn't hurt us to protect and secure that information."

Nodding with slight smile, Ramirez stood thinking —
thinking that his commanding officer was either more patriotic or a
better player than he had imagined. "Honor and integrity, sir?"
Ramirez snickered and shook his head, "We're all so fucking noble."

Puffing up his chest and raising his chin just a little, Medlin
looked through narrowed eyes and shouted, "Move it!"

The Lt. Commander knew that everything he did from this
point on could be relevant to mitigating the damage to his career in
what he assumed would be the upcoming Courts Marshal. Even
though he had been communicating with Admiral Collins for most
of his direction on this mission, he was also disobeying direct orders
from his superior officer at Little Creek to fully cooperate with the
admiral. Commander Kirk had hinted at the impending investigation
while giving him instructions to cooperate with the rescue and to
secure the MK6C dolphins.

When Angela closed her phone, she turned and looked down
from the tower and at Medlin. She opened her arms to the rescue now
in progress and mouthed, "Thank you." He nodded back and
smiled — secure in the knowledge that he had done the right thing.

Medlin's gaze moved back out over the water, *At least the right
thing for the dolphins.*

Chapter 102

Coast Guard Helicopter on Route to Saint Anthony's Hospital
St. Petersburg, Florida

"Adam? Did anyone...?" Nicely squirmed in the litter and tilted his well-packed head towards the hovering Coast Guard medic. The medic shook his head and pulled the Res-Q-Air mask away from Robin's face. Weak-voiced, Robin tried again, "Adam? How is...Adam?"

Gesturing out the window with his thumb, the medic answered, "MacDill. They are taking him to MacDill. But, Dr..." He referred to his notes, "...Dr. Nicely, the report we got was that it did not look good. He was under a few minutes, severely hypothermic...but had some serious blunt trauma that deformed his chest and abdomen. Not a good combination. At least—from what I heard—his weak vitals weren't getting any worse."

"He needs to...I think he really has information...other information..." Robin was gasping—his breathing raspy—as his arms strained to move under the blankets and straps of the litter. "My pants...where are...?"

Sliding the oxygen mask back over Robin's nose and mouth, the ensign added, "Relax. Slow, deep breaths. I'm sure someone on the boat has your clothes. At least you're warming up—more coherent. We'll be at the hospital in less than five minutes, sir." Robin obeyed the medic—he took slow, deep breaths and closed his eyes.

Virginia Aquarium, Virginia Beach, Virginia

"Ed!" There was a knock on the curator's door frame—Dr. Caruso, the lead veterinarian on the necropsies stood in the doorway—a metal pan in his hand. Bordon swiveled his desk chair and looked.

Dr. Caruso held up the pan. "Is this what you were looking for? What that Dr. Clarke was looking for?"

Bordon's eyes widened as he stood and took the few steps to the door. Taking the pan into his hands, his head began to bob. "Shit. I think so. Where?"

"One of the second group—the ones you said the surfers found. It was right where you wanted us to look—four centimeters anterior and to the right of the blowhole. No scar, but the slightest of lumps."

The befuddled curator continued to stare at the metallic cylinder.

The vet prodded him, "What now?"

Breaking out of his stare, Bordon walked over to his desk and set the pan next to his computer. "You continue as planned. I'll contact Dr. Clarke...thanks."

Now alone, Ed pulled his digital camera out of a desk drawer and readied the chip for a photo—laying it out on a blank sheet of paper. He then hooked up the USB cable and downloaded the photo. After attaching it to a short email and hitting send, he dialed Dr. Clarke.

"Ed? Sorry, there's a lot of background noise." The rescue was now in full-swing and boats were all over the area off Egmont Key. "There, I'm in a quieter place. I'm assuming...well, I don't assume. What's up?"

"We've recovered one of the Navy chips. At least that's what I think it is. I've emailed you a photo. Dr. Caruso found it right where you suggested—in one of the dolphins from few that were recovered after the report from the surfers...one of the one's buried under piles of snow after the storm. What....? What do I do with it now? Do I need to contact the Navy?"

"Photos-then, secure it. Put it in a locked, limited-access safe or vault or whatever you have. I'll contact the Navy. Just make sure that the chain of custody sheet is properly completed—make sure you fax or email me a copy so that we cover our bases." Angela sighed.

"You sound disappointed. I thought you'd be thrilled to have more evidence."

"Usually, I am. But something...we discounted the chip in Texas...well, it seems like a long time ago. I guess I'm still a little skeptical."

"But, you've got the chip from Texas..."

"I don't have that chip."

"Okay, you *had* a chip in Texas. The Navy has admitted to there being chipped dolphins in the Tampa Bay group. Now, you have a chip here--pretty compelling evidence."

"Except that I'll never get real verification of those chips in the Tampa animals. I'll never see those chips removed from the dolphins. I'm taking the Navy at their word."

"Seems like that's all you have."

Angela sighed again, "Seems you're right. Thanks for the quick work—I appreciate you moving things ahead. Thank your team for me. Now, I need to get ready for my press conference."

Chapter 103

MacDill Air Force Base, Tampa, Florida

"We'll take it from here, gentlemen." The doctor from the Air Force's 6th Medical Group shouted through the side door of the Coast Guard helicopter.

"Sir?"

The doctor pointed to four waiting MPs. "We're taking custody of the patient at this time. I'll be responsible for his care and treatment from this point on."

Adam's litter was transferred to a stretcher and the Coast Guard medic passed his files along to the attending doctor. Flipping through the pages, the doctor sighed and looked at the seaman. "It looks like you've done all that you could…" Rolling back some of the hypothermia packaging, the doctor examined Adam's chest and abdomen. Upon palpation, there was no response from Adam. "He's breathing, but he appears unresponsive. He may have lapsed into a coma."

After nodding at the medics, the doctor turned to his team and shouted, "Let's move people! We have work to do!"

With that, the MacDill medical team wheeled Adam away and left the Coast Guard medic standing on the tarmac.

St. Anthony's Hospital, Saint Petersburg, Florida

"Lt. Commander Medlin, the Navy team commander, he requested that I stay with you, sir."

"I'm Robin Nicely."

"I know, sir. Seaman Chaffe, sir. I'm the rescue swimmer that directed your treatment, sir."

"Any news on Adam Reich, Chaffe? Is he here?"

"Sir? I told you on the flight that...that he was taken to MacDill—the Air Force base. He..." The Coast Guard rescue swimmer looked away.

"Don't tell me he didn't make it...he had to have made it...he was..."

"He was in a coma...last I heard...sir."

"A coma?"

"Yes, sir. When a hypothermia patient's temp drops below 32 C—32 Celsius—they slip into a coma. Hopefully, the Air Force team at MacDill can get him warmer quickly. If his temp drops anymore..."

"Fuck." Robin's eyes darted around the room, "Where...where are my clothes?"

"They were bagged and left on the boat. I believe the Navy Master Chief took care of them, sir."

Robin looked at the nightstand and the phone, "Chaffe, would you mind stepping outside for a minute or two? I'd like to make a personal call."

"Certainly, Dr. Nicely."

Taking a deep breath—testing his lungs—Robin dialed.

"Robin! So, good to hear your crazy South African voice! How are you...?"

"I'm well—as well as can be expected. Have you got my clothes, love?"

Ignoring the question, Angela told him about the chip found in the Virginia Beach dolphins.

"Another chip? I really...Another chip? I really don't think the chip is it. Ramirez...Well, I've had a little time to think about this, love. Ramirez...Adam, they were whispering about something else. A top secret file. I'm sure they were talking about it." Robin took a slow, deep breath and continued, "Adam was either very convincing in his argument—made something up completely plausible---or, he wasn't talking about the chip. I don't think he would have reacted that way on the boat—got nearly as frantic--if the chip were really the cause...if *he* were the real cause."

Angela sighed. "Unless he was being *really* defensive—caught lying."

"No one knew—for sure—what else he had postulated. Ramirez was the only..."

"Hey, Robin, I'm getting ready to head to the news conference. The boat is almost here. There's no other evidence to support your theory..."

"In my pants. Get in my pants!"

"Wow, that's something you've never had to demand."

Ignoring the innuendo, Robin continued with his instructions, "There is a baggie in my pants pocket. Adam gave it to me. In the baggie is a flash drive—a thumb drive. He passed it to me while Ramirez was otherwise occupied—wasn't looking. He made sure of that. It really might be something." Closing his eyes and shaking his head, Robin continued, "I was hard on him, love. When I found out that he worked on the chip with the Navy…I…anyway, I hope that whatever he gave me isn't damaged." Taxing himself, Robin gasped for a few raspy breaths.

"Okay — relax. Slow down and breathe — slow down. I'll find the bag and your pants and look for that thumb drive."

Robin exhaled. "I hope it's usable — I was in the water a long time."

"I'll see and let you know. If it's anything, I'll share it. Try to watch the press conference on TV. Do what the doctors tell you…I love you."

"I love you too. Now, find that ….."

"I will."

With the droning dial tone in his ear, Robin hung up the phone and grabbed the TV remote.

Egmont Key, Tampa Bay, Florida

In the command boat's forward compartment, Angela sorted through her and Robin's pile of stuff — sleeping bags, duffels, toiletries--and found a heavy plastic bag of wet clothes. In the right front pocket of his pants she found the heavy-duty, military grade Ziploc bag.

Angela was frozen — staring at the bag and wondering what to do next. She knew Robin expected her to examine what was on the thumb drive. She knew that would take time. She also knew that she had never been late for a press conference.

"Shit—Niceleeeeeeeeee." Drawing his name out as she whispered to herself, Angela pulled out and booted up her laptop.

There was a knock on the compartment door. "Dr. Clarke?" It was Lt. Commander Medlin. "Your boat is here to take you to St. Petersburg." With no response, he knocked again. "Dr. Clarke?"

"One minute, Medlin. I'm...I'm changing." So as not to be caught in a lie, Angela dug out a fresh NMFS button-down shirt and exchanged it with the polo she had been wearing. Her laptop went back in its case. The thumb drive went back into the baggie and then into her pocket.

Briefcase over her shoulder, Angela exited the compartment and boarded the inflatable boat for the ride to the press conference. Looking back at Medlin now on the tower, she nodded and shouted over the diesel engines, "Thank you!"

Chapter 104

Office of Admiral Collins, NOAA

Silver Spring, Maryland

"Ensign Ramirez, it's good to hear your voice again, son. Email and texting just isn't the same."

"Sir, as per Lt. Commander Medlin's orders, I've secured Adam Reich's gear and equipment and am now at MacDill. I'm assuming..."

"Medlin gave that order? Change of heart?"

"Sir, Lt. Commander Medlin has served our well for most of his adult life. He has always been a strong, respected commander among his peers. His operational record at MSOT speaks for itself. He..."

"I'm aware of his service record — that is why he was chosen to lead this mission. Still..."

"Begging your pardon, admiral, but he has always commanded my respect. And, with all due respect to you, admiral, sir, he made an error of judgment...these...well, these were extraordinary circumstances...sir."

Collins clenched his jaw, stood and paced around his desk. Unclenching his jaw and licking his lips, he responded, "Need I remind you, ensign, that extraordinary circumstances are exactly what MSOTs are trained for? The Navy, the people of the United States, invested a lot of time and money into training Lt. Commander Medlin to deal with and excel in *extraordinary situations*. But, he made a very serious error in judgment—in a high value, high stress situation. His decision may have compromised the security of the nation and certainly has caused us to compromise—to go public with--an important top secret program. There *will* be severe consequences, Ramirez. We can't have someone with lapses in judgment commanding elite forces—any forces—in the field."

"Sir?"

"I'm afraid that will be the final word. Now, secure that gear in what was Adam Reich's lab. Someone will be along to…

"And the kid, sir? Reich?"

"You provided an important service, ensign—but do not forget your place." Admiral Collins paused just long enough for Ramirez to digest his annoyance at being interrupted. "Now, my latest update has him in a hypothermic coma and receiving treatment. But, that is none of your concern—you did your duty. Reich knew the potential consequences of his actions. He may look like a teenager, but he is an adult—a very smart adult. You knew the consequences as well—but, you made the correct decision. That has been duly noted. Now, *Lieutenant* Ramirez, secure that equipment and return to your team to await further orders."

"Sir, yes, sir!"

With Ramirez sorted out, Admiral Collins returned to his desk chair and his computer. Mouse in hand, he opened the live video page of GlobalReport.com and waited for the NMFS press conference. In the interim, he sent an email update to the Director of National Intelligence:

BLADE
Reich's equipment being secured at MacDill. Transport to San Diego will be arranged. Reich receiving intensive treatment.
ACRET

Chapter 105

NMFS Southeast Regional Office, St. Petersburg, Florida
Sarah Meehan, the Director of the NMFS Office of Public Affairs, looked at her watch and then at Director Hamilton — it was 1:20pm and Angela Clarke was yet to arrive.

Grinning, Jake whispered, "She'll be here. It might be 1:29:59, but she'll be here — she's never late."

The conference room at the NMFS office in St. Petersburg was filled to capacity. Reporters and camera crews from around the world were crammed into the space.

At 1:29pm, Sarah again looked at Director Hamilton.

He shook his head and shrugged. "Uncharacteristic."

"Unacceptable." Sarah looked out over the crowd of reporters and then back to Jake. "Let's get started, director."

Director Hamilton nodded and stepped behind the podium. "Thank you all for coming. I'm Dr. Jake Hamilton, Director of the National Marine Fisheries Service. I wish we were meeting under better circumstances, but…"

Jake paused and looked up from his notes. Disheveled from the fast open-boat ride, Angela entered through the door at the back of the room. Narrowing his eyes just a little, the director looked at Angela and then back into the audience. He continued, "While the loss of dolphins in Texas and Virginia were unprecedented and disturbing, we're hoping that Dr. Clarke will have some more positive news with regards to the rescue operations here in Tampa Bay." Again, he looked to the back of the room.

Angela was busy — hooking her laptop up to the projector that she had requested. Seeing Jake's glance, she held up her finger — she needed another minute or two.

But Jake had nothing further to say, so after a long, uncomfortable silence, he continued, "Now, without further delay, I'd like to introduce Dr. Angela Clarke, our National Director of Marine Mammal Health and Stranding. Dr. Clarke will give us an update on how the rescue is proceeding." Angela was finishing with the projector — slipping the laptop remote into her pocket. "Dr. Clarke?"

Angela made her way through the close rows of folding chairs. At the front of the room, she doffed her damp windbreaker and stepped behind the podium. After pushing a few stray strands of blonde hair behind her ears, she bent over and pulled a legal pad out of her briefcase. With a crooked smile, she started, "Thank you, Director Hamilton. But, prior to my update on the rescue operations, I'd like to bring everyone up to speed on another important matter…"

After looking at Sarah Meehan and Director Hamilton, she continued, "I'd like to talk about the cause of this event and the events in Galveston and Virginia Beach." Setting her notes on top of the podium, Angela took the remote for her laptop out of her pocket, pressed a button and an image appeared on the screen on the screen — it was Adam's note briefly outlining his suspicions — his conclusions — about *Wendall*.

For the moment, Angela ignored the rude murmurs from the press — and the image — and continued, "According to Rear Admiral Hancock, at SPAWAR, San Diego, the cause of these events — the cause of the extended dolphin sleep in these groups-- has been the malfunctioning of a subcutaneous telemetry chip implanted in several individual dolphins. According to the Rear Admiral, the chip was designed by Dr. Aldo Menke and Adam Reich and Adam Reich was brought to Tampa Bay to troubleshoot the potential malfunction."

Glancing over at Jake, she could see that he was focused on reading the slide on the screen. "We did recover a chip — a metallic cylinder — in Texas that was subsequently lost in an accident — an explosion — at the NMFS laboratory in Galveston. We've recovered no such chips in Tampa Bay as the MK6C dolphins are being handled by teams escorted by Navy personnel only. We have only the word of Rear Admiral Hancock that there are chipped dolphins in the Tampa Bay group." Taking a deep breath, she continued, "We *have* recovered one chip from a carcass in Virginia Beach. The images emailed by the team there seem to match the object from Texas and would seem to support the Navy's admission that MK6C dolphins were active in each of the event areas. What this does not prove..."

"Angela." Jake whispered and stared. "I can't allow you..."

Looking out at the reporters, Angela whispered back, "It's too late."

Turning back to the cameras — the press conference was being broadcast live-- Angela stood tall and continued, "What this does not prove is that these chips were the cause of these Unusual Mortality Events or of the behavior of the dolphins in Tampa Bay. The Navy would like us to assume guilt by association — circumstantial evidence--in science we look for more than that. Frankly, we don't have it."

Angela clicked to the next slide. "The slide you were just looking at — that I'm sure you've digested by now — was a note from Adam Reich of Dolphin Towne. It was a regrettably quick outline of what he believed to be the real cause of the UMEs and of the event here in Tampa. As you read, he was convinced that some unforeseen problems with a top secret sonar net — *Wendall* he called it — were creating a compound sound wave that stimulated and kept the dolphins in an extended sleep-state."

"According to Reich, this system was designed to avoid the past *issues* the Navy has had with sonar and marine mammals — on its face the project was to be innocuous. Reich pointed to flaws in the research methodologies — Dr. Aldo Menke's testing on dolphins at the Navy Marine Mammal Program — that would have rendered the later environmental review of the project essentially moot." Angela looked at Director Hamilton — knowing that somewhere, somehow, at some time, he was the duped reviewer.

"Whether it was a sloppy, rushed research design or an intentional omission, Mr. Reich has pointed out that the two sonar waves used in *Wendall* were only tested individually — never as a compound wave as they would appear — at times--in the field. It is this compound wave that Mr. Reich has pointed to as being similar to a type of wave created to induce sleep in humans. Mr. Reich has also noted that the testing of *Wendall* did not entail exposing dolphins to the sonar waves as they would appear in the final operational system — those waves originating from a network of multiple sources."

"In all honesty, I have to say that while Adam Reich's argument is compelling — and I agree with my colleague from South Africa, Dr. Robin Nicely, that we should give his work serious consideration — we have no hard evidence beyond these files and Mr. Reich's summary."

"That said, ladies and gentlemen, if this *Wendall* was the cause of the prolonged dolphin sleep — the cause of the mortalities in Texas and in Virginia and of the unusual behavior here in Tampa Bay — and, if it is functional in other U.S. coastal waters…well, it needs to be shut down now. *That* would be my recommendation — to err on the side of caution. There may already be similarly massive, pre-stranding pods in other U.S. coastal areas…"

The reporters talked loudly amongst themselves and shouted out questions. Dr. Clarke looked at Director Hamilton and Sarah Meehan and held up her hand to quiet the crowd. "Please, please — there will be time for questions. I'll answer all of your questions when I am finished." The noise level dropped to a whisper and Angela continued, "But, before we get to that, I'd like to give you a more concrete report–an update on the rescue and rehabilitation operation."

Chapter 106

Office of Admiral Collins, NOAA

Silver Spring, Maryland

Sitting at his desk, Admiral Collins stared over the top of his computer screen. His eyes were focused on nothing, but in his mind he kept replaying the press conference. He knew they had no hard evidence of a link with the defensive sonar network — yet, he knew there would be an investigation. He knew the program would have to be suspended. After a moment, his thoughts focused on *Wendall*. "Wendall?" The Admiral's head shake morphed into a repeated nod as he repeated the original code name for the sonar project originally conceived by his late son.

"Wendall..." Collins stood, circled his desk and stopped. Sitting on the corner, he leaned over to look at the small photo of his son and closed his eyes. "I'm sorry we let you down, son. I'm sorry Menke couldn't get it right...two projects lost...the dolphins...Wendall, I'm sorry we couldn't get it right..." Straightening up, Collins stared at the dark, wood panel walls of his office.

"Shit!" Grinning, Collins walked the rest of the way around his desk and sat. He had remembered one of the many messages from Ramirez — "Reich sure he can fix Wendall. Reich can fix Wendall." Looking again at his son's photo, the admiral whispered, "Menke didn't get it right — maybe Reich can."

With that thought in mind, Collins typed:

BLADE
Priority: Reich's survival, anonymity and evacuation.
ACRET

Dolphin Towne, Tortola, BVI

Kurt walked to the open door, stepped out onto the balcony and paused, "Jasmine." She didn't reactt's...it' — continuing to scan the bay with her binocular. "It's been all over the online news outlets." Dolphin Towne's entire electrical system was fried, Rachel had packed her bags and left, so Kurt was now relying on an underpowered cell phone borrowed from one of the resort's staff for news. "Dr. Clarke is saying that the cause of the strandings might not be the chips after all. She's saying that Adam..." He stepped closer and touched her on the shoulder. "She's saying that Adam may not have been involved — other than to have found this potential other cause. It may have been some sonar system malfunction — Adam discovered it. Sounds like her Dr. Nicely agrees it has some credence — that Adam wasn't just covering his ass or his mistakes with the chip."

Jasmine pulled away from his hand and slid a few steps to the side. She put the binoculars back up to her eyes.

Staying put, Kurt continued, "There's other news. It's not good. Adam...well, all they were saying...he was injured somehow. The details of how he was injured are rather sketchy. There *were* rumors that he was in a coma."

Jasmine set her binoculars on a table on the balcony and stood silent. She had been searching the waters of the bay for Bee.

Kurt's voice cracked as he stepped closer, "Adam... I'm...sorry. He was...Summers, CNN...they just started reporting...someone from MacDill leaked..." Shaking his head, Kurt continued, "Shit. They're reporting that Adam didn't make it."

Collapsing to the deck of the balcony Jasmine didn't hear anything else — the beating of her fists on the floor was too loud. Her crying was too loud. Jasmine could feel it — Adam's death — and her whole body spasmed as she sobbed. Kurt took a tentative step towards her — towards comforting her — but instead, quietly turned and walked back inside to his room.

He didn't want to be there for Jasmine. He didn't want to be there for anyone. Back in his room he stuffed his clothes and all the clutter on top of the dresser into his duffel bag. It wasn't neat or organized and he didn't care. He just needed to get out of Dolphin Towne. Rachel had packed her things and headed for the airport soon after Jasmine had released Bee — soon after she had released *him*. He didn't want to run into her at the airport, but he did want to run.

Day Nine

Thursday, February 27, 2008

Chapter 107

MacDill Air Force Base, Tampa, Florida

"Admiral, sir. The MK6C dolphins have been recovered and are on route to San Diego. Adam Reich's equipment and personal effects are also secure and on route to San Diego—as per your orders, sir."

"I'm surprised to be hearing directly from you, Medlin. I thought for sure that you'd relay that information through MSOTs Commander Kirk." Medlin shifted his weight from foot to foot in the silence—he knew the admiral would continue. "Very well. The Coast Guard is now the lead agency on providing perimeter security?"

"Yes, sir. They are keeping the area clear of all but the few rescue boats dealing with the animals that beached last night on the bay side of Egmont Key, sir."

"Yes, that is unfortunate—but it seems Dr. Clarke now has many of the dolphins on the way to recovery. Her latest update had the number captured and in tanks at 83. She's sure to get those few more off the beach." The admiral paused.

Medlin could hear Collins sigh through the phone and took the opportunity to ask a delicate question, "Sir, is it true what they are reporting? Is it true that Adam Reich is dead? Is that *really* an acceptable sacrifice?"

Collins ignored the insubordinate question and continued in an even, measured tone, "I'm in a difficult spot. In some ways you did a fine job—at Virginia Beach you did an exemplary job. In Tampa, well...you didn't handle the extraordinary circumstances like an elite special operator. I'm disappointed in you and I'm disappointed in our MSOT training regime."

"Sir, I thought…I was sure you'd be furious with me and the team."

"You don't get to be in my position by flying off the handle at subordinates who can't clearly follow orders—no matter how flagrant or how damaging…because I know you know how damaging your actions have been. Though they have no hard proof— yet—that *Wendall* is what caused the dolphin mortalities, there is enough evidence for them to figure it out…enough evidence for us to preemptively shut down the system—to cancel systems that were just about to go online. Our national security will be severely compromised. Assets will need to be reallocated and will be taxed to their limits—and they still won't provide the level of protection we had."

Medlin leaned against the side wall of the guest barracks and waited for more—the admiral continued, "I'm disappointed in you. I'm angry with you. But I'm also extremely disappointed in myself. You were *my* pick for this. But, I neglected to see through your string of promotions and mission successes—to see the vulnerability—the insecurity—buried deep."

Unsure as to what character flaw was being addressed, Medlin asked, "Admiral, sir?"

"Lt. Commander Ricardo Medlin'." Medlin had no words— he paced between the corner of the building and a rusting dumpster- -so Collins continued, "You anglicized your name just before you enlisted. Maybe at the time you thought it might draw a little less attention to your ethnicity? Maybe you thought you'd have a better chance at a Special Forces slot?"

"Maybe I was looking for a way around the subtle racism I knew still existed in the Navy, sir."

"You should never deny who you are—Richard, Ricardo. Not your family, your name...or your being an MSOT. You forgot that years ago—you forgot it in Tampa."

"Admiral Collins, sir—I...I have never forgotten..."

"Enough! I'm afraid your days of MSOT are over. Commander Kirk will have new orders for you today. You will be debriefed, reassigned, your men will get a new commander and they will be deployed.

Admiral Collins hung up and Medlin found himself next to the rusting dumpster. He leaned back on the barracks and slid to the ground. He fingered the small, round blue pin on his chest. The plain emblem was nothing as recognizable as the golden trident worn by a Navy SEAL—MSOTs were not supposed to be recognizable.

"Lt. Commander! Commander Kirk has been trying..." Master Chief Petty Officer Samson came around the corner and stopped. "Sir?" He took three quick steps closer and stopped again. "What did the admiral say, sir?"

Medlin shook his head and stood up. He brushed the dirt from the seat of his pants and took two steps towards Samson. Unbuttoning his shirt, he reached in and unpinned his emblem.

Samson just shook his head when his commander held out the insignia.

"Yes, Master Chief." He pressed it into Samson's hand and paused—the two men a little uncomfortable with the prolonged contact. "I want you to save it for me. I *will* earn it back. Somehow, I will earn it back."

Samson held the pin in his fist and just shook his head. "You could have just done what he wanted, sir, you could have obeyed his…"

"…his highly irregular and possibly illegal orders?" Medlin's body stretched as he stood a little more erect and shook his head. "No, Master Chief—no. Average men might take that route—the easy way…*just following orders, sir*--in hopes of saving their skins. We're *MSOTs*, Samson—we *are not* average men. I had to come up with a better solution because *I'm* not an average man." Frowning, Medlin's eyes drifted to Samson's hand.

"It won't leave my person, sir. And…and *when* the time comes…I didn't say "if"…*when* the time comes I will be honored to return it to your chest."

Chapter 108

Eckerd College, St. Petersburg, Florida

"Robin!" Angela stepped away from the above ground swimming pool with pastel starfish painted on the sides and marched over to the edge of the parking lot. "Nice of you to call! How'd you get here? Where'd you get clean clothes?"

Dr. Robin Nicely pointed his thumb over his left shoulder. "Seaman Chaffe and his buddy, Seaman Wright. Chaffe was…"

Angela wrapped him in a hug. "How are you feeling?"

"I'm fine, love. Mind if Chaffe and Wright look around — they're curious as to how things are working out. I am too."

Stepping back, Angela waved at the Coast Guard men by the car and said to Robin, "Of course. There are plenty of people around to keep them from getting into trouble."

The seamen stepped up to the couple and expressed their thanks. Nicely responded, "No, thank you — Chaffe for taking such great care of me and Wright for lending me the jeans, t-shirt and sweatshirt…well, a complete outfit — thank you. I'll have them laundered and returned ASAP."

"Take your time. We're going to look around, okay?"

"By all means." When the men passed, Angela pulled Robin close for a long kiss.

Robin smiled. "I missed that. I missed you."

"We've been together for how…what day is it?"

"Thursday." Grabbing her hand, Robin started them walking through the bustle of the makeshift rehab center. "I meant that I missed you...since the last time we were together. I really missed you, love."

Angela was silent, but with subtle pressure on Robin's hand steered him through the student volunteers, tents and tanks, past the sandpit volleyball court, and to the campus' concrete seawall. She sat—Robin remained standing.

With the silence stretching, Angela fidgeted on the concrete. Taking a deep breath, Robin sat. "I should have called. I should have emailed. I know that wasn't..."

Still looking out over the water towards Indian Key, Angela put up the hand. "I really don't have time for this right now, Robin. I've got to get back on the phone and check on the strandings at Egmont. Some of the animals we didn't net hit the beach overnight. It's a small group, but amazingly we still have room. And, we'll have more room as the really weak animals continue to die..."

She put her hands down on the concrete—preparing to boost herself up—but Robin took her closest hand in both of his and looked at the side of her head. "I built us a house. I built *us* a house...in Plettenberg...on the water..." One of his hands touched Angela's cheek and gently turned her head. "For us."

Chapter 109

Operations Center, National Counterterrorism Center Virginia

Jenna Damne approached her boss. "Sir. CONCH was disabled—as per your orders—at 1800 hours EST on Wednesday, February 25. My team has now secured the necessary physical and electronic files and completed the necessary debriefing."

"Well done—your team's performance has been exemplary." The Director of National Security and his team leader stood overlooking the theatre-like room of dormant workstations and several blank, big screens on the wall.

"Then, sir...I don't understand, the system...my team...was working...we had new regions coming online...it was successful and the threat is still...credible and imminent. I can't believe this was the system they were alluding to on the news, sir—the sonar net that killed all those dolphins." Jenna fidgeted with her security badge.

"I don't argue with an Executive Order. And, we *have* put other defensive precautions in place. But, be assured the shutdown has nothing to do with the work of your team—nothing. Their work was exemplary—apparently someone else's work was not." He started walking towards the door to an overlooking office, when he stopped and turned back to the team leader. "Your team's reassignment...well, just don't get too settled in..." He looked at the office's opaque glass that everyone knew was a one-way window, "We're hoping it is very temporary."

With that, he quickly turned and moved through the door — closing it behind him and frowning at the men in the room. One wore a neat, navy-blue suit with a triton pin in the lapel; another, sat board upright on a black sofa; off to the side, sat the third--in a wheel chair with several IVs, a nasal cannula supplying supplemental oxygen and wearing a warm, red stocking cap.

"Well done, Shaw. They'll never be able to verify that CONCH ever really existed. They'll never link it to what they are calling *Wendall*." Collins smiled and looked at the pale young man in the wheelchair. "And, we'll be able to modify the system — improve the system — and, make sure the research covers all the bases this time." He looked at the only seriously morose man in the room, "Right, Doc?"

Dr. Aldo Menke did not respond. Instead, there was a weak, raspy whisper from the wheel chair, "I can fix it. I will fix it. Some minor shifts in the amplitude and frequency..." There were a few wheezy deep breaths. "I've already started to work out a simulation that will provide us with a safer — more optimal — pattern of placement for each source." Adam Reich closed his eyes and took three slow, shallow breaths — both arms wrapped around his ribs.

"And now?" Shaw looked at Collins.

Collins looked at Adam. "And now?"

Opening his eyes, Adam scanned all the men — his eyes settled on Doc. He shook his head and shifted his gaze to the admiral. "Now we get to work. Barring any medical complications...I think I can have a new version ready for testing within a week — ten days max." Once again he grasped his chest and wheeze-whispered, "Three weeks of testing in San Diego. Using slightly modified existing infrastructure--including the New York City approaches--we'll have CROWN CONCH up and running a month and half from now. Maybe sooner. New regions can come online..."

"CROWN CONCH?" Admiral Collins stepped closer to Adam. Shaw also moved closer. Menke stayed on the sofa on the far side of the room.

"Not to take anything away from Wendall, sir." Adam managed a weak grin. "But, the new system will be a significant upgrade to his work. I thought the project name required an upgrade as well."

The admiral walked behind the wheelchair and held the genius' shoulders firmly. He looked at Dr. Menke. "Doc may have judged you correctly, after all. At this point, it appears you're the only one who can do this."

Turning his head just enough to see Collins out of the corner of one eye, Adam whispered, "At this point, sir — this is all I have."

EPILOGUE

March 19, 2008

The New House, Plettenberg Bay, South Africa

Robin had just returned from his third surf ski paddle since arriving back in South Africa — a quick 10 kilometers out and back from the house doing 30-second on, 30-second off intervals. After showering, he was standing in a towel on the deck. Hearing some shuffling in the bedroom he glanced quickly over his shoulder — sure Angela would razz him about lounging about in a towel again.

Without looking toward the bedroom again, he teased, "Nice of you join me — finally."

Officially, they had slipped back to South Africa for some rest and relaxation prior to what they thought would be a month of grand jury testimony, Congressional hearings, and news conferences. Angela wanted to stay in the U.S. — to keep managing the recovery of the 36 dolphins that managed to survive the rescue. The Department of Justice wanted them to stay in the U.S. — because they were key witnesses in what was shaping up to be a controversial and far-reaching government investigation. But somehow, Robin had convinced them that they would better serve justice if they were well-rested. After what they had all been through — their initial strandings, flights, injuries, the incident in Tampa Bay, two days on-the-water, the beaching of 22 animals on Egmont Key, the dolphin rescues and the subsequent rehabilitation management and four days of preliminary   interviews with various government and law enforcement agencies — it was well worth the persuasive effort and the long flights.

And, Robin had another motive as well. "The view is spectacular — even with our FBI liaison milling about the grounds. You like...?"

"Everything." Her voice trembled as she looked at her left hand and the tastefully set one carat diamond. "The house is just what I wanted. *You* are just what I wanted."

Robin swaggered from the deck railing to the bedroom door where Angela was leaning and took her hands in his, "Then why the look, love? No comment about my towel? Why the red eyes and unhappy tears? I know the difference and...and, you can't still be brooding over the dolphins we lost. There was nothing that could have been done in Virginia. In Texas you saved four. In Tampa...in Tampa your actions saved 36 out of..."

She pulled him close and started to cry. Through the tears she mumbled, "New York. The Navy sank one mini-sub within sight of the Verrazano Narrows Bridge. The other...the other detonated...South Street Seaport — about 50 meters from Pier 17...Robin, it was a small nuke...low-yield. Oh Robin."

"A nuke? Where?" Robin whispered.

Through her sniffles, Angela replied, "Manhattan. The pier was obliterated—300 people dead. Luckily, it was crude and relatively weak—some fallout...it went off in the water. We didn't save all the dolphins...we shut down *Wendall* and something got through...people are dead and..."

"Fuck!" He pulled back slightly to see her face—to look into her eyes. "No." His voice was firm. "No. *You* did the right thing. *We* did the right thing."

Still, she buried her shaking head into his chest and sobbed.

The End

About the Author

Wendall's Lullaby may be **Kip Koelsch's** first novel, but he wrote his first "books" in Mrs. Cook's second grade class in Leonardo, NJ. His love of and interest in dolphins also developed early--by reading National Geographic, watching The Undersea World of Jacques Cousteau and through family beach vacations to Anna Maria Island in Florida.

Koelsch has a BA in Journalism and Mass Media from Rutgers University in NJ and a Master's Degree in Humanities and American Studies from the University of South Florida in Tampa, FL.

Over the years, Koelsch has been a collegiate rowing coach, an adjunct professor in Environmental Studies, a "manatee watch" coordinator, a salesperson in two outdoor retail stores, a canoe guide, an outdoor fitness and adventure program coordinator and a trail running and triathlon race director.

Through it all, he has been an on-again, off-again freelance magazine writer, blogger and keeper of a journal of "other writing ideas" — including the seeds for a follow-up to Wendall's Lullaby and more works of fiction.

https://www.facebook.com/WendallsLullaby/
https://kipwkoelsch.wordpress.com/

Made in the USA
Middletown, DE
07 August 2022

70305990R00357